This Deceitful Light

Collected, Curated & Corrected

BY

MR JEMAHL EVANS

Paperback ISBN: 978-1-910688-33-5
Kindle: 978-1-910688-34-2

Cover design by Julia B. Lloyd
Typeset by B. Lloyd
Published in the USA and UK
Caerus Press
An Imprint of Holland House Books

Holland House
47 Greenham Road
Newbury, Berkshire RG14 7HY
United Kingdom
www.hhousebooks.com
caeruspress.wordpress.com

Printed and bound in Great Britain by
TJ International Ltd, Padstow, Cornwall

For Ben, Frankie, and Jake.
(I'm a terrible uncle who forgets your birthdays and neglects his duties, but I adore you all!)

ENGLAND
AT THE END OF
1643.

Kilsyth
Dunbar
Glasgow
EDINBURGH
Carlisle
Newcastle
Marston Moor
York
Hull
Leeds
Manchester
Whinceby
Chester
Nantwich
Newark
Nottingham
Shrewsbury
Lichfield
Leicester
Naseby
Worcester
Northampton
Colchester
Gloucester
Edgehill
Oxford
LONDON
Pembroke
Bristol
Lansdown
Newbury
Roundway Down
Maidstone
Cheriton
Bridgewater
Poole
Exeter
Lyme
Lostwithiel
Plymouth

Parts held by the King.... White
Parts held by the Parliament
and the Scots; shaded thus.........

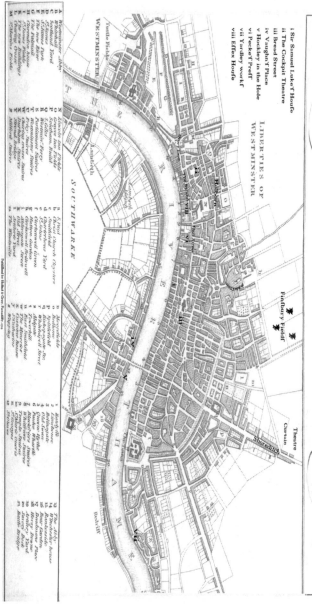

A Plan of London with Some Places Related to the Adventures of Sir Blandford Candy, together with other Noted Buildings and Quarters of that City

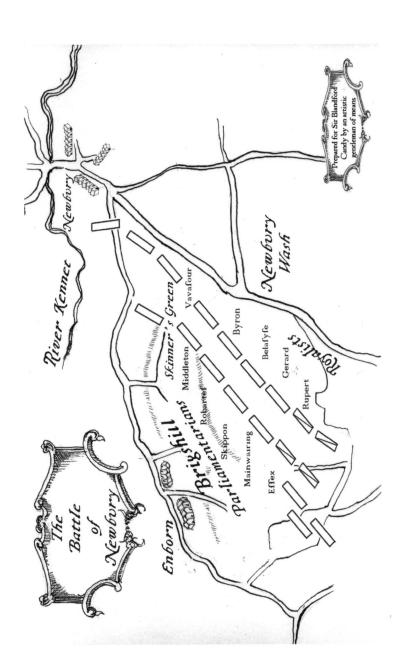

The Battle of Newbury

River Kennet

Newbury

Enborn

Brigshill

Skinner's Green

Parliamentarians

Middleton

Robartes

Skippon

Mainwaring

Essex

Vavafour

Byron

Belafyfe

Gerard

Rupert

Newbury Wash

Royalists

Prepared for Sir Blundford Candy by an artistic gentleman of means

Cross Deep, Twickenham, 1719.

There are some certain people (who roar well)
That in their drunken cups are apt to tell,
Strange stories what they did, and mean to do,
And they intend you should believe them too.

(John Clavell, *A Recantation of an Ill Led Life*.)

Mr Colley Cibber is an effete fop. He is an abominable actor who can only ever play one part, that of himself. His poetry is a dirge, his plays are derivative tedium, he is vain, self-serving, and a grasper. His fashion is French; his manners uncouth; his speech nasal and whiny. A pointed sausage for a nose, weasel little eyes, and a permanent sneer fixed upon his pale thin lips. His wig is oversized, full of powder, perfume, and piss, and his company is detestable. Mr Colley Cibber hates Mr Alexander Pope.

Mr Cibber is a wonderful man!

My idiot nephew has business with Cibber—an investor in this South Sea scheme—and I insisted, upon threat of eviction, that he gain me an interview. The actor lives but a short walk away for a normal man, a continent to me. I made the servants carry me in a chair; they huffed and puffed all the way down the road—a bare few hundred paces—complaining all the while, and deposited me in Cibber's tiled hallway, where I sat awaiting the great man's pleasure. There was not a soul about, dark and cold. I hauled myself out of the chair and shuffled over to the closed door into the study.

The idiot and the actor had been ensconced there for an hour or more, leaving me alone with nothing to drink or eat. Whatever the business, it seemed to have finished

1

satisfactorily (with laughs and the clink of glass) then I heard my name mentioned as I pressed my ear to the cold wood.

'Your great uncle is a vindictive old drunk, Mr Candy. A liar, a cheat, and a thief.'

Insolent little snotjockey; I swived his mother, twice, once bent over a cushioned chair and once in his father's bed—she was an eager little hoyden. There were murmurings from the idiot that I did not catch—it did not sound as if he was pleading my case.

'Very well, I can bear his company for a short time, if I must.' Cibber's voice scraped like a knife on a plate. 'Bring the sly devil in.'

I could hear the sound of steps. I scuttled back to the chair, cursing my arthritic joints, sat down, pulled up the blanket, and fixed an innocent look upon my face. The door opened and the idiot came out to me. Christ's blessed foreskin he looks like his father; blonde hair, blue eyes and pretty features. I looked like that once. I could seduce a nun with my smile, and did, more than once. If only he would show some industry; at thirty-four I had won and lost three fortunes. Mayhap his upcoming nuptials will put some jam in his trumpet. By God, I pray so; he wastes his time as a stockjobber* for the company.

'You will be polite, Uncle?' he said, helping me out of the chair.

I snorted and stood up straight. My back and knees creaked their complaints—the cold plagues the bones, y'know. I followed the boy into Cibber's study; the room overflowing with dross. Pictures, playbills, and posters covered the walls— all about Cibber: Cibber the actor, Cibber the comedian, Cibber the playwright, Cibber the poet. There were books

* Broker

spread about, and French ornaments, and an ostentatious gold leafed desk. Framed mirrors at every angle so the man could admire himself. Twenty or so expensive white candles flickered on a gilt bronze chandelier—alit in the daylight. Cibber is a tradesman with far too much money, and far too little breeding, aspiring to be a gentleman—tasteless.

He did not stand to greet me, but lounged on a green divan with one arm posed on his knee.

'Sir Blandford, it has been a long time. Not long enough, would you say?' He gave a high-pitched giggle. 'Your nephew tells me that you wish to ask something of me, let us be quick about it, shall we?'

'Hullo, Colley,' I said. 'I have known you since you were a bratling; I will be damned if I call you mister.' I am most assuredly damned anyway; one more black mark will not alter the tally.

He did not like that, sat up, and started shovelling snuff from a silver box up his nose. I sat down in a comfortable chair, with plump embroidered cushions, and waited through the snorting and sneezing. The idiot looked to the floor in embarrassed silence—I am an embarrassment. Cibber made a god-awful noise down his throat, picked up a pewter pot and spat out the effluent. He composed himself and turned to face me.

'What do you want, Candy?' He spoke normally, in a lower tone, the affectation dropped away.

Damnable actors, do you see, you cannot trust them. You can never truly know an actor, for he does not truly know himself. I reached into my pocket and drew out the petition, leaning forward and passed it to him. He glanced at it.

'Mr Pope and his tunnel? I have heard of it.' The screech was back.

3

'I want you to put in a complaint to stop the licence. It would carry more weight if put by you.'

'Why would I do that? Pope is a spiteful little man, he would be certain to pen some nasty ditty to mock me. He criticised my Lord Foppington.'

Cibber made another girlish giggle, passed the petition back to me and grabbed at the snuff again. I saw his Lord Foppington, and in truth 'twas excellent, but it was Cibber being Cibber and never realising that we laughed at him and not with him.[1]

'You owe me a debt.'

'An acting part a quarter of a century ago? I think not.'

'You detest Mr Pope.'

'I detest you the same and more.'

Well, he asked for it; I had tried to be reasonable. The idiot covered his face with his hands, expecting a profane abusive tantrum, no doubt, but I relaxed back into the comfortable chair—no tantrums today.

'I still have the original document for the theatre, did you know that?' I said. 'With the King's seal and my name upon it. A half share in the profits, not redeemed in fifty years or more. How is the company financially?'

He sneered at me. 'That is not worth the parchment it is written upon.'

'It would make a court case—create a scandal—other things would come out. Your mother was...' I paused. 'A friendly woman, Colley.' Ha! That wiped the scorn from his face. 'I have letters from her—letters that the gossips would adore.'

'You are an evil old man. I want those letters and the patent.'

'Then you will submit the complaint, and I will give you

the documents.'

'How have you stayed alive so long? I marvel that nobody has murdered you or called you out.'

'I fought a duel once.'

'And yet you still live. Somewhat fortunate for you, if not for the rest of us.'

'You could call it providence.'

'I was unaware the Devil traded in such goods. Very well, Sir Blandford, I will make this petition against Pope's tunnel. The man is little more than a poisonous pamphlet puppy that needs to be spanked, but after that I want the papers and I never wish to see or hear from you again.'

'Have no fear, Colley. I am sure I have not long left.'

He rang a little bell and his man appeared to take us away. Cibber rose and grasped the idiot's hand warmly, but turned away from me, gazing adoringly at his face in a mirror instead.

The idiot led me away; the valet had already taken my chair into the cobbled drive. Cibber did not follow, and I shuffled out behind my nephew without another word. I paused as I got to the steps—six plunging granite cliffs to scale—climbing carefully down them, one at a time. I could ill afford to humiliate myself by falling; I wanted Cibber worried. Safely down, I sat in the chair and breathed deeply. A boy was sent to fetch servants from the lodge to carry me, leaving the idiot and me alone in the cold. I pulled the blanket up over my legs.

'Will you give him the documents, Uncle?'

I glanced up at him. 'There are no documents, witless boy, but he knows that not.'

The boy began to chuckle. Perhaps there is hope for him yet.

'Did you truly fight a duel, Uncle? Or is it just another of your stories?'

'Yes.'[2]

1. Newbury: 2oth September 1643.

I fear no plots against me,
I live in open cell;
Then who would be a king,
When beggars live so well?

(Traditional, *A Jovial Beggar*.)

The plain before Newbury is bordered by two rivers running east, the Kennet to the north, and another—whose name escapes me—to the south*. Heavy rains had soaked the ground but 'twas not boggy. The Royalist army, just waking, filled the fields with their numbers. I could smell the wood smoke from their fires. Horse, Foot, and Ordnance blocking the London Road and our way home.

'There you are,' said Everard, as we viewed the scene. 'The King's whole damned army.'

The shabby little poacher was exultant. He took off his scarf and waved for our Foot to come up. Gilbert was silent beside me, gazing down at the enemy host. War was a new experience for the scribe.

Everard had scouted the night previous, and found the hill overlooking the cavalier encampment. The Earl of Essex, hearing that it was unguarded, for once in his life acted with purpose. Lord Robartes and Fortescue marched to seize the hill, and our Horse swung south supported by two infantry brigades.[3]

My Uncle Samuel, Scoutmaster General and Colonel of Dragoons, had assigned me to the infantry centre instead of riding with Essex. He said it was my penance.

I was in disgrace, you see; unfairly, in my opinion.

---

* The River Enbourne.

Fortescue's musketeers ran past us, taking up positions in the hedgerows and fields below the brow of the hill facing the Royalists, their mixed coats and hats a jumble of colour. They began lighting and blowing on their matches, twirling them around their heads to raise a glow. Armoured pikemen joined us, big burly men with iron breastplates and shining morions*. A tall officer, dressed in a red coat, barked orders to them as they crouched nervously with the musketeers.

It had been a quite remarkable few weeks. The King looked to win the war in the summer of forty-three. The north was his barring a few outposts, and only Plymouth and Gloucester remained as bastions in the west; lonesome roundhead islands in a cavalier ocean.

Parliament roused itself to stop Gloucester's fall, and sent our last field army of worth to the town's relief. We saved Gloucester and avoided disaster, but His Majesty had one last chance to end the war before Christmas: block our return to London, watch our supplies dwindle, and our men desert.

Our arrival on the hills above Newbury sparked consternation in the camp below. Royalist Foot were swarming together at the base of the slope, trumpets tootling out a call-to-arms, drums beating a rhythm.

'There are so many of them,' said Gilbert.

The scribe looked wretched at the sight of them: no hat, nor weapons, and in a suit of purple velvet, his face white, brown hair wild and slender frame shaking. Had he pissed himself? I think he had. I was the same at my first sight of battle, but had seen too much blood spilt already that year, and was strangely exhilarated by it all; terrified, but exhilarated nonetheless.

---

*   Open faced helmet popular in the Sixteenth and Seventeenth Centuries.

More of our Foot arrived taking up position at the hedgerows. Four small drakes carried behind them onto the hilltop, barrels thrust towards the mustering Cavalier host.

Everard pointed at the enemy bluecoats. 'Byron's Foot by the look of them, good troops. Think you the King will send them up against us, Captain?'

William treating me as his commander was new, and strange, given his experience. He had refused the commission, calling it a vain gentleman's bauble, and then handed it to me. I studied the ground that the Royalists would have to take, dense copses, banked hedges, and sunken lanes. They would find it hot work.

'His Majesty has little choice. More cannon on this hill will wreak bloody murder in their ranks.'

'Let us hope Skippon hurries along with the reinforcements then; I fancy not these odds,' said Everard.

'Amen to that.'

We both dismounted and handed our horses reins to a waiting trooper. I looked to the scribe.

'You had best dismount, Gilbert,' I said. 'You be a perfect mark atop the beast.'

'Of course, forgive me.' He clambered down then started retching, heaving up his breakfast. Everard looked on with disgust. The trooper led our three animals to the reverse slope.

'What did you bring him for?' asked Everard.

'He wanted to see the battle; said it would make a good story for the newsbooks.'

'People will pay more for a first-hand account,' said Gilbert, weakly between heaves. 'Mr Rushworth says that is why we are here.'[4]

I turned away from him; his retching was contagious. My

9

own stomach felt as tight as a drum—it always does before battle.

'Here they come,' shouted a man in the line.

Everard and I turned from Gilbert to watch the Royalist Foot make their first assault.

'Hold your fire, wait, wait,' shouted our officers.

Men were praying in the ranks, blowing on their matches, pissing themselves with fear. A battle is a terrible thing. Byron's blue-coated Foot came up the hill in a rush, climbing over hedges and through sunken lanes, with no attempt to hold their formation together. At every obstacle, we met them with a hail of shot. I could taste the familiar burn of powder in my mouth, smell the sulphur, blink as the white smoke made my eyes water.

'Sit in the hedge and stay out of the way.' Everard pushed Gilbert back from our line. He did not argue—a good story was worth nothing without his head.

William and I joined the pikes and muskets, clashing with Royalist infantry at a hedge, throwing them back, stabbing and thrusting at them with pike and sword. Musketeers bludgeoned the enemy at close quarters with their matchlocks. I shot one Cavalier in the mouth as he tried to push through the hedge, bone and grey brain splattering across my face. One of his companions slipped in the mud before me. A soldier set upon him, swung the butt of his weapon at the man's head, caving in his skull, smashing out his life. Blood spraying around at the blows; a fine mist of red hanging in the air. I could smell shit, as men's bellies opened up in the fight.

A hand grabbed towards me, I slashed at it, taking the fingers off with my blade. The bright flash of a muzzle scorched my cheek, blinding me for a moment. I parried a pike thrust—by instinct—and staggered back. There was a roaring in my ears, and I could feel the burning sting on my face. My eyes were streaming water; I shook my head to clear my sight, cursing all the while. Two men stepped past me to plug the gap in our line.

We were slowly being driven back up the hill by weight of numbers, but the Royalists were taking heavy casualties. From hedge to hedge, we grappled in brutal combat; the bluecoats cursing and shouting as they drove into us, weapons bloody, and carbines hot.

Standing with our backs to the last hedge before the hilltop, we faced down Byron's advancing infantry. Massed volleys of muskets shredded their ranks, ripping through armour, maiming and killing, until the Bluecoats broke. Turning, running back down the hill, throwing away their weapons, and leaving behind ground littered with dead and dying. Broken bodies, like bundles of rags, sprawled across the field.

A wave of short-lived relief rolled over me. More Royalists were forming up at the base of the hill, but not yet ready to assault. We had a pause. Everard looked at my face.

'You need this.' He reached into his pouch and passed me a small vial of clear liquid. 'Dab it on with your scarf.'

I did as instructed—William was a wonder with his remedies. It cooled my skin in an instant.

'Captain Candy.'

A boy tugged my coat: one of our young ensigns—a kitten amidst the lions—running messages for Lord Robartes. Perhaps twelve years of age, dressed richly in a tailored buff coat, and fine boots. A wealthy London merchant's son, I assumed.

'His Lordship requests your presence, sir,' he said, white-faced at the sight of dead and dying.

'Very well.' I nodded, and turned to Everard, who was lighting his pipe from a musketeer's glowing match. 'Look after Gilbert; I am away to his Lordship.'

The boy led me back to the brow of the hill. Lord Robartes was directing the defence with his staff. His red-coated deputy lay dead at his feet, face torn away in the battle. My stomach flipped at the sight.

'Candy, get yourself to the Major General, and ask him to hasten up the support,' Robartes told me brusquely.

'Yes, Milord.'

I hurried down the reverse slope to my mount, past the wounded, the dying, and those rushing powder and shot to the front. Apple was tied to a hedge with other horses, quietly munching at the ground, and treating the sound of battle with disdain. Taking his reins, I mounted, and rode to Major General Skippon at the rear.

It was barely organised chaos as regiments were fed into the line. Men and horses jumbled together with little picture of the battle but their own small part. March, and hold, and fight, and march, aware only of the small space around them. I spotted Franny Cole leading a column of Foot southwards down a sunken lane. Mainwairing's London Redcoats— Muskets and Pikes—singing psalms as they went, and podgy bespectacled colonel at their head.

'Hullo, Franny, where be the Skipper?'

I paused to speak to him as if we passed down the Strand, rather than midst a hot fight. He lifted the frontpiece of his pot and gave me an amused grin—all big nose and big mouth. Franny rarely took anything seriously, even a bloody battle just over the hill.

'What ho, Sugar. He is organising the reserves.' Franny

gestured behind him, and then looked at my singed face. 'You have burned your pretty cheek. 'Tis hot up there?'

'Aye, Robartes wants support to come up.'

'Essex wants the same in the south. I take these boys down to him. The Prince Robber* is pressing hard, but we have held him thus far. Hurry is with him.'

Sir John Hurry was my nemesis, a lowborn Scots Judas with fetid breath and dark countenance: a venal turncoat, who had tried to have me killed and caused the death of my best friend. I had sworn to kill him twice over.

'Tell our boys, if anyone sticks that bastard, I will give him ten pounds.'

'You have no coin to your name.'

'Do not tell them that,' I said.

'They already know, Sugar,' said Franny. 'Your losses are legendary. Try not to get yourself killed —'twill only annoy your sister.'

I bade him farewell and cantered to the Major General. The Skipper turned to me as I dismounted. Tall, with dark hair and moustache, dressed in expensive armour and surrounded by his sycophantic staff. He did not like me—not my fault; 'twas all a misunderstanding—but he was a man of influence and second in the Army under Essex.

'What is it, Captain Candy?'

'Message from Lord Robartes, General. He requests support. Byron's Foot have been beaten off but the Royalists gather to assault once more.'

'Two brigades of infantry are already moving up, Candy. Get yourself back to Milord Robartes; request of him that he move north with Fortescue and secure the fields to our left.'

I bowed and turned—with difficulty in my corselet of

---

*   Prince Rupert of the Rhine.

armour—and rode back up the long slope to round top. More wounded men, bloodied and broken, brought back from the fighting. Two brigades of Foot followed on behind me: the Skipper's own and Springate's. They were good troops, veterans who could be relied upon to hold the hill.

I gave Robartes the orders and he organised his men into columns, leading them down from the brow of the round hill. I followed them into enclosed fields to the north, as they took position along a sunken lane. Fortescue's musketeers were with still us, crouched behind the great hedgerow running along the road. Opposite, Royalist musketeers did the same. The green walls formed a barrier none dared cross. To step into the lane invited instant death.

Instead of assault, 'twas constant fire-play. The musketeers loading and reloading, rods clattering as they rammed home powder and shot, explosions popping as they discharged their piece and round went round again. It became a desperate struggle of volley and counter-volley; pistol and musket shot; men falling as the iron balls tore through armour and flesh, leaving great gaping wounds, smashing bones, staining the ground dark with blood.

More musketeers joined us, men from the London Bands, brave men, good men, but not enough. It went on and on, two hours and more of bloody musketry. The sulphurous white smoke rose like a mist, stinging the eyes, burning the nose and mouth with each breath. 'Middleton's Horse have come up to support us, Milord,' Everard told Robartes.

''Tis powder and musketeers we need, not cavalry,' said Robartes. 'Captain Candy, get yourself back up the hill and request men and shot from Major General Skippon. Tell him how hard pressed we are.'

'Yes, Milord.'

I rode Apple along the ridge that ran behind our whole line up to Roundhill, cantering behind the lines of battalia, infantry, cannon, drake, and bloody mêlée. There was a narrow lane leading up to Skippon's position, and I could breathe more easily out of the smoke. The hill was besieged, assaulted by lines of Royalists charging up the steep slope. They crashed over the defenders like waves in a storm breaking over rocks and receding to form up once more.

'Here come the Horse!' I heard the shouts and turned in my saddle.

Royalist Horse pushed through a gap in the hedge to the front. At first, it was only big enough for one rider to force his way through, in the face of musket and case shot. A richly dressed officer was shot from his saddle, another had his horse killed under him, but their troopers cut away at the hedge, widened the gap, and more came through. Thundering at a charge towards our pikes and veering off at the last, discharging pistols, rather than headlong into the phalanx. They formed up at distance, firing carbine and pistol, as red coated Foot came to join in the assault.

Our own men also wore red coats—Springate's Foot— which only added to the confused jumble of battle.

I would have to fight my way through to Skippon—that was disappointing—but a scout's lot is never a happy one. I tied Apple up at a gatepost behind Roundhill. Any semblance of control had broken down behind our lines, and I could only pray to God's mercy that he would be safe. Loading both of my pistols, I holstered one and carried the other in my left hand, a sword in my right, and tried to make my way to the Major General.

A group of soldiers—more of Springate's I decided— carrying groaning wounded back to the surgeon, appeared through the choking white smoke. I could hear the shouts and clash of steel, pop of musket, and roar of drake behind them.

'Where be Major General Skippon?' I asked one—a sergeant by the look.

He grinned at me. 'At the heart of the fight on the hill, Captain.' Rivulets of sweat had run down his smoke-blackened face, leaving white streaks. They all looked exhausted from the battle, but their eyes were still bright—they were not beaten. I thanked him and turned to run up to the battle at Roundhill.

'Who is that?' I heard one ask as I left.

'Sugar Candy, the Golden Scout.'

'He shall make the damned royalists sorry. God bless him.'

That puffed at my vanity. I straightened my back as I ran, but did not turn. 'Tis flattering to have the adoration, but too often it ends in trouble. Gilbert's pamphleting made me out to be some golden-haired Apollo, and the truth was rather more prosaic. The masses wanted heroes, so the scribe told me. In my youth I was only too willing to indulge them; a name and a reputation was what I craved. If that involved taking damn silly risks, then so be it. Young men ever believe in their immortality.

I have learned with age, that if you put your head over the parapet too often, eventually it will get blown off.

I was panting heavily in my armour as I crested the hill, and saw the whole battle spread before me. Two lines crashing together—north and south—whilst the ranks of Royalist Foot charged the centre. The mêlée at the summit had been vicious; dead and dying sprawled around as the fight went on. Soldiers on both sides snarling like dogs as they killed. War makes beasts of men.

Standing in the centre of it all, calm in the heat of battle, was Skippon. He was a cold one, I grant him that. I gave him Robartes message, ignoring the dark scowl that crossed his face at the sight of me.

'You can wait for my reply,' he said, turning away.

From my vantage point on the hill, I could see the Londoners of the Red and Blue in squares to the south, with Essex embattled beyond. Prince Rupert was canny; he knew that the Trained Bands were the hinge of our line. If he could break them, our southern flank would collapse, Essex would be destroyed, and the war finished.

The Royalist cannon pounded the Red and Blue, men decapitated, bodies torn and broken, but still they held. The Royalists would pause the barrage, and Prince Rupert's cavalry would swarm around them hacking at the pikes, discharging their pistols and carbines close up, but the Londoners swatted them aside. Charge after charge, until the Horse fell back exhausted, and the cannon started roaring again with murderous intent.[5]

Our own great guns were being dragged up to round hill to return the fire; the entire Royalist line exposed to their shot.

'Get yourself back to Lord Robartes, Candy,' said Skippon. 'Tell him we have no more reserve to spare. All turns on the battle there.'

He pointed to the Red and Blue formed now into one square so great were their casualties. The Royalist Horse charging once more, and Skippon dismissed me.[6]

I found Apple (praise be) and rode back north to Robartes, and the bloody stalemate on the left flank. The ranks of our men had thinned, bodies of dead and dying piled up around them. It went on and on, a day of battle. *Bella horrida bella.**

As night fell, I expected the two lines to fall back from spitting flame and fire in the darkness, but neither side was so disposed. Only the Horse, unable to charge for fear of broken legs, retired. It was late when exhaustion finally called a halt to the battle. The Royalist attacks all down our line petered out. They had failed to break us.

We stood down in the killing field, our dead all around us, our wounded drawn off to the rear. Franny and quiet Sam Brayne arrived, as we crouched around a small fire, and huddled down with us.

'Why does Skippon dislike you so?' Gilbert asked me.

'Has Sugar not told you?' said Franny. 'It would make a good story for the newsbooks.'

'It was a misunderstanding,' I said.

Franny burst out laughing. 'Our Sugar had a bad case of the squits in Gloucester; spent most his time running to the privy.'

'I thought I would die,' I admitted, 'and I was not the only one.'

'You were the only one to be caught using Skippon's book of religious tracts for bum fodder,' said Everard.

''Twas the only paper to hand,' I said.

'Blasphemous and insulting, Skippon said,' Franny told Gilbert. 'And the Skipper is one to hold a grudge. Our new Captain is beloved of the London mob that read your pamphlets, but the Major General considers him... What was it, Blandford?'

'An impudent fop and probably a heretic,' I said, to my friends' mirth.

There was no sleep that night. We took up our positions

---

*   Virgil: war horrid war.

18

before dawn, ready to continue the fight. We had no choice. The King stood between us and London. To get to safety we would have to battle once more. Men determined to fight on for God and Liberty.

Dawn broke, a rising sun obscured by grey clouds, and we could see no enemy to stand against us. The Cavaliers had slipped away in the night leaving only their dead and the smouldering remains of their campfires.

The road to London was open.

2. Ophelia: London, October 1643.

When blustering Boreas with impetuous breath
Gives the spread sails a wound to let in Death,
Cracks the tall mast, forcing the ship (though loathe)
On its carv'd prow to wear a crown of froth;
Will face all perils boldly, to attain
Harbour in safety; then set forth again.

(Henry Glapthorne, *For Ezekiel Fenn on his first acting a Man's part*)

It was late when I arrived at the brew house—a smoky little hovel overlooking the river—near the Globe in Southwark. 'Tis called the Anchor now, has been since the Sixties; then, 'twas just called Vaughn's place. It had been Vaughn's place for nigh on fifty years, passed down from father to son, serving actors, whores, and their pimps for decades. What was left of London's acting fraternity would gather there in the evenings to ply their trade; it stank of wood smoke and sweat, French perfumes, musks and citrus, and stale ale, and I loved it.

Vaughn's was one of my regular haunts—you were always assured a riotous evening with wine, song, games of chance or skill, and willing women. I fought my way through the malodorous throng until I found a table at the back, but remained standing so that I could see the end of the performance.

The playhouses remained closed, but the taverns south of the river put on shows of drolls* to bring in the crowds. The puritans loathed it, but did not wish for riots and so tolerated the pastime; the lower orders loved the spectacle, flocking

---

*   Short scenes from popular plays

nightly to see the players. It was also one of Mr William Beeston's more lucrative money making schemes. I think 'schemes' is the correct word; he was ever the schemer. Beeston managed the Phoenix Theatre, and his family had shares in the building with my sister, and William Davenant—the royalist poet, gun smuggler, and syphilitic mangelwurzel.

Beeston stood on Vaughn's little stage, surrounded by onlookers, in his dirty scarlet suit; oily black ringlets dangled down his back, his face caked with makeup, and a spade held in his hands. John Rhodes the bookseller was with him—a grey haired man, middle-aged, and dressed in shabby black—playing his partner. Ophelia lay on a bench behind, covered in a thin shroud, his eyes closed, a silent corpse awaiting burial.

The audience watched on in rapt attention, and Beeston held them with his eyes, deep voice rolling around the packed bar room like thunder. He could act, that Mr William Beeston, blackguard and scoundrel that he was.

'Who builds stronger than a mason, a shipwright, or a carpenter?' said Rhodes, leaning into Beeston.

'Ay, tell me that, and unyoke,' Beeston replied, dismissively waving his hand and turning away.

'Marry, now I can tell,' said Rhodes.

Beeston turned back to face the bookseller. 'To't,' he said, urging Rhodes to speak.

'Mass, I cannot.' The bookseller looked befuddled like a simpleton.

'Cudgel thy brains no more about it,' bellowed Beeston in response, slapping Rhodes on the back. 'For your dull ass will not mend his pace with beating, and, when you are asked this question next, say...'

Some wits in the crowd shouted out various insalubrious

occupations like punk, pimp or poxmonger, as he paused. Beeston flashed them a quick smile and continued.

'A grave-maker!' He roared. 'For the houses that he makes last till doomsday.' He gave Rhodes a boot up the arse. 'Go, get thee to Vaughan and fetch me a stoup of liquor.'

The crowd screamed in delight at that, even though they knew it was coming, and Mr Vaughn passed up a frothing flagon of ale to the raised stage—just as his grandsire did for Shakespeare. Beeston took a great gulp, and bowed to the cheering audience.[7]

When he stood, he fixed them with a stare; the dross quieted, and Beeston sang out in a clear tone. He had only a passable voice, but his presence on the stage was so powerful that you were fain to keep your eyes upon him.

'In youth when I did love, did love, methought 'twas very sweet. To contract–o–the time, for–a–my behove, Oh, methought, there–a–was nothing–a–meet.'

As he finished the song, he gave a final deep bow and the crowd went wild. Huzzahs, shouts, and more drinks passed to the actors. Beeston stood straight and revelled in the adulation, his eyes shining. Ophelia rose from his grave, dressed in a fine green satin robe my sisters would have adored, and held hands with Rhodes. They both gave the audience a little bow as well, but 'twas Beeston's triumph—he had already taken up with his flatterers; some richly dressed woman was draped all over him.

Ophelia noted me watching at the back, flashed me a smile and gave a wave. If you knew him not for a man of an age with me you would surely have taken him for a beautiful maid; petite, pale and slim, with big brown eyes, long lashes, red lips, and straight brown hair as fine as mist. He grabbed a bottle of wine from Vaughn and pushed through the crowd to me.[8]

Perhaps we recognised kindred spirits, Ophelia and I, for we bounced along well enough. He took his lovers, men and women, with little thought or care—together we seduced brothers and sisters, husbands and wives—and I was certain there was more to his love of Beeston than mere comradeship. Whilst I was ne'er his suitor, yet I will claim him as a friend. I sat at the table as he joined me, still wearing his lady's gown and courtesan's painted face.

He threw me a little pout. 'No kisses for Ophelia?'

'Your admirers give you kisses enough, Zeke.' I said, blowing him a kiss nevertheless.

'You are late; you missed Rhodes play Faustus to my Helen—Beeston was Mephistopheles.'

'A devilish part he was born to play. You made a pretty corpse.'

'Such flattery,' said Ophelia. ''Tis a truth the pamphlets tell: there is no sugar as sweet as Candy.'

I sniffed at that—the newsbooks were full of it—Mabbot's fault.

Ophelia poured me a cup of sack from his bottle, and one out for himself, then pulled up a chair. I supped away at the wine—the sack had a delightful taste, thick like nectar—'twas surprisingly good for the waterfront stew.

'What is this?'

'Spanish, it is wonderful is it not?' said Ophelia. 'Vaughn tells me 'tis from the city of Malaga. Created by Moorish wine makers for the Turk Sultan hi'self.'

'Then Vaughn tells you fables. The Moors make no wine, Malaga is Christian, and the Sultan drinks no grape nor grain.'

Ophelia grimaced. 'Oh, dear heart, I know all that, but 'tis such a beautiful tale for a beautiful wine. Why do you have to spoil the dream with reality?'

'Perhaps I am just a practical man.'

He laughed. 'Then you are the most impractical practical man I know, Sugar.' And blew me a kiss back. 'Have you met the fishmonger's wife? She is most pretty, and does not smell of fish at all; I wager she tastes most sweet.' He winked and nodded to a buxom blonde woman, slim waist, with sweet little dimples and full red lips.

'No?' I said, my interest piqued.

'Then I shall introduce you... If you buy me another bottle of the Malaga wine.'

I called Vaughn over and reached into my purse.

The hammering was getting louder—damnably loud. Please let it not be the husband, I said to myself. I did not wish a duel before breakfast. Leaving the woman asleep in my bed, I took down my sword and stepped into the main room.

Bang! Bang! Bang! Bang!

My chambers in Bread Street (only three small rooms at the top of a rickety old wooden tenement) had become a bawdyhouse for the scouts. Sam was snoring in a cot by the fire and the door to Franny's room was firmly shut. A stale odour of wine and men's farts, mixed with smoke and sweat, hung in the air. Bodies of men—and women—slumbered beneath blankets on the floor, surrounded by the debris of bottles, and all ignoring the racket downstairs.

Bang! Bang! Bang! Bang!

I needed a servant.

'I am coming! For the love of God, stop that damn awful

knocking. I have a headache,' I shouted, then stumbled down the three flights of narrow stairwell.

The fishmonger's wife was a foolish dalliance. Uncle Samuel would not be best pleased at yet another scandal, but she was pretty and buxom, and her decrepit cuckold husband thrice her age. If only I could remember her name. Polly? Was it Polly? Or perhaps Molly? I could not be certain; my head was befuddled. Holding the sword behind my back, I drew the bolts and pulled open the front door.

Gilbert stood in the courtyard in his purple suit and bubbling over with excitement.

'There has been a murder at the Phoenix.'

I rushed back upstairs to my bedchamber, pulling on stockings, boots, and doublet. I had spent more time with Gilbert since Newbury and liked him well enough, but trusted him not. He was more than a simple recorder of the news—a London agent with contacts in trade, and Westminster, and tame lawyers to do his bidding. No man's pie was free from his ambitious finger. Information was his currency and he sold it to the highest bidder.[9]

'You shall have to be away home,' I told the fishmonger's wife. 'I have urgent business.'

A sweet moan of protest as she sat up, stretched her arms, and yawned. Her pretty face and blonde hair all perfectly messed up. The blanket fell away to reveal plump white breasts. Jilly? Was her name Jilly? Or was it Millie? She was a rum distraction—I can tell you that. I kissed her, grabbed my cloak and hat, and rushed to rejoin Gilbert. Madam Fishmonger I left pouting and naked in my bed.

'Tis only a mile or so run from Bread Street to Drury Lane; our boots pounded on mucky cobbles in the early morning sun: ducking between stalls, horses, and carts, cutting through the churchyard of St Pauls and out of the City at Ludgate, leaving behind the narrow streets and smoke blackened old buildings.

Down the Strand are houses of a richer sort—over the Fleet air be cleaner: new builds of brick, stone, and stucco decoration; the mansions of aristocrats, merchant palaces, and expensive shops. We jostled with carriages, sedan porters, and delivery boys until turning into Drury Lane and the theatre. I called a halt and puked in the road, retching out yellow bile, and sweating like a docker with a thick head.

The Phoenix Theatre was enclosed. Not like the wooden rounds across the river—designed by Mr Inigo Jones himself—built of red brick and three stories high with white pointing and slate roof. The entrance, like a Roman temple, had pillars and porch. Plaster statuettes of the muses beckoned from alcoves to passersby. Come rain or shine, 'twas fit for performance. Well, until the Puritans banned fun and performances along with it.

The new Lord Mayor had not even been sworn in, but was already throwing his weight around. There were men from the Yellow Regiment all over the building, their coloured badges proclaiming allegiance. They herded watching onlookers away from the frontage.

A herd of street urchins loudly abused the guardsmen by the entrance. Some of my sister's waifs and strays, I assumed. The soldiers were not gentle in sending them running with a couple of swings of the pikestaff. The brats scrambled back out of range and carried on with the jeers and catcalls. One ragabash, dressed in rags with dark face and black curls, picked up a stone and readied to toss it at the guard sergeant.

'Stay your hand, boy,' I said, as I pushed past. 'The Lord Mayor's men will tolerate insults cast, but a stone will see you whipped.'

'Got to catch me first,' said the cheeky little beggar, lobbing his missile and striking the sergeant in the face.

The soldiers came out in a rush at that, charging the children, who scattered pell-mell in different directions. The men had no hope of catching them. I strode over to the old sergeant, ignoring his pikemen. Tall, well dressed but running to fat, and hair dyed an unnatural shade of black; his eye already swelling from the boy's stone.

'What the devil goes here?' I said to him. 'Let me pass, damn you.' Two guards blocked my path.

Gilbert trotted behind in my wake. I noted he already had his journal and pencil, and scribbled as he walked.

'Do you have to?' I gestured to the journal.

'There could be a good story in this. People will pay more for a murder.'

I turned away in disgust. His obsession with a good story was not seemly when it touched on my theatre. He would make me pay to keep this out of the pamphlets. I turned back to the soldiers.

'Let me pass, I say.' I called again. ''Tis my damn theatre.'

The guard sergeant finally took note, and waved us past his men.

'You are Candy?' he asked.

'I am, sir. Captain Candy... Where be my sister and what goes here?'

I could pull rank if he wanted, and be as pompous as a bishop.

'Your sister is inside, sir. She has had a fret but is unharmed,' he said. 'Come with me.'

Gilbert and I followed the soldier into the theatre. The shutters were drawn and it was dark, as if for a performance.

More guards at the entrance to the pit; the sound of raised voices carried from the stage inside.

'The woman is in a bustle, Reggie,' one of the guards told the sergeant.

I followed 'Reggie' onto the stage. My sister—dressed like a servant—was loudly berating a richly dressed merchant. White haired and dripping with gold, a chain of office displayed proudly upon his breast: the new Lord Mayor - Sir John Wollaston.[10]

Elizabeth trembled with anger, and her blue eyes flashed. Golden wisps of hair slipped, unpinned, across her face. She absently brushed them away, raging at Sir John all the while, every sentence punctuated with a jab of her finger into his wobbly belly. He huffed and puffed, hemmed and hawed, all whilst turning a bright shade of vermillion.

'This be no bawdy house, Sir John, 'tis a schoolhouse. The teachers are not, as you so charmingly put it, trulls and strumpets, and there is no crime teaching poor children to read the catechism. Instead of seeking salacious acts where there are none, 'twere better you investigate the poor unfortunate in the gardens.'

'Which catechism, Mistress Candy? Not the King's, I wager,' said Sir John. 'This is a Scottish invention.' He pointed to some papers scattered across the stage.

What has she done now? I thought. I had been against the idea of turning the theatre into a schoolhouse but Elizabeth had insisted, much to the disgust of Mr Beeston.

'The Scots have now turned ally, Lord Mayor,' I said, interrupting before Elizabeth slapped his face. I could see the explosion building inside her.

He turned to me. 'Who are you, sir?'

'I am Captain Candy, Sir John. This lady's brother. You

know our uncle, I am sure?' 'Tis always wise to remind people of your connections and rank before you are arrested.

'Where have you been?' said Elizabeth. 'You stink of wine and vomit.'

'Sleeping. Where is Beeston? Has somebody finally killed the rogue?'

'Mr Beeston is missing,' said our rotund Lord Mayor. 'And where were you last night, sir? Were you with the victim?'

'What victim, if not Beeston then who?' I said.

''Tis Ezekiel,' said Elizabeth.

'Ophelia?' That was a surprise.

'And your whereabouts, sir.' Sir John asked again. 'Can you account for them?'

'I was with my uncle.' I had been briefly. 'Then supped with friends. I have a witness who can vouch for me.' A witness whose name I remembered not; a witness with a husband. That could prove vexatious.

Gilbert coughed politely for attention. Sir John paused, as if noting him for the first time.

'I will not be answering your questions today, Mr Mabbot. You, and the troublesome scrivener that employs you, can find your stories elsewhere. Keep him here,' he said to one of the guards, and led me and Elizabeth out the rear of the theatre.

The gardens at the back of the Phoenix were small, with niches and nooks that made it perfect for a night-time dalliance. The back gate should have been locked, but never was. After performances—and certain illegal performances there still were—whores would flock there to pick up clients, and their pockets. More guards with pikes in hand stood watching the scene.

All this for a single murder? There must be ten a day in

London.

Poor sweet Ophelia was not a pretty corpse in death. He lay, spread-eagled on his back, beneath the willow at the centre of the garden, shrouded in the golden autumn foliage. He was dressed fashionably in a dark blue satin suit, loose unconfined breeches, and frilled shirt, but the skin on his hands and face was scalded and red. Bootless, and no stockings, but the feet were not burned. The rest of the body and dress covered in a white waxy substance, in his mouth, up his nostrils, over his blistered eyelids, but not his feet. He must have been dunked in the stuff. I knelt before the body, scraped off a smidgen, and tasted it. Sir John looked at me in disgust.

'Tallow,' I said, in explanation. 'He has been drowned in hot render.'

A guardsman started to heave at my words.

'It did not occur here then,' said Sir John. He sounded disappointed.

'No.' I searched the actor's pockets. 'No purse or coin, but it has not the look of a robbery.'

I looked around studying the ground. There was a knot in the bole of the willow tree. It reminded me of Elizabeth's hiding place for messages in an old oak that she used as a child. I stood up and walked over, reaching into the hole as if from some forgotten habit. I felt a piece of parchment and drew it out. The Lord Mayor gasped.

'What is this?'

I opened the parchment and read.

*There is special providence in the fall of a sparrow.**

The words were written in a strong bold hand, and one that I recognised, but I could not place it. The Lord Mayor went

---

*   Hamlet Act V Scene II.

bright red when he saw the script, and called for his black haired sergeant.

'Was this here when you arrived?' asked Wollaston.

I thought that a strangely worded question, but wondered no more on it. Sergeant Hairdye was as bemused by the note as anyone else, and Wollaston sent him away with a flea in his ear for not searching the ground properly.

'Ophelia drowned and found under a willow tree? Someone is playing games, Lord Mayor.'

I am not so witless I did not see the links to the play, but if Ophelia was drowned, where was Hamlet? And what was the note? A line from the play only yards from the body could be no mere coincidence.

'Nevertheless, until we can find why the body was deposited here, your *schoolhouse* will remain closed, Mistress Candy.'

My sister looked enraged at that, but remained silent.

'Uncle Samuel will want to hear of this,' I said.

'Your uncle has no authority in the city, Captain Candy.'

Technically, we were not in the city, and I was not sure that the Lord Mayor's writ extended this far, but I was not about to argue when he had soldiers at his back. I took Elizabeth inside the Phoenix before she started another storm with Sir John.

'We go to Uncle Samuel, Sister. He will know what is to be done.'

My uncle's mansion on Thames Street was a grand four-storey residence with its own wharf on the river. Dwarf Hall the newsbooks dubbed it. Elizabeth had taken up residence there upon arrival in London. The house was largely empty, my aunt and cousins preferred the manor in Cople, and only two or three servants remained. Mr Butler still guarded access to Uncle Samuel, like a fat balding Narcissus, but he had learned quickly enough not to challenge Elizabeth. I smirked at him as she led me to the study, but the secretary ignored me.

Uncle Samuel was alone writing his journal; dressed simply in a grey woollen doublet, and perched on a high chair with four cushions so that he could sit at the desk, his-feet-a-dangle, not touching the floor. We sat and told him of the murder, the Lord Mayor, and the missing Mr Beeston. He continued to write as we talked, brows furrowed, long grey hair swept back, and spectacles perched on his beak. When we had told him every detail, showed him the note from the willow, and been questioned thrice over, he sat back and took off his glasses.

'What has Mr Beeston done now?' he said to us. 'It would be better if you sold your share of the place, Elizabeth.'

'Who would buy a share in a theatre?' she said. 'Besides, I have plans for the building, Uncle.'

Uncle Samuel smiled indulgently at her. 'You have your father's mind for trade, so I will not press the point.'

She be spoiled and stubborn, I thought to myself. Indulging her only ever causes trouble.

'In the meantime, Blandford, I want you to stay in the city and look into this,' my uncle said. 'It may be nothing, or merely some criminal scheme of Beeston's that has gone awry. Nevertheless, 'tis best to be sure.' He sighed. 'Sometimes I think I see Royalist plots everywhere.'

That was a notion I did not contest. The army was to move on Reading once more, in spite of the late season. I preferred a murder in London to that, and I did not wish Ophelia's death to go unpunished. We had been friends, and I had seen too many friends die of late.

'Keep Cole and Everard with you; the others I need for the campaign. I will inform Mr Darnelly that you will remain in the city. Report to him with any information.'

'Yes, Uncle,' I said. Every silver lining has a sable cloud, I thought. Darnelly was a misery.

Elizabeth and I left our uncle with his journal and walked together in the long room, family paintings were displayed along one wall, and a row of arched windows on the other. A portrait of my mother hung alongside other forgotten ancestors. The painter, Larkin, had captured her beauty: long blonde hair hanging loose, shining blue eyes, a pearl earring my eldest brother now wore, and a pretty dress embroidered with flowers and trimmed with gold lace. Every time I saw it, I was reminded how much Elizabeth resembled her—or would, if she made up her face and wore some fashion.[11]

'Ezekiel's murder angers you, Blandford.' She linked her arm in mine. 'I can tell, even if Uncle Samuel noticed not.'

'It does not anger you?'

'Not in the same way. I barely knew him, and I know he rests in the Lord's arms now.'

'He was my friend,' I conceded. 'I do not like to see my friends murdered.'

I have many faults, but I am loyal to my friends—as long as they have not a pretty wife, sister, or daughter. With the mothers you are generally safe—generally.

'You think it was Beeston?'

'No, but I wager 'tis his fault.'

Elizabeth led me away from the portraits to the windows facing out over Thames Street. It was busy with carts, and barrows, and people bustling up and down.

'Look at that boy out there,' she said, pointing out of the

window to a child waiting on his own at the gates.

'Twas the little chittiface from the theatre; the mulatto stone thrower.[12]

'His name is John,' she continued. 'He can read and write and is clever. His mother was taken from a French ship but died when he was born. His father was Thomas Coxon, a sailor and villain.' She put on a mournful look. 'Hanged for theft two months since.'

'Like father like son,' I said. 'What has this to do with me, sister?'

She gave a look I knew well enough. Elizabeth was after saving someone's soul. Some design to make my life a misery; I could see it coming.

'I want you to take him with you, and give him employ as your page.'

'No.'

'You were complaining only yesterday that you needed a good servant.'

'A good servant, not a child, and certainly not some guttersnipe.'

''Tis your choice of course. Just as 'tis mine to withhold your allowance, should I choose.'

'You would blackmail me, Sister?' Spiteful mendacious witch! Today had started badly and was getting worse.

She smiled at me. 'I have told him you will be a gentle master and his tasks not onerous. He is most anxious to meet you.'

''Tis unkindness itself to set me such a burden, Elizabeth. I have no need of a dead thief's brat.'

'Unkindness is a world that casts children aside to starve. Suffer little children and forbid them not to come unto me, for such is the kingdom of heaven."*

There was no arguing with her. I left the house and walked out to the gates, to where the boy was waiting. I took more note now that he was mine: twelve years or so of age, puny and underfed, tight black curls, barefoot and clothed in rags. I would need to dress him properly and feed him up.

'Come with me, boy,' I said to him. 'You are to be my page, it seems.'

He gave me a white toothed grin and jumped to his feet, following me down Thames Street.

'Art thou named John Coxon?'

'Yes indeed, Master. Oh, indeed yes,' he said, bowing three times and tugging his forelock as he walked. He was overdoing it on purpose.

'You are from the Africs; when did you come to England?'

'I was born in Wapping, sir. I am an Englishman; my father was an Englishman.' He looked at me as if I were a fool. I remembered what Elizabeth had said about his parents.

'Well,' I said, gruffly to cover my embarrassment. 'If you do your work well you will be rewarded. Annoy me and I will thrash you, boy.' That should put a stop to his cheek.

'No, I think not,' he said, without even a hint of fear.

I stopped to look at the little brat, and he smiled sweetly up at me.

'If you beat me, I could just slip poison in your luncheon, but most likely I would tell your sister.'

I would rather the poison take me, I thought, but I could not stand for such a flagrant challenge to my authority. I made to grab at him, but he stepped aside, and I expected him to run. Instead he fell, banging his arm on the cobbles,

---

*   Matthew 19:14

scraping away the skin.

'Oh, please do not beat me again, Master!' he wailed at the top of his voice. 'I will let you bugger me, even though it hurts my bum hole.' He rolled around on the floor, screaming and beating himself in the face. Elizabeth would think I *had* thrashed him, the onlookers worse.

'What? No! You sly young turdlet.'

More people were starting to look over at the scene he was making. I could see myself being hauled up in front of the Beck*. Damn it! A child had outflanked me.

'Enough, boy! You make your point.'

John Coxon, a hanged man's son, stopped rolling in the mud and came to his feet with a big smile on his chops.

'We understand each other then, Master. I pledge to be your good and loyal servant and you my fair and honest lord.' He spat in his hand then held it to shake mine—a thief's bond.

I snorted as I took his grasp. I had been cozened.**

He was no servant; he was my sister's spy.

---

*   Magistrate - probably the origin of Beak.

**   Tricked

A True and Exact Relation of the great Victory obtained by the Earl of Manchester, and the Lord Fairfax, 19th October 1643.

The Earl spent all that night in the field, for the better drawing up of his body together the next morning. Having received intelligence that the enemy would march next day to Bolingbroke for the relief of the castle (the next morning being Wednesday the 12th of October) the Earl drew all his horse and foot into battalions upon Bolingbroke Hill, having a very safe place of retreat into Holland.*

About twelve of the clock on the Wednesday, notice was brought that the enemy was marching within three miles in a full body. Whereupon, the Earl marched towards them and met them midway upon a plain field. The armies faced one another for about one hour, and then the forlorn hope had a very sharp encounter, and my Lord Manchester's regiment, and Colonel Cromwell's, gave their body such a charge as they would not abide a second.

Colonel Cromwell charged at some distance before his regiment when his horse was killed under him. He recovered himself from under his horse, but afterwards was again knocked down. Yet, by God's good providence, he got up again. The enemy's forlorn hope were charging ours, and a good body of horse following them.

Sir Thomas Fairfax, being in the rear of Colonel Cromwell's regiment with his first body, fell in towards the flank of the enemy's body, and so Sir Thomas had the chase and execution of them a great way. Our men fell upon them and pursued them four miles, killing many and taking prisoners all the way.

All told, 1200 were slain, wounded, or taken prisoners, and, as the countrymen report, betwixt 100 and 200 drowned in Horncastle River. The Earl pursued the enemy to Horncastle and there quartered

---

*   The Parts of Holland is in Lincolnshire.

for the night. Very many of our men are wounded, but we do not hear of above twenty killed.[3]

3. The Canting Crew: London, October 1643.

So rais'd above the tumult and the crowd,

I see the city, in a thicker cloud,

Of business, than of smoke, where men like ants

Toil to prevent imaginary wants;

Yet all in vain, increasing with their store,

Their vast desires, but makes their wants the more.

(John Denham, *Cooper's Hill*.)

Franny was alone when the boy and I arrived back at Bread Street. The other scouts had gone to their billets or been despatched on tasks for my uncle. Coal burned in the grate of the main room, warming the chill, and he had even made the garret neat—that was a welcome surprise. I told him of Ophelia's death and Uncle Samuel's orders, and introduced him to my new page. He was most unimpressed with the boy. He also had word of an unwelcome visitor.

'The fishmonger called upon you.'

'Oh, tiresome fate, save me from a vengeful husband.'

'You are to stay away from his wife. He was quite insistent upon it.'

'Did he mention her name?' I had decided it must be Sally.

'You remember not even her name? That is a rum affair; she would be heartbroken.'

'Sally,' I said.

'Polly,' said Franny.

The door downstairs slammed and the sound of boots came pounding up the narrow steps. Uncle Samuel used the floors below as storage, but I knew they were empty. Had the cuckold fishmonger returned? He may have been a decrepit, but some of his workers were bulky fellows. I looked to the sound and back at Franny.

'Everard,' he said.

I breathed a sigh of relief, and offered a silent prayer to mend my ways.

William's arrival prompted another round of introductions, explanations, and recriminations. He was not best pleased at being kept in the city, although he could hardly blame me for Ophelia's murder. The fishmonger's wife was a different matter, of course.

'Thou shalt not commit adultery. Thou shalt not covet thy neighbour's wife. Do these words mean nothing to you? 'Tis a wonder that no husband, father, or brother has called you out.'

In faith, he was correct. I was, am, a sinner. I adore women. 'Tis a petite misdemeanour in the grand scheme of things. Tall ones, short ones; fat ones, thin ones; big breasts and small titties—they are all beautiful. I have kissed pert lips and squeezed plump buttocks from every race and creed. 'Tis no empty boast to say that they adored me in return. There were some I cared for more than others; some that I loved, some who broke my heart. I do not begrudge them that. I probably deserved it.

The poet Davenant told me once that he thought the loss of my mother as a child was the cause. I was seeking my mother in the breasts of the women I chased. I told him he was damned insulting.

I took John Coxon to Birchin Lane—a row of dark shops in

the city selling cheap and sturdy clothing. Above the shops, men and women would sew together the clothes, cutting cloth, stitching, mending, and patching. I could not let the boy disgrace me by looking like a vagabond's brat, but I was not about to waste a fortune dressing him.

Franny tagged along and was busy charming the seamstress's daughter—a pretty little thing, as I recall, but not so enraptured by my friend's wit. John, stood on a stool in his bare feet, wore an old woollen suit of faded blue and complained to her mother.

'I shall not wear them. You will make me a laughing stock.'

The suit was too big for the boy—he was but skin and bone—but perhaps with alterations would work. I looked over to Mother Seamstress.

''Tis a tad over large.'

'We can raise the breeches and cuffs,' she said.

'You will fill out with some food,' I told him. 'And I will buy you a belt.'

'Why must I wear them? I have my own clothes.' He snorted and looked longingly at the rags on the table.

'Because you look like a gutter rat,' said Franny, making the daughter giggle.

'And your nose looks much like a potato, yet I bid you not wear a mask,' retorted the boy, making her laugh some more.

'It pains my sister to see you so ragged,' I said, before Franny clouted him. 'Now, you would not upset Mistress Elizabeth, would you?'

That worked quickly enough. The boy would have presented his own head to her on a platter had she requested it. Like Salome, she beguiled him. 'Twas not healthy.

'Mistress Elizabeth says that you are a wastrel, Master.'

That was cheeky.

'Mistress Elizabeth talks too much,' I said. 'And so do you.'

'She says you have spent enough on whores to buy a galleon.'

'He has spent enough in them to float one,' said Franny, with a laugh. The girl did not look impressed with his smuttery.

I gave them both a look of disgust, and the mother tutted, digging a pin into the boy. His yelp of pain offered me a modicum of satisfaction—cheeky little ragabash—but he remained silent as the woman finished her work. Tuppence to alter his suit, and he looked respectable enough. A couple of spare shirts, stockings, a pair of musketeer boots, and he was fitted out better than a soldier. I placed a brown leather hat on his noggin for a couple of shillings more.

We strolled back to Bread Street carrying our parcels. Pamphlet sellers crowded Cheapside, where the cross once stood before the zealots tore it down. It was sixpence for a copy of *The Civicus*. I took one and read as we walked.

The news was grim. Royalist councils were a bickering mess but our leaders no better. Lord General Squeaky* argued with General Waller over primacy instead of taking advantage of the Cavalier disarray. The attack on Reading was abandoned; instead, the army marched on Newport Pagnell. The war became a multitude of petite sieges and skirmishes, but neither side could strike a killing blow. Neither side really dared to. The Scots promised to invade the north, and the King threatened to bring a papist army from Ireland. For each move, there was a counter.

---

*   The Earl of Essex.

'And have I a bilhoa?*' John asked.

'No,' I said.

'Why not?'

'Because you are a child, not a soldier,' said Franny.

'Am fifteen.'

Franny and I both stopped and looked down at him.

'Fifteen?' I said. 'You look ten.'

I was only nineteen, barely more than the boy, but a year of war had made me a veteran. I turned to walk on.

'So,' he asked again, 'may I have a bilhoa, Master?' He said the last grudgingly.

'No.'

> *'A body was found this day in the grounds of the Cockpit Theatre, most foully done to death'*

The report in the *Civicus* gave Ophelia's name, but nothing more of worth. Mabbot's version of events was bound to be more colourful. I would have to get the boy to buy a copy when the *Perfect Diurnal* next came out.

The walk up Cheapside did not take long. The bells of Mary-le-Bow rang us home. Sermons in the church had become ever longer, ever more haranguing, of late. I was relieved Elizabeth had not dragged me to the service recently. We climbed the narrow stairs to my chambers laden with purchases. There was a note from Everard left under a half-full bottle of the Malaga wine on the table. He knew that I would find it there; he knew me too well.

Come to the Phoenix. WE.

---

*   Sword—originally from Bilhoa, Biscay, which had a reputation for steel blades, but used as a generic for swords by the criminal classes.

It was misty and drizzling, thick and sticky, by the time we reached Drury Lane. I led Franny and the boy around to the back and let us in through the stage door. My key rattled in the lock as it turned. The mechanism needed oiling—Beeston was letting the place go to rack and ruin. A lantern burned inside the entrance, the flickering tallow candle cast a dull light. I took it down from the wall and walked past the boxes of decorations and costumes backstage. We followed the sound of voices. Everard was in Beeston's small room, just off from the stage, with Elizabeth and Gilbert. Seated around an old table, they turned as we entered.

'Oh, you look absolutely wonderful,' said Elizabeth, clapping when she spied John. 'Turn about so that I may see you properly.'

The boy blushed, but did as instructed.

'You be very smart indeed, John,' she said finally, inspection over.

He near swooned at the praise from my sister, but I was more interested in Everard and Gilbert's news. John opened a bottle of Beeston's Malaga red and filled our cups.

'See, Blandford, he pours the wine like a footman born,' said Elizabeth.

'Bugger,' said John, spilling some.

My sister winced. I bit back a laugh, took a cup and sipped at the wine—a good vintage, sweet as nectar. Ophelia adored the stuff, and I had developed a taste myself that past week, but 'twas exceeding expensive sack. For a man with little income Beeston was extravagant. I do not damn him for it; I am the same, but where he acquired the funds was a question. I took a playbill from the table; it had Beeston's writing scrawled all over it, a near undecipherable mess of black ink. It was not his hand on the message in the willow.

'Beeston is in debt,' Gilbert said. 'To some very unsavoury characters. Many angry fellows are searching for him. Informers at the wharves told me he was in a brewhouse east of the city the night before Ophelia was found, but has since vanished.'

'They have been playing The Gravemakers south of the river, all this week past,' I said. 'I saw them both in Vaughn's four nights past. John Rhodes* was with them.'

'How very apt,' said Franny. 'Beeston is dead or in hiding now.'

'We should speak to Rhodes,' I said. 'Do we know who the creditors are?'

'He owes the Boswells,' said Gilbert. 'Gyptians,' he added, seeing my blank face. 'Haniel Boswell is their leader; he calls himself the King of the Beggars. A most disreputable rogue.'[14]

'He is Judas reborn,' said John, with some venom.

'You know this man?' asked Elizabeth.

'He betrayed my father to the constables, Mistress. If it was not for him, my Da would still live.'

The Gyptians have a sorry reputation. They are wanderers, with contacts all over England and Europe. They follow the seasons as tinkers, or drovers, or to harvest crops, but no honest man would trust them. Wherever they went, trouble followed—thieving, witchcraft, prostitution, and murder. My father had turned them off our land more than once. London was home to some; beggars, whores, and villains, periodically purged by the authorities.

Naught else is left to them; barred from any lawful occupation, considered heretics, or criminals, or worse— always the first to be accused and condemned in times of

---

*   See The Last Roundhead.

trouble.

Englishmen are ever suspicious of foreigners. They shake our smug sense of superiority. Roma, Jew and Turk, Italian, Frenchman, German, and Spanish, we sneer at them all. Do you know what they think of us? They laugh at us, think us pompous and dull, our opinions coarse and insignificant, our customs backward, our women ugly, and our land cold and wet. They be mistaken about our women.

'Whatever the Gypt interest in this is,' said Everard. 'Beeston has come to the attention of Mistress Jane again. I saw Mr Darnelly today. One of her agents is in the city looking for Beeston and Ophelia.'

'Perhaps this agent discovered Ophelia and murdered him,' I said.

'Where? Not here,' said Everard. 'And why? If it were just Beeston and the beggars, I would say back to the army with us. But the Washerwoman's agents being involved make it of more concern.'

That was true enough. The Washerwoman—Mistress Jane Whorwood—was like a spider in her web, weaving the threads of royalist plots together. Too often, I had been the fly.

'This whole affair makes my nose twitch with trouble,' said Franny.

''Tis a big nose,' said the boy.

A loud hammering on the front doors to the theatre boomed out in the big empty space. We all looked to each other.

'Who calls so late?' asked Elizabeth. 'Go and tell them there are no performances, games of chance, or any other of Mr Beeston's unsavoury entertainments from today onwards, John.'

'Yes, Mistress.'

He skipped out of the room to the stage and out to the front doors. Before the closures, the audiences would wait there for the plays to open and cutpurses and pickpockets would run amok in the crowd. The players performed in nervous excitement—food and jokes cast at the actors onstage, and a raucous night's entertainment had by all. No longer, with the theatres closed, baiting and games of chance banned, and drunkenness frowned upon; morality and decency reigned supreme. Puritans and war sucked all the joy from the world.

We followed John out onto the stage. Elizabeth took a taper and lit the candles, casting a flickering light in the great space. The boy was not long in returning. We heard a yelp, then a crash and the door to the pit opened. A man—some rough vagabond—and his sturdy beggar friends entered. The leader was holding John by the coat, a knife held at his throat.

'Why does this always happen to us?' said Franny.

Franny, Everard, and I straightened and faced the beggars—hands on our swords. Elizabeth and Gilbert got behind us; I could see the scribe slyly edging off into the darkness backstage. I turned to the beggar crew in the pit.

'John's captor was a wretched creature in patched cloak and muddied breeches, his wide brimmed hat half covering his face—and a dark face it was too, with hollow cheeks and long moustache.

'Let the boy go,' I said, firmly enough although my stomach fluttered.

'Who asks?'

His companions numbered seven ruffians, dressed similarly to workmen, and bore clubs and daggers—but no firearms, I noted. Seven bashers and thieves to three trained men; I wondered how used to steel they were. Perhaps we had the advantage, if the boy could escape. Gilbert had slipped off into the darkness; he would be next to pathetic in a brawl.

I gave the leader a flourishing bow—trying to buy a few seconds with my charm.

'Captain Candy, at your service. Now, if you please, let my boy go.'

I could see Everard in the corner of my eye edging around the stage—a better angle for a shot. I hoped Franny was doing something similar, and cursed that I had only a sword to hand. I was damn useless with the weapon.

'Beeston owes us money,' said the rogue.

'Well, sir,' I said, 'as you can see Mr Beeston is not present.'

'Then we shall shake the money from you.'

'Sadly,' I said. 'There are no such monies here.' I gestured around, noting that Franny and Everard were ready. 'And if there were, it would not be for you. Now, let my servant GO!'

John stamped on the man's foot, jamming the heel of his new boot onto his captor's flimsy shoe. The beggar howled and let go of the boy, who jumped away. Everard discharged a pistol at another of the ruffians—knocking him from his feet. Franny did the same—and missed, his shot leaving a dark scorch-hole in the whitewashed wall behind.

The boy darted away towards the gallery, and I dived from the stage onto the leader, throwing him to the floor. Smashing the basket hilt of my sword in his face, I felt a satisfying crunch as his nose exploded, but another jumped on my back, pulling me away.

I should not brawl. I am strong enough, and taller than most, but no match for a common street basher or muscled workman. The man knocked me sideways, and started pummelling away at my belly. Franny and Everard leapt into the pit to help, swords in hand. Franny stabbed my assailant in the back and he fell to the side with a groan.

I struggled to my feet, heard Elizabeth scream, turned and saw her crack one of the bashers with a piece of wood on the skull. The beggar fell senseless to the stage floor.

We had won this battle. The miscreants could see which way the fight was heading. There were only three still standing, but the bastard leader was one. They left two of their comrades dead, two others senseless, and took to their heels.

'Was that Boswell?' I asked, still panting from the fight.

'No, Master,' said John. ''Twas his lieutenant Running Jack.' The boy's knowledge of this crew from the streets could prove useful.

'Well, he ran quick enough,' said Franny, with a half-hearted laugh. He was bleeding heavily from a shallow cut to the head; it streamed down his face. I handed him my kerchief to mop it; he saw my look. 'It seems worse than it is. A couple of William's stitches and I will be right enough.'

More banging on the theatre door interrupted us.

'What now?' said Elizabeth. 'Not more trouble, I pray.'

Gilbert was late in bringing help—if help it was—Sergeant Hairdye and some of the Lord Mayor's men came into the theatre. Partisans at the ready and wet from the night's rain. Reggie took one look at the bodies of the beggars, and the two captives, and ordered his troopers to take them into custody. Then he turned to me and took his hat off, shaking the rain from it. The grey roots showed in his hair; he needed to dye it more frequently.

'Captain Candy,' said the sergeant. 'What is this here?'

'You are somewhat late, Sergeant,' I said. 'We could have used your help with these scoundrels.'

'I found them just down the road a way,' said Gilbert.

'A fortunate occurrence, Sergeant?'

'The Lord Mayor wishes to see you,' he said. 'We were happened upon by Mr Mabbot as we came down The Strand.'

He looked guilty. I can sniff out deceit—it hangs like a stale fart in the air. Did they watch as we were attacked, I wondered, and wait to see the outcome of our battle? Were they in with the beggar crew? I knew I trusted not the Lord Mayor.

'Fortuna* be such a fickle wench,' I said. 'If only you had *happened* along quicker we may have had them all in chains. Your last name, Sergeant? I never did catch it.'

'Plucker,' he said.

'Plucker?' That was rich. Franny and the boy choked back a snigger.

'What of it?' He was going red.

'Nothing at all, Sergeant. Sergeant Reginald *Plucker.*' I stretched the surname on my tongue. His face went a pretty puce—perhaps not the best time to bait him.

'Our venerable Lord Mayor has some matters he wishes to discuss with me?'

'Yes, sir,' he said. 'Urgent matters, said His Worship.'

Urgent for whom, I wondered. Our Lord Mayor is far too concerned with this business. That worried me further. This whole affair had powerful interests taking note. The Washerwoman, the Lord Mayor, the King of the Beggars. All were dangerous people for Beeston to be involved with. I cursed internally.

Everard and the others watched us leave with worried glances at each other. Gilbert came along with me; Plucker would have to be careful he did not appear in tomorrow's

---

*　　The Roman Goddess of Luck.

newsbooks. Mr Darnelly had warned me to expect Sir John's attentions, and I was passing confident that he would not risk confrontation with Uncle Samuel. This would be merely a testing of the waters.

I whistled as we walked through the drizzle. Gilbert badgered Sergeant Plucker with incessant questions, but received only sullen silence in return. By the time we arrived, I would wager the good sergeant was sick of the sight of both of us. He took an inordinate pleasure informing Mabbot the Lord Mayor did not want him, and to be on his way. The scribe winked at me and left without an argument; he had his story already.

4. The Lord Mayor: London, October 1643.

When I consider life, 'tis all a cheat;

Yet, fooled with hope, men favour the deceit;

Trust on, and think to-morrow will repay:

To-morrow's falser than the former day.

(John Dryden, *Avreng-Zebe*.)

The Guildhall was full of fat merchants, and their clerks, secretaries, and advocates all scrambling together—buying this, selling that, and rubbing their hands with glee at profitable deceits. Reggie led me across the courtyard and through the great entrance, with two guards following behind, and sat me with other supplicants in the hall. The old stone building is the home of London's merchants. It displays wealth and power as virtues—carved masonry, clear glass windowpanes, and great stone arches holding up the expensive vaulted roof; dripping with rich paintings, and guild arms, and statues of the great merchant princes—a temple to Mamon*.

I sat quietly, with Reggie watching over me, waiting on the Lord Mayor's pleasure. I still had no idea of Sir John's interest in this matter. He was an Anglican, but did not seem devout. He was no supporter of Parliament, but nor the King, and whilst a rich gold merchant, was not, according to Darnelly, suspected of supplying His Majesty with funds. I turned to the Sergeant.

'So, what business is this, Sergeant Plucker?'

'You are wanted, Mr Candy. Sir John requests your presence. 'Tis all I know,' he said.

'Captain Candy,' I said. ''Tis the second time you have made

---

*   The personification of greed.

that error, Reggie. Thrice and I may take it as an insult.'

'Indeed, *sir*,' he said, uncowed.

The London Trained Bands were a mixed bag. Some, like the Red and Blue, were amongst the best infantry in the army. The Whitecoats under Pennington were an efficient garrison at the Tower, and when he was Lord Mayor useful enough. The Yellow regiment were not of such quality. They wore no uniform, merely a yellow sash or badge in their hats. Buff jerkins on a few like Reggie Plucker, but most in their workaday clothes and little armour. They were but middling tradesmen and shopkeepers, too old and fat for campaign, and only good for breaking a riot.

I sat pondering the fight in the theatre. Could all of this be for one of Mr Beeston's schemes? I did not think so—Everard was correct, too many powerful names were showing an interest.

Ophelia's demise was a mystery. The actor had been a Royalist for sure, most anyone who worked in theatres was. But, after Waller's plot*, he seemed happy enough performing drolls in taverns. He had certainly shown no sign of worry when I had seen him last. A pretty corpse?

Oh my prophetic soul.**

Then there was the willow tree missive. I knew the hand that had scrawled the message out but 'twas not Beeston, nor Ophelia who had a small neat script. I also knew John Rhodes' writing well enough from Waller's Plot, and knew it was not him. 'Twas not Elizabeth's which I would recognise in an instant. So, all those regularly at the theatre could be ruled out—a testicle twisting annoyance—how many hands did I know?

---

*   See The Last Roundhead.

**   Hamlet, Act I Scene V.

After a lengthier wait than I liked, a clerk called me to a small chamber off the great hall showing me into the room announcing:

'Mr Candy, Lord Mayor.'

'Captain Candy,' I said.

Really, it was starting to tweak at my tit-ends. I may have been young but I had earned the commission—Everard had not wanted it but that was barely the point. The clerk raised an eyebrow at me, said nothing, turned and closed the door on his way out.

Sir John sat on a carved throne behind a table covered with papers, inks, and quills. The room of an official, and from my experience officials do not often like soldiers. A roaring fire full of coal, in spite of the shortages, raised the heat and there was a large canvas of London along one wall showing the spread of the city west and east. The new defences were marked on the map in recent ink, a dark ring surrounding the city, and brightly coloured pins were stuck into the paper in unfathomable design. I had no time to wonder on it; Sir John stood to greet me.

'Captain Candy, do please take a seat,' he said, a half-smile on his round red face.

I took a seat opposite him in a high back chair, hard and uncomfortable. He sat down and looked me over, scrutinising me, intelligence in his piggy eyes.

'You are a promising young officer, it seems,' he said, after a pause.

I said nothing.

'You took a colour at Edgehill; Mr Edmund Waller's treason exposed in the spring, and the army's pay column saved before Chalgrove Field.'* He looked at me as if waiting

---

*   See The Last Roundhead.

for a response. When I remained silent, he continued.

'You were commissioned Scout Captain after the relief of Gloucester*, you captured royalist ammunition stores at Cirencester, and fought well at Newbury. Feted by your friend Mr Mabbot in the newsbooks, and adored by the London mob who dub you The Golden Scout, but you also have some powerful enemies, Mr Candy.'

'Captain Candy.'

'Forgive me.' The Lord Mayor smiled again, like a shark. 'Your own brothers have disowned you.'

I disowned them years ago, I thought to myself.

'Sir John Hurry?'

True enough, he was a turncoat bastard.

'Even your allies find you troublesome. The Lord General is said to dislike you, whilst Major General Skippon describes you...' He looked at a piece of paper. 'As an impudent fop.'

''Twas a misunderstanding,' I said.

When 'tis all laid out like that bare, well, it looks bad enough, but I had fair reasons for all of those petite feuds. Sir John was not finished, however.

'Mistress Jane Whorwood of Holton? The King's washerwoman, the King's Spy Mistress.'

There was a hint of a sneer when he said that. I still had no idea which side of the coin this man played, but if he knew of Mistress Jane, he was well informed indeed. Darnelly would want to know that.

'She is very unhappy with you, I am told, but given no reason for her distaste?'

''Tis no secret,' I said. 'I upset her designs around the poet Waller and killed her brother in the course of my duty.'**

---

*   See Davenant's Egg and Other Tales.

**   See The Last Roundhead.

'Ah yes, well, that brings me to your own sister.'

'Which one?'

'The troublesome one, Captain Candy.'

'They are both troublesome in their own special ways.'

There is something about authority that makes me want to bait it—and Wollaston bit.

'The theatre owner; the presumptuous and wilful young woman who badgers aldermen as if they were servants to do her bidding,' said Sir John, going red-faced at my impudence. 'She should be married off, though I pity her future husband. If she were of lower rank, I would see her in a scolds bridle.'

Well, we had *some* common ground.

'Then we have your uncle, of course. Both the late Mr Hampden and, soon to be late, Mr Pym spoke well of you. Mr Bulstrode Whitelocke is a friend, and now you and your associates are set to investigate the murder of the actor Fenn—one of your playmates in debauchery. Have I missed anything?'

He had omitted the delightful, spiteful, Countess of Carlisle, but I was not sure if she was friend or foe, or both, depending upon her whim. I did not enlighten him.

''Tis a reasonable summation,' I said.

I did not understand the nub to all this; was he merely showing off his knowledge to impress? He leaned forward, resting his elbows on the table.

'We are at a crossroads, you and I,' he said.

I said nothing. He stood up and walked to the map, pointing to it.

'This is the greatest city in the world. Not the biggest—I have been to Constantinople—but the greatest; the beating heart of world trade; three hundred thousand souls. 'Tis agreat responsibility.' He turned back to me. 'To be Lord

Mayor of such a wonder.'

'I am sure,' I said. 'But what has this to do with me?'

'Because I must keep the peace in a time of strife. Civil disorder threatens trade, and without trade, there is little point in London. Now I find you and your sister at the centre of a mystery that has the potential to turn this,' he waved his hand at the map, 'into a bonfire. Have you ever heard of Gerald Polman?' He turned away from the map and sat in his cushioned throne once more.

'No, the name means nought to me.'

'You are too young perhaps. Polman was a Dutchman, a rich gold merchant and East India Company trader. He died voyaging, oh, ten years or more ago.'

'I was nine, ten years or more ago.'

He was irritated at my interruption to his soliloquy—as if he had practiced his lines. Was this just a play act?

'You and your sister do not come into this sorry tale until more recently, Mr Candy.'

'Captain Candy!' I said.

'Of course,' and he carried on regardless. 'When poor Mr Polman passed into the arms of the Lord, he left behind a quite considerable amount of wealth; gold and silver, a great many precious stones and well worked pieces—a collection of immense value.'

That piqued my interest.

'After Polman's unfortunate demise from some tropical malady, his treasure was purloined by one Adams, a first mate on an India Company ship. Four years ago Adams returned from the Indies, absconded from his ship, and brought the treasure to London.'

A mask of gold hides all deformities. [*]

---

[*] Thomas Dekker, *Fortune giving Fortunatus his choice of goods.*

The Lord Mayor paused in his tale—for dramatic effect I am sure—and pulled out a bottle and two glass cups from under the desk. He poured out one cup then looked to me.

'Malaga wine?' he asked. 'You are partial to it, I hear.'

I nodded and he poured out another cup and continued his story.

'Adams split the treasure into three chests, but such a rogue could not keep such wealth to himself without drawing notice, was soon arrested and imprisoned.'

'And the chests?'

'Everyone asks about the chests,' he said.

'So?' The wine was delightful; I took a sip and swilled it around my tongue.

'Adams buried the chests separately; one was recovered and taken by the Earl of Lindsey as treasurer of the East India Company, and the other two remain missing. Adams died in the Fleet Prison before he could be released, the Earl was killed at Edgehill, and the chests remain unrevealed. Until now, perhaps.'

'You think I have them? I would that I did.'

'No, Captain Candy. Had you the chests, I would need look no further than the illegal gambling dens of Southwark. The Earl of Lindsey did not know the location, but he knew one person that did—Adams' wife Betty; a lunatic, bedridden in her home and speaking only gibberish.' He gestured to parchment rolls on the table. 'Her testimony is worthless, and she died recently confined in Southampton. She spoke to only one person before passing, her younger brother—Mr Ezekiel Fenn.'

'Your pardon?' I had thought Ophelia London born, he knew the streets so well.

'I see I have your attention.' He supped at his wine then

continued. 'The same Ezekiel Fenn who resided until recently in your theatre. The same Mr Fenn found murdered upon his return from Southampton.'

'You think he was killed for the treasure.'

'He is murdered, his partner Beeston disappears, and Madame Jane's agents flood the city asking for them both. I make no assumptions, merely calculated odds from the evidence. Now, we come to that crossroads, Captain Candy.' He sat back in his chair once more, leaning on the armrest.

'Polman owed a considerable amount to the Goldsmiths Company. The chests, if recovered, will be held on behalf of the family by the Goldsmiths Company until such debts are settled.'

Now I understood. By rights, Parliament would want the treasure. It would be broken down and sold off to finance the war. Mistress Whorwood would want the same for the King. Polman's family and the East India merchants could claim it as their own, with some justification, and now Sir John and the Goldsmiths had thrown their hat into the ring.

'You want me to help find the treasure?'

'You desire to foil Mistress Whorwood's agents, do you not?'

'Yes,' I admitted. 'That does not mean I wish to help you get rich.'

'You have no witness for your whereabouts on the night of Fenn's demise.'

'That is not true.'

'None that you can produce, Captain Candy, none that you can produce.'

He knew of the fishmonger's wife. I needed to learn discretion. I nodded but said nought.

'Have no fear, Captain. I will not hinder your investigation.

I merely expect you to report to me your findings. Are such terms agreeable?'

I nodded again; there was little option.

Sir John beamed with pleasure. 'Very good, Captain Candy—then I will have no need of this.' He picked up a piece of parchment and cast it on the fire.'

'What was that?'

'That was a warrant to seize your sister's theatre and have you both arrested for the murder of Mr Fenn. I am so very glad 'twas not required. Willing compliance is much more agreeable than induced.'

He deliberately let slip the mask. Uncle Samuel's absence from London with the army made the Lord Mayor bold. Such an explicit threat was clumsy, but enough to concern me.

There was little more to be said. I finished my wine in one gulp, and assured Sir John that I would, of course, inform him should I find anything of the Polman hoard. He assured me that he would, of course, keep a close watch over my affairs. What we both wanted, and knew no way to discover, was the whereabouts of the theatre manager—Mr William Beeston.

The next morning I sent Franny to speak to John Rhodes, while I took a sedan to the Tower and Mr Darnelly—my uncle's unofficial deputy—Clerk of the Office of Ordnance and Armouries. Darnelly was a choleric sort, never given to compliments or praise, and far too serious for my liking. Always soberly dressed, hair cropped short to his scalp, excessively lean with skin drawn tight on his face. His grey countenance gave me the impression of an animated cadaver.

Darnelly's chambers in the White Tower were orderly and

neat. The clerks were used to his fastidiousness. His desk, like my uncle's, covered in papers, but all organised into little piles and weighted down with stones banded in leather. He remembered the Polman treasure.

'It is a ridiculous notion,' said Darnelly. 'I recall the case well enough, but 'tis years ago.'

'So Ophelia did not come from Southampton?'

Darnelly's clerk butted in. 'That is the strange thing, Captain. Fenn actually was the brother of this Betty Adams and procured a passport in the summer to travel to the coast. The Lord Mayor spoke the truth in that regard.'

Darnelly sat back and pondered for a moment.

'Mistress Whorwood's associates would not be in London chasing a wild goose,' he said finally. 'Yet I doubt Polman's treasure is involved. It has all the semblance of a decoy. I will look into it. In the meantime, I want you to find Beeston. He is the key to all this, I believe.'

I agreed with him, but had no idea where I would start with that. Beeston had friends who could hide him if needed. Gilbert would have to start throwing money around for information. That would be costly.

'What if I have to spend coin?' I had precious little of my own and did not wish to go begging to Elizabeth. She would only demand to know on what I had wasted my allowance.

Darnelly sighed—my request was predictable. 'I am sure I can provide funds, Candy.' He reached into a draw and took out a purse, casting it on the table—it clinked. 'There is five pounds or more here. Try not to spend it all.'

I took up the purse. That was exceedingly generous of Darnelly. He was normally more miserly than a Dutchman— a sure sign that this affair worried him.

'What of the Gypts?'

'I suspect they will give your theatre a wide berth now,' said Darnelly. 'We have contacts among them that I shall press for information.'

That would have to suffice. I took my leave of Darnelly and walked the mile back to Bread Street. Franny was home—half soused—and eager to hear the news. There had been no word of Beeston all over London. He had either gone to ground or fled. I decided he was unlikely to be dead. Too many people were looking for the swine and the body would have turned up.

'I saw John Rhodes,' said Franny. 'He knew nothing of worth, but will see to the boy's funeral. The actors will make a collection.'

'The brotherhood of the stage always look after their own,' I said. 'Anything else?'

'We have been invited to the football on Sunday,' he told me.

'Football is forbidden.'

''Tis the forbidden fruit that is most sweet, Sugar.'

'Have you told William this?'

'No, I thought it best come from you. Mabbot will be there; he hopes for more information on Beeston and Ophelia.'

'My thanks, let us hope that persuades William to be reasonable.'

Everard would rather report an illegal gathering than happily attend. He was becoming ever more radical of late. Everyone seemed to become bitter, full of piss and vinegar, as the war dragged on. Mayhap watching a game of football would lift our spirits.

From Anne Candy to Elizabeth Candy.

Dearest Sister,

I am relieved so to receive your missive. I confess I have quite terrified myself with dark imaginings. I thank you for the purse as my resources are much diminished, but I am blessed in the friendship of Mistress Margaret, whose family, as you know, have suffered much to their fortunes, but whose generosity and kindness can only be praised.

You will forgive me, I am sure, my questions. Our home burned to the ground, our father dead, and James speaking ill of Blandford to any who will listen. Oh, you need not fret about me. Henry wrote and told me that, for once in his life, B acted honourably and bore no blame for Father's death. Nevertheless, Blandford should know of the slanders James spreads.

You have asked for a description of the court, which I am fain to give, though I profess that you will disapprove. To be in Oxford is to be betwixt extremes. There be gaiety and music and joy, and some quite scandalous behaviour. Alongside that is the misery of war. Not a day passes without word coming of someone killed, a fortress lost, or a plan gone awry. Even when there is some joyous victory, the melancholic cost counts out the lives of our men folk.

Her Majesty's apartments in Merton College are quite filled to the rafters with her ladies and favourites. Mistress Margaret spends much of her day waiting upon the Queen, as required by her position, but the other ladies of the court are not of the same character. Anne Harrison and Lady Rich are the two leaders in the dissolute gaming of the Queen's ladies. Mistress Margaret calls them Wagtail and Wanton. For such be their worth.

I will tell you a story of Wagtail, so you may understand the character of some here. On one occasion, in bacchanalian procession, they so vexed one Doctor that he is said to have told Mistress Harrison that though she were not a whore, she was a 'very woman'. Wagtail merely scorned the poor Doctor, flaunting herself at him. Mistress Margaret keeps herself apart from such scenes, but has to endure the taunts of Wagtail and Wanton who name her eccentric and strange.

They parade their nakedness as if it were virtue, egged on in their games, though it saddens me to say it, by the poet Davenant and the Queen's schemer-in-chief, Jermyn. Another is Hudson the dwarf. I walked in upon him rutting with a kitchen drudge this Sunday past. 'Twas like watching a shaved monkey swive a pig – for such is the salacity of many at court. Mistress Margaret says that the courtiers all run up debts of vanity, and their mistresses flatter, cozen, dissemble, profess, protest, and then betray. They have too little time to pray and only enough to intrigue, hiding their sinfulness with gallantry and deceits with fine words.

Mistress Margaret is very miserable with her position at court and stands apart. She says she would rather be a meteor alone than a star amongst many. Wagtail and Wanton may cast their barbs at her, but for whom is their honour held?

I keep the door to my bedchamber firmly locked at night, I assure you.

I will write again soon, Elizabeth, but I confess it

becomes increasingly difficult to find reliable carriers at such time.

Anne, Oxford, Oct 24th 1643.[15]

5. The Football Match: London, October 1643.

Am I so round with you as you with me,
That like a football you do spurn me thus?
You spurn me hence, and he will spurn me hither:
If I last in this service, you must case me in leather.

(Shakespeare, *A Comedy of Errors.*)

I looked out at the crowd packed into Smithfield, all dressed in their Sunday best after service. Some were standing on carts and others on horseback, straining to see the battle begin at the middle. The open space on the edge of The City was perfect for the game, part enclosed by encroaching houses and shops, but gardens and open fields to the north before the new defences. Food and drink was being sold from some of the buildings, and by vendors from carts—pies, sausage, ale, and the like.

The match in the centre of the field was about to start: two gates set up about two hundred paces apart as goal, and the players just taken to the field. Each side was a squadron of twenty men wearing a token bearing their troops colour— red or white. Some were spurning* and tossing the leather as others made ready for the game by smoking a pipe or drinking tankards of ale handed over by the crowd.

''This is sure to cause trouble,' I said.

''Tis a grudge match,' said Franny, missing the point.

''Tis blasphemous,' said Everard. 'This is the Sabbath.'

It was a deliberate attempt to whip up a storm in London. Football had been banned since the summer, along with other unruly entertainments. The authorities, scared of large crowds gathering in a disgruntled city, dared not risk

---

*   Kicking.

such pastimes causing a riot. The capital smouldered with increasing taxes and regulations. This gathering had been promoted by Royalist malignants daring the authorities to do something. It probably would cause a riot.[*]

I wondered whether to get a wager on; the red squadron were bigger, watermen and carters by the looks of them. Perhaps I could make up some of my losses at the table.[16]

'Let us see what the odds are,' I said.

'He that loveth silver shall not be satisfied with silver; nor he that loveth abundance with increase: this is also vanity,' said Everard.[**]

'We are only mixing with the crowd, William,' Franny told him. 'It would be suspicious not to ask.'

'You are each as bad as the other.'

I worried about Everard. His widow woman did not seem to make him happy and he gave himself up more and more to wonder on sin, and the state of our souls and nation. I knew he thought London nothing more than Gomorrah reborn, but his mood grew more radical by the week, and more sour. The happy poacher I had first met seemed weighed down with the worries of the world, as if seeking some inspiration—a solution to our woes. It was damned irritating, I can tell you.

Franny and I jumped down from the cart to lay wagers and buy refreshments.

'This be different to the game we play at home,' I said. 'There, whole villages take part. 'Tis merely an excuse for a brawl, if truth be told.'

'That is mob football,' said Franny. 'This is London rules.'

We found a broker running a book. A small man with a big, drooping, ginger moustache, such that he resembled a

---

[*] The football match probably took place on Sunday October 24th 1643.

[**] Ecclesiastes 5:10

tomcat, and bright green bonnet. The odds were not good. Everyone was laying wagers on the Reds, but at five pence down for seven returned it did not look a worthwhile wager.

'What about the Whites?' I asked.

'Shop-boys and street-rats,' he said, and then spat. 'A penny down, I will give you three back if they win.'

I handed over a shilling and took my token then made my way back to the wagons around the edge of the crowd. I bought a flask of ale and a blood sausage to share between us and we rejoined Everard.

'So, how is this game played?' I said, climbing atop the cart.

'The judge tosses the ball into the middle of the field, and the two teams need to drive it towards the other goal,' Franny told me. 'The team that makes a goal first wins. No hands and no spurning each other in the whirligigs.'

'I have seen no sign of Gilbert,' said Everard.

'I am certain he will be along shortly, William,' I said. 'Let us enjoy the spectacle.'

He snorted in response to that and turned to watch the game. The two sides had gathered in the middle of the field for the kick off. The leather thrown between them and a great mêlée struck up. The Red team kept around the ball, throwing elbows and kicks, and drove it hard towards the White goal. The Reds seemed confident enough, leaving only one player back to guard.

The Whites were bundled out of the way. The ball kicked high and fast and a rush of players following. Reds looked certain to score after only a minute of play, but a White player got into the middle of them, taking a good few boots and kicks, and gave the ball a great hoof back towards the Red goal.

One of the White players was swift. He ran fast after the ball trying to reach it before the Reds fell back—too slow. The Red Guard came from his goal, knocked the ball calmly to one of his own players, and the Reds went on the attack once more.

That set the pattern for the contest. The Reds would drive the ball up to the White goal time and time again, but at the last moment a white boot would kick the ball away. The Reds would have to build their attack once more. The swaying crowd whooped and shouted with every kick and shove.

I chewed on my sausage as I watched, taking an occasional gulp from the ale. This was all a new experience for me. The crowd adored the action, roaring, chanting, and shouting out insults to the players—their own and the opposition. Some of the boys watching knew the players names and called out to their heroes as they ran past, screeching with delight when one responded with a smile or a wave.

A rare attack by the Whites, as one small lad, following up his own kick, rushed onto the ball. The Red Guard, seeing he would not reach the leather in time, barged the white player, knocked him sideways and kicked out at his leg. The lad screamed, clutching at his shin as he fell to the floor and the Red Guard took control of the ball.

Three or four Whites charged across the field, jumped onto the Red Guard, and started to pummel him. Red and White players joined in a mass brawl - kicking, punching, and stamping. By the time it was over, both the Red Guard and White attacker were carried off unconscious. The ball tossed back into the middle by the umpire* and game on once more.

---

*   The word umpire in a sporting sense is first attested in 1714. They would not become referees until the Nineteenth Century.

'Is that not your boy?' said Franny, pointing out one of the white players.

I followed his gesture and there was John, dressed in rags once more. He stayed on the edge of the battle around the ball, throwing in a boot now and again. He was covered in muck but wore a wide grin on his face.

'Gad! Cheeky little beggar should be shining my spare boots.'

'There is Mabbot,' said Everard, and jumped down off the cart without another word, turning away from the game.

Franny shrugged at me and we followed him. Mabbot had promised us information on Beeston from his myriad of contacts. We were all keen to find the blackguard, but Franny had also noted William's morose mood. He was reading too much, I decided. Too many of those radical words flooding his head with foolish notions. He was not alone; there were many like him, angry at injustice and envious of their betters. Voices growing ever louder as the war stumbled on with no sign of end.

Gilbert was stood at the back of the crowd on some boxes, straining to watch the action. Every now and again, he would scribble in the journal he carried everywhere.

'Another pamphlet, Gilbert,' I said as we joined him.

'If there is a riot 'twill be worth more,' he said. 'Is that not your boy?'

'Yes, he is for a whipping when my sister finds out.'

I pulled an empty barrel over and stood up beside Gilbert and Franny to see the game. Everard sat down on his arse and started packing a pipe, his back to the game. The Reds were on the attack once more, hacking the ball towards the White goal, rushing any White player in their way. It looked like an easy win but the White guard was damnably brave. He dove into the middle of the Red players, taking a few hits, booting the ball as hard as he could away from his goal. Then the oncoming rush crushed him.

The ball flew high and long towards the Red goal, but their guard was nowhere near; he had joined the last attack on the White goal. I saw John running as fast as he could up field. He was certain to get to the ball first; the lumbering Red team were too far behind to catch him. As the ball bounced, he caught it square on his boot and spurned it straight into the goal.

The crowd roared their approval and rushed the field. John lifted up high on the backs of some of them, whilst scuffles and fights broke out amongst others. The Red team stood about, mouths gaping at the sudden nature of their defeat.

'Where is the man with my winnings,' I said, looking for Red Moustache.

'Over there,' said Franny.

I saw him walking off towards the open fields beyond the city. As I watched, his green bonnet disappeared and the red moustache was removed.

'Sly bastard! After him, Franny!'

The two of us jumped down from the barrels and ran after the man, leaving Everard and Gilbert behind. The cozener did not get far; Franny had his hand on the man's collar, quick as you like, and he grudgingly handed over the three shillings at the threat of our steel. There were others waiting for their winnings, grateful we had caught him before he disappeared. John had cost him money with that goal at such long odds. Red Moustache was having a bad day. I felt no pity for him as he counted out my winnings.

With the end of the football, fighting had started between supporters of the two sides. The players threw themselves into the violence as well. Franny and I rejoined Everard and Gilbert and watched on. Pushing and shoving, men struggling on the floor, flurries of punches and kicks as the crowd descended into a mob.

'Here comes more trouble,' said Gilbert, pointing with his pencil, then making some jottings.

At the southern end of the field, coming in from Little Britain, were the buff coats and pikes of the Lord Mayor's Yellow Regiment. They quickly became the focus of the crowd's ire. A pitched battle got under way between the football spectators and authorities. The Yellowcoats breaking heads and arresting anyone they could lay hands on. The crowd threw stones and jumped unwary guardsmen, kicking and punching them to the ground. There were some digging up cobbles and tearing down buildings for makeshift weapons.

'Grab the boy and let us away from here,' said Everard.

John was with the crowd tossing stones, and curses, at the Lord Mayor's men, but more troopers were coming into the field. They were starting to block off side streets, keeping people penned up in Smithfield and away from the city. I grabbed the boy.

'Come along, my lad,' I said. 'We are away from here and you have chores to do if you do not wish Mistress Elizabeth to hear of this?'

The boy came meekly as a full-blown riot broke out. We headed to the gardens at the northern end of the field away from the troops and the arrests. It is strange now to think how close Smithfield was to the farms beyond London. Now, it is all enclosed with buildings around the marketplace. London swallows up so much, but grows greater every year; 'tis bigger than Constantinople now.

Safe from the fighting, Gilbert gave us his news. It was good news indeed.

'It would seem that Mabbot's information is correct,' said Mr Darnelly. 'Beeston has been arrested in Southampton.'

'What of the Polman hoard?' I asked. 'Mabbot has heard nothing of it.'

'The detail of the case matches our records, but I think the Lord Mayor lays a false trail,' said Darnelly. 'Yet such an obvious deceit begs the question why? Wollaston is no fool. Get yourselves to Southampton and bring Beeston back. He will have the answers to Fenn's murder and why it has aroused such interest.'

'There are two armies between here and Southampton,' said Everard.

'Then you shall have to be careful, Mr Everard, will you not.' He handed a warrant to me bearing the Earl of Essex's seal. 'Take this. It should ease your passage.'

We left the tower in a sour mood. A journey in those times was not to be undertaken lightly. Quite apart from random ambush or the poor weather, was the Hoptonian army (my eldest brother Henry among them) pushing on Winchester and threatening the southern approach to London.

'How the Devil are we to get past Hopton,' said Franny once we were clear of the citadel.

'Cut south first,' I suggested, 'and travel along the coast.'

'It would take too long,' said Everard. 'Mayhap General Waller will assist us. Best we get to Farnham first and see how the land lies. At least it gets us out of London and into the fresh air.'[17]

Franny and I grimaced. Both of us preferred a night in a city tavern to one spent in some barn or under canvas, especially with the weather so foul, but William believed grubbing in the dirt more godly. At the very least, I hoped it would lift his recent dark mood.

6. Farnham Castle: November 1643.

Love is the fart
Of every heart;
It pains a man when 'tis kept close,
And others doth offend when 'tis let loose.

(Sir John Suckling, *Love's Offence*.)

In happier times, the ride to Southampton would take only two days of easy riding. We set out early the next morning, and in foul weather, made our way to Kingston and onto Farnham by nightfall. We kept to a trot, passing columns of marching infantry and carts of supplies, with rain, sleet, and snow beating hard down upon us, and the road slick with mud and waters. Apple, made miserable by the weather, kept his head low.

'I like this not at all,' I said.

There were grunts of acknowledgement from Franny and Everard, but no conversation forthcoming. I pulled my hat down and watched the stream of rain drip from the brim. All of us, men and horses, were soaked to the skin.

Waller's new army was in Farnham, but beyond that, Royalist cavalry raided with impunity. Sir Ralph Hopton's cavalier force (my oversized, witless, brute of an eldest brother amongst them) had advanced as far as Winchester. Much of England seemed at the King's command. Royalist armies slowly pushed on the capital, ringing London and the South Eastern shires. Look at the maps: the Royalist noose tightened around our necks but control was a doomed notion. No place was truly for the King, just as no place was truly for Parliament. Ambush, murder, and sabotage could strike anywhere, even in your own bed.

'There are soldiers up ahead,' said Franny.

A barricade of carts was set up as we descended the ridge before Farnham. Dragoons, well-equipped veterans from their demeanour, waved us off the roadway to check our papers. I pulled out the soggy parchment bearing the Earl of Essex's seal and warrant, and handed it to one. A young trooper stood dripping in the rain squinted at the note, slowly reading the words to himself. He looked up at us.

'You will have to come and see the major, sirs. You are expected,' he said, and handed back our credentials.

He directed us off to the buildings where most of his troop was billeted—an old farmhouse of rough stone, with upper floor of wood and a shingle roof in no good condition. We took our horses to a lean-to—a makeshift stable beside the house. There were cowsheds and barns behind taken up with men and beasts hiding from the elements.

'How the buggery are we expected?' asked Franny as we tied up our mounts. 'We only decided to leave last night, and only Darnelly knew our plans.'

I shrugged but Everard looked glum.

'It means that we are playing to somebody else's rules,' he said. 'Say nought of our need to go to Southampton. We are on a mission for the Earl, is all we tell.'

Franny and I nodded in agreement and followed Everard to the farmhouse. Tents pitched behind the house with at least a troop of goons billeted, waiting. Two sullen, soaked, guards on duty at the doors showed us into the building. As we entered, dripping wet on the flagstone floor, a booming Scots voice greeted us.

'All the fountains of the great deep are broken up and the windows of heaven open, and here arrive Shem, Ham and Japeth!* Come out of the rain, my friends, and into our ark.'

---

*   Genesis chapter 7.

'Twas Archie Strachan. A major of dragoons in Waller's army, and a good officer who knew us all well enough. I owed him my life, and my sister's, and liked him—even if he did talk like Milton in his cups.* He grasped my hand and shook it. His normally neat dark beard was untrimmed and he looked thinner, his slender frame bony and gaunt.

'Well met, my friend,' I said, shaking his hand.

'Hullo, Archie,' said Franny.

'That is Major Strachan to you, Francis,' he replied with a twinkle, then turned to one of the men huddled around the fire. 'Fetch us some of that honey-mead and bring it into the parlour.' He shrugged at us. 'Farmers mead is all we have or some dried biscuit if you are hungry? 'Tis not so dry but fit enough to eat...'

We shook our heads.

'Just as well; the biscuit is awful. The mead is passable though.'

'What are you doing here, Archie?' I asked. The normally taciturn Scot sounded like he had been much-at-the-mead already.

'Set to watch for you gentlemen as I know you by sight. Come, let us talk where we can be seated.' He took us through into a small room with rough chairs and table. Closing the door behind us, he added quietly. 'And not heard.' He put his fingers to his lips.

We divested ourselves of wet cloak and hat. A trooper brought a jug of hot mead and cups, set them on the table and left. I sat and poured us all drinks and Everard turned to Strachan.

'What goes here, Strachan?' he said in a low voice.

'I know not, friend. I was put here to watch for you

* See The Last Roundhead.

yesterday with my men, and told you would be along in a day or two. When you arrive, I am to take you on to the general.'

'We told none of our coming...' started Franny. I kicked him under the table and he stopped talking.

'The general has his own informers,' said Strachan. 'Worse, he thinks you are part of some plot of Essex's.'

'Ridiculous!' said I.

'Ridiculous or not he believes it,' said Strachan. 'The general has changed since the Roundway. He sees enemies everywhere and is convinced Essex tries to undermine him. His own clerk stands condemned on a charge of mutiny. Waller will hang him on the morrow'[18]

The dislike between Waller and Essex was well known; the pamphlets were full of the feud. Waller thought Essex vacillating and weak, whilst Essex believed Waller wanted his role as commander. Both were in the right; both played out their petty jealousies with armed men at their backs—to the detriment of our cause. After Waller's defeat at Roundway Down, and Essex's fortunate victory at Newbury, the Earl was in the ascendant. Waller, embittered, blamed the Earl for every slight real or perceived.

'What will he do?' asked Everard.

'Question you, and hold you if your answers are not satisfactory, I would hazard,' said Strachan. 'Waller has determined to march on Winchester and thinks you are sent by Essex to interfere.'

'He marches out in this weather?' I said, surprised. 'The elements alone will defeat him; he needs no interference from us. Why have you not stopped him from this course, Archie?'

'He thinks me of no more use than riding picket or garrison duty,' the Scot replied with a wry smile. 'I am too much the radical independent for his Presbyterian ways.'

That was worrying news indeed. I could see from Franny and Everard's face that they took it as ill-omened.

'This army is no good,' Strachan continued. 'But the general will not see it. Most are untried militia from the London bands. Good enough playing at soldiers at home, but they will not march happily in this deluge, nor stand under fire, and none paid for weeks past. Waller knows it in his heart too, but is driven to prove himself after the defeat. He is become reckless.'

'So, what are we to do now?' asked Everard.

'I will take you up to the castle to see the general,' said Strachan. 'If you will take my advice, answer him true and hope he sees good sense.'

Farnham Castle is well defended from all but the most determined assailant, with its strong wall, great towers and ditch, keeping safe the fine red palace within. By the time we rode through the gatehouse with Strachan and his escort, it was very late indeed. Inside was busy with people, beasts, carts, and soldiers. There were smiths hammering away at a forge, and camp followers, food vendors, and whores plying their trade. The furnaces, smoke, and seething shadows gave it a hellish aspect in the darkness.

We dismounted, handed our horses to Strachan's men and he led us up to the palace entrance. Guards stood watching, but they nodded us through without question. Strachan took us up some steps to a hall with three great windows looking into an inner courtyard. There were benches along the other wall. He pointed to them.

'Wait here,' he said. 'I will let the general know you have arrived.'

He was not gone long, soon returning with a clerk and beckoning us to follow. We went through a doorway and down some steps into a large hall with carpeted floor and paintings of bishops in their robes on the wall.

I heard Everard mutter, 'Papist priests be damned!'

There was a roaring fire and chairs around a table covered in papers and maps. Standing by the fire, warming himself, was the General. William Waller—William the Conqueror as the London newsbooks had christened him.

I would not judge him on newsbooks opinions—not when they dubbed me The Golden Scout—but Waller did not impress. The circumstance of war had brought him low, and whilst as a battlefield commander he was better than most, that night he was embittered and suspicious.

He turned as we entered; a man of middling years, hair still thick and brown, beard and moustache trimmed and neat. In spite of his rank, he was dressed like a captain of 'goons in buff coat and riding boots. I noted the dark circles under his grey eyes and furrowed brow—this was not a happy man.

'You are Essex's spies,' he said, coming straight to the point.

'No, indeed, Sir William,' I replied. 'I am Scout Captain Candy and these are two of my officers. We are on...' I paused. 'An engagement that takes us to Southampton.'

'You just happen to arrive as I prepare to march on Winchester?'

'A sorry coincidence, I can assure you, sir.'

'What, pray tell, is this mission in Southampton?'

'We are ordered not to divulge that information, sir.'

'I am your superior, sir!'

'That is as may be, Sir William. Yet, my warrant is from the Earl of Essex. I am sure he will be happy to give you the information you require, should you request it of him.' That was bold, but I had no choice.

He glared back at me. It was perfectly in his power to hold us and request confirmation from Essex, but I think he simply wanted rid of us. He turned to Archie, stood quietly behind Everard and Franny.

'Do you vouch for these men, Strachan?'

'I do, Sir William.' There was no hint of hesitation; Archie was a true friend.

'Then, 'tis your responsibility to see them to Southampton at good speed. If they are not here to spy for Essex, there is no need for them to tarry. Take a troop of your dragoons and hurry them along.'

'Yes, Sir William.' I was sure from his face Archie was regretting our friendship.

With that, we were dismissed. Short and sweet, the way I like meetings with general officers. Strachan was not so happy as he led us back to the farmhouse.

'Every time we meet it leads to trouble, Sugar Candy. If we were aboard ship, I would cast you overboard for the whale.'

'My apologies, Archie,' I said, with at least some pretence of remorse.

*So they cast lots, and the lot fell upon Jonah.**

There were thirty men and horse ready the next morning under Strachan's command—well equipped with carbines, and pistol, and all veterans. They stood patiently waiting to

---

*   Jonah I: VII

ride out before dawn. The army was to be arrayed for the clerk's hanging, and none of us wished to wait for that.

'Where are the rest?' I asked Strachan.

'This is all there are—not enough horses—most troops are half strength,' he said. 'Come along, gentlemen, let us away from here.'

Our small column clattered down the muddy road to Alton. The clouds above us were heavy with rain that looked set in for the day. A company of musketeers held a small village down the road, about an hour's ride Strachan told us. We would break our fast there.

From Farnham, the road descends into a wooded vale alongside the River Wey, before rising up to the village where our men were placed. Some of Waller's veteran infantry in a far-flung outpost greeted us there. They were nervous, but had no word of Royalists on the road. The cavalier commander in Winchester had drawn his men back to the city to ready for Waller's assault and no traffic had come down the road for two days past.

'I like it not,' said Franny. 'We would be better advised to ride across country on our own.'

'Once we arrive in Alton we can take the road to Southampton and Strachan will lead his boys back,' said Everard. 'Let us just pray we have no trouble meantime.'

People often complain that their prayers are never answered. What they mean is their wishes did not come true. The Lord our Father always answers your prayers. 'Tis just the answer most often be no.

By the time we neared Alton, I began to believe that our prayers had been answered in the affirmative. We saw none on the road. The weather too foul for casual travel, and locals hid from the soldiery. Strachan pulled us to a halt outside the town and sent one of his men in on foot to check nearby buildings. He was not long in returning, running back to our position at a low dry-stone wall. The crack of musketry started up and Archie had us off our mounts with carbines returning fire.

We three huddled behind the wall, hiding from the crack of stone splintering shot, fumbling with damp powder and cartridge.

'How do we know they are Royalist?' I said, loading a pistol.

'They are shooting at us, Sugar,' replied Franny. ''Tis generally a tell.'

Everard rose up above the wall, and in one movement aimed his carbine, discharged and ducked back down before the enemy returned his shot. Strachan's men were keeping up a steady fire, crouched in ditches and behind walls, but the enemy had greater numbers.

'We are pinned here,' said Everard.

I grunted and rose up myself, firing blind at a building before crouching again.

'Well what are we to do then?' I said.

'If Strachan can keep them occupied for a time, we can slip off south through the fields and then pick up the Southampton road,' said Everard. 'We will have to ford the river and 'tis in full flow. What think you?'

'Misfire be damned!' said Franny as his carbine failed to ignite. 'Let us be gone quickly then before these beggars decide to charge us.'

I nodded. 'I will go and ask Archie.'

I ran crouched along the wall. Strachan himself was keeping up a steady stream of biblical encouragement to his men, despite the odds. I could see no fallen among our ranks, the rain and cover keeping casualties down. I explained our plan to Archie.

'Well then,' he said. 'We will give you a few minutes, Candy.' He took my hand. 'God be with you, my friend.'

'And with you, Archie.'

I ran back to Everard and Franny and then to our horses, held by some of Strachan's 'goons. We swung ourselves up into the saddle as the troopers started up a great volley of shot. Franny led us down to the river that runs alongside the Alton Road. 'Twas running fast, foam and fallen branches rushing past in the flood. We had no time to reconsider. For a moment, I thought Apple would refuse to enter the bitter cold water. He trembled as we stepped into the river but walked forward, ever deeper, into the middle of the waterway.

The water went as high as his chest, over my riding boots, soaking my saddlebags and me, but no deeper. Making the other side, slipping and stumbling up the muddy bank into open fields beyond, we gathered ourselves together. The sound of musketry was ongoing back at the road, but Strachan would want to be away safely soon enough. After a brief pause, we started at a gallop to make good our escape.

We kept up a good pace for a few miles, across fields to the south, and then cut west to meet up with the road to the port. It is hilly country for the most part, and we avoided the villages and hamlets along the road. Everard scouted ahead, sometimes on foot, and we slowly made our way. It was dark by the time we reached the last rise before the coast. The plain spread out before us and in the distance I could see the city lights of Southampton.

The Parliament Scout.

We heard Tuesday that Sir William Waller had set upon Basing House Sunday last, by way of storming, and had lost one of his captains and twenty-five men. The other side say he lost five hundred.

Had his London bands come on, then the house would that day undoubtedly be taken. His other soldiers did very bravely, especially the Sussex. His own Dragooners even venturing to lay hold upon the muskets of the enemy as they were shooting. But the Londoners failed and could not be persuaded to fight on.

Some say the fault was one Captain Whitekeeper of my Lord Peter's House, and say he would not go on for fear of displeasing his prisoners, and that had he been killed he had lost a place worth fifteen hundred pounds per annum. Others say the soldiers would not fight for fear of hurting His Majesty, whom they expected to come shortly.

On Thursday, we understood that Sir William had had another bout at Basing House, but it did not succeed, and therefore he has come off a little. Instead, he keeps it blocked up, so that provisions of no sort can come into it. We do not hear that Colonel Hopton doth draw towards him, but we do hear that forty sail of ships are gone from Bristol to fetch over a Catholic army from Ireland.

Printed by G Bishop and R White, 7ʰ November 1643.

7. Mr William Beeston: Southampton, November 1643.

Had I ever thee forsaken,

putting thee out of my mind,

Then thou might'st have justly spoken,

that I to thee was unkind.

(Traditional, *A Pleasant New Song betwixt a Saylor and his Love*)

Southampton was a poxy little port full of poor unfortunates fleeing the war—shabby streets, shabby houses and shabby people. The town walls were in a wretched state, the ditch filled in and weed-ridden cracks in the stonework. Towering over the town is the castle and white stone spire of St Michael's, but both buildings were empty husks. A smell of rotting fish and brine hung on the air and a chorus of gulls cried overhead. Compared to London or Bristol, Southampton was a midden.

The town thronged with Puritans, in every house and building, waiting for the good weather. Ships stopped crossing to the colonies during the winter, but soon a new wave would depart in search of a new world. Six weeks spent bobbing on a bit of wood only to be greeted with disease, starvation, and savages—an exodus of the godly.[19] War and devastation at home, or an uncertain future in a new land; many preferred the latter option. If 'twas not the Americas, then 'twas Paris, or Florence or Rome. The great cities of Europe overflowed with English *émigrés* upsetting the locals, demanding their mutton and ale.

Beeston was held in the Bargate, that great flinty gatehouse built like a castle to guard the city's entrance. He had been arrested seeking passage to France, carrying unmarked bars of gold.

We sat on simple chairs with Beeston on a stool before us, and a table between us. Everard lit his pipe and looked on, puffing quietly, whilst Franny and I questioned the scoundrel. Captain Bettesworth, a local officer, sat in there with us. I looked around the stone built chamber: a thick oak door, reinforced with iron bands; strong walls and bars on the open windows; the stink of mundungus* and sweat reeked.

Beeston was transformed; gone was the mask of make-up and oily black ringlets, no ring in his ear, and a dishevelled suit of dirty brown wool instead of his usual scarlet attire. He glared at me. Much of the stench was coming from him I decided, wrinkling my nose.

'I hardly recognise you, Mr Beeston. 'Tis almost as if you did not wish our attention.'

'What do you want, Sugar? I have been detained with no charge! This is an outrage. I have been maligned, I tell you.'

'You were detained trying to board a boat to France with false papers, carrying a considerable amount of gold,' said Captain Bettesworth before Beeston began weeping in faux outrage. He pointed to a box sat on the table.

Bettesworth was a solid man in his forties with greying hair and moustache. He had been brave at Newbury but was too godly for my liking. It showed in his plain dress and no fripperies, and I am always one to judge a man by his clothing. Beeston could have no complaints about his treatment, however; Bettesworth was one to play by the letter. [20]

'What about this gold, Mr Beeston?' I said.

I flipped open the box and looked at the five bars of gold. They gleamed in the lamplight, each one small enough to fit in the palm of my hand. No mark—the goldsmiths had

---

*   Foul smelling type of tobacco.

not seen these ingots. That point made me think of our Lord Mayor and Polman's treasure. The hoard was gemstones and worked pieces, not unmarked gold. This little windfall was something new.

'There are more than a thousand crowns* here, and you near destitute and a debtor?' I said, mildly.

Beeston's mouth opened and closed but he said nothing.

'Just start cutting off his fingers,' said Franny. 'I wager he speaks before we get to a thumb.'

'Twas an old ploy. Franny would play his part as a bloodthirsty rogue and I would be more reasonable. Darnelly played the same game of cat and mouse with prisoners often enough, but Bettesworth put a stop to it.

'There will be no torture here, gentlemen.'

I nodded to him and sat back in my chair. Franny grunted but said nothing.

'We know you owe money to the gypsies, Beeston. We have already had a visit from them,' I said, gesturing to the gold. 'Ophelia found murdered at the Phoenix and you as elusive as smoke. Zeke and I were friends, it would be remiss of me not to ask what occurred.'

Beeston sat in silence for a minute or so, the four of us staring at him waiting an answer. With no make-up, his normally impassive mask ripped away, I could see the internal struggle as he made a decision. Then I remembered he was a brilliant actor; any emotion could be false.

'Twas Ophelia's idea,' said Beeston finally.

'What?' I leaned forward.

'We owed money to the Boswells—one hundred pounds—

---

*   The crown was worth five shillings. A thousand crowns would be £250 (around £35,000 at 2015 prices) See Appendix for money. Beeston would have been carrying approximately 5lb in gold, which today could cost in the region of £60,000.

from the baiting and performances. They demanded a share from the spectacles we had put on.' He raised his palms. 'But no way of paying.'

'How did you manage to get this past my sister?'

'Your sister comes but rarely to the theatre on a Saturday or Sunday, whilst wonderfully my clientele prefer those evenings. The place was cleaned and returned to a schoolhouse by Monday morning and none the wiser.' He sniggered the word schoolhouse, proud of his deception.

I must admit I was impressed. 'Twas no mean feat to cozen Elizabeth.

'And what of the profits from these ventures?'

'Sadly, I have poor fortune. Failed investments, losses here and there, it all adds up you know.' I did. 'Then the Boswells wanted the money from me.' He opened his arms again. 'And no gold left to pay them.'

'You have gold enough now?' I said.

'Ophelia's suitor,' said Beeston, 'is a rich man. He would not be happy if his family discovered his dalliances and would pay to keep the matter quiet. A little word with him, then we planned to go to France and on to Italy.'

'Which suitor?' I asked. 'Ophelia had so many, and enough were rich men.'

'A soapmaker from Wapping.'

'So you decided to blackmail this suitor?' I said.

'What of your wife whilst you drank the Tiber dry?' said Everard, outraged. 'The unrighteous will inherit not the kingdom of God..."*

'What is the soap-makers name?' I said, before Everard started ranting.

Beeston looked up. 'Yardley, Jonathan Yardley. He always

---

*　　　　Corinthians 6:9

stinks of Lavender oil.'[21]

'So, the gold came from Mr Yardley?' I asked. 'And he killed Ophelia?'

'Yardley is a noddie mecock,' said Beeston. 'He wouldn't kill the boy himself. He was to hand over a final payment, but men were waiting for Ezekiel at the soap factory. Yardley had tipped them he was coming. I waited at a brewhouse by the wharf for him. When I heard the screams I decided to make myself scarce—go to the continent until the hue and cry died down.'

'That is truly despicable, Beeston,' I said. 'You left my sister to face your criminal debtors and Ophelia to his fate.'

'I have committed no crime,' said Beeston.

'Blackmail,' said Franny.

'Yardley would not stand in a court and testify against me and I will not testify against him. *Testis nullus.*'**

'Testicles to you!' I said. 'Ophelia was my friend; I assumed that he was yours.'

At least Beeston had the good grace to look guilty at that. He had loved the boy too, you see, not that he would admit it to me.

Was this no more than a little blackmail gone wrong? I asked to myself. No, Mistress Jane would not be interested in such.

The source of these unmarked ingots interested me also. Perhaps it be my innate greed, but something did not sit right and I wondered still on the Dutchman's treasure. Yardley would have to be questioned on our return to London, but what to do with Beeston? He was correct, despicable as his action had been; there was no crime we could prove and no

---

**   Effeminate weakling

**   No witness.

Royalist plot. Even so, I decided, Darnelly would want him brought to London for interrogation—I owed Ophelia that.

'I have seen your woman, you know,' said Beeston, breaking my thoughts.

'What woman?' I asked. 'I know so many.'

'Your friend's sister. The one that got hi'self killed. Russell, was it not?'

I went cold inside. 'Emily?'

'Aye, she left with one of the groups travelling to the New World.'

'When?'

'Before Newbury,' said Everard. 'Widow Russell wrote to Sir Samuel after Peter was killed. They have family in New England.'

'You knew?' I asked.

'We did not think it would do you any good to know, Sugar,' Franny said. 'You took Peter's death hard.' He looked to Everard then back to me. 'We worried about you, friend.'

'You as well?' I half expected Bettesworth to be in on the secret. I was angry at the deception.

'They had already left when Sir Samuel received the news, and us all on the march to Gloucester with the army,' said Everard.

Beeston started chuckling at the argument he had caused. I looked over at him sitting smugly on his stool. He had known the impact his little snippet would have and had happily sown the discord.

'You are an unashamed recreant,' I told him.

'I think we have already established that I am somewhat lacking in scruples, Sugar,' he said.

'What know you of Gerald Polman?' asked Franny.

'Goodness, that is a name I have not heard in many a

year.'

He was lying; I was convinced of it. 'You should ask our Lord Mayor on it; he could tell you more about Mister Polman, I am certain.' He winked at me; the bastard actually winked at me.

'You will come back to London with us,' I said. 'Mr Darnelly will wish to speak with you.'

That wiped the grin from his face.

It was four days of riding, in foul weather, to get back to London. None of us had any desire to return via Farnham and Waller. There was fighting around Alton and Basing House, and Royalists in Winchester. We took the road along the coast to Portsmouth then on to Chichester. Burned out houses around the walls of the town gave dark testimony to the passage of war. We stopped, sodden from the rain, but there were Parliament men on the gates and our papers saw us safely through.

We took rooms just inside the town walls near the Northgate, eager to be away early in the morning. The inn was two storeys high with a red tiled roof, whitewashed walls, oak beams, and glass in the bay windows. There were stalls for the horses and a large courtyard to the rear. I tipped the stable boy a penny to rub the animals down and find some oats for a mash. 'Twas also my coin that paid for the room and food for the night. I noted, sourly, that since my being made up captain, the others rarely opened their purses.

There was only a young maid looking to the rooms and a tapster serving ale; the place empty of other travellers; a roaring fire in the bar room. Franny and Everard threw off their cloaks and hats, calling for sack and food. The maid led Beeston and I upstairs to the room.

The girl was dressed in a loose-fitting gown of blue wool over a linen shift and skirts; sleeves rolled up her shapely pale arms, mousey hair under a white cap; a heart shaped face and brown eyes full of interest. She pointed Beeston into the room and smiled at me—a pretty smile.

'Twas a light chamber with windows overlooking the back courtyard and a high ceiling, a well-strung bed made up for guests and fireplace with coal ready to light.

'You get the floor by the fire,' I told Beeston. 'I take the bed.' I looked at the maid and winked. She giggled and turned to leave.

Beeston grunted, snatched some blankets from the bed and started making up a bunk on the floor. He had been mostly silent since leaving Southampton. No doubt, contemplating his approaching fate at Mr Darnelly's hands. I turned back to the maid, following her out to the corridor.

'You are a soldier, sir? she asked. 'There are always such terrible stories of the war hereabouts. They smashed the cross and the cathedral in town.'

I had no need to ask who *they* were. Puritans, zealots, and independents were like a plague of locusts.

'The evils of war are everywhere,' I told her. 'I fear sometimes that I may go blind with all that I have seen.'

She looked horrified at that, reaching out to touch my arm, taking my hand in hers.

'If the Good Lord doth take my sight,' I continued. ''Tis the vision of your beauty, my angel, that I will hold as a picture in my heart.'

That was glib, and she blushed red, but was no innocent

fooled by sweet words.

'I finish work at midnight, sir. Mayhap you can tell me more then,' she said with a saucy wink, and hurried away.

I smiled to myself. Emily Russell may have fled to a new world, but the pretty girls still flocked to Sugar Candy like bees round the honey pot. I returned to the room with a smug little smirk on my face. The chamber was empty, the window wide open. The bird had flown.

'Nooooo!' I wailed in a panic, sick to my stomach. 'No, no, no, no, no! Damn you no!'

I ran out of the room and down the stairs, jumping them two and three a time, praying to mend my lustful ways if only we could find Beeston. I was half-convinced 'twas God's judgement for trying to seduce the maid. Downstairs, I pushed open the bar room door, took a deep breath, and went into the room.

'Beeston is gone!' I said.

'Gone? What do you mean gone?' said Everard, rising from his seat by the fire.

'Gone is gone, not there, absented himself, departed the premises, gone!'

'Bum-nuggets!' Franny said, gulping down his sack.

We all rushed back upstairs to the room. It was still empty. A part of me had hoped we would find Beeston in his billet and me mistaken.

'You were supposed to watch him, Blandford,' said William.

'I stepped out of the room for less than a minute —not even that,' I said.

'Why did you step out of the room?'

'The maid...'

Everard cuffed me as if I were a raw recruit.

'Franny and I will check the streets and find through which gate he left the town,' he said. 'You see to the horses. We will need to be on the road and away if we are to find him again. Darnelly will not be pleased if he is lost.'

We ran to our tasks. Everard and Franny out into the rain swept streets of Chichester, me to the stables. The pretty maid watched on, an amused grin on her face, as we bustled around grabbing boots, and hats, and weapons.

As I entered the courtyard to the rear of the inn, I could hear shouts from the stable. I rushed into the building to find Beeston trapped in the stall nearest the door—the stall with Apple in—a mistake on his part. The stable boy looked aghast as my horse pinned the actor in the corner. Apple stamped his hoof and snorted, nostrils flared, bared teeth, ears flat back in rage at the intruder. Beeston, white with fear, cringed away from the roan's gnashers. I thanked God and promised again to mend my ways—another broken promise.

'Get me out,' he yelled. 'The monster is crazed.'

Reaching out to calm Apple, I rubbed his neck and back, letting him know I was close. He moved back a tad to allow Beeston to slip out beside him. As the actor stepped past to get out of the stall, Apple moved his head and nipped the man's buttocks. Beeston squealed, leapt over the stall-gate, and fell face in the dirt.

I looked down on him and doffed.

'A sorry state indeed, Mr Beeston,' I said. 'I fear the animal has taken a dislike to you.'

We came at London from the South towards the great star fort that guarded the approach to the bridge. An endless flow of traffic pouring into the city—carts and wagons full of goods, cattle and pigs driven to market, all crowded around the entrance to the defences. The earthen bastions bristled with cannon and men from the Trained Bands. We passed inside the gate, our papers checked, and rode on towards the city.

I was well acquainted with Southwark, and the drinking dens and brothels that line the port roads. It brought a smile to my face to be back. I had missed London and planned on more than a few bottles once we delivered Beeston to the Tower. There would be women too. I would bury myself between the legs of a few admirers and memories of the Russell girl would dissipate.

'Master! Master Blandford!'

I turned in my saddle. It was John's voice. The others pulled up their horses.

'Is that not your boy?' asked Franny.

'Aye, do you see the little beggar?'

'There he is.' Franny pointed.

I caught sight of him darting through the crowds in his rags once more, not the blue suit I had left him in, and covered in filth.

'John, what do you here and in such dress?'

'Mr Darnelly set me to watch for you, Master. Mr Mabbot watches the fort at Constitution Hill lest you came that way to the city.'

'What is amiss, John?' asked Everard.

''Tis Mistress Elizabeth, sir. She has been taken by the Boswells.'

Beeston started to laugh.

Cross Deep, Twickenham, 1719.

THE time for payment came; the money used;
The cash our factor would not be refused;
Of writs he talked, attorneys, and distress;
The reason: heav'n can tell, and you may guess;
In short, 'twas clear our gay gallant desired,
To cheer the wife, whose beauty all admired.

(Jean De La Fontaine, *The Cobbler*)

It is a truth in life, that when you acquire a new suit of clothes you should always purchase a new pair of shoes. Nothing spoils the effect of fine expensive brocade better than worn-out cobbler-patched old flyers*. The upcoming wedding means I am in for a new suit. The idiot is paying.

'Spare no expense Uncle,' he told me.

Where he gets the coin is not my concern; perhaps he embezzles from his investors. So, I have spared no expense on a fine bottle green silk coat with gold thread and buttons, and a white waistcoat and tight breeches with no room for my whirligigs. As you age, the cod expands in proportion to the pizzle's shrinkage—cross your legs too quick and you'll sing castrati. The obsequious tailor persuaded me, with little difficulty, a new beaver skin tricorn hat would be just perfect to go with the new long heavy itchy wig that I am required to wear.

Once the tailor and hatter had left and all else had been purchased, I sent for Bennett the cordwainer**. A local man, but well respected and praised for his work, so I saw no need to send to town for a London shoemaker. I wished afterwards

---

*   Shoes.

**   A shoemaker who uses new leather, rather than a cobbler who would repair and patch old shoes.

that I had.

Bennett was dressed in his workman's brown, with a leather apron and coarse woollen shirt under his coat. Of medium build and height, broad faced, with thick yellow hair tied back. He kneeled in front of me measuring up my feet.

'I want slippers,' I told him. 'None of these high heels otherwise I will be tottering around the stage like a tuppenny whore.'

'Yes, Sir Blandford.'

'And I want soft worked leather. I will not have blisters at the end of the day, else I will have you thrashed.'

'Yes, Sir Blandford.'

I noted a faded green ribbon pinned on his coat, so I poked him with my cane, and made sure the bell for the servants was near—just in case.

'You are too young to be wearing that?'

He looked up at me, glassy blue eyes shining. Damn me a fanatic, I thought to myself. I can smell them out. A wave of fear came over me. Was he here for me? No, he was too young. Bennett smiled—an honest smile. Honest men are the worst.

'I wear it in honour of my Leveller Grandsire, Sir Blandford. And yourself, of course. He told me you were a hero of the Good Old Cause, and friend to Lillburne and Digger Everard.'

I relaxed; this man was not seeking vengeance.

'I was no friend to Lillburne,' I said. 'The man was a damn troublemaker, always whining about one thing or the other. He could cause a brawl in a solemn church funeral with his constant objections. And Digger Everard went lunatic. Did your grandsire tell you that?'

'No, Sir.' He looked crestfallen.

'What drives you, Mr Bennett?'

'I am unwilling to leave the world a worse place than I found it, Sir Blandford.'

'An idealist then. The world is oft a better place for us departing it, Bennett.'

'Do not say that, Sir Blandford, you did much good, changed things for the better.'

'We changed nothing!' I need no reminding of my failures.

Bennett was taken aback at my venom and finished his work in silence. When he was done and sent back to his shop in Hampton Wick. I poured myself a cup of brandy; the shoemaker had unsettled me. The idiot came into my study with a concerned look on his face.

'Uncle? I saw the ribbon.'

I sighed. 'He was no would be assassin, my boy. He would have been but a child.'

I poured myself another drink, and a cup for my nephew. I handed it to him and we raised our glasses together.

'God damn the Duke of Monmouth,' we said in unison.[22]

8. Haniel Boswell: London, November 1643.

Then we'll return home, with triumph and joy,

Then we'll be merry, drink sack and sherry,

And we will sing boys, God bless the King boys,

Cast up our caps, and cry, Vive Le Roy.

(Traditional, *Vive Le Roy*.)

The Fleet River is a foul brown porridge of effluent that slides into the Thames—the rotting waste from butchers and fishmongers, dead dogs, and piss pot emptyings. Noxious vapours rise up like steam, powerful enough to overcome a strong man, and the taste of shit in the air makes you gag and retch. On the north bank, at Hockley-in-the-Hole, is a labyrinth of narrow streets and run-down tenements, courts, blind alleys, dark seedy taverns and warehouses.

'Tis an area renowned for its thieves, cock-bawds, whoremongers, and highwaymen. Young girls of fourteen or fifteen, half-naked with matted hair, empty slops from upper storey windows; boys of all ages, in no coats and barefoot, run on errands for their masters and paters—criminals all. Men and women, dirty and scantily dressed, drunk and bickering, wallow in profanity, lasciviousness, violence and vice. 'Twas not an area I frequented. That be no affectation of superiority, merely self-preservation.

I followed the boy along a wooden walkway slick with excrement and down some steps. The dull glow of torches set into the wall our only light.

'Are you certain on this, John?'

'Yes, Master.'

The Boswells had agreed to meet with me, alone, on their

territory. If I wanted my sister returned safe, there was little choice. Everard and Franny had taken Beeston to Darnelly, whilst John took me to the beggar crew. I did not trust the boy, but was certain of one thing: he would see no harm come to Elizabeth.

We came to a stone archway, down near river level, and John led me through into a dimly lit tunnel with a door at the end. The torchlight showed a figure sitting by the door. A beggar, about John's age I would guess.

'I have been waiting for you, Brighteyes,' said the boy, as we approached.

'Well, now I am here,' said John. 'What of it?'

The beggar stood up; he was about a height with my page, dressed similarly in ragged cloth and no shoes.

'We have a score to settle,' he said.

'I will stand in the ring with you, Eddie, and your Da can watch as I cut slices off your skin.'

The beggar boy looked cowed at that. I was quite proud of my little page; he showed his mettle.

'I will not interfere with the king's business, Brighteyes, but when 'tis done, then we shall see.' He nodded to the door. 'Down you go then.'

John pushed open the door and stepped inside as the boy glowered at us; I followed my page, and nodded politely to the beggar.

'Charmed, I'm sure.'

Inside there were more steps down, into darkness, as if to the bowels of hell. Too dark to see; we felt our way, step by step, holding the dank walls.

'Brighteyes?' I asked, as we descended.

''Tis my moniker. I would watch for the tribe.'

'How delightful. You are one with this gang then, John?'

'Was, till I took your sister's shilling.'

'My shilling,' I pointed out.

He sniggered in the darkness at that.

John was opening my eyes to a world I had not known existed. With its own laws, language and, it seemed, own king.

We reached the bottom of the steps. Thanks be, there was a dim rush-light burning at yet another door. We were deep underground; it was damp, and the sour smell worse. John knocked on the door three times. A hatch opened, and a face peered out, before it snapped shut again. I could hear the sound of bolts drawn back, the door swung open, and a figure stood illuminated. I blinked at the sudden bright light, but my arms were seized, and a hood thrown over my head, thrusting me back into darkness. There had been others hidden; John complained as he received the same treatment.

'I am the gatekeeper, Brighteyes,' said a rough voice. 'I do not know where you stand on the road. That is for the king to decide. So, you go hooded.'

A hand led me; I could hear the noise of people close. I stumbled up a couple of steps, given no warning by my guide. The noise grew louder, as if a door had opened—a cacophony of shouts and catcalls.

The hood lifted from my face, revealing a grotesque parody of the royal court. An ancient cellar with flagstone floor and vaulted roof and lit by burning torches. Full of people barking and chattering at me like animals. Men, women, and children, all delinquents, and dressed in a spectacle of strange fashions, from beggars' rags to the mismatched clothes of quality and every style and colour in between. John was still with me glowering at the audience, but before us on a raised platform sat Haniel Boswell—King of the Gypsies.

He stretched out on rugs and cushions in a yellow silk shirt unbuttoned to his waist and wearing a farrier's leather breeches—strong athletic frame, black eyes, thick black hair and whiskers, but shot through with white. He must have been in his fifties. A blue 'kerchief was tied around his neck, and gold and jewels at his breast.

The King flashed a white smile and beckoned me forward, past the leering faces of his courtiers.

'Afraid?' asked the gatekeeper.

'Of course not,' I lied.

'You should be.'

He pushed me forward towards the dais; a hush came over the rough crowd as I stood before their chief.

'We have before us The Golden Scout,' Boswell said in a loud voice to his audience. 'A man who owes the tribe blood and gold for his partner's debt. With him I see John Brighteyes, kinchin-coes,* who stands accused of betraying the tribe.' He smiled at John. 'Like father like son.'

I thought the boy was going to spring at Boswell, but he composed himself. There was some history to this. 'Twas just typical of Elizabeth to entangle us with this crew by her do-gooding. That was not to abrogate Beeston of any responsibility; I would take this out on his hide—if I survived.

'So, what have you to say for yourself, Golden?'

'If it pleases you, sir, I would like my sister returned.' I said it bravely enough, but I was shaking like a leaf.

The crowd bayed at that, shouting and screaming, at each other and me. There was some disagreement then.

'If only it were that simple,' said Boswell, hushing the crowd. 'Running Jack and Moll Cutpurse say you should be

---

* An orphan - the lowest rank of the Canting Crew.

theirs for the two lives taken, and two boned* by the mayor's crew.'

He gestured to two of his attendants: one seated, a solid built crone in a man's attire, stout and vulgar looking. She smoked a long clay pipe, and stroked a mastiff at her side. That would be Moll Cutpurse then, I decided. Beside her stood a tall thin rogue with ragged beard, dressed as a workman. I recognised him as one that had attacked the theatre—Running Jack.[23]

'They assaulted me, unprovoked I might add,' I said.

'Beeston is your man,' shouted someone from the crowd.

'Do you have any in the tribe that will speak for you?' asked Boswell.

'I will speak for him,' said John.

Wonderful, I thought: a beggar-thief's approval.

'Be silent! You have no standing in the tribe and recompense for your betrayal is yet to be taken,' said Boswell to him.

The crowd went wild again at that. I noted the young boy from the tunnels above had arrived and squeezed in near the beggar king. A clear female voice cut above the shouting.

'I will speak for him.'

I turned to face my timely advocate. She was dressed as a lady: emerald green satin with a tight bodice and fur-trimmed cloak. Her raven hair, unconfined by cap or bonnet, curled around her shoulders. She brushed a ringlet away from her face—a fair complexion, pretty features, and stunning violet blue eyes. There was a lithe body and sweet cuckoo's nest** under her clothes that I knew well enough. She was no lady; she was a punk, albeit an expensive one. Her name was Megan, mostly; it could be Lady Sarah depending on the quality of her custom.

---

*   Arrested.

*   Euphemism for female genitalia.

'What is your interest in this, Welsh Meg?' asked Boswell.

'I like a pretty boy.'

She certainly did, I thought!

'But more than that I like an easy life.'

'Aye, on your back,' shouted someone. She ignored them and carried on.

'Moll Cutpurse and Running Jack threaten that with their foolishness and greed. They threaten all our livelihoods.'

That caused mayhem. Everyone was shouting; Running Jack started screaming at her, calling her unclean, a whore. John and the boy Eddie had started scuffling. I stood there not knowing what to do or say in the confusion. Boswell allowed the arguments to carry for a minute and then raised his hand for silence. One of his men separated the two fighting boys, slapping them both down.

'In what way do they threaten our livelihoods?' asked Boswell.

'The war has been good to us,' said Megan, coolly. There were some mumbles of agreement at that from the court. 'Shag-poll locusts* and dour-faced puritans, all intent on fighting each other, leaving us free to our trades. We stayed out of it, but now they...' she pointed to Jack and Moll '...have ended that.'

There were shouts of 'No!' Running Jack spat at her but Megan continued.

'Christ's blessed foreskin! They have kidnapped the Dwarf's niece and brought her to us. They attacked the Phoenix openly. Now the new Lord Mayor sends his men into our streets and the Dwarf's agents hunt us down.'

There was some agreement in the crowd of cutthroats. Our new Lord Mayor was not popular with the criminal tribe,

---

*   Royalists.

nor was my uncle.

Meg walked forward to stand beside me as she spoke, defiantly staring down Moll and Jack. 'Release the woman, blow off the loose corns*and pray to God they have not brought disaster upon us.'

'Beeston owes me a debt of two hundred pounds,' said Moll. 'Should we walk away from that, Meg?'

Lying bastard! I thought. He told me a hundred.

'I will pay the debt,' came my sister's imperious voice.

My heart sank. Someone had brought her to the soirée. I turned to see Elizabeth standing to the side of the hall. A couple of large well-armed men stood beside her, clearly guards, but she looked unharmed.

'What of my men?' shouted Moll Cutpurse standing up, her mastiff growling, its hackles up.

'You care nothing for your men; you only bring this complaint because you are bought with Pindar's gold,' Meg shouted straight back at her. The two boys had started fighting again, rolling on the floor, punching and biting. The crowd argued and screamed amongst themselves.

'I challenge!' shouted Running Jack over the noise. 'I challenge, Golden!'

I stood, stripped to my waist, on the edge of the ring—a chalk-drawn circle in the hall of the gypsy king. Six paces in width and surrounded by a baying mob. Running Jack stood opposite me, he looked more muscular and taller; he would outreach me.

---

*   Lie low

'You have to survive two turns of the glass, Master,' said John to me. 'Stay away from him; he has challenged, so must knock you down. If he cannot in the time, we walk away free.'

"'Tis easier said than done.'

I am not a brawler, I never have been, and my prospects in a fistfight with a street-basher were not good. However, I had no real choice. Win and we could all get out of this nightmarish den of iniquity; lose and—well, I did not think on the consequences of losing.

The king stood up for the first time on his dais. I noted his strong muscular frame and thanked God I did not face him. He took the neckerchief off and raised it above his head.

'When I drop the 'kerchief, the glass will turn and the contest will begin. When the round ends I will shout turn,' he cried above the din.

I saw a movement and the hand dropped. Running Jack was already stepping up to me, a fist jabbing at my face. I leaped back to avoid his blows, but only a couple of paces before I was pushed back into him by the crowd. He aimed a vicious right swing at my head and I ducked, straight into another fist cutting up at me, smashing into my jaw.

It felt like a horse had kicked me; lifted from the floor with the power of the blow, but still standing, I staggered back, trying to clear my head, eyes watering. Running Jack came on again. Desperately, I threw out a punch. He knocked it aside with his fists and then he hit me, one and two. Pain exploded in my face, and I could only see darkness and stars. I ducked, sticking out my elbow and caught him. I had poked him in the eye.

'Twas not hit with much force, but enough to drive him away for a moment. I shook my head, trying to clear it as he stepped up again. He worked my body with hammer blows to the side and belly. I was being badly beaten, and not even a single turn of the glass.

Desperately, I tried to grab hold of him, get inside the fists that kept pummelling me. As I stepped in, I lifted my knee into his whirligigs with as much force as I could muster. Running Jack collapsed to the ground, gasping, and clutching at his crotch.

'Foul!' screamed Moll, 'He fouled.'

The King agreed, ordering me to the other side of the ring as Jack composed himself. By the time he was able to stand again, the turn was over.

'Do not try that again,' said Meg in my ear. 'Boswell will add another turn.'

I tried to give her my most charming smile, but winced at my cut lip. John looked up at my face.

'Not too bad, Master, small cuts and bruises is all.'

The break over, I stepped back into the circle and faced Running Jack. I heard the shouts around me and instead of circling away from him as I had done before, I stepped up and threw a punch at his face. He had not expected that from me and I caught him just above the eye, throwing all my weight behind it. It was like punching a wall, my hand was in agony and I stepped back.

Running Jack was shaken by that and a cut over his left eye streamed blood. He came on though, determined to knock me down. I threw another punch straight at him with my right, but nearly passed out in pain when it connected - a blacking at the edge of my vision. Had he hit me then I would have collapsed. Instead, he screamed; my thumb had caught his eye again.

I jumped forward, jabbing my left at him, trying to put

him off balance. For the first time he stepped away from me, and I followed him up. I could not use my right hand, the pain was too great, but I hit him again, and again, with my left.

He withstood my barrage of blows, as if they were midges swatted away, and once his eye cleared came on at me once more, swinging his great hams. I knew in my heart, that I was going to lose this fight. I dipped and swerved, desperate to avoid his iron fists, then he caught me on the jaw and I staggered back. I could feel my legs giving way, but I heard a shout.

'Turn!'

Another blow to the top of my head sent me to my knees and out.

Elizabeth cleaned my swollen face with a cloth dipped in vinegar, making my cuts sting and me wince.

'It hurts.'

'Be not a baby,' she said.

After the fight, I had been carried out, barely conscious. Boswell had declared us free to leave and pandemonium broke out. Meg and the boy rushed us away, back down tunnels and up the stairwell. Meg had a carriage waiting; we climbed in and she knocked for the driver to move on.

From Clerkenwell to Uncle Samuel's manse on Thames Street was no more than a mile distant, but I swooned, only coming round to be helped into the house. Then Elizabeth set to cleaning my cuts and binding my hand.

'You have broken the knuckle on your little finger,' she said.

''Twas like punching a stone wall.'

'You won, Master,' said John. 'I can scarce believe it.'

'You do not look happy about it, boy?'

'Wagered on Running Jack,' he said. 'You cost me a shilling.'

'You mustn't gamble, John. 'Tis sinful,' said my sister.

'It is not over yet,' said Megan.

We all looked to her at that. She was sitting in a chair by the fireplace, a cup of wine in her hand.

'What interest have you in this, Meg?' I asked.

'I work for your uncle, Sugar. Mostly I provide him with information. Saving your sorry hide will be a tad more expensive.' I must have looked surprised. 'Oh, poor lamb, you did not think 'twas because of your pretty looks?'

I must admit I was a smidgen hurt at that.

'You are so vain, Blandford,' said Elizabeth. 'So Miss...'

'Powell,' replied Megan.

'Miss Powell, why do you think this is not the end of the matter?' said Elizabeth. 'The money will be paid to the Boswells and no more said. I will squeeze it back from Mr Beeston over time.'

'Moll and Jack were not doing Boswell's bidding. The 'Gypt tribe want no part of the war, but Moll is for King Charles and Jack is Sir Paul Pindar's creature. You have upset some design of his, that is for certain. Tell Mr Darnelly to look into Sir Paul's interests.'

I had never even heard of Sir Paul Pindar; he was another name to add to this puzzle. I was starting to think garrison duty in Newport Pagnell would be preferable to this mystery.

'Now, it is high time I should be leaving.' She stood up. 'Stay away from your old haunts, Brighteyes. You will not be welcome.'

The boy nodded, and Meg leaned over to me and kissed

me full on the mouth. She tasted of sweet wine and honey and smelled of expensive French perfume. My heart raced, beating fast at her touch.

'Adieu, Sugar.' she whispered in my ear.

Then she stood back up, smoothed her dress down, and nodded to my sister. 'Mistress Candy.' And she swished out of the room.

'I like that woman,' said Elizabeth.

'She is a punk, Sister.'

'So was Rahab.'[24]

'Have you not saved enough souls?'

'The fruit of the righteous is a tree of life, and he that winneth souls is wise."*

'What means this?'

'I have noted something about you over the years, Brother. The many vapid little creatures that you dangle on your arm are mostly always blonde and mostly discarded without a seconds thought. I doubt you even remember their names.'

I often questioned whether Elizabeth's honesty was such a virtue.

'The women that entrance you, that can match you, the ones that lead you into trouble...'

'Trouble?'

'Our sister-in-law, and Emily Russell by all accounts, and that little maid whose family Father had to pay off.' Elizabeth counted them off on her fingers. 'They have all, without exception, had raven black hair and blue eyes. I wonder why that is?'

She was correct in her observation, of course—'twas <u>damnably irritating</u>—but I would read little into it. Like most

*   Proverbs 11:30

men, I find certain features alluring. Most women are the same, I suspect.

A Great Over-throw given to Sir Ralph Hopton's whole Army by Sir William Waller.

On Tuesday last, being the 28th of November 1643, Sir William Waller having stated his Army in several quarters to prevent the passage of Sir Ralph Hopton into Surry and Kent.

Sir Ralph Hopton marched with the whole body of his army towards Farnham, where Sir William Waller then was, having only six troops of his Horse then present with him, besides the Foot, the rest being quartered at other places.

Sir William Waller, having a watchful eye about him, had some scouts who first discovered this great army of the Cavaliers marching towards him. The which caused Sir William Waller to address himself to fight, and accordingly ordered the station of his army.

Sir William let the Cavaliers march up very close to him, before they realised he had descried them, and then let fly a piece of ordnance against them. This ordnance did good execution, and after that another. The Cavaliers let not many bullets fly against our Army before they began to retreat. As they retreated, Sir William Waller marched upon them, and through the loss of many men, in few hours the Cavaliers began to retreat in great disorder.

Sir William marched up to their dead corpses, where many horse lay dead, and the riders by their countenance and habit seemed to be of worth. By this time - which was about two of the clock in the afternoon - the Cavaliers began to fly, some one way, some another, but the greatest part of them towards Basing.

Sir William Waller having no more but six troops to pursue them, did notwithstanding follow on, as full of valour and outrage as ever. The service which his Horse did in the pursuit of them was most wonderful, and the enemy flight most desperate. Sir William pursued them five miles, and is still in the pursuit of them.

Sir William Waller hath slain in this fight many hundreds of the Cavaliers, amongst which it is thought there are many commanders. It is reputed by the prisoners that Sir William Waller hath taken, that they saw Sir Ralph Hopton carried away as if he had been dangerously wounded.

There is but one man yet missing in our Army, and very few hurt. Sir William Waller is still in pursuit of the Cavaliers, and is resolved with his whole army not to leave them even though they be already routed. He follows the execution against them so close, that he will not permit them any time to gather again in any place.

ANON.

9. Jonathan Yardley: London, November 1643.

He ne'r consider'd it, as loath,

To look a gift-horse in the mouth;

And very wisely would lay forth

No more upon it than 'twas worth.

(Samuel Butler, *Hvdibras.*)

I told Elizabeth to go to our grandfather in Cople; she said no. I begged her to hire a guard; she told me I was a dunderhead. I threatened to *send* her to Cople in shackles; she threatened to slap my face off if I were so ill mannered. She started attending some dissenting group with an old woman named Kitty Chidley—a tailor's widow of all things—and it made her more stubborn and wilful than ever. In the end, I gave up pestering. I would wait for Uncle Samuel to return to London. Elizabeth would at least obey him, I concluded.

Beeston was carted off to Marshalsea Prison whilst our investigations into Jonathan Yardley continued. Mr Darnelly was as concerned as I was about the unmarked gold, although he still dismissed the idea of Polman's treasure. The news from Welsh Meg that Paul Pindar was involved piqued his interest. Pindar was a rich merchant and known Royalist supporter. So, my uncle's deputy hatched a plan—a ridiculous and foolish plan that had little chance of success, in my humble opinion.

'Just play the fop,' said Darnelly, dabbing powder and rouge onto my face. 'You were born to the part. Besides, we need Cole with Brayne in Oxford.'

'I have never been so humiliated.'

'Oh, Sugar, of course you have,' said Franny.

'Why can we not simply arrest him?' I said. 'He is guilty of

Ophelia's murder, or at the least collusion in it.'

'Because we want to know where this gold comes from, who his contacts are, and we do not wish to arouse their concern,' said Darnelly patiently.

'Well, why do I have to do it? Franny is better suited to this work.'

'Because he likes pretty little boys, Blandford,' said Franny with a grin. 'And you are a very pretty little boy.' He blew me a kiss.

'I like it not.'

''Tis no sin to play this role, Blandford,' said Everard, earnestly. 'You will not be condemned.'

As if that was what concerned me!

'What if he should, you know...?' I made a vague gesture with my hands.

'Know what?' asked Franny, innocently.

'You are not there to be his catamite,' said Darnelly. 'Merely catch his interest and ask a few questions. Yardley provides soap to the court in Oxford. I want to know when his shipments go and who carries them—so buy some soap. Your uncle believes they are using the deliveries to smuggle gold to the King. 'You are the bait for the trap we set.'[25]

East of the city, downwind of The Tower, are the factories, warehouses, and yards of noxious industry. Melting tallow, slaughterhouses, and tanners all add to the stench—a noisy ant's nest of workers, and boats, and carts, watermen and dockers.

Yardley's premises was a tall warehouse backing onto the river, built of rough-hewn wood and shingle roof. A high fence surrounded an outside yard filled with barrels of suet. I walked from the street through the open gates and asked directions to Yardley from a pair of workmen unloading a cart. They gestured towards the warehouse.

Long and high roofed, with tall double doors open to the courtyard. Inside, suet was rendered down and mixed with lye and oils to make soap. It was hot; great copper vats of tallow boiling on the ground floor with leeching barrels and mixing set up beyond them, and a raised wooden walkway around. By the river end, the mixture was being poured out into tuns* and loaded onto boats. I took note of the copper vats—big enough to drown a man in. One as slight as Ophelia would fit with ease.

Yardley was in a small room, high up, overlooking the whole process. I took the steps up, after asking another sweating workman, and along a walkway to his office. There was no door to his chamber, just an open frame. A bare room with a table covered in dockets and some rickety chairs for seating. I noted a cross and rosary on the wall—a papist then.

He stood at the table, open shirted. Thinning yellow hair and snub nose gave him the look of an ageing lion.

'Mr Yardley?' I doffed my hat and gave him a smile.

He gave me a strange look. 'Do I know you, sir? You seem familiar.'

'I do not think so, sir,' I said. 'My name is Ca...' I caught myself. 'Catchpole. Arthur Catchpole.'

He took my hand and shook it. I held it just a tad longer and tighter than was appropriate and smiled again. I was trying to be coquettish; I was unconvinced that it was working.

'How may I be of assistance, Mr Catchpole?'

---

*   240 gallon barrel.

'Soap,' I said. 'As much as you can spare.'

''Tis difficult to procure the supplies for demand,' he said, and gestured to the busy workers below. 'I produce a hundred tuns* a week, but all are accounted for.'

'I would need at least forty barrels,' I said.

'That would be exceeding difficult,' he said. 'Please take a seat. When would you need it for?'

I sat down on one of the chairs. 'By Christmas Eve. Would that give you some time?'

He sat down opposite me and pulled some papers to him scrutinising them quickly. I absently touched his foot and with my own and then drew back.

'I may be able to produce enough' he said, ignoring my foot. 'But 'twill cost. I would need at least half up front.'

Darnelly had prepared me for that. 'Could you deliver to Henley?' I said. 'You ship along the river, I believe.'

He nodded, 'I can add it to one of the weekly deliveries upriver. It may have to come in two loads,' he said. 'Space is at a premium.'

'That would be most satisfactory, Mr Yardley,' I said with another smile.

I handed over twenty-five pounds in coin and arranged for the balance to be paid upon delivery in Henley. As an afterthought, I scrawled down Mabbot's address as means to contact me when the first shipment was ready. I pressed the address into his hand and urged him to contact me if he there be any need.

This had been easier than I had expected.

I left Yardley's warehouse, walked back to the street, and turned toward the city. After a hundred yards or so Everard fell in next to me and we trudged back to the Tower.

---

*   A Barrel is 1/8 of a Tun. 100 Tuns would be 800 barrels a week.

'Did he take the bait?' he asked.

'Aye, 'twas easy,' I said. 'Darnelly will be pleased. He pushed the price up with some corn-jobbery* but 'tis to be expected with the shortages.'

'What of the actor?'

'Great vats of boiling render big enough to drown him in,' I said. 'Ophelia was murdered there, I am certain, but why would they take his body across London to the Phoenix?' It was a point that bothered me—like a fleabite on my cod. 'Had they thrown him in the river, I doubt any more would have come from it.'

'Perhaps as a warning to Beeston,' said Everard.

'Perhaps; there is the note in the willow also, that is still unexplained.'

I was unconvinced by William's conclusion. Murdering the boy would be warning enough for Beeston, and carting a corpse through busy streets across the city—day or night— risked discovery. Yardley and his associates would not wager their necks on a pointless warning to the theatre manager. So, if it be no warning, then what exactly was the message? And who was it for?

I am honoured to have counted Bulstrode Whitelocke a friend. He was much older than I, but had a fun-loving spirit. Age, and a brood of pretty daughters, had not put a grey hair in his head, and his dark beard and long curls were always neatly trimmed. He was quick with a smile and a lover of fine wine and good conversation. Bulstrode was a member of the Commons and garrison commander at Henley near his own lands; we would need his help if Darnelly's plan were to

---

*   Similar to the modern carpetbagger.

work.

'We can stop the barges at Henley and search them,' said Bulstrode. 'That is easy enough. And if there is gold, take it. What then?'

'I will have the soapmaker arrested once the shipment has left for Oxford,' said Darnelly. 'Yardley is a papist so few will take note. Once we have the gold, I can become more persuasive.' He had a dark smile on his face.

I think both Bulstrode and I were a pinch sickened by that; we all knew what it meant. Darnelly had always been a choleric sort, but the war brought those tendencies to the fore. I half wondered if the man enjoyed his duty. Darnelly continued with the design.

'At the very least we shall have closed one of His Majesty's more lucrative sources of income. If Yardley talks, we may find who is at the heart of the operation.'

'Would that not be Mistress Jane?' I asked. 'And what of our Lord Mayor?'

'Mistress Jane will be a part,' he said. 'Who is providing gold from the city in such weight is of more interest, certainly. Even Sir Paul Pindar does not have such wealth. And no, I do not think the Lord Mayor's fable is involved, but best you go see him and tell of Beeston's arrest.'

'Why do we not arrest Pindar as well,' asked Everard.

'On a whore's word?' said Darnelly. 'We need more than that to take one of Sir Paul's stature.'

'And we are certain they are smuggling gold in the soap?' I asked. It seemed an obvious flaw to me.

'Cole's contacts in Oxford are most certain,' said Darnelly. 'Every day boats arrive in Oxford carrying goods, but Yardley's are always taken off to a separate wharf with its own warehouse, and unloaded under a heavy guard. Cole and

Brayne will be able to see what consternation is caused when this shipment does not arrive.'

Franny and Sam both had good contacts in Oxford, and I knew Uncle Samuel had more than one informer in the King's court. If they could confirm our suspicions, then 'twas too good an opportunity to miss; Darnelly was in the right: we could deprive the King of monies vital to the war. That would be a victory for Parliament worth ten regiments.

The Lord Mayor kept me waiting, kicking my heels in the busy Guildhall. When he finally deigned to see me, and I told him of Beeston's imprisonment, it felt like we were both performing a play. It was clear he already knew the actor was held in Marshalsea.

'Of the Polman treasure I have found nothing, Sir John.'

'Really? That is such a terrible shame, Captain. Well I am sure you will let me know if anything comes to light.'

He did not look as if it were a shame. He could barely conceal his amusement. 'Tis bad enough when people laugh at you, 'tis worse when you have no understanding why.

I left the Guildhall in a sour mood and walked back to the manse on Thames Street. The weather was vile, and had been for weeks, biting cold and driving rain. My cloak pulled tight around me, hat down, as I trudged through the dark wet streets. Since Elizabeth had been returned from the Boswell clan I made certain to see her every day, at least whilst I was in London.

Upon arrival, I divested of hat, cloak, and boots and wandered into the parlour in my stockinged feet, calling for a cloth to dry myself. The Chidley crone was with Elizabeth, with John in attendance looking bored. There was a fire, though, and some blessed warmth. The boy had been teaching me his gutter cant and I attempted a phrase.

'Greetings, Mistress Chidley, Elizabeth.' I rubbed my hands at the hot fire. ''Tis rum-bustling chamber-pots* out there,' I said to them.

The boy shook his head, rolled his eyes, and looked to the heavens.

'I understand not this idiom,' said Chidley, looking to Elizabeth.

'We call him an idiot,' said my sister.

The gulf in rank was obvious from their clothing. Elizabeth, dressed demurely, but in a crushed damask dress of deepest blue that matched her eyes. Her golden hair tucked 'neath an embroidered white cap, and delicate little slippers on her delicate little feet. Chidley was a shapeless sack of wool, linen, and sturdy boots; grey hair, big nose, and eyebrows like hedgerows.

I confess it openly. I did not like the woman—a fanatic—and I did not like to see Elizabeth so dazzled by a malignant. Freedom of conscience? Freedom to make trouble more likely. She, and her son, pamphleted, preached, and raised tensions. No bishops! No divines! No church! No dashed nation! A no to everything ideology. [26]

I wondered sometimes what they actually said yes to. Do you know what the answer was when I ventured to ask?—a godly England. Pish!

'So, what be your discussion today, ladies?' I asked in as polite a tone as I could muster.

'Antinomianism,' said my sister. 'What is law and what is gospel, and how to reconcile ourselves to them.'

---

*   Very agitated urinals? This seems to be of Blandford's own design.

122

'Is that not heresy?' I asked, reaching for an unopened bottle of sack.

'Is that not the point?' said Mistress Chidley.

I had fallen into the trap, out of my depth and floundering about topics of which I knew little and cared even less. I poured myself a cup, downed it, poured another and regretted my decision to converse.

'Have you heard of the Family of Love, Captain Candy?' asked Chidley.

I looked at her suspiciously. This was surely another trap.

'Well, I have heard of it, of course,' I said. 'But, 'tis not the kind of premises I frequent; there are better stews* in Southwark.'

Behind their backs, the boy buried his face in his palms. What had I said? The two women looked at me; a blank look on Chidley's face, but my sister was furious, angry that I might embarrass her.

'The Family of Love are a dissenting sect,' said Elizabeth, before I could say anything else. 'Antinomians who believe that the spirit be of the highest precedence, above even that of the scriptures.'[27]

I hemmed and hawed in response to that.

'Can we seek salvation without the guidance of the scriptures, Mr. Candy? What think you?'

I hemmed and hawed some more.

''Tis a world of contradictions,' I said finally.

They both looked in askance at that.

'Look at Elizabeth,' I said. 'A puritan who owns a theatre.'

'Schoolhouse,' said Elizabeth, caustically. 'And that answers not the question, Blandford.'

Something struck a chord in my head; a way to change the

---

*   Brothels.

conversation to matters of more interest.

'Talking of your schoolhouse, sister, when you found Zeke's body...'

'I did not discover the poor unfortunate.'

'Your pardon?'

'The militia man—what was his name—Sergeant Plucker. He and his men were at the theatre when I arrived that morning. They discovered the body, not I. The Lord Mayor arrived not long after.'

I cursed internally at my negligence. Who found the victim? It should have been the first question I had asked. However, I doubted that Sergeant Plucker or the Lord Mayor would submit to an interrogation.

Even so, Elizabeth's little snippet only raised more questions and provided me with no real answers. And then, my sister added another layer to the mystery.

'Another note has been placed in the willow tree, just as you expected; I found it this morning,' she said, passing me a piece of parchment with the same bold hand written upon it.

He shall not depart out of darkness; the flame shall dry up his branches, and by the breath of his mouth shall he go away.[*]

'It is from Job,' Elizabeth said.

'Not a play this time, then.'

I tucked the note into my doublet, I did not wish to discuss it in front of the Chidley woman, and seeing that the two ladies were settled in for an evening of theological debate, I grabbed my page and bade a retreat.

As we left the manse, the boy looked up at me gratefully.

'Thank you, Master.'

'What for?' I asked.

'Rescuing me from the autem-cacklers.'[**]

I snorted, but he was right. Elizabeth could be terrifying

---

[*]   Job 15:30

[**]   Dissenters from the Church of England, of any persuasion

on her own, but that Chidley woman would have given Cromwell a run for his money if they had not been two turds from the same pot.

Mark you, that was the way the world turned. The scribes of history would have you believe in two sides, King or Parliament, but in truth, there were only factions—factions within and factions without. Royalists, Parliamentarians, Independents and Presbyterians, moderates and radicals, aristocrats, merchants, and yeoman, every rank and every trade grasped for power in the absence of authority. The only result was confusion and bitterness—a nation collapsing in upon itself.

Mercurius Aulicus, 9th December 1643.

We are constrained to be larger in the relation of this day's intelligence than we expected, because of the remarkable news of John Pym's death. The most eminent of those five members so justly accused by His Majesty of treason, the fruits wherof are so visible to this distressed kingdom.

This, I cannot say famous, but notorious man, loaded with other diseases, died this very day, chiefly of the Herodian visitation*, as he was certainly a most loathsome foul carcass. However, a preacher at Warwick sensible this might open the eyes of some well meaning but seduced persons, prayed that master Pym might not die of this disease, lest the Cavaliers should cry it up as God's Judgement.

I will denounce no more of it, but, it is remarkable how this man died, observable how Master Hampden received his deaths wounds in Chalgrove Field (where he first appeared in arms to exercise that unjust and mischievous Ordinance of the Militia), and that my Lord Brooke, who loved not our church, was slain from one.

Neither living nor dead, have the prime authors of these miseries cause to rejoice. For those that remember what feeds the present mischief, of Sir John Hotham and his son, and how active and fruitful to this faction Master Nathaniel Feinnes was, would think it strange and wonderful that they should, all three, be now facing a sentence upon their own lives.

But they are the sort of men that apply nothing to themselves that befalls others. They may smart soon enough themselves, and then they will have more sense of the condition this kingdom is brought unto.

I will let Pym and the others rest in peace, though they first disturbed the peace of our flourishing kingdom, and pray to God that he will remove his judgements from us.

Peter Helyn.[28]

---

*   An infestation of pubic lice.

10. A Masked Ball: London, December 1643.

In spite of masks and hoods descry
The parts denied unto the eye.
I was undoing all she wore,
And had she walked but one turn more,
Eve in her first state had not been
More naked or more plainly seen.

(Sir John Suckling, *Upon My Lady Carlisle's Walking*.)

Samuel Pecke was an old scrivener with a stall selling cheap pamphlets and books in Westminster Hall. His own publication was *A Perfect Diurnal*, one of the less lurid and more reliable in the torrent of pamphlets vomiting forth from London. Gilbert would provide him with stories from the army and around the city, and Pecke would have them in a pamphlet the next day. The press itself was set up off Fleet Street, near the Inner Temple: a noisy little chamber with the constant clackety-clack of the press and an overpowering smell of ink that left me giddy.

Gilbert read out his tales and Pecke set the type. The old man was quick; 'twas only minutes before a boy would be daubing the letters in ink, setting the paper in its holder and running off copy after copy—instant news, day or night. There must have been a hundred presses of the like in London, and a new breed of men like Gilbert Mabbot fed them.

We walked to Fleet Street for our supper and he told me his information.

'Pindar is in debt,' he said. 'He has borrowed fantastic amounts from nearly anyone who will lend it. East India merchants in the main, but some other names as well; Sir John Wollaston among them.'

'How much debt?' I asked.

'Eighty thousand pounds,' he said.*

I whistled. 'Damn, that is a lot of coin. Where did you get this information?'

'Oh, Sugar, you know I cannot tell you that. If I revealed my contacts, they would soon stop feeding me their snippets.'

I shrugged. ''Twas worth a try. So, Sir Paul provides the plate, it is melted down into unmarked ingots, and then Yardley hides them in his soap barrels to ship to Oxford. The only link in the chain we do not have is the goldsmith.'

'Our Lord Mayor is a goldsmith.' said Gilbert.

'He is indeed, Gilbert, my friend. He is indeed.'

There was, however, only suspicion. What was it Beeston had said? *Testis Nullis.*

'What of the Polman treasure?'

'Every time I mentioned it, I was laughed at,' said Gilbert. 'Darnelly is in the right, 'tis the Mayor's flight of fancy.'

We reached the Fountain Tavern[29]. It should have been busy with lawyers, but was half-empty with the Inns of Court closed. Gilbert took a table and I ordered sack, mutton, and a penny loaf from a yellow-haired serving girl with buck teeth; she looked grateful for the employment. We took a table by the window, looking out on the road. The girl brought the victuals and I poured us both a cup. A sweet Malaga red, thick and dripping of fruits—Ezekiel's favourite.

'What of Ophelia?' I asked.

'The actor? Nothing that Beeston has not already told. There were none that cared much for him, excepting the bookseller and Beeston; none of influence at least.'

'I cared for him.'

'I like that,' he said, pulling out his journal. 'The Golden Scout sheds tears for his fallen comrades, but girds his manly

---

*   At least twenty million pounds today. See Appendix II for money.

breast for war.' He scribbled down the words.

'I gird my manly breasts?'

'A poet's embellishment,' he said. 'Running Jack and his crew are the hired bashers for Pindar. I would wager it was they who did for the actor - since you care. Foolish, it exposed the smuggling.'

I was not convinced Ophelia died such, but I did not tell Gilbert that. A dark suspicion had occurred to me but I had no proof, and I could still fathom no reason for leaving the body at the theatre. He was certain to be found, and certain to attract Uncle Samuel's attention—and mine.Was it just a foolish mistake?

'Pecke did not print your account of Ophelia's murder,' I said. 'And I have not read it elsewhere, why not?'

Gilbert grimaced. 'The Lord Mayor can be most persuasive; gold and veiled threats were enough to stop that being published. Gold for Pecke if he did not print, and offers to look into my friends business interests for me, if I did.'

That was interesting—our Lord Mayor once again.

'On something of a more personal note,' said Gilbert. 'Your sister has been cutting swathes through Oxford's gentlemen.'

'Little Anne? That surprises me not. Has she hooked herself a rich husband?' Even a cavalier brother-in-law could prove useful—if he had wealth.

'No, quite the opposite. She is bodyguard to Margaret Lucas—one of the Queen's Ladies in Waiting.'

'Bodyguard?'

He laughed. 'Companion then. It seems she slapped some fellow for calling Lucas dull and witless; she claimed that he had less intellect than a turd, despite both looking and stinking like one, and then struck him. Are all the women in your family so contrary?'

Anne was not normally so forthright, but as children, she would hold a grudge to the bitter end. Elizabeth would always forgive my misdemeanours. Little Anne would explode into a rage followed by days—sometimes weeks—of silent stares and poisonous tales told to Father. All her spite delivered with simpering sweetness: a flutter of her eyelashes, a suck of the thumb, a toss of her golden locks and she would get her way.

She had fallen under the spell of Margaret Lucas in Oxford. I did not think much upon it, back then, but poor Anne would suffer for her witless devotion. Some workers came into the tavern - scrivener's apprentices and rude clerks, noisy and calling for ale. I turned back to Gilbert.

'Have you anything else? My uncle and Darnelly like good value for their coin.'

'Let us not sully the evening with talk of payment, Sugar. There is news that the London Brigade have abandoned General Waller at Basing, but that will be everywhere by tomorrow.[30] However, I do have something strange—a threat to Fairfax in London. Our friends Running Jack and Moll Cutpurse named again. An attack on the highway it seems. They are very busy rogues.'

'Lord Fairfax is in Hull, not London, and his son in the north.'

''Tis why I said it was strange, Sugar, everybody knows that. However, the source is reliable in the main.'

I shrugged and handed him the purse under the table. He took it, and pocketed it quickly enough, sullied or not.

'I will pass it on to Darnelly,' I said. 'I am sure he will look into it. Now, since you have some coin, I would say 'tis your turn to pay for supper.'

He laughed and called over to the girl for more sack.

I was drunk. Not falling-down-stupid drunk, but soused enough to feel warm in the cold air as I left the Fountain. Mabbot had taken up with the serving girl—he had lower standards than I—and it had started snowing. A thin layer of white settled on the rooftops and streets. 'Twas not a long walk to the city, I decided, and the boy could earn his keep by cleaning my boots. I trundled up Fleet Street towards Ludgate, cursing each time I stepped into an icy puddle of slush.

I cursed again; a coach had pulled alongside splattering me in snow and muck. Footmen jumped down from the back, and the door was thrown open. Before I could protest, they grabbed me, pushed me into the carriage, and sent me sprawling on the floor at the shoes and skirts of a woman. She giggled; I knew that laugh.

'Well, arise, Blandford, my sweet,' she said. 'We have so much to do.'

'Hullo, Megan.' I climbed into the seat opposite, even as she tapped the cushioned place beside her. She threw a mock pout at me once we faced, then scrutinised my dress.

'Not too bad,' she said. 'Do up your doublet and shirt, and tie your falling band. 'Tis good fortune you are so vain.' She passed me a cloth and told me to wipe down my boots.

'What is this, Meg?' I asked as I tidied myself. The coach was turning around in the street and heading back down Fleet Street towards Westminster. 'You need not kidnap me if you wish to dally.'

'I need a *gentleman* to accompany me to a dance, dunderhead. And I am Lady Sarah this eve.'

'I do not dance.'

'And you are no true gentleman, Sugar, yet here we are. Much better,' she said when I had finished wiping my boots clean.

'Whose party do we attend?'

'Oh, that is the most wonderful thing, my sweet. We go to sup with Lucy Hay, the Countess of Carlisle.'

I stared back at her in horror. 'Have you lost your wits?'

'Be not so silly.'

I began to sober up quickly, I can tell you.

Lucy Hay was the most beguiling woman of the age - England's Sempronia. In her youth, she inspired poets, and even with fading charms her grace and wit, big brown eyes, and big soft bubbies could enrapture. They had enraptured me, I confess it freely. She was an inveterate plotter. *A woman who had committed many crimes with the spirit of a man*[*]. I had not seen her in half a year, and had hoped to avoid her machinations ever again.[**]

Her apartments were at Essex House, not far down the Strand, and we were not long in arriving.[31] I combed my hair back, put on my hat, dabbed perfume on my wrists, and chewed on a sprig of thyme to take away the taste of sour wine. There were other carriages, and hackneys, filling the square as we arrived. Meg reached above her head and took down a box. Reaching in, she took out a pair of masks, one yellow with a golden mane and in the countenance of a lion, the other a black cat with sharp little ears. She passed me the lion.

'Put this on.'

---

[*]   Sallust.

[**]   See The Last Roundhead.

'At least it matches my hair,' I said, taking the mask from her and tying up the ribbons.

She turned away from me and flapped the silk bands of her own mask.

'Tie the ribbons for me, Blandford, if you please.'

I tied them for her. 'So Meg, what are we to do here? Daniel is not my favourite bible story, and I fear the good Lord would be less disposed to me than he.'

She giggled again. 'Your disguise marks you the lion in this story, Sugar. We do nothing but keep our eyes and ears open. Your uncle wants to know who the Countess draws into her web.'

'Everyone will be wearing masks,' I said.

'So? That only hides the features, there is more on display.'

The door opened, her footmen stood in place as she stepped down and I followed. She nodded to another carriage and other waiting footmen in a smart livery.

'The Earl of Loudoun is also a guest it seems,' she said, in a low voice. 'How very interesting.'

The Earl of Loudoun was the Scottish ambassador to Parliament, a strict Presbyterian, and implacable opponent of the King. That was interesting indeed.

'Come along, my sweet.'

I followed Meg up the steps and into the rambling old building. Servants, in Percy colours of red and black, took my cloak and hat, as Megan unbuttoned her coat and slipped it off her shoulders. Her dress was of green and gold satin; she had pearls, and a deep neckline to display her obvious charms. Her raven ringlets tied back with a fine-wrought gold headpiece, atop her cat face and violet eyes. I tried to think of some smutty comment, but in faith, my wit deserted me—

she was beautiful even masked.

Meg took my arm, and we walked into a great hall, fair bursting with people. Men dressed like peacocks in their finery and women in their silks and satins, feathers and jewels. Behind the tall columns were waiting servants with titbits of food, kickshaws* and the like. Musicians and boy-singers high in the galleries above played a brisk French dance.

I took a goblet of wine from a waiting lackey.

'Where be our hostess?' I asked Meg.

'The butterfly that flutters by? She is over there.'

Lucy Hay stood near the end of the hall by some great double doors with a crowd of suitors and attendants around her. Her mask, in the shape of a golden butterfly, matched her cloth of gold dress, but there was no disguising identity. Megan had been right; there was more on display than individuals' faces.

'Pym's body is not even cold in its tomb and here she is throwing a party, 'tis heartless.' I was faintly disgusted.[32]

'Oh, how little you understand women.'

Meg took a goblet of wine and led me to the side of the hall, to where we had a better view of our hostess. Next to Lucy Hay was another figure I recognised. I could tell from his saggy frame, the way he stood, the piggy eyes behind a strange blue mask—Sir John Wollaston.

'There be something rotten in the City of London,' I said.

'Indeed, I think I should try and engage good Sir John.'

'Looking for clients?' I said, slyly.

'This is not a buttock-ball**, my sweet, and you are impolite. See if you can find Loudoun.'

'I have never seen him.'

| * | 17th Century pastry. |
| ** | Orgy. |

'Listen for a Scots accent, it should be a tell,' she said, and then walked away.

I followed Meg's advice and walked around looking for the Scots ambassador.

For the next hour or so, I wandered through the rambling old building with the other revellers. I merely sipped at the wine, not wishing to lose control of my senses. That was unfair; a party like this in wartime London was a rare delight. Normally, I would have thrown myself into it with wild abandon. Instead, I ignored the attentions of maidens and became a watcher and listener—all to no avail. I overheard and saw nothing of consequence. The usual grumbles about shortages, complaints about restrictions on trade, and heavy moans from couples clinched in dark corners. It may not have been a buttock-ball, but 'twas debauched enough. Lucy Hay was openly cocking-a-snook at the puritans.

I watched Lily, the astrologer, pontificating and holding court over the dunderheaded devotees of false hope. Dressed in robes of blue wool as if he were a Roman senator, and a white mask that did little to disguise, he twiddled with his wispy moustache and gibbered.

'I do carefully take notice of every grand action betwixt king and parliament, and every eve do measure the conjunctions.' He said to the men and women drooling at his feet. 'I am inclined to the belief that, as all sublunary affairs depend upon superior causes, so there is a possibility of discovering them by the configurations of the superior bodies.'

The audience clapped their hands calling for more of his wisdom, as a prophet of old returned to them.

I walked away in disgust. By God, the charlatan could talk—so many words with such emptiness of meaning. Lily was like a papist relic salesman, with twenty of the messiah's foreskins in his sack.

'Twas coming back to the dancing, after taking a piss in the jakes, when I saw him. At first, I could not believe it. There he was, wearing a red mask, but 'twas most certainly him. He walked quickly to the back of the hall. I followed, past copulating couples and vomiting drunks, down some steps to a doorway. I waited a couple of seconds and then followed on.

It was a different part of the building; servants quarters, I decided. I skipped down the corridor, through more doors, into an open courtyard. There were ornamental gardens beyond. I saw him again through the trees, walking briskly down towards the river. I picked up the pace, but kept to the shadows. My sword and pistols were in Meg's carriage: the last thing I desired was a fight.

He reached the water gate, burning torches illuminated him against the carved stone—there was no mistake. He took something out of his pocket. It must have been a key, for the gate swung open with a groan, and I heard him call out. There was an answering reply, and he stepped through the gate and disappeared.

Heart beating, I paused and composed myself, then retraced my steps back to the ball. I soon located Megan, fluttering her eyes at some old man, and begged her indulgence and his leave. She looked annoyed.

'What is wrong with you? That is Loudoun.'

'I have just seen my brother.'

11. Plots: London, December 1643.

Corruption is a tree, whose branches are
Of an immeasurable length: they spread
Ev'rywhere; and the dew that drops from thence,
Hath infected some chairs and stools of authority.

(John Fletcher, *The Honest Man's Fortune*.)

Uncle Samuel looked grim. The news that my brother had been seen in London was the least of his worries—if the most pressing of mine. He returned to the city for Mr Pym's funeral, only to find bitter division in Parliament. The radicals and independents like Henry Vane, Cromwell, and Oliver St John pushed for outright victory still, but also freedom of conscience in the church—the same ideas as the Chidley crone. Such moves terrified the Presbyterian Lords and rich landowners in the Commons.[*]

Pym's last gift to the cause had been Scottish alliance, signed on the condition that England became Presbyterian. Worded vaguely enough for the Independents to demand religious freedom. The Presbyterians were outraged, the Scots thought they had been cozened, and the Royalist newsbooks gleeful at the differences.

I poured myself a cup of sack, and one for Franny, as Uncle Samuel outlined the situation to us in his study on Thames Street. We were all sat around the oak table. Darnelly was there, Everard, Sam and Franny back from Oxford, Megan and myself. He had not brought Mr Butler with him—to my relief—leaving him in Cople.

'The Countess of Carlisle thinks she can draw the Scots away from Parliament, if the King will support a Presbyterian Church,' Uncle Samuel told us.

---

[*]   See Appendix II for Religious factions.

Uncle Samuel was a known Presbyterian but a pragmatist first. He wished for the King to be beaten and a settlement forged after. Everard, my sister, and Franny, even Darnelly leaned to the Independents. I was no radical, and happy to follow my uncle's lead.

'There is talk in Oxford that the King wavers over bishops, and the Scots will support him,' said Franny. 'I have it on good authority that pressure is put upon His Majesty, even from his damned wife.'

'That would cook our goose, indeed,' said Uncle Samuel. 'But the King has too much principle and too little wit.'[33]

'The Scots ambassador has no interest in serving Charles,' said Meg. 'I think he is true.'

I did not question how she got that information. Meg was rather persuasive.

'However,' she continued. 'There are others amongst the Scots who do not trust we can win the war, who feel only the king can guarantee the church. Loudoun waits on despatches from Scotland.' She grimaced. 'The Countess of Carlisle was not best pleased with his stance.'

The Scots had promised an army to invade England and bring ruin to Royalist hopes in the north. Yet, if Lucy Hay could draw the Scots to the King, then it would be all our heads on a spike.

'What of the Fenn boy and Beeston's gold?' asked Uncle Samuel.

I outlined what we had discovered: the soap smuggling, Sir Paul Pindar, and my suspicions about the Lord Mayor. Beeston was still in Marshalsea and would stay there until the matter was settled—one way or t'other.

'Ophelia was killed on Yardley's premises,' I concluded. 'Gilbert believes they dumped the body as a warning to

Beeston. A mistake, as it exposed the smuggling to our scrutiny.'

'It has the all the mark of Mistress Whorwood,' said my uncle. 'And your brother James is her creature. There is some plot afoot, 'tis certain.' He paused for a second as if in decision, then. 'Well, we shall spring this trap upon them, and see what can be discovered. Mr Cole, we will need you back in Oxford with Mr Brayne. If the Countess and the Washerwoman have made common cause, there is trouble indeed.'

Franny nodded.

'I will have a watch placed upon the Countess,' said Darnelly. 'Wallis has not broken the Percy code, but we can still hope to find something of use. Pindar has not moved from his house in Bishopsgate for days, and taken no visitors of note.'[34]

'He is old and foolish,' said Uncle Samuel. 'It is his contacts that concern me, and how deep he is in with Whorwood and the Countess.'

'What watcher watches which witch?' I said jovially, to irritate my uncle's deputy.

There was something about Darnelly that made me want to bait him. 'Twas childish, I admit it, but immensely enjoyable.

'Be not a child, Blandford,' said Megan.

They were all looking at me with disapproval, except perhaps Franny who seemed lost in his own thoughts.

'Forgive me,' I said.

My uncle sighed and spoke again. 'It seems our Lord Mayor has been to Marshalsea twice to visit Mr Beeston. I received word from the governor that Sir John left on the second occasion in exceeding good spirits.'

'Polman's treasure?' I asked.

I confess it was greed on my part.

'It would seem so, or at least the Lord Mayor believes so,' said Uncle Samuel. 'I want your boy to watch over Sergeant Plucker—he is Wollaston's lackey in this. Mr Darnelly, you will have our informants in the guildhall watch the Lord Mayor himself. If God wills, we can deprive the King of his income and gain some for our own cause.'

Uncle Samuel detailed our tasks to the rest of us: Franny and Sam would return to Oxford to watch over Mistress Whorwood; Everard and Whitelocke would stop the barge at Henley and seize the soap and gold; I would take a squad of men and arrest Yardley and his workers. Uncle Samuel was satisfied and dismissed us.

'Mistress Powell, if I could have one last word whilst the others wait without,' said my uncle as we were leaving.

Meg waited with Uncle Samuel whilst the rest of us trooped out of the chamber, our plans set. I wondered what our Lord Mayor would think of our design. He wanted Polman's treasure for himself. I also suspected he was involved in smuggling gold to Oxford, and I wondered still on Ophelia. Sir John was a consummate politician, and a politician's greatest skill is artifice. It runs like blood through their veins.

Franny danced, madly and badly; drunk, flushed red and laughing. The people around him, men and women, swayed and bounced along with the music. Meg grabbed my hand and pulled me into the swirling mass of people, the drums and pipes beating out a quick tempo.

'A Scots jig in honour of our allies,' shouted one of the musicians and the tune changed, even faster with a heavy beat. The floorboards bounced as people jumped and twisted to the music.

We were in the Old George,[35] one of the many cheap inns that line Borough High Street, in Southwark. Everard had gone home to his widow, but Franny and Sam had insisted on taking ourselves over the river where puritan displeasure had not yet pierced the drunken haze of delinquency. It was busy, full of people looking for entertainment. A roaring fire away from the cold weather enticed them, and music, and drinking, and women—our very own Elysium. Compared to the Countess of Carlisle's ball a rough affair, but rich or poor, the enjoyment was the same.

I held Megan in my arms spinning her around, making her laugh aloud. Franny cut in: taking her hand he kissed it, and led her away deeper into the jig. I am not a good dancer, so slipped back to our table where Sam sat watching the dance with a strange smile on his chops.

Sam had changed in the year I had known him. His sandy hair was now cut more fashionably, and he wore good clothes. Still quiet, rarely given to speech without need, and no conversation was forthcoming. I sat for a while watching Franny and Meg, sipping at my wine. The woman was almost as stubborn as my sister, but her beauty and wit made me forgive that. I would say I was enamoured, but part of me still yearned for Emily, lost across the ocean. Like most men, I made some women into cold statues—a perfect image that can never be attained—whilst missing what is right under our noses.

Franny came to sit beside us, sweating from his exertions, mopping his brow with a cloth and unbuttoning his doublet. Meg was still dancing, another partner now; a tall youngster but others were lining up to steal a turn. She smiled at me as she span past, sparking a smidgen of jealousy, I confess.

'You look pleased with yourself,' I said to Franny, looking away from the dance.

'Oh, do not fret, Sugar,' he said, reading me. 'Your lady dances well.'

'She is not my lady.'

He laughed at that. 'For one with such a rakish reputation, you are curiously naive with women at times, my friend.' Then he burped and leaned forward to whisper in my ear; his breath stinking of beer.

'I know something you do not.'

I laughed. 'The names of all the bawds in London Town?'

'There is a ledger,' he said. 'With the names of all those that have lent the King money. I know where it is.' Then he sat back and put a finger to his lips.

I looked at him in surprise; he had not mentioned this at the meet earlier. Franny leaned forward again.

'If we can get that, we can cut off all of His Majestic Stammerer's funds and round up the traitors. And I know where it is,' he said again, and then started chuckling to himself.

'Where?'

'Tis in the office of the King's secretary at Christ Church.'

That was perhaps the best-defended place in Oxford. I realised why he had not mentioned this before.

'And you are going to try and get it? You take too many damn risks, Franny. My uncle would not ask this of you—'tis a fool's quest.'

'That ledger could end the war, Sugar, do you not see?' Of a sudden, he was deadly serious 'All this misery would be over. It will have Sir John Wollaston's name in it, I wager that with you.'

There was no denying his words, as he saw from my face.

'Have no fears,' he said, smiling. 'I will not do anything foolish. I will leave that to you and your Welsh punk. Sam will look out for me and he is always careful.'

Megan curled into the crook of my arm and kissed my chest. Grey light through the shutters marked the dawn of a new day. The smell of her perfume was on my tumbled bedclothes, our clothes discarded around the room. I breathed the scent of her in—honey and expensive perfume—but said nothing as she pulled away the blankets and stood up. A toned naked body and pale white skin, tendrils of black hair curling around her white breasts. Once again, I wondered at how beautiful she was. Like a creature from legend, a nymph, or goddess, or queen.

Was this the face that launch'd a thousand ships, And burnt the topless towers of Ilium. *

'Do not leave.'

She smiled back at me. ''Tis past time to arise, my lover.'

I reached for her but she slapped my hand away.

'I said arise, not arouse.'

She slowly dressed as I watched, pulling on her underskirts and shift, then tying back her long hair into a ball and pinning it. She pulled her dress over her head and pulled the strings of her bodice before lifting her skirts, pulling up her stockings, and tying her garters. She put on a cap and tucked her black curls underneath. Then, she brushed herself down and looked at me.

'Do not pout, Blandford.'

I sat up on the bed and reached for my shirt and

---

*   Christopher Marlowe, Doctor Faustus.

breeches.

'I am not pouting.' I was pouting. 'But what need have you to arise at this time? 'Tis damnably early?'

She leaned over and kissed me. I prayed my breath did not stink of last night's sour wine, or the garlic sausage I had wolfed down. She broke away.

'I am to York in a few days, Sugar. Your uncle wants someone in Cavendish's court when the Scots come south.'

I must have looked even more disappointed, because she took to laughter.

'Oh, look at you. You are like a little boy whose favourite toy has been taken from him. I am nobody's toy, my sweet.'

'You will be safe?'

'As safe as any in this sorry world,' she said. 'Now, stop being so miserable. You have enough to worry about with the gold and your brother.'

'My brother is an emetic.'

She leaned over and kissed me again, long and deep. I pulled her into me, but a polite knocking on the door to my chamber put an end to that tryst. We broke apart and both looked over.

'Come in,' I said, after a sigh.

The boy entered, looking flustered, as if he had been running.

'Well, what is it, John,' I said, irritated at the interruption.

''Tis Mr Mabbot, Master. He has had word. The soap barges leave tomorrow; our delivery will be among them.'

'And so it begins,' said Megan.

12. The Soap Factory: London, December 1643.

Seek not to know what must not be reveal'd,

Joys only flow when hate is most conceal'd.

Too busy man would find his sorrows more

If future fortunes he should know before.

(John Dryden, *Seek not to Know*, from *The Indian Qveen*.)

We gathered at the White Tower before dawn on Christmas Eve. It was cold with a heavy frost. I had bundled myself up in warm clothes, and a thick cloak. A troop of Whitecoats came with Darnelly, and I noted he buckled on his own sword and pistols, and wore a buff coat.

'You are coming with us?' I asked.

'Indeed, Captain Candy. You do not object?'

'No, no,' I said. 'The more the merrier. 'Tis Christmas Eve after all.'

''Tis just another day,' said Darnelly.

I looked over the twenty or so soldiers gathered beneath the wall. All armed with sword and pistol, a couple with new flintlock muskets, and the sergeant carrying a partisan.* They handled their weapons well and looked disciplined, not like the Lord Mayor's tapsters and bullyboys. Sergeant Plucker, and his company of witless wonders, would be useless on a raid like this.

'The barge left upriver with yesterday's tide,' said Darnelly. 'It should be in Henley by tonight. We have a man watching Yardley's premises.'

I nodded—my uncle had men watching everyone, it felt.

Darnelly led us from the tower; the men's hob nailed boots cracked in unison on the cobbles as we marched. The stalls

---

*   A type of polearm still carried by the Yeoman of the Guard today.

and shops were just starting their day. Shopkeepers opening doors and setting out their wares, all watching in sullen silence as we trooped past; our breath like puffing smoke in the cold air. London's merchants grew ever surlier with the cost of the war. The city bore the brunt of Parliament's demands for money.

We reached the factory in the grey light of dawn, the clouds dark and heavy with snow. A man in a shabby cloak joined us at the gates; Darnelly recognised him and waved him past the soldiers.

'Well?'

'There are ten or so men in there, Mr Darnelly,' said Shabby. 'They went in an hour ago.'

I peered through the wooden gates; a padlocked chain held them closed. The great double doors to the building inside, and few windows were closed tight. I could smell boiling tallow and smoke in the air. There was work going on inside, it seemed. Darnelly gave me the nod.

'Break it down,' I said to the sergeant.

He lifted his partisan and brought it down with a smash onto the gate chain. I took out my pistols.

The few locals and bystanders, realising what was happening, made themselves scarce. 'Tis always the best policy in such situations. There is no point in getting yourself arrested in error. You may unwittingly expose your real crimes.

Finally, the links of the chain gave way and gates swung open with a kick from the soldiers. A hail of shot met us. I stepped back behind the fence, but the sergeant fell down dead, pierced through more than once. A Whitecoat dragged his body back.

'Bastards!' I turned to the soldiers. 'Right, this is how it happens. We go through in a rush, muskets at the back to pick off the marksmen. Get up against the factory doors as quick as you can. Ready?'

They nodded at me.

'Go! Go! Go!' I shouted at the top of my voice.

Darnelly and I led them in a mad dash towards the building. I discharged both of my pistols blindly at windows, sprinting as fast as I could to the cover of the factory wall. Behind me, Darnelly and the musketeers did the same, stopping the inhabitants from returning fire. We crossed the yard and gathered by the double doors. Only one of our men lay prone on the frosty white cobbles, a pool of dark blood spreading out beneath him.

'Smash them open,' I said, reloading my pistols.

The men used their muskets to break down the double doors: the wood soon cracked, and they swung them open to reveal the soap factory. My men stood back as more shot poured out at us, and then we charged again, straight into the long building.

I stepped inside and discharged my first pistol, with care this time. There was a moment of satisfaction as my mark screamed, holding his belly, and fell to the floor. I paused and took in the rest of the scene.

The Royalists were outnumbered and outmatched. They looked like some of Yardley's workers given pistol and club, and against trained men had no hope. My soldiers cut down the ones that stood their ground. The rest, already retreating towards the river, discharged pistols at us as they ducked behind the great copper vats of render.

I looked up to the small office above the works; I could see movement up there. That was where Yardley would be—if he were still here—and any incriminating papers.

'Up there,' I pointed, and took off at a run.

Darnelly followed me as we went up the steps and along the walkway to the office. Halfway along, I heard screams and glanced down. One of the vats of boiling tallow tipped, hot render catching light, and a wave of liquid fire swept over the battling men. Whitecoats and Royalist alike went up in flames. I turned away—it reminded me of my father's death.

From my vantage on the walkway, I could see right down to the river wharf. There were men clambering into a longboat —Yardley amongst them.

'Damn it!' I swore.

My brother stepped out of the office onto the walkway. Dressed in leathers, his long blonde hair tied back, and murder in his eyes. I noted the crooked nose I gave him at our last meeting, discharged my second pistol—hitting the wall beside his head—and drew my sword. He ducked away from the splinters, drew his own steel, and came on at me. He was holding something in his other hand, papers of some sort.

'That sniffer of yours is damnably ugly, James,' I told him as he approached.

'Merry Christmas, Runt.' He thrust at me with his sword.

I stepped to the side, almost tipping off the walkway, but regained my balance and slashed out at him; he stepped back. James was better with a blade, but I had improved enough over the last year to hold my own, and my men were crawling all over. I decided to taunt him.

'I wager the ladies call you Crooknose behind your back.'

He thrust at me again forcing me to parry, stepping back as he followed up, his blade flashing at my face.

'Do not talk to him, you feeble-minded fop, stick the bugger!' yelled Darnelly behind me.

I launched an attack, thrusting at my brother's face, forcing him to step aside, and then sweeping a slash at his knees. He parried my blade easily, and turned on the balls of his feet to strike at me; the tip of his sword caught my coat and tore a hole. I stepped back but he did not follow up. He sneered at me instead.

'Arthur Catchpole,' he said. 'Did you think I would not recognise our old schoolmaster's name, dunderhead?'

'You should,' I said, aiming a wicked slash at his head— missing. 'He whipped you often enough.'

The fire was spreading through the factory. Tallow and suet, oils, rope, and lye-soaked barrels all caught easily, and the wooden building engulfed in flame. It was getting too hot for my liking. I could see the Whitecoats getting out, away from the flames, and the boat pulling away from the wharf with Yardley.

'You lose, Brother,' I said. 'There is no escape.'

'Foolish, Blandford, I always win.'

'Rara est concordia fratrum,* I said.

'Mori in igni.'**

He stepped back as I made to slash out at him, threw his sword at me, tucked the papers inside his doublet and dived off the walkway. For an instant, he was suspended in the air as if from an invisible cord. The cord severed, and he plummeted to the floor. I rushed to the edge to see. The acrobatic pig-nose caught a chain hanging down from the rafters, and swung himself to the ground. Without a glance behind, he ran for the wharf and the boat, leaping onto it. Then he turned to wave back at me.

'Arsehole,' I said.

---

*   Ovid. Agreement among brothers is rare.

**   Die in a fire.

They were heading for a ship anchored out in the middle of the river, a Dutchman by the look, but there was nought we could do. The warehouse was burning; we had to be quick or the flames would roast us all alive. Darnelly and I ran back down the walkway and wooden stairs, even as flames began to lick around them, and out of the doors into the cobbled courtyard. What was left of our men gathered, smouldering and bloody. A couple of Yardley's were held as captives, the rest dead or escaped.

The fire had already sent the local merchants and business owners into a frenzy. A blaze in London is a deadly thing. Rows of men pressed into bucket lines, passing water from the river, to make sure the burning did not spread. Darnelly ignored them, sent the soldiers back to the Tower with our prisoners, and turned to me.

'They knew we were coming,' said Darnelly. 'Can you ride?'

'Aye,' I told him.

'Get yourself to Henley,' he said. 'This was nought but a trap for us. I fear the same for Whitelocke and Everard.'

There is no sense galloping off all in a rush if you have distance to travel. Your horse would be winded after a league. Henley was forty or so miles away. At a trot, it would take me six hours. I took Apple down the Great West Road out of the city. We kept up a good pace on towards Brentford despite the bitter wind near freezing my gloves to the reins.

I pondered my brother as I rode. James had been triumphant when he saw me in the factory, gleeful even. The

150

whole thing had been a trap, but perhaps also a decoy. What I worried on was whilst our gaze had been fixed upon Yardley and the gold smuggling, something else had been taking place.

A road vendor sold me a cup of hot cider on Brentford High Street, spreading some warmth inside me.

'Merry Christmas,' I said, to thank him.

He gave only a non-committal grunt in response.

These were the contradictions of the war. Some people treated the time as of old—a holiday with drinking and feasting. Others, like Darnelly, saw the celebrations as blasphemous. It is true, there is nought in the bible that says to make a sacrament of Christ's birth—'tis his messy death that is important—but there is no need to be damn surly about it. Where is the sin in eating a fat goose or some figgy pudding?

The heath at Hounslow is a lonely stretch. I skirted around its northern edge on the Bath Road—bare skeletal trees and brown grass, wisps of mist, the odd snow flurry, and only the screeching crows for company. A tarred body in a creaking gibbet gave testimony to the highwaymen and bandits that preyed upon travellers. I loaded my pistols. [36]

'What a sorry way to spend Christmas Eve, Apple,' I said, and scratched behind his ears.

A year ago, I had spent it with my friends, with Emily and Peter. Now Peter was dead, my friends scattered and Emily lost across the ocean. I was tired, and dozed in the saddle as I rode along.

'If you can ride him, you can have him,' Father told James. 'He has

an ambling gait, so is good for long journeys.'

The horse was a blue roan, tall, thirteen or fourteen hands, fine mane and tail. It was typical of Father to spoil James with it. I made do with Elizabeth's nag. I bit into my apple and chewed on it, sourly contemplating the fate of a third son.

'I wager James cannot ride him, Father,' said Henry. 'He does not have the seat.'

'He will need a good horse if he is to go up to Oxford,' said my father. Perhaps he sensed my jealousy.

'I will show you, Fatty,' said James to Henry.

James climbed over the fencing into the paddock. The seller watched on anxiously; twenty pounds was a good day's earnings if he could get it. My brother reached up to the horse's bridle but the beast flinched back and stamped his hoof. The stallion was nervous and twitchy; James reached again, and the animal took a step back. I started to laugh. My bother turned away to curse me, and the horse nipped him on the shoulder. Henry and I guffawed as James, screeching, backed away.

'You could not ride him, Runt,' said James to me, with murder in his eyes.

'I wager he can,' said Henry. 'The runt knows horseflesh better than you, Bookworm.'

I put the apple in my pocket, climbed over the fence, and walked away from the horse. Figgis had taught me a trick or two; James would never lower himself to address the man. My father knew what I was about though; a rare smile crossed his face.

'If you can ride him you can keep him,' called Father.

Looking at the ground—never the animal—I walked around as if searching for something. That pricked the stallion's interest. A horse is always thinking of himself and they are damnably stubborn about it. The beast knew James wanted to ride him, but saw no reason to let him. I gave him a reason.

As I ignored the beast, he started wondering what he was missing. I could hear the hoofs thump on the grass as he approached from behind. Slowly, as if I had just found something on the floor, I bent down and at the same time reached into my coat pocket. I thanked God for the half-eaten apple.

His great head peered over my shoulder, eager to see what I had found. I softly raised my hand, palm open, with the apple free for him to take. He reached forward, sniffed, and then took the apple gently from my hand. As he chomped, I stroked his neck, whispering quietly to him—what a great horse he was; so strong, and such a fine mane, and would he let me ride him, please?

I took the bridle in my hand, and stroked his back down to the saddle. He was tense, but there was no more than a shiver as I put my foot in the stirrup and swung myself up. We stood like statues for a couple of seconds, and then I twitched the reins, and rode him around the paddock.

'What will you call him?' asked my father.

'Apple,' I said, smiling at James's angry look.

By early afternoon, we were near Maidenhead. I scanned nervously along the river looking for a sign of the soap barge, but there were few boats. I stopped at the flash lock to rest the horse. The old lockkeeper was the first person I had seen since Brentford, wrapped up warm in a heavy wool coat and scarf.[37]

'Has there been much traffic on the river today?' I asked.

'Not too much, Master,' he said, 'A few boats went upriver an hour or so ago.'

I tipped him a silver sixpence for that snippet and swung myself back onto Apple's back. I waved goodbye as we rode away.

'Merry Christmas!' he shouted.

I picked up the pace after crossing the Thames at Maidenhead. The river takes a great north loop, a grand meander before turning back towards Henley. By road, I could cut that loop out and overtake the barge. I kicked Apple into a canter and prayed I would reach Everard in time.

I came out of the woods above the town and took out my spyglass. Whitelocke's manor was on the other side of the river—a fortified bastion. I had visited more than once. He kept a fine table and cellar and was good company.[38] I could see right down to the river but nought looked untoward. Packing the glass away, I rode down into Henley. There were guards at the entrance—a gate set up with gabions and earth entrenchments, but no ancient walls to protect the town. Whitelocke's men, they waved me through, my face well enough known.

There was a wooden bridge over the Thames, and I crossed it—I was barely half-way over when there was a shaking explosion to my right, startling Apple, who reared in panic. I struggled to control him and keep my seat; smoke was rising along the river, shouts of anger and surprise.

I was too late.

I kicked Apple into a gallop, riding past the taverns along the river, to Phyllis Court. This was our last outpost before Royalist Reading. The stone outer wall had been reinforced with earth and there were men on guard; alert, as if expecting attack. I was stopped at the gate and checked again, before being waved through. There was a palpable sense of panic in the place.

I handed Apple over to a groom and ran down to the riverside. Along the Thames, Bulstrode had a stone embankment with steps down to a wooden jetty. Even before I reached the water there was the broken dross of the explosion. Shards of jagged wood, some still smouldering, splinters as long as my arm, twisted metal and—to my dismay—bodies.

There were others helping, wounded being carried up to the house, soldiers standing watch with muskets at the ready. All scanned up and down the river. I saw Bulstrode, unharmed, directing the rescue. He came over to greet me as I arrived.

'Hullo, Blandford, you have missed the excitement.' He sounded jovial enough, but looked more than vexed.

'Excitement? What, in the name of Satan's left testicle, happened?'

'The barge just slammed into the wharf,' said Bulstrode. 'Nobody on it. I sent Everard and some men on to check it out, and the damn thing went up.'

'Everard?'

'Is alive,' said Bulstrode. 'Singed a tad, a dislocated shoulder and broken leg. Thanks be, he survived the blast.'

I walked back up to the house with Bulstrode and he gave me a fuller account. The barge had come on the long straight stretch of the Thames before Henley. Bulstrode had men hidden back from the river, only a couple dressed as workmen —and Everard—at the wharf. When it crashed into the wharf, Everard and the others went on board. The rudder was strapped; the crew had slipped overboard when it entered the straight.

Everard poked his head in the cabin, saw four barrels of powder with candles for fuse about to go off, and went straight over the side. Of the others, only one was alive, and him not expected to last the night.

The whole thing had been a debacle from start to finish.

We had been played for fools.

William was battered and bruised, his face swollen, leg splinted by Bulstrode's physician, and his arm in a sling. He would be in no fit state to travel for some weeks. He was alive, though, and I gave thanks for his deliverance. I had already lost too many friends.

'What will you do now?' asked Bulstrode.

'Rest up awhile,' I said. 'Then try and make Windsor tonight. Darnelly will want to know what has happened; I can be in London early tomorrow.'

Whitelocke gave me an escort as far as Maidenhead. We made good time, but it was still late when I climbed the hill in Windsor and stopped at the Mermaid. I got Apple stabled and fed and went into the inn. There were no rooms spare, the other guests all abed, but good food and a seat beside the fire in the empty common room. I took a plate of pork pie, bread, and cheese, and a flagon of ale gratefully from the maid. The strains of drunken singing carried down from the castle.

'Soused soldiers?' I said to the girl.

'Aye, sir. They will not trouble us here. The master sees to that.'

She took a seat opposite me and removed her coif—dressed in brown woollen skirts and tight green bodice over a plain white shift, with copper hair, pale skin, freckles on her nose, and full red lips, perhaps the same age as me, perhaps a little younger. She shook back her hair, letting it fall in shining ringlets around her linen collar.

'I shall make up some blankets when you are ready, sir,' she said.

I smiled and leaned forward.

'I do beseech you—chiefly that I may set it in my prayers—

what is your name?'*

She laughed. 'You like the theatre, sir?'

'I own a theatre.' A good line—even if technically untrue. 'It is of little use in these times, I fear.'

'Come woo me, woo me, for I am in a holiday humour and like enough to consent,' she said, with another pretty smile.**

I never did catch her name, but I remember her as Rosalind.

*   *The Tempest*. Act III Scene I.

**   *As You Like it*. Act IV Scene I.

Anne Candy to Elizabeth Candy.

Beloved Sister,

I thank yov for the letters and cloth – I will make a fine dress if I can acqvire the thread and bvttons – they are most very welcome. I send this short missive with the only covrier I can find.

I hope yov will not take it ill if I wish yov good cheer. I remember how we once loved this time so. I confess I oft tvrn my mind back to those happy days. It is a pleasant distraction from ovr cvrrent trials and depredation. We hear in Oxford that London has become a qvite sorry city for the holiday. It is said that ovr perpetval parliament does take every goose, and close every tavern, on pain of imprisonment. Mistress Margaret says that I shovld not believe all that I read in the newsbooks.

Her Majesty has grown ever frailer with the seasonal chills that sweep Oxford. Her sickness in the morning is powerfvl, bvt the physicians tell that the child is strong. In the afternoons, His Majesty comes to Merton, and sometimes the yovng princes, bvt never enovgh for the Qveen. Mistress Margaret says she grows short tempered with her condition, bvt svch is the lot of all women.

Sir William Davenant – who came vpon me when hearing of yovr bvsiness with the Phoenix – tells me that there will be bvt few celebrations in Oxford this year, bvt we shall still make merry. In times past Mr (Inigo) Jones wovld devise spectacvlars and their majesties wovld dance and hold masqves, bvt for now resovrces are too diminished. Sir William is exceeding bombastic, and the pox scars his face so. His nose – if nose it be – is so horrid to the sight that he covers it with a silk mask. He does have the saddest eyes behind it.

Sir William has asked for your credentials, in order to open correspondence with you over shared concerns. With your permission, I would forward such?

I received word from Henry that he was with General Hopton near Basing House, and that he will be returning to Farleigh for the holidays. His wife's family will be imposed upon – the Hall is gone and estate ruined. He tells me that monies from our tenants and cloth are ever more diminished. Of James I have – thanks be – seen little; he rides in the North on business for the Washerwoman. I leave off only wishing you a Merry Christmas, and Blandford of course. He always was so full of boisterous cheer at this time of year, I quite miss his company – you must not tell him that of course, it would only puff his vanity. Oh how I wish this war finished.

Your affectionate sister,
Anne.
Oxford, December 13th 1643.

13. Highwayman: Hounslow Heath, December 1643.

If they ask who would have pulled the crown from the king's head,

taken the government off the hinges, dissolved monarchy,

enslaved the laws, and ruined their country, - say, 'twas the proud,

unthankful, schismatical, rebellious, bloody city of London.

(John Berkenhead, *A Letter from Mercurius Aulicus to
Mercurius Civicus*)

The snow was sticking—a muffling blanket of white that covered Windsor. I watched it fall from the windows of the Mermaid. It would make travel difficult in the morning. The sounds of carousing soldiers had died away and silence descended upon the town. It is always quieter when the snow falls.

Rosalind snored gently, naked under blankets by the fire. I had managed to doze a little and felt somewhat better for the relaxation, but could not sleep deeply. I poured myself a tankard of ale from the barrel behind the bar and finished my supper by the glowing embers in the fireplace, watching over her. She had a soft smile on her face as she slept—I took it for a compliment.

A shouting outside, a couple of loud bangs—gates opening. Curious, I went back to the window. A carriage came out of the castle, turned and then headed down the hill, right past the inn. I had seen the coach before, and the guards livery. That was Loudoun's coach! What in the devil's arse was he doing in Windsor?

I ran out in the snow in my bare feet, slipping and sliding over to the gatehouse. There were two guards standing there in the cold. Both looked young, one tall, the other round and short. He had not been suffering long on army stew. They were dressed in thick overcoats, with morions*and pikes, and both looked quizzically at me as I arrived, half dressed and bootless, like a lunatic.

'Who was that?' I asked them.

'Who is asking?' said the lanky one.

'Captain Candy; now tell me, was that the Earl of Loudoun?'

'The Golden Scout?' said the other.

I sighed; they were clearly idiots. I would wager the drill sergeant just loved this pair.

'Yes,' I said. 'The Golden Scout. Now, was that Loudon?'

'How do we know you is the Golden Scout?' Shorty asked.

'I have just told you.'

'Ah, but you could be lying; you is a tad young for the *real* Golden Scout,' said Lanky.

'And not tall enough,' said Shorty.

'And not tall enough,' agreed Lanky.

'Listen, you dungwitted pair of turnips, if you do not tell me where the Earl was going, I shall have you both scrubbing out shit buckets for the rest of your sorry lives!'

They both looked taken aback at that. Shorty started mumbling something under his breath about officers no longer being gentlemen, but Lanky answered.

'He was meeting with Colonel Fairfax and now goes back to London.' He added 'Captain,' after a pause.

'Fairfax is in the north, you fool.'

'Not Black Tom, sir—his younger brother. He has brought despatches from Scotland for the Earl.'

And, of a sudden, all fell into place.

I turned without a word and ran back to the inn, stubbed a toe, cursed and rushed to get my stockings and boots,

---

*   Open faced helmet, also known as the Pikeman's Pot in England.

falling over as I tried to drag them on. I followed that with my doublet, hat, coat, cloak, gloves, pistols, powder and shot. I buckled on my sword, cursed again, took off my boots and put them back on the correct feet. Rosalind woke with my bustling about, but there was no time for amorous farewells. I kissed her once upon the lips, and dropped a couple of silver sixpence on the counter—one for her, one for the house.

'Farewell, sweet Orlando,' she called after me.

I ran out into the back courtyard. Apple did not look impressed as I saddled him up, pulled the straps tight, and mounted. I rode him out to the courtyard, cursed a third time before the cock crowed, dismounted, opened the gates, remounted and rode into the night.

I followed the tracks out of the town; the wheels left dark ruts in the snow. Loudoun was heading south to the Staines Bridge. With a lead of thirty minutes or so, they would make the bridge before me. There was only one way for them to go after that—Hounslow Heath. If I was correct, the ambush would be set there.

We clattered over the bridge at Staines, and took the long straight road to Hounslow across the heath. The tracks were just visible in the snow, but more was falling. If I did not catch them soon I could lose the scent. I did not pause in Bedfont, galloping through the hamlet. It was not far past when I heard the crack of shot boom out, followed by more gunfire. I pulled up Apple, checked my pistols were primed, and slapped his rump, urging him into a gallop again.

It was less than a hundred paces before I came upon the coach, waylaid and tipped into the side of the roadway, two of the horses down, the others struggling at the traces. A guard fighting with one malignant on the ground, but his comrade lay dead in the snow. Another bandit atop of the coach, throwing down bags to a figure on horseback, whilst yet another was at the coach doors, fighting a man dressed in a buff coat. I assumed Fairfax.

I pulled my pistols, and put a shot in the man on top of the coach, an easy mark. He tumbled down behind. A hand reached up for my horses reins, another robber in the dark, but Apple reared, striking out with his hooves, and smashed out the man's brains. I held on tight with my knees as we plunged to the ground. The bandit struggling on the floor had finished the last guard. He stood and faced me. I recognised him—Running Jack. He saw me and laughed.

'You are dead, Golden!' He pointed his bloody knife at me and came forward.

I shot him in the face with my second pistol and he fell down dead without another word. I holstered the gun and drew my sword.

'Arsehole,' I said to the corpse—too smugly and too soon.

I was smashed on the back of the head; stunned, and knocked off my horse to the floor. I rolled and came to my feet. There was another coming for me with a club, and my own blade lay out of reach. I stepped to the side to avoid his blow and tripped him as he swung. He went sprawling and I dived for my sword.

The rider came in, and I recognised her—Cutpurse Moll. She screeched and discharged her pistol at Fairfax, hitting him in the arm, making him drop his sword. Fairfax went back into the carriage, leaving me alone to face Moll and the last attacker.

The buffoon facing me was ill prepared to fight a swordsman—even with my poor skills. I easily parried as he swung at my head, and punched him on the nose with my left fist. That shocked him, made him slow, and he did not raise any defence as I cut him in the belly. He fell to the floor, screaming, clutching at his innards as they spilled out. I turned to face Moll but she saw the game was up. Their plan had depended upon surprise, quickly killing the guards, but I had put paid to that. She still had a pistol in her hand, but unloaded, for she merely threw it at me, cursed, and spurred away.

'My Lord, Colonel Fairfax, it is over,' I called out to the carriage.

I heard the sound of bolts drawn back and the carriage door opened. Fairfax stepped out, coat bloody and bleeding from his arm—sword at the ready. He ignored me, checked above the carriage, and spoke to the earl inside.

'They have the case, My Lord, and my money.' Then he turned to me. 'Where did they go?'

'There is only one left, sir, the rest are dead, and she be known to me.' I gestured around.

'Well, get after her, man. The woman has taken important papers and my money!'

I wanted to tell him to go bugger himself after the ride I had had. Instead, I nodded and called Apple to me. The horse came and I mounted, slapped his rump, and charged off after Moll Frith. There was no way I would catch her, whatever Fairfax wanted; Apple and I were both blown. I pushed him though, as hard and as fast as I dared on the dark road.

We rushed through Hounslow, following the great west road into the city; buildings flashed by in a blur. It was near Syon House when I saw her; Apple almost spent, but her horse had gone down, and both rider and mount were sprawled on the floor. There were people around rushing in to help, but I put paid to that, riding up with a pistol out.

'Let me through,' I shouted. 'In the name of Parliament!'

Apple pushed past the few bystanders, who quickly absented themselves seeing an armed man. I looked down on the woman on the floor, and pointed my pistol at her.

'You are under arrest for murder and robbery, Mistress Frith,' I said. 'I look forward to seeing you dance a jig at Tyburn.'

'She glared up at me.[39]

'Merry Christmas,' I said, and smiled back.

Darnelly pushed his chair away from the desk and sat back, contemplating me for a moment.

'You killed four men.'

'The horse accounted for one.'

'Still, it is impressive, Captain Candy. Colonel Fairfax was certainly impressed; he has sent you a reward.' Darnelly took out a small bag and passed it to me. He sounded quite impressed himself; that was a first for me. He rarely called me captain.

'Two hundred pounds, Captain. Something for you to waste in the stews of Southwark before you return to your uncle, no doubt.' The adulation had not lasted long.

'What of Yardley and the gold?'

'There, I must offer my apologies.' Another first. 'Yardley recognised you as soon as you met. He knew your brother and the two of you are similar enough in looks. When you appeared asking about a soap delivery, they decided to bait us.'

He relayed the whole scheme to me. How Beeston's

little attempt at blackmail had led to Ophelia's murder. The body dumped as a warning to Beeston foolishly exposed the gold smuggling. My brother then decided to play on our investigations as a distraction. Whilst we watched for the gold, the Royalists would murder the Earl of Loudoun and ruin the Scots alliance.

'It was clever of your brother and the Washerwoman, and would have come to pass had you not seen Loudoun in Windsor. Your uncle and I dismissed the rumours about Fairfax, and the Earl slipped out of the city unseen by our agents.'

Too damn clever by half, I thought to myself, although I was still unconvinced the body had been a warning to Beeston. 'And the Lord Mayor?' I asked.

'Has been giving money to the King's cause through Pindar. He was not involved in the attack on Loudoun, though, and merely wished to ensure his name was not exposed. However, your boy tells me that the Lord Mayor also had two strong seaman's chests delivered to premises in Goldsmith's Row on Christmas Eve.'

'So he found the treasure.' I cursed internally.

'It seems so. He has also arranged for Mr Beeston's release from Marshalsea.'

'Then we shall arrest them?'

'We can hardly set aside another Lord Mayor, Captain Candy. Our evidence is slender, and the guilds would not stand for it. We would have apprentices rioting in the streets. No, Sir John can keep his head, and his treasure, but he will do as we say from now on. Mr Beeston has found passage to France, where I am sure he will soon outstay his welcome.'

And there we had it. Right and wrong barely mattered anymore. The Lord Mayor, if the accounts were true, was much enriched by Polman's haul, and had played us for fools. I also had my suspicions about Ophelia's death. Happen that was no murderous mistake. Now, the Lord Mayor would be protected—more use alive than dead. The man deserved to hang for treason and murder, but politicians are as slippery as eels.

'So what am I to do now?'

'You are to return to your uncle in Newport Pagnell once the weather improves. No doubt, he will have something interesting for you to do. You have done well here, Captain Candy. He will be pleased, I think. There is a column of new recruits leaving in a week or so. Mayhap you will see Cromwell.'

Cromwell was already becoming known as a cavalry commander. In those dark days, when it looked like the King would soon win the war, only Oliver seemed able to stand against the Royalists. He was the new hero of the war party and the independents. The lords, landowners, and moderates all still thought he could be manipulated for their own ends. They planned to praise him, reward him, and discard him once his usefulness was served—the idiots. [*]

Someone was hammering on the door of the tenement. I shouted at the boy to answer it; my head pounded. I was sweating like a docker and felt nauseous. Charles Fairfax's reward was burning a hole in my purse I spent it so quick. The banging carried on unabated.

'John!'

---

[*]   Cicero on Octavian.

Bang! Bang! Bang!

'John!'

Bang! Bang! Bang!

'Where in damnation is the boy now?' I dragged myself up off my bed, swearing and stumbling down the narrow stairwell.

Bang! Bang! Bang!

'What is the point in a servant if he is absent when required?'

Drawing the bolts back, I pulled the door open and blinked at the daylight. Sergeant Plucker stood there with some men, his freshly dyed hair glistening in the sunlight. The men behind had new muskets, and helmets, and swords. Someone had been lavishing coin on the Mayor's crew.

'The Lord Mayor wishes to see you now, *Captain* Candy.'

Well at least he remembered my rank.

'Have I time to put on my boots, *Sergeant* Plucker?'

'Of course, sir.'

He was jovial with his insolence.

The stone building was busy as always, but for once, Wollaston did not keep me waiting. A clerk led me into his hot chamber with the grand map of London on the wall. Wollaston was seated behind his desk; a wide grin came over his face as the clerk showed me in.

'Mr Candy, Lord Mayor.'

'Captain Candy, Ezra,' said Sir John. 'He can be quite sensitive about his rank.' Then to me. 'Please take a seat, Captain.'

I sat in the chair opposite him as he scrutinised me with his piggy eyes. Then he leaned forward with a friendly smile.

'I hear that you are to return to the army, Captain?'

'Soon—in a week or so.'

'That would intimate the Fenn business is now concluded.'

'You know that it is, Sir John. You had the boy killed in the first place.'

'Why would I do such a thing, Captain Candy?' He sat back; the smile had gone.

'Yardley came to you, did he not, with his little blackmail problem? A golden opportunity. Betty Adams's brother, just returned from Southampton, with whatever his sister may have revealed.'

His eyes flickered for just a second—guilty.

'I hazard Ophelia told you some but not all, and Beeston had the key to the rest. Why did you dump the corpse at the theatre? That is what I do not understand—it exposed the gold smuggling.'

A sly smirk crossed his face, and then I understood.

'You wanted the smuggling discovered—if you could keep your name out of it.' I was impressed at the deception. 'At the same time you used me to seek Beeston? Uncle Samuel's contacts and agents could find him much quicker, and help you get the Polman treasure.'

I hate being played.

'Ah, Mr Polman's treasure. I fear I was overly eager in that regard.' He waved his hand dismissively. 'An old man's vain fancy, I assure you; it must have been lost in the oceans.' He had a wide grin on his face. He could barely conceal his glee. Bastard!

'I know you supplied gold for the King.' That wiped the smile off his face once more.

'These are extremely grave accusations. Do you have any evidence of such murder and treason?'

I thought of Franny's gold ledger in Oxford.

'No,' I replied.

'No, I thought not. You should beware such slander, Captain. Your sister remains in London whilst you go off on your travels?'

A barely veiled threat.

'Yes.'

'Then you must pass along my regards. I am happy that her schoolhouse may reopen now that the Fenn case is closed. It is closed, is it not, Captain?'

'Yes,' I said, sourly, and prayed Ophelia would forgive me.

'Then good day to you, sir,' said Sir John. 'And fair weather on your journey.'

Cross Deep, Twickenham, 1719.

What though I spend my hapless days
In finding entertainments out,
Careless of what I go about,
Or seek my peace in skilful ways
Applying to my Eyes new rays
Of Beauty, and another flame
Unto my Heart, my heart is still the same.

(Sidney Godolphin, *Cloris, it is not thy disdain*)

My great nephew's wedding was an immensely enjoyable spectacle, in spite of the itching periwig: drunkenness and fighting—men and women all—cracked plates, smashed furniture, and broken heads.

There was a saucy matron of seventy-five—the bride's aunt—with pretty blue eyes that twinkled when she laughed, and dark hair with only a touch of grey. I charmed her with my tales whilst the hurly-burly raged. She told me that she had been born in the month before Marston Moor and left her hand resting softly upon my knee.

'I spent the month before Marston Moor cooped up inside York,' I told her.

'You were with the Marquis of Newcastle and his Lambs?'

'Oh, no.' I remembered their screams as they died for him, though.

'There is a story here, I think?'

'I rode with Cromwell.'

There were few who would admit that in the years following, and all excepting myself long dead.

Auntie clapped her hands together in delight. 'Goodness! What was he like?'

Would a petty legionary know Caesar? I have had no

171

answer on Oliver these decades past. He was no fixed thing. He changed, as fickle as any man over time. Marston Moor was early; I believed in him then. Auntie was waiting for my reply.

'A monster,' I told her. 'A wicked monster of legend, eating babies and murdering kings on a whim.'

For such is Noll Cromwell's legacy, the truth matters not.

She laughed at that; a great belly laugh. It was a shame about her smile—she still had all her gnashers. 'Tis a rum pleasure to have your pizzle chewed by toothless gums. Remember that when you are in your dotage. You will thank me for it.

Did I? At my age? What think you?

The idiot and his bride plan to go on the tour, but his investments in the South Sea Company must be settled first. A sure thing he tells me; all the profits from cloth, coffee, and slaves, and dividends aplenty. He thinks I read not the newsbooks; he be a witless dunderhead. I hold out little hope for his intellectual redemption.

I know all merchants are thieves, we are at war with Spain, and there are no sure things.

They both reside with me in Twickenham, for now. His bride is a carping, bloodless, little flower—always complaining. 'Tis too hot; 'tis too cold; oh how damp it is; oh how dry. I am bemused at what he sees in her. I hear no moans, or gasps, or giggles of passion from their bedchamber. The boy needs reminding that he is the last of our line.

I mind not overmuch. 'Tis good to have company of an evening, even such dullards.

You go through life accumulating people and possessions. Then, you reach a point where time starts to rob them from you and only mortality remains. In the end, loneliness is the killer.

The servants carry me down to the study to write every morning. My ancient legs are too weak to walk the stairs. They think it an old man's vanity to record for posterity the folly of youth. A pox on them! I have always been vain.

'Tis not just my testimony, 'tis the testimony of all; all of us who stood by the monster's side, swung our swords for him, spilled our blood in the dirt, and for what? For this? To be a muse for a third rate poet; a pensioner to a third rate monarch. A beggar in a third rate land.

What is that? The duel? Worry not, we shall get to it.

14. Franny: Newport Pagnell, January 1644.

Yet once more, O ye laurels, and once more

Ye myrtles brown, with ivy never sere,

I come to pluck your berries harsh and crude,

And with forc'd fingers rude

Shatter your leaves before the mellowing year.

(John Milton, *Lycidas.*)

I tarried in London longer than I should despite the mood of the city being anything but merry. Megan left for York after Christmas, and Franny and Sam had gone to Oxford, but I took time to celebrate. I went to church with Elizabeth once or twice, so my soul will not burn eternally in hell, and compelled the boy into attendance, but mostly it was stews, and taverns, and drolls and singing. You could still raise up a roar in Southwark if you knew where to look. I had money to spend and I spent it with wild abandon!

Everard recuperated with his widow. She liked me not—condemned me as an unrepentant sinner—and the incarceration made him miserable and tetchy. I went to the house before returning to the army and found him propped up in bed, leg in splints, reading a book. He put the book down and greeted me warmly; the widow tutted and left us alone. I glanced at the cover—Peter Ramus' *Logica*.

'That looks a dull tome,' I said.

'I find it most interesting. Mr Barker brought it for me.'

Barker was my sister's tame lawyer—an owl-eyed, tufty-browed old dodderer, and yet another radical independent.[*]

'*Bene disserere est finis logices,*' I said.[40]

---

[*]   See *The Last Roundhead.*

He looked at me blankly.

''Tis from a play.'

No need to tell him which play; it would only upset him. The last thing I wanted was a sermon.

'I saw the dead, small and great, stand before God, and the books were opened, and the dead were judged out of those things which were written in the books, according to their works,' he intoned at me. 'That is from the bible; perhaps you should spend more time with the Lord's word than some playwright's.'*

I got a sermon anyway.

'I worry about you, my friend,' I said, shaking my head.

He looked surprised. 'Why do you worry about me? You are the one away to war. I worry about you.'

'Then we are both taken for a pair of fools,' said I, laughing.

Everard laughed with me, and it broke down the barrier that had grown between us. I told him about my meeting with the Lord Mayor—how he had killed the boy, cozened us, won Polman's treasure, and would still escape justice for his part in the gold smuggling. I could see it made him angry, but he just shrugged.

'What did you expect?' he said. 'The rich always look after themselves. But a day of reckoning comes, Blandford. God's hammer will smash the unrighteous.'

'Malleus Dei?** Let us hope it does not get caught on the way down.'

'You are incorrigible.' But he smiled.

'The boy will remain behind to wait on you whilst you recuperate. I am away to Newport Pagnell.'

| * | Revelations 20:12 |
| ** | Hammer of God. |

'I need no man as my servant.'

'It will keep him out of trouble. Elizabeth would be furious with me if something happened to the little ragabash.'

He laughed and raised his cup.

'Here is to Newport Pagnell, and to keeping boys out of trouble,' he said, then reached for his pipe and weed. He looked at my new clothes and shook his head. 'Ah, Blandford, you are the gaudy fop. Is that a new hat? Bright blue—'tis colourful indeed.'

We spent the rest of the evening in pleasant conversation— no lectures, or sermons, and only faint disapproval of my vanities. For once, he was like the man I had first met, fun loving and not so devout. He told me of his designs for the war's end. A holding near his home in Reading, away from this city he hated so. It was a fine last night in London together. That is until his woman turned me out with a belly bloated from ale. I pissed in the street, farted, and walked home.

The next morning I left London, joined a column of new recruits, and rode through the snow to Newport Pagnell. Elizabeth had been unusually subdued at my leaving. I took Apple from the stalls at Thames Street to saddle him up. She stood watching me in the courtyard, wearing only a thin shawl to keep out the shivers, pursed lips and sour look on her face.

'You will be careful, Blandford.'

'Of course I will; there is no need to fuss. The boy can remain here with you and Everard for now. I want you to check the willow tree regularly. If any new messages appear, write to me.'

She nodded. 'And you will pray every day and write often,

promise me.'

'I promise, Elizabeth,' I said it too glibly and she glared. 'Would I lie to you, dear sister?'

'With only short pauses to catch breath, dear Blandford.'

But, she held me tight before I left, and I swear there was a glistening in her eye as I rode away.

Thick snow still covered the country roads, and mud and ice made the journey hazardous. Lonesome travel was foolish, and the company of numbers better than the risk of ambush. It meant four days of trudge, with muskets and pikes struggling through the slush and ruts; few repairs had been done for a year or more.

That is something to think upon. Roads are the arteries of a nation; when they are well maintained, the nation is well governed. As they fall apart, so does trade and commerce, so does the state—each pothole and rut is a sign of regression. Throughout parish and shire in our three kingdoms, the roads crumbled.

It was dark on the fourth day when we reached Newport Pagnell. The town surrounded by half-finished outworks and ramparts, tenailles,* and bastions. The Ouse River** was a natural moat around the south and east. When the defences were complete they would make a formidable citadel, but it would take all of my uncle's skill and diplomacy to bring that about. I crossed over the old wooden bridge at Tickford, showed my papers to the sentinels at the gates and passed into the town. The infantry and carts—my companions from London—remained in the fields south of the town until billets were found.

Guards at the gate directed me into the town. The High

---

*   Defensive earthwork advanced from the main ramparts.

**   The Great Ouse rather than the Yorkshire River Ouse.

Street overflowed with soldiers and miserable looking locals bewailing their fate. Buildings become taverns and drinking dens, stalls served cheap food, and stews full of pox-ridden punks. Crude rough sorts filled the garrison of Newport Pagnell. I sniffed, preferring a better class of drunkard. Uncle Samuel would be hard pressed to keep order with this mob of villains.

The Saracen's Head on the High Street was the governor's residence and headquarters. A large red-bricked building with three floors, and expensive tiled roof, that had become Uncle Samuel's lair. There, he received reports from spies, scouts, and informers all over England. People in the court in Oxford, Bristol, Gloucester, and York, all sent their tidings on to him. Every little scrap and snippet was scrawled down in a leather journal, and fed to the Earl of Essex. And, our squeaky Lord General did nothing with the precious gift.

I handed Apple's reins to a waiting boy, told him to stay away from the gnashers, and skipped up the steps to the inn, glad to be at my journey's end and already planning my entertainments for the evening; through the doors, into a large common room with high ceilings and painted beams. The supplicants and penitents who wished to petition my uncle waited for him there, even at that late hour.

Guarding over this *petite* kingdom was Mr Samuel Butler. I had not missed his companionship those last months. Jammed behind his desk, and arse grown so fat the poor chair groaned like it would shatter when he rolled a cheek. His sandy hair had thinned more, a little bald crown gave him a monk's tonsure. I smiled, and his bulbous lower lip drooped when he caught view of my happy visage.

'Mr Butler, what a sorry sight you are,' I said. 'I am surprised you can fit behind your desk you are grown so tubby. I wager it is some time since you caught sight of your pizzle when you piss. Do your young gentlemen have to lift that belly to get at it?'

That was sly, I admit, but he was an odious shitling and I was full of whimsy.

'So, you have returned, have you, Mr Candy.' He knew that would dig at me.

'Captain Candy.'

'Such terrible news about your comrade, *Captain*.'

'What are you talking about, you fat oaf?' Butler looked unspeakably smug.

'Have you not heard?' He said it innocently. 'Poor Mr Cole was captured in Oxford. They hanged him, just a week past, for a traitor.'

I wanted to punch his fat face in, but his words had pierced my soul. I could not believe it, praying that there was some mistake.

'Mr Butler!' Uncle Samuel had caught the end of that exchange. 'Have you no shame, sir? Such a display is most unworthy and cruel. I will speak with you on this again.' He turned to me, and gently. 'Blandford, my boy, come through to my chambers.'

He gave Butler a withering stare and led me to his chamber.

'What happened?' I asked, once inside.

Uncle Samuel perched in a chair by his desk—covered in the usual papers—and gestured for me to do the same. I stayed standing; I was stunned that Franny had gone. Of all of us, he had seemed invincible. Taking the most risks, but when he fell into shit he always came up smelling of roses. Now he was dead, snuffed out, just like that.

'He was captured coming out of Oxford; a Royalist officer

recognised him,' said my uncle, and then sighed. 'Franny had been in and out of the city too often over the holidays and drew attention to himself.'

'Who recognised him?'

He paused before answering. 'John Hurry,' he said finally.

All composure left me; I cursed, kicked a chair, and cursed again. While I had been carousing in London, Franny had been swinging from a gallows.[41] And bastard John Hurry was to blame. Another of my friends that man—that Judas—would answer for. I swore to Franny's shade, as I had sworn on Peter Russell's corpse, that John Hurry would pay. Uncle Samuel let my tantrum run its course. I smashed the chair in my frustration, and that pricked my bubble of anger. Suddenly embarrassed, I looked at my uncle.

'Now I have nowhere to sit.'

He smiled at me, palpable relief on his face, and called Butler into the room.

'Bring in your chair for Blandford to sit, Mr Butler, and take this one away to be repaired.'

The White Swan stands next-door to The Saracen's Head on the busy High Street.[42] An older building, not so spacious, but warm food and ale, and packed to the rafters—soldiers, tapsters, cardsters, and women—in the common room. The scouts and officers had made it their mess—an effusion of drunkards. I nodded to the few faces I recognised, but most had joined since Newbury and were new to me.

I saw Captain Temple—a decent sort from Suffolk. He had been on the Gloucester march and I knew him well enough to talk.

'What ho, Temple. This place be a rum bustle.'

'Well met, Candy. You are back from London and come to Sodom's stew.' He had a grin on his flushed red face, a woman in one hand, and a bottle in the other. I was not in the mood for a revel.

'Have you seen Sam Brayne?'

'In his garret.' Temple gestured to the stairs. 'He has been sulking there for days. Carpe Diem, I told him. He told me to bugger off.'

The tapster sold me two bottles of sack at an extortionate price, and I grabbed a brace of cups and climbed the stairs. Sam was right at the top of the building in a small room, with only a straw mattress for a bed and thin blanket for warmth.

He looked broken. Always quiet and reserved, but now withdrawn and dark. He had not shaved in days, nor emptied the piss-pot in as long. I threw the waste out of the window leaving it open to clear the air. Then I sat on the pallet next to him and tried to open one of the bottles.

'How did it happen?' I asked him.

'He stayed in Oxford; I told him not to.' He did not look at me as he spoke. 'There was information he wanted from a woman at court. We arranged to meet at a tavern outside the city walls. I waited and waited but when he did not return...' Sam started sobbing.

'What information? What woman?'

'I know not; I did not ask. Franny said he trusted her.'

'Was it that damned ledger?' I asked. 'I told him 'twas a fools quest.'

Sam looked up, eyes red. 'We had the ledger, Sugar. It was in his bag when they took him. We were clean away; Franny said he would come out at the next change of guards. We had done it so many times before. 'Twas but poor chance Hurry came through the gates and recognised him.'

I cursed. 'So Hurry has the ledger now?' The man would sell it, or use it to blackmail the names inside. Of that much I was certain.

'He can do nothing with it,' said Sam. 'It was written in cipher.'

'He will know it is important though,' I said. 'He could have handed it back to the King's secretary, but I wager it is kept safe till he can make some gain.'

'Oh, Sugar, I loved him so,' he repeated. 'I should have stopped him.'

I realised what he meant by his love. I should have been shocked by it, Sam so quiet and Franny always full of laughter, and both chased women like huntsmen. They had been so close and I had never noticed. I thought of all the times I had mocked or made sly comments, and wondered at the hurt a casual barb can cause. I even felt somewhat guilty of my jibing at Butler earlier. I forgave myself that; Butler was a turd.

'You know that we are the only ones left,' he said.

'What do you mean?'

'You and I and Everard. All the others are dead.'

The scouts who had been first had paid a bloody butchers bill. Franny, Peter Russell and his father, Zeal Miller, and more were on the tally. Sam was right, there were only three left who had stood together at Kineton.

'Everard is lucky to be out of it with his broken leg then,' I said. 'Though I am sure he would say providence not fortune.'

'I wonder if we are to be next.'

I had the same thought but said nothing. Sam had become like a man at the bottom of a well, who can see life and light above him, but has no way to reach for it. I did not like to dwell on my mortality as a young man. As a decrepit relic, I find it is all I think of. Death is so damn final, you see, and life too damn short.

I finally managed to open the bottle of wine and poured us both a cup.

'Drink this.'

He took the cup without argument; I swigged mine back and poured another. I knew of only one way to shake this melancholy. Looking over at Sam, I took a stern tone.

'Enough of this despair, my friend,' I said. 'We cannot waste our lives crying for the dead; I will not allow it.'

'And who are you, Sugar?'

'I am your poxy captain, and I order you to drink.'

That finally raised a half-hearted smile from him. Sam necked back his cup, reached for the bottle, and poured himself another.

Mercurius Civicus:
Sir Alexander Denton's House taken.

On Tuesday 16th January, it was advertised by several letters from Newport Pagnell, that the Earl of Manchester's Foot came there last week, in place of the London Trained bands that returned home Friday last.

Since arriving, they had intelligence of a party of Cavaliers who had possessed themselves of Sir Alexander Denton's house in Hillesden, between Newport Pagnell and Aylesbury. The governor-in-chief sent forth a party of Dragoons under one Captain Abercrombie to beset the house.

The Cavaliers, having notice of them about half an hour before they came, fled away in all haste to Brackley in Northamptonshire. They left most of the arms and many of their horses behind in the house, wherof the dragoons possessed themselves upon their entrance. They also took a great store of ammunition, provision, and treasure that was left behind.

They have since taken eighty of the Cavaliers that they found straggling in small parties. This is the first action the successful forces have achieved since arriving at the garrison. It is not doubted that, with God's assistance, we shall find them willing and ready to take all advantages upon the enemy. They can do good service by joining with the forces of Northamptonshire to clear the county of the Cavaliers.

London, January 17th 1644

15. A Brave Bad Man: Ely, January 1644.

I preached and prayed for Oliver,
And all his vile abettors,
But curs'd the King and Cavalier,
And cried 'em down for traitors.

(Traditional, *The Religious Turncoat; Or, The Trimming Parson.*)

Ely Cathedral dominates the fens. The great limestone towers erect, fucking the sky. Set on an island in the marshes and meres; a beacon for travellers as they take the road north from Cambridge. 'Tis a flat country—monotonously dull when I compared it to the Wiltshire Downs. I told Sam how I would ride out to the horse carving at Westbury as a boy, with luncheon in a basket, and watch the land around for miles. Here, there was nought but reeds, brackish water, and flooded icy pasture. Even the bare trees looked stunted.

I was sure Uncle Samuel was having some private jest in sending us to Cromwell. The man was a renowned terror, even then—plain speaking, rude in manner and dress, and unbearably godly. My uncle held him in high regard, however, and Cromwell returned the honour.

'Make a good impression,' Uncle Samuel told me.

We took the regular despatches sent up to Ely. Cromwell—without the lethargy of our generals—used every titbit Uncle Samuel could feed him. The war in the east had broken down into raid and counter raid, ambush and skirmish, houses burned out and cattle stolen. Old Wart Face and his men showed themselves masters in these *petite* battles. Soon, they would be masters of all England.

Sam proved a miserable companion as we plodded along. Two days on muddy roads and he hardly said a word. We crossed the Ouse at St Neots, a solid roundhead garrison town, and spent the night by the fire in a tavern. Whilst the black mood of Franny's passing still weighed on us both, I tried to cover it with babble and japes. By the second day, Sam's patience was wearing thin.

'The Devil take you and your chatter! Would that I had some soft cheese to stuff my ears and free me from your noise.'

'Soft cheese?'

'Aye, soft cheese.'

It was growing dark, we were still four or five miles from the Ely, and it had started snowing again. The road took a couple of sudden twists, past a crossroads, and into a hamlet —squat tiled houses built of dirty yellow brick, a small parish church with pointed spire, and opposite, an old papist cross cracked and broken by the iconoclasts. I noted a garland of dried flowers at its base—customs die hard.

A wood-built inn sat beside the road with moss on the roof and ivy curling up the walls, but good stables, and rooms for travellers. A wooden sign, with the head of a lion daubed in peeling red paint, hung above the doors. The windows were of glass, not hide, and seemingly clean. I turned to Sam.[43]

'Let us rest here and carry on in the morning. Cromwell can wait on our despatches.'

'Do you promise not to babble at me?'

'I make no promises,' I said, dismounting. 'Mayhap they will sell you some soft cheese.'

We rubbed the horses down, stabled them, and stepped down into the inn. I paid for the rooms, ordered food and wine and bread, and Sam took a table beside the fire. There were only a couple of locals drinking cider, but the place was well kept and the innkeeper's goodwife blonde, buxom, and welcoming. She quickly brought our food—smoked eel baked in red wine—and drinks.

'If there is ought else thou need, masters?'

'Soft cheese, Sam?'

'No thank you, Mistress,' said Sam politely, ignoring me.

We ate in silence; the food was good, and the wine passable but expensive—everything was expensive in those times. Belly full, I belched, and thanked the woman when she came to clear away the platters. We gave her a couple of pennies on top for the service, and I ordered another bottle of wine. The wind had picked up outside; I could see the trees swaying in the lamplight through the windows. Drinking by a fire was better than riding in that. Perhaps a game of cards.

'A trick or two of Put?' I suggested, pouring out sack for us both.[44]

'Not with your deck.'

Instead, he loaded a pipe and lit it from the fire. He had picked up that foul habit from Everard, but had less pungent taste in tobacco. I sniffed then turned in my chair as the doors opened letting in a blast of cold air. Four men in soldier's coats entered, all bearing green tokens in their hats and wearing high cavalry boots—well armed with sword and pistol, but no armour, noisy—and already the worst for drink by their look.

Goodwife hurried to serve them, nervously, and the two local men quaffed their drinks and left. That was not encouraging: these intruders had a reputation. I turned back to Sam, as they spoke sharply to the woman, calling out their orders. One of the troopers noticed us sitting by the fire.

'Are you the gentlemen with the fine horses that I saw in the stalls?' he asked, in an insolent tone.

I looked over; the one who had spoken had pimples

bursting across his face—another beardless boy out to prove himself. I kept my temper in check. His friends looked solid enough and I saw no need for conflict.

'We are,' I said. 'Be that your business?'

The others came to join Pimple, standing around Sam and I with drinks in their hands.

'It is our business,' said another. 'You are strangers, by your dress and voice; you could be spies.'

It was becoming the regular line touted by miscreants on both sides: accusation and condemnation—it worked mostly. People were scared of being caught in the wrong faction and lynched. When the enemy speaks the same language, wears the same dress, and is probably married to your cousin, well, then paranoia becomes the bully's best friend. Sam and I were not so easily cowed. I showed them our passport and commission from Uncle Samuel.

'Happy?' I asked.

'Samuel Luke?' one of them sneered. 'He is a deformed dwarf. Not a soldier—a grotesque.'

The insult to my uncle prickled me. I should have bitten my tongue, but—well you know me better than that by now.

'He fought well enough at Newbury and Edgehill,' I said. 'Where were you boys there? Happen we missed you.' I looked over at Sam. 'Quis est haec simia.'*

Sam glared at me. Unfortunately, the soldier knew his Latin.

'Are you saying I am a monkey?'

'We should take them in, Zachary,' said one of the others. 'Colonel Cromwell will want to check their story—they could be spies. He looks too young to be made a captain.'

That grated even more; I had earned the poxy

---

*   Who is this monkey?

commission.

'Colonel Cromwell can kiss my hairy arse,' I said, and took a drink from my cup. A hammer blow to the side of my face made me spill wine across the table.

My insult to Noll had given the bullyboys an excuse for a fight. No surprises—they had wanted one all along. A couple of them began pummelling me, knocking me from my chair, while the others went at Sam.

The innkeeper's wife screeched for her husband, and shouted: 'This is no bawdy house! This is no bawdy house!' I could have told her that good bawdy houses have big bastards to keep the riff-raff out, but a beating distracted me.

A lesson there: endeavour to not start a tavern brawl when the odds are set against you.

One of the men left off pounding me, to grab at Sam, who had smashed the bottle of wine over his comrade. I struggled with Pimple, hitting him, grabbing at his collar. The innkeeper waded in finally, fat bellied, and swinging a cudgel at the soldiers. I rolled on top of my adversary, and started pounding him in his spotted face. That did not last, one of his friends kicked me—right on the kidney—and I slumped to the floor in agony.

I rolled around squealing at the pain in my back. Sam had downed another with a swift kick to the balls, but other men were arriving, charging through the doors—more buff-coated troopers, and their young captain, who set about us with gusto. We brawlers were grabbed and boned, a few broken heads handed out, and soon we were stood outside in the dark. Our horses taken from us, we were tied behind and forced to march. I made to explain our business but the young captain ordered me silent.

'That got out of hand rather quickly, Sam,' I said, somewhat remorsefully. He did not respond.

As we walked to Ely, I heard the name of the captain but could not believe it. He was too young, a boy of my own age not the country squire of reputation. Then, I realised the son must have taken the father's—Oliver Cromwell.

How many stout cells have I occupied in my long life - too many to count. The one in Ely was better than most. The usual thick stone walls and a strong door banded with iron, no windows, but dry, and most unusually clean. It is more typical to find the smeared faeces of former inmates when in a pound.

'This is entirely your fault.'

I looked over at Sam. They were the first words he had spoken since we had been dumped in the cell. The brawlers who had caused the fight were marched off under guard, making vain protests, whilst I hurled insults and curses at them. I took some comfort in that, but we were locked up and left alone for rest of the night—our despatches and papers taken by Young Oliver. My back hurt from the kicking and there had been blood in my piss.

'They broke my pipe and took my baccy. I cannot even take a smoke.'

'My apologies, Sam,' I said.

'Your fuse has grown too short, Sugar. There was no need for this. We could have spent a night on feather bolsters instead of a bare bench,' he said. 'And they broke my pipe.'

I was surprised by that, I had not realised my temper had changed. I have always been prone to the odd tantrum, but considered myself a happy sort in the main. Yet, as I thought on it, I realised Sam was true. The war was making me tetchy and giving me bad dreams. We sat in silence for a time as I contemplated that.

The lock rattled and door creaked open; a couple of men entered, both in uniform coats—one with an officer's sash.

'Captain Candy?' said the officer to Sam. He shook his head.

'I am Candy.' I might have to start wearing a beard to look older.

'You can come with us, if you please, sir.'

I stood up and brushed myself down, nodded to Sam, and followed the officer. Then I stopped.

'Good, sir, could I beg a clay pipe and some tobacco for my comrade? It would soothe his nervous disposition.'

I thought Sam was going to spring at me from his evil stare. The trooper fumbled around in his coat, pulled out a pipe and tobacco pouch, then handed them to him. He took them gratefully enough but offered me no thanks. In truth, it was a test—and Sam knew it. Had they dismissed my request, or worse, then we would have been in trouble. Their polite demeanour and easy acquiescence reassured us both.

They led me out of the lockup—an old monkish storehouse in the shadow of the cathedral—over lawns busy with men exercising horses and drilling with swords. We crossed a road to a small church and, in the gardens, a plainly built house, two stories high, wood and plaster, stone and tile. This was Cromwell's home: an old vicarage with a leaky roof. [45]

They took me through into the kitchen—a neat tiled affair, with a long table, great hearth, and a roaring wood fire. Standing at the table, eating eggs and toasted bread, was the man himself. Young Oliver was with him—being lectured about something or other.

Cromwell's shirt was open at the collar, no shoes on his feet, at ease in his own home. He turned to face me as the guards led me in. The woodcuts did not do him justice. Lean, and of medium height, mousey hair turning grey, a long face with a ruddy complexion, big bulbous nose, and the most piercing grey-blue eyes.

He stared at me as if weighing my soul; fixing me with a most penetrating glare. It was both frightening and fascinating in equal measures. This man exuded absolute power. Even in a plain kitchen, in his stockings, with egg yolk on his shirt.

'You are Candy?' He asked with no polite introductions.

'Yes, Colonel.'

'My men say you provoked a brawl, caused damage to property, and upset the locals.'

I paused before answering. Depending upon the view of the incident it could be seen either way—that is a lesson in context. Cromwell carried on before I could conjure a suitable response.

'You said that I could kiss your hairy arse?'

'Yes, sir, but now I have made your acquaintance, I withdraw the invitation.'

That was glib, and I thought he was going to bawl me out, but he stared at me for just a second and then guffawed.

'Your uncle tells me you have a roguish wit,' he said, in his big booming voice. 'Do you fear God, Captain Candy?'

I damn well fear you, I thought, but gave him my most roguish smile and stayed silent. He carried on.

'I have already spoken with the innkeeper. I know it was not you who caused this disturbance. The other men will be made examples of in the stocks.' That was harsh even if they started it. 'Still, it is not the best introduction, Captain.'

'I can assure you, Colonel, that neither I nor my comrade

intended such an arrival.'

He nodded. 'Why do you fight, Candy?'

The answer to that was one I knew well enough. 'Twas something we all worried on: treason tends to fix the mind. It always boiled down to two reasons—money or religion—I cared little for God.

'I say the King is a tyrant who raises illegal taxes and makes bloody war on his own people.' I believed it then and I believe it now. I met three Stuart kings—they were all stubborn shitholes.

He smiled and nodded again at that.

'At least (God be praised) you know why you fight. Too many have no idea and it makes them weak. The Lord of Israel abhors weakness of spirit, Candy.'

I did not know how to respond to that.

He looked to his son, and then to me, and finally explained his and my uncle's design. Young Oliver would return with us to Newport Pagnell in a few days, with supplies and troops promised to Uncle Samuel. In the meantime, we were to show them the work of the Scouts. He wanted our opinions, indeed, he ordered us to be honest and forthright in our assessment, both of his son and his men. I thought that would be the end of the interview.

'They call you The Golden Scout?'

'Yes, sir,' I said, somewhat bashfully.

'They called my grandfather The Golden Knight. He was a vain spendthrift. Are you a vain spendthrift, Captain Candy?'

'Yes, sir.' A reputation is akin to a suit of old clothes—more comfortable when a trifle stained.

He guffawed again. I was starting to wonder if Cromwell's fearsome reputation was perhaps a little exaggerated. He had decided that I was an honest rogue and, I think, kept that opinion until the end. He was wrong of course and I told him often enough, but he would just laugh and pinch my cheeks. He thought pinching cheeks was funny—lunatic; it damn well hurt, I can tell you.

The man stood preaching to the other soldiers in the shadow of the cathedral. No ordained priest or minister, just one of Cromwell's troopers inspired to speak on God. My uncle would have clapped him in irons for the impudence. The soldier was no great orator; I had heard it all before. Fear this; fear that. Sin! Sin! Sin! How the march of the godly would sweep the idolaters away.

The idolaters, meanwhile, were inside enjoying their usual Sunday morning prayers. I could hear strains of the choral liturgy coming from the cathedral. The men grumbled about that, making the odd threat to 'cast out the vicar', but I did not think much on it until I caught sight of Cromwell storming across the lawns.

This was not the reasonable, guffawing, country gentleman of the day before. His face was dark red in anger, brows furrowed, and mouth twisted in a cruel snarl; dressed for war, in buff coat and cavalry boots, sword at his side, and hat on his head. Some of his captains were trailing in his wake, now joined by others, until a whole crowd were behind him. Old Wart Face led the stampede towards the west tower of the cathedral. I nudged Sam.

'Let us see what this is about.'

We followed the troopers into the cathedral itself, our boots stamping on the tiles, like drums to battle, the noise echoing through the high vaults. Cromwell pounded down the long nave before us, screaming at the top of his voice.

'Mr Hitch! Mr Hitch!'

Mr Hitch stood at the pulpit, singing along with the rest. An old man, tall and bony, and wearing a forbidden surplice—the man wanted a scene. His congregation stammered to a halt in their caterwauling, but Reverend Hitch was a bravado, he continued intoning the liturgy, even as a raving angel of destruction bore down.

'We pray that the light of the glorious gospel of Christ may dispel the darkness of ignorance and unbelief, shine into the hearts of all your people and reveal the knowledge of your glory in the face of Jesus Chri...'

'I warned you, Mr Hitch!' shouted Cromwell. 'To forbear altogether your choir service that is so unedifying and offensive to God.'

Hitch finally came to a halt as the Colonel turned to the stunned worshippers.

'I am a man under authority and am commanded to dismiss this assembly.' And, when not a person stirred, he raged: 'You are dismissed!' and gestured to the troopers to start removing the people.

Hitch now started up again with the singing, but on his own.

'As it was in the beginning...'

A determined martyr, then—a modern Thomas Becket. A couple of the choirboys started warbling along with him, and Oliver lurched towards the carved pulpit.

'Leave off your fooling, Hitch, and come down, sir!' bellowed Cromwell.

Two of the troopers made to drag Hitch down from the pulpit and that was enough to end his dreams of heaven. To be a martyr takes bravery, or stupidity, or both; they were not mutually exclusive in the martyrs I have met. Mr Hitch was neither brave enough nor lacking in wit. The subdued reverend trawled out with the choir and the rest of the congregation. I stepped aside as they passed me, a troubled look on Hitch's face. I know not what became of him, but the great House of God was locked up and used for stores and stables from then on.

It was an important lesson in Cromwell's character. At first, he was always reasonable even when he thought you damned. But if reason did not work, then by God, he would force you to his will. For his design was that of God. With every victory that he won, every triumph against the odds, he became more convinced that he was divinely blessed.

Post hoc ergo propter hoc,[*] of course, and damned difficult to argue against.[at]

---

[*]   *After this, therefore because of this*. The idea that because Y happened, it was caused by X.

16. Young Oliver: Hillesden, February 1644.

Gather ye rosebuds while ye may,
Old time is still a-flying:
And this same flower that smiles to-day
To-morrow will be dying.

(Robert Herrick, *To the Virgins, to Make Much of Time*.)

Sam and I watched Cromwell's regiment as they drilled on a grey morning in Ely. Young Oliver manoeuvred his men in the fields below the cathedral. Noll was sending these troops to Uncle Samuel—earnest greenhorns like their captain. Most were just learning to ride, as well as use a sword for the first time. Others, veterans from the regiment, were instructing them in the drill.

'They may well stand in battle,' said Sam. 'But are useless for scouts.'

Sacks packed with straw had been set up on poles, about the height of a rider, and the men were riding at speed, trying to cut them. They knew what to do, holding their swords steady, letting the speed and weight of the charge do the rest. Straw was soon flying through the air, but instead of whoops of excitement, they exercised in silence. It was most disconcerting.

'They seem stout enough,' I said. 'And they do what they are told—a tad quiet.'

'When did you do what you were told, or any of us?' he said. 'These boys are too god-fearing. Rupert's Horse will eat them alive.'

Sam was wrong about the Ironsides.

I have seen many a horse-soldier in my time, some good, and some bad. Regiments follow their officers in temperament. John Hurry's company of cutthroats were the worst, regardless

197

of which side the turncoat was fighting for; Leslie's Scottish lancers were a wild-eyed rabble and dangerous, George Goring's Horse the most prone to looting, womanising, and drunkenness—I liked Goring. Prince Rupert had the best of the Cavaliers; moulded into the image of their leader. Brave, reckless, and unbearably arrogant—my brother James fitted in well.[47]

Cromwell and his regiment were different. There were rogues amongst them, no doubts about that, and religious malignants, but in the main they were sober and stubborn. Oliver cast his net wide and far, and cared not if you be Anabaptist or agitator, only fear God and follow his lead. England's Gideon—God's Captain—for that is how Cromwell saw himself, even then.

It would be admirable, had he not been such a consummate bastard.

Young Oliver did not follow his father—excepting the blue eyes and mousey hair. He had the curse of children born to overbearing parents: decent, honest and single-hearted, but uninspiring. He lacked confidence in himself, was nervous of making mistakes, and too timid in general. I told Cromwell all this, stood in his kitchen, and he pondered a while before answering.

'I only hope to prove myself an honest man and single-hearted to our cause,' he said, eventually. 'I can ask no more of my son.'

'Perhaps his time in Newport Pagnell will temper him, Colonel,' I said.[48]

'Perhaps, perhaps; I appreciate your candour, Candy.' His fierce blue eyes blinked, he nodded, and I was dismissed.

The journey back to Newport Pagnell passed without incident, and the weather was cold and bright. Young Oliver and his troop rode with us. Away from his father, he seemed more at ease, but still serious. He had brought a book of histories with him, to study the great generals of the past. It was his father's suggestion of course, but Oliver was enjoying the book and enthused by the tactics and strategies of Hannibal, and Caesar, Scipio, and Alexander.

'Who do you read about today?' I asked, as we rode.

'Philip of Macedon,' he said. 'Alexander's father.'

Did he think himself Alexander to Oliver's Philip, I wondered.

'Philip sent the Spartans a message,' Young Oliver continued. 'If I win this war, you will be slaves forever. Do you know what the Spartans said?'

'If,' I answered. 'I remember from school. 'Tis a good reply.'

'What did Philip do?' asked Sam. His schooling had been done in a village church and his Latin and Greek history poor.

'Left them be,' Oliver told him.

'Wise man.'

'Until he was stabbed by his bodyguard on the orders of Alexander's mother,' I said. ''Tis the women you need to watch.'[49]

That raised a laugh from them, but given my experiences with Mistress Jane Whorewood, the captivating Countess of Carlisle, and even the bewitching Meg Powell... Well, you can see why I might have been a little biased.

Hillesden is a small hamlet in West Buckinghamshire with a few red-bricked cottages, an old church, and a manor house. It lay in the hinterlands between Oxford and Newport Pagnell. Sir Alexander Denton—a Royalist—owned the great house itself. We had stationed a small garrison of dragoons there in January, but a cavalier company forced them out—now it was our time to return the favour. Uncle Samuel decided that this would be Young Oliver's first test and sent me to accompany him. We led his troop south to Aylesbury and then turned our horses to Hillesden.[50]

'How many do you think there will be, Jeremiah?' Oliver was nervous.

Jeremiah Abercrombie was a Scots Covenanter, with estates in Ireland, and a captain in the Earl of Manchester's Dragoons. He was lean, in his middle age, with a big shining dome of a forehead and greying hair receding back to the crown. Jeremiah had been garrisoned at Hillesden before being beaten out. He came from Aylesbury with his men and his local knowledge. That made a hundred or more of us, all mounted, provisioned, and well armed.

'There were no more than fifty,' said Jeremiah. 'We had no powder to stand against them, but now—if God wills it—we shall prevail.'

He knew his business, had spent time in Germany, and fought with Adolphus. We passed the previous night in a barn near Aylesbury. Jeremiah regaled us with tales of Lutzen and Breitenfeld in his lilting accent.[51] Young Oliver had lapped it all up, eagerly asking questions, and the Scot had been happy to oblige. Loquacious is the word for him, but he was pleasant enough.

The land around Hillesden is flat with narrow lanes, only wide enough for two abreast on horseback, and enclosed by tall hedgerows. A perfect terrain for ambush; our column was exposed.

'Send some men into the fields, Oliver, and up ahead,' I whispered it quietly to him. 'As outriders and scouts.'

'Yes, yes of course,' he said, and hurriedly detailed a squad to the task.

We approached Hillesden from the East. Abercrombie told us that the estate was bordered by a brook, in full flow after the recent rain, but with a small wooden bridge and tree cover. It could not be seen from the church spire, where the Royalists had a watch. As we got close, Oliver explained to the men what he wanted from them. He was nervous, so were they all, but they listened intently to him nonetheless.

'The dragoons will go in on foot, and secure the bridge.' He nodded to Abercrombie. 'We wait for their signal, then we ride across with pistols at the ready, and fan out into loose order. Any questions?'

'If we ride in and take the bridge quickly, we could surprise them,' said one.

'If,' replied Oliver.

Perhaps he will do after all, I thought. Riding in blind would only lead to disaster, and whilst he was nervous he was determined. We reached a farm before the bridge—small, only a couple of thatched buildings, and broken down. Abercrombie sent a few men on foot into the buildings, but there was nobody home.

'Could they have been warned of our coming?' asked Oliver.

''Tis possible,' I said.

We carried down the straight lane, past a crossroads, to another farmhouse—burned out by our own forces when made to retreat from the hamlet, Abercrombie told us. The blue-coated dragoons dismounted and checked their weaponry. Some of them took their comrades mounts whilst the others shouldered their carbines and lined up waiting for Abercrombie's orders.

'Wait for our trumpet call,' Jeremiah told Oliver.

'No,' he said, dismounting. 'I want to see what is down there.'

Abercrombie shrugged and led half of the 'goons in file down towards the brook. I dismounted, made sure my pistols were loaded, and then joined Oliver at the back of running soldiers. The rest of Abercrombie's men scrambled over the hedges and into the fields, down to the swiftly flowing waters. They would cover the flanks of our attack on the bridge.

My boots were not made for running, and I cursed as I kept pace with Oliver.

We ran straight into Royalist guards at the narrow bridge. An overturned cart had been made a barricade, a wall behind which enemy musketeers unleashed a rain of shot . We scattered into ditches, and behind bushes, and began returning fire. I grabbed Oliver by his coat, pulling him down, and took aim with my pistol.

A trumpet call went up, but not from our dragoons; it came from the Royalist musketeers defending the bridge. Abercrombie ran at a half-crouch to join us. We could hear the musket shot buzzing through the bushes around us, and a couple of our boys had fallen.

'There are at least fifty on the bridge and brook alone,' he said. 'We have not the numbers to take this place.

'They must have been forewarned,' I said, 'and brought in reinforcements.'

Oliver looked crestfallen. His first chance to win his spurs had ended with a reverse. Now he had to make a decision whether to press on with the attack, against unknown odds, or to withdraw in good order. I had fretted on this moment.

Would he blindly follow his orders and lead us all to disaster? Oliver closed his eyes for a moment, and then nodded, as if receiving divine advice. He opened his pale blue eyes—so like his father's —and looked to us.

'We should withdraw,' he said, reluctantly.

I hid in a ditch, took out my spyglass and checked the land around the narrow crossing. I could see the ranks of enemy musketeers forming up on the opposite bank. At least a company, ready and waiting, their officer on horseback waving his sword—a full one hundred paces away—no breastplate, just a buff coat.

I took my second pistol and made careful aim at the figure. The rifling in the barrel gave my piece more range and accuracy, but this was an almost impossible shot. I held it steady and on the out-breath squeezed the trigger. The flame roared through the weapon, hurtling the shot towards my mark. I missed; the officer did not even notice. Cursing, I ran back to the horses and Oliver. He looked miserable at having to retreat.

''Twas a good decision not to ride in,' I reassured him. 'It is a reverse only, not a disaster. I am certain that we will be back.'

We took the road back to Aylesbury. Hillesden was being fortified and reinforced, that was clear. Uncle Samuel would want to snuff it out before it became an unassailable stronghold like Basing House. For that, we would need more men than our little company.

Oliver was silent during the ride back to Newport Pagnell. He still looked desolate at the reverse, his eyes red as if he had been crying. As we crossed the bridge into the town I turned with a jest to cheer his spirits, but before I could say ought, he toppled glassy-eyed from his mount.

They took him to a house off the High Street, a lazaretto* for all the sick soldiers. Young Oliver was dying, only a week after we rode to Hillesden, from Smallpox—a damnable fever. In the confined garrison at Newport the disease was rife.

His rank secured a room and bed, but he faded fast. I knocked on the door of the house, and was allowed to enter. Only those who had survived the disease could visit him. I had endured a mild dose as an infant when it had taken my mother. Uncle Samuel sent word to his father and we said prayers for his soul. Young Oliver understood what was coming.

He lay on the bed naked but for a cloth to cover his modesty. Hard pustules covered his skin, seeping pus. Face a livid red with the lesions, eyelids scabbed so they could not close, and the whites of his eyes turned to blood. His torso arms and legs were similarly afflicted. There was a dark colour to him from bleeding under the skin.

'I am dying, Blandford.' His voice a rasp.

I thought of pithy falsehoods to reassure him. Tell him that all would be well, but he would know my deceit. Young Oliver was not stupid.

'Yes, my friend, to my sorrow.'

'Tell my father...' he stopped and moaned, wracked with sudden pain.

I wanted to grasp his hand and give him the comfort of touch, but even the slightest pressure on his skin would be

---

*   Leper colony.

agony. There were tears in my eyes.

'Tell my father, I did my duty,' he croaked out. 'Please, and pray for my soul, Blandford.'

They were the last words he said. His breathing became heavy and ragged, as if fighting for every gasp, and he went quietly in only a few minutes. I pulled a sheet over his body, and said a prayer for his soul. There was noise and confusion outside, but I sat in silence for a while and shed a tear. He had proven me wrong. Young Oliver was no Alexander, and it would be unfair to measure him against his father. Yet, if I can say ought about him, he was a good man.

I left the sick house; left the dead, dying, and diseased, and stepped into the fresh air. I took note of the shouting men, finally, wildly running about, waving newsbooks in their hands. The London papers were delivered every week, and pamphlets heavily thumbed by a garrison desperate for word of the wider war.

'What is occurring?' I asked one. 'Has all the back pay arrived?'

''Tis the Scots,' he said. 'They have reached the Tyne. Soon they will be in York.'

Megan was in York, I was reminded. I hoped she got out before the siege began. A woman near was what I desired. I needed to swive, swive, and swive again. Some blessed comfort, away from the damned war, buried between the legs of a lover.

Damn it! Perchance, D'Avenant was correct about me.

I took the despatch to Cromwell that told him of his son's death. He was as distraught as any father would be. He took my hand, holding it tightly, and together we prayed for Young Oliver's soul, kneeling on the tiles in his kitchen. Cromwell's eyes filled with tears as I left; he looked broken by his loss.

His faith would give him comfort and stiffen his resolve. It was all God's will, he would decide—an infuriating fatalism to me. But I noted he kept his next son away from the war and soldiers. A mistake, as that turned out, but we are a long way from tales of Tumbledown Dick.

On my return to Newport Pagnell, I told Uncle Samuel how distraught the Colonel had been. My uncle had hoped for Cromwell's support in reducing Hillesden, but we both doubted he would ride out any time soon.

Mercurius Civicus: News from Northern Parts.

In the next place, I shall go farther off and present unto you the affairs of Northern parts, and principally from the Scots Army. I need not tell you about their taking of Coquet Island (Northumberland) where they captured the governor, and above sixty soldiers which kept garrison in the castle, seven pieces of brass ordnance, several barrels of gunpowder and much other provision and ammunition.

On Monday last, the Scots Commissioners here in London had letters concerning the revolt of Colonel Grey (Brother to Lord Grey) who, with a complete regiment of Horse, is come to the Scots. He and the rest of his soldiers have cheerfully taken the Covenant. The Scots have designed that Colonel Grey will remain in Northumberland for the better securities thereof.

The same letters do further certify, that upon Sir Thomas Glenham (The Royalist Governor of Newcastle) quitting Anwicke, he caused all the cattle in those parts to be carried away. Whereupon, the Scots sent out a strong party, rescued the cattle, and took several prisoners. The Scots restored the cattle to the owners, which made a deep impression in the minds of the inhabitants of those parts. Because of that, many of the most eminent men, with four thousand of the county have come and taken the Covenant.

On Friday last, the Scots made their first summons of Newcastle, whereupon Glenham required five days respite before answering. Since which time we have no further intelligence from thence. I am confident that before the next (issue), you will hear not only of the surrendering of Newcastle, but also of the Shields and diverse other places of consequence in those parts.

15th February 1644.

17. Hillesden House: March 1644.

I had six oxen t'other day,
But them the Roundheads stole away,
A mischief be their speed.

(Anon, *A Somersetshire Man's complaint*.)

A few weeks after Young Oliver's death, at the start of March, his father appeared before Newport Pagnell. Uncle Samuel led our dragoons out to join him, leaving only Foot and a single troop of Horse under Temple at the garrison. Our combined forces made a strength of more than two thousand. The army moved in force on Hillesden, spending the night nearby, and surrounding the Denton estate in the early morning. This time, the enemy had not been forewarned.

The brook proved no obstacle. Abercrombie led two companies across the bridge, clearing away defenders, whilst Cromwell went to the north. I took two troops of dragoons over the ford at Claydon—a village to the south—and approached on foot, carbines at the ready.

The rest of our men went into the fields to the west with Sam. The Royalists had fortified the church and there were half finished entrenchments around it and the house. Hillesden was invested on all sides. We were ready to assault, but a white flag and two figures on foot appearing from the house called a halt.

'Let us see what they are about then, Blandford,' said Uncle Samuel, and spurred his horse into a trot towards the Cavaliers. I followed him on foot after ordering my 'goons to spread out in loose order.

Uncle Samuel went thirty paces forward and waited for me to join him as the two royalist heralds approached. Both were finely dressed, one of an age with my uncle, with dark curls and beard streaked with white. The other had the look of a mercenary—well-armed, broad, and not much older than me.

'Colonel Smith, a good morning to you, sir. I trust we have not spoiled your breakfast.'

The older man grimaced. Uncle Samuel was acquainted with him, it seemed.

'What terms do you ask for, Luke?' he said.

'No terms, Colonel. It is surrender and captivity for you, else we assault and no quarter will be offered.'

Colonel Smith looked appalled at that.

'That is most uncivil. You will not let us leave under arms?'

'No, sir.'

'Then assault, Luke, and be damned.'

He turned away from us and the mercenary followed. Uncle Samuel smiled at me.

'Now we shall leave them stew a while. The colonel may be determined to die, but I wager the rest of them will not be so eager.'

We waited for no more than a quart of the hour. Then, Uncle Samuel nodded to a trumpeter who blew out the signal to attack, loud and clear in the bright morning sun. We advanced on the village from all sides. I led the dragoons on foot towards the trenches at the house, sword and pistol in hand. The Royalist defenders discharged their matchlocks at us long before we were in range: a wasted volley. They bent down to reload.

'Charge! Charge! Charge!'

I screamed out the order, waving my sword in the direction of the house. The Royalists broke as we pounded towards them firing our carbine and pistol. Some went for the house, some to the church. I pistolled one fleeing enemy in the back. He fell to the floor with arms flailing. Halting at the trench—no more than a knee-deep ditch—I made a pause. The sounds of fighting roared all around. Abercrombie led his men in from the east, down a tree-lined avenue, right into the heart of the estate. Cromwell and his men rode into the village and assaulted the church.

'Twas all too easy.

A few moments to reload our weaponry, and I led the men against the house and stables. The few Royalists standing against us, we cut down without mercy. One threw away his weapons and begged for quarter, but two dragoons stabbed him through the body and clubbed another down. Cromwell's men smashed at the great door to the house with a wooden bench as ram. It boomed against the door with each strike. The crack of shot and taste of gun-smoke merged with screams from the defenders inside; women and children were crying—their voices carried over the thunder of battle. I looked around for a Royalist but there were none left standing.

It was all over so quickly. A white flag hung out from the house and the defenders in the church calling out: 'Yield! We yield!'

Hillesden House had fallen.

The final assault on the church left it peppered with shot. The windows smashed, and roodscreen torn down by Cromwell's victorious troopers. Our own dragoons were less pious but no less destructive. They began ripping the house apart looking for the spoils of war.

The defenders were led out of the church—Colonel Smith and the house's owner Sir Alexander Denton were among them. Uncle Samuel would have been justified in having them all shot there and then in the graveyard, but none was harmed. That is the truth, whatever the lies you may have heard. No crime took place—there was no bloody murder! No more than thirty soldiers were killed in the assault, the rest taken prisoner and marched away.

Uncle Samuel led me into the house after the attack was finished. The great door lay ripped off its hinges in the courtyard. The occupants, men, women, and children herded outside - Denton's daughters, sisters, and nieces with misery drawn on their faces. We separated off the officers, weapons taken, and put them under guard in the church. The ordinary men—villagers and servants—we stripped of everything of worth, even the clothes off their backs, and turned out.

Denton's study was full of papers. A large room with oak wainscoting and flagged floor; bookcases stuffed with literature, and a great desk—a haul of information that made my uncle near weep with joy: Denton's private letters—full of information on enemy dispositions and garrisons. Some of it in cipher (that could be broken), but most in open hand.

'They had no time to burn the papers before the battle was upon them,' Uncle Samuel said. 'Put some men to guard this room. You and Brayne go through this treasure.'

I detailed a couple of dragoons to guard the room: men that could be trusted. The house was being stripped of anything of value. Barrels of powder were found in the cellars, with match and ball, along with stores of beer and wine; fifty horses in the barns and stables, and cattle, all driven off as the spoils of war. Wagons were called from nearby villages, and filled to the brim with the booty to be taken back to Newport Pagnell.

Sir Alexander Denton was not a happy man. His daughter added to his woes in public. Captain Jeremiah Abercrombie, hat off and bald forehead shining, stood hand in hand with her. A crowd of people, prisoners, family and dragoons , watched on in rapt attention as the drama played out. She was no great beauty—more ageing spinster to my eyes—but she seemed enamoured with my comrade. Denton did not share her enthusiasm.

'He is a rebel and a Scotsman; married be damned.'

'I love him, Father.'

'I care not one jot for your love.'

'I will pledge him my troth,' she said, 'and...'

'And what? Out with it, girl.'

'I bear his child, Father.'

Denton sat down in shock, his chains rattling.

My-oh-my, I thought to myself. Jeremiah has been a very naughty boy. Seducing Denton's daughter was a rum affair. No wonder Sir Alexander looked broken; he had seen his house taken, his family beggared, and men waited to cart him off to prison. Now, his daughter presented one of the very officers who had done this to him as her lover. I could not help but smile at the situation.

'Why have you got that silly grin on your face?' whispered Sam.

'I adore a good romance.'

'Coxcomb.'

It was a miserable little betrothal. Sir Alexander insisted that it took place before they took him away, and Uncle Samuel acquiesced. Denton and his weeping family, Jeremiah in his buff coat, the bride-to-be in a stained dress; all stood before the altar in the broken church. Cromwell's own chaplain performed the ceremony. He made the couple declare that they were not foresworn to another, and they both clasped hands to make their declaration. She gazed into Jeremiah's eyes with adoration, clearly smitten, and he did the same.

'I, Jeremiah Abercrombie take thee, Susan Denton, to be my espoused wife, and do faithfully promise to marry thee in times meet and convenient,' he said in his lilting accent.

'I, Susan Denton take thee, Jeremiah Abercrombie, to be my espoused husband, and do faithfully promise to marry thee in times meet and convenient,' she replied, with a nervous smile.

I raised a solitary huzzah but the family's silent glares soon quieted that. There were no rings to exchange; the couple looked around not knowing what to do. Taking a gold jacobus from my purse (the last of Charles Fairfax' reward money), I chopped it in two with my dagger.

'Let it be my gift to the happy couple,' I said, with a bow, and yet more glares from her father *et alii**. Bugger the family's sensibilities!

Jeremiah, and his bride-to-be, each took a half of the coin to be matched when the marriage ceremony was eventually performed. Jeremiah pierced his later and wore it on a leather cord around his neck. Susan Denton, her sisters and family were taken to the Verney house nearby. I was sure recriminations would soon begin. The woman seemed oblivious to the pain her actions had caused the family.

'She seems happy with her match,' I said to Sam. 'No fears for the future; Abercrombie looks terrified.'

'A woman worries about the future until she catches a husband. A man worries not about the future till he be caught.'

'Cynic.'[52]

---

*   And others.

Sorting through someone else's letters holds a strange fascination, a secret intrusion into the lives of others. Denton had been most careless in letting his cache fall into our hands. We placed anything in cipher in a chest to take to London and break. Sam and I sifted through the rest searching out anything of interest.

'Do you think there could be anything behind the panels?' asked Sam.

I grunted in response. Denton's letter book was proving quite illuminating. He had provided copies of all his letters in open hand. Sam started to check the oak wainscoting, knocking against panels and listening for a hollow. I returned to the letters. One worried about providing for his many daughters' weddings; he had one less to worry about—I chuckled to myself over that. A loud bang from Sam drew me away from my mirth.

'Do you have to be so loud?'

'There is something here; I need a crowbar.'

He left the study to search for something to pry back the panels. I went back to the book. The next letter detailed plate and stores sent to the King in Oxford. Sam returned and started on an oak panel half away up the wall. Smashing it with the crow and trying to rip back the panel. I turned the paper. It was a note signed JB, written in February at Chester. A description of the Battle of Nantwich that was interesting enough. Perhaps JB was John Byron; the letter was certainly from one who was well informed. Another smash and bang shook the room.

'Sam, for the love of God!'

I was about to berate him further, but a stream of coins came from the panelling—gold and silver. They tumbled to the floor clinking and rolling on the flagstones—hundreds, nay, thousands of them. Sam turned to me with a big grin on his face.

'There is more.'

He pulled out a small chest banded in iron. Locked, but he shot off the mechanism, bringing troopers running. Inside was more plate, gemstones, and jewels. The troopers looked on—mouths wide open at the sight of so much wealth.

'We will need sacks and more guards. Sir Samuel will be pleased with this haul...'

But, I was not listening. The final paragraph of the letter from JB had sent me cold.

Colonel Hurry said something most strange. I know not if threat or offer were intended. It seems he has some book of the Washerwoman's - or at the very least, that she desires. The man cannot be trusted and I brushed him away. I advise the same to you should he make any approach. [53]

Hurry and the Washerwoman's ledger had come back to haunt me.

Cross Deep, Twickenham 1719.

WE scorn to spend money on queans,[*]

Though sometimes we hunt the fox,

For he that so wasteth his means,

At last will be paid with a pox.

(Traditional, *A Messe of Good Fellows.*)

Most servants are mercenary sycophants. Keep them happy, pay them well, and they will still desert you when a wealthier patron appears—I do not pay mine well. The carriage pulled off Cross Deep and drew up outside my lodgings; I watched it through the window of my study. Ornate and pulled by a team of four stunning animals—this was a very rich man's transport. One of the idiot's South Sea investors, I assumed. The staff, despite orders that I wanted no disturbances or interruptions, ignored my instructions and showed the visitor into me, bowing and scraping all the while—traitors.

I recognised the garishly dressed old man without introductions: Sir Gottfried Kneller, the painter and local magistrate. A slightly built man in his seventies running to fat, richly dressed but no wig—all his own hair. He looks good for his age; I look better for mine, bald pate or no.[54]

He came forward to greet me; I did not rise. Kneller is in for twenty thousand pounds in the South Sea Company, or so the idiot tells me. 'Tis amazing how much coin a second rate portraitist can make. The boy has callers nearly every day thrusting their tickets at him, wanting more and more of the company stock. 'Tis even more amazing not a soul asks how a company can trade exclusively with an empire with which we are at war and make any profit.

---

[*]   Prostitutes

'Sir Blandford, it has been too long since we saw you at St Mary's,' he said, only a hint of his German origins in his accent after a lifetime in London.

'I was there for the wedding, Sir Gottfried.'

Damn! I forgot he is the churchwarden as well as magistrate. Surely he cannot be here to chastise me for non attendance?

'Ah yes, married life seems to be suiting the boy.'

'He is disgustingly naive. You are here to see him?'

'Indeed, but I thought I should take the time to pay my respects.' He sat down in the chair opposite me and smiled. 'I wanted to speak to you after the court case, but felt the timing was not correct.'

'You bound me over like a criminal.'

'You are a criminal, Sir Blandford. The horse smashed up a stall in King Street and caused twenty pounds worth of damage. We could hardly ignore that, and Mr Pope has important friends, and well...' He paused. 'You have a less than savoury reputation.'[*]

I grunted at that; there is no denying the truth of my past—whatever the justification. Kneller looked at me intently for a moment, as if studying my face with his painter's eye. I waited in uncomfortable silence.

'You never engaged me to paint your portrait, I have always wondered why?' He said finally. 'Nearly all the others in the club did.'

'Lely painted me,' I said. 'I posed for him in the Fifties. He did not do a good job of it. That daub is around here somewhere.' I waved my hand dismissively. 'I never wanted another.'

'You seem determined to cause local problems with your feud, Blandford. Engaging Cibber to present the petition at

---

*   See The Last Roundhead

least muddies your involvement, but 'tis vexing still.'

'What care you? Pope is a Tory and no friend of yours.'

'True, I find him odious and spiteful, but times are uncertain, friend. We are at war; the Stuarts wait ready to pounce should our new King show any weakness, and too many would be happy see them back. You upsetting Pope at every opportunity is only agitating matters.'

'A pish on all Tories and all Stuart kings,' I said, quite unrepentantly. 'I have spent a lifetime wiping my arse with their bills, why should I change now?'

Kneller sighed. 'Have a care, Sir Blandford. His Majesty's patronage protects you only so far; you cannot make a game of baiting Tory scribes. We will stop the building of this tunnel—as a favour to an old comrade—but not indefinitely. If Pope can prove a need, and will take steps to minimise disruption, the permits will be passed. This is but a friendly warning.'

'I should be grateful for such small mercies, should I?'

'Perhaps you should, Sir Blandford,' he said, standing up. 'Now, I should pay my respects to your great nephew. Have you seen the price of the stock?' He looked gleeful. 'It rises as high as the Tower of Babel.'

'Is it churlish of me to point out that the Tower of Babel fell?'

He laughed at that as if I were a Grub Street wit, and called for a servant to show him to the idiot. The boy uses rooms on the other side of the house as his offices; I should charge him rent. Kneller went off to see him rubbing his hands together with delight at the prospects of more phantom earnings.

A collective insanity comes over men when money is involved. It is a herd-like nature that is particularly pronounced in the English—and by that, I mean Welsh and

Scots too—of gazing enviously at our neighbours. We must have better than they, and flaunt it for the world to see, and if (heaven forbid) one of them manages to rise above us, we will cut them down. 'He has changed,' we will say. 'The money has gone to his head,' or 'he forgets where he comes from.' All the while wishing we were in their place.

This company is such a madness: everyone scrambling to be a part of the big thing; everyone desperate in case they miss out on the fabulous earnings; everyone gloating to their neighbour how clever they have been, and feeding the insanity. All of them are like blind mad sheep not noticing the wolves are driving them to destitution, and the shepherd be drunk on gin.

Is the idiot mad, drunk, or a wolf, I wonder?

18. Sir Hudibras and Walter Raleigh: March/April 1644.

When civil dudgeon first grew high,
And men fell out they knew not why?
When hard words, jealousies, and fears,
Set folks together by the ears,
And made them fight, like mad or drunk,
For Dame Religion, as for punk.

(Samuel Butler, *Hvdibras*)

Uncle Samuel placed the letter on the desk, took off his glasses, and looked up at us. It was late the next evening, but my uncle was still at work in the back room of the Saracen's Head. Sam and I had decided—after considerable discussion—to wait until returning to Newport before revealing our news.

'Are you gentlemen actually telling me that John Hurry is in possession of Mistress Whorwood's gold ledger, and that Cole had it on his person when he was captured?'

Sam and I both nodded ruefully.

'And why, pray tell, did neither of you think to mention this before?'

We had no ready answer to that other that Franny had sworn us to secrecy. We told him of Franny's plan and how he had managed to steal the ledger before Hurry captured him. When he had been arrested, there had been no word of the ledger. Uncle Samuel opened a draw, took out a small brass key, and handed it to me.

'In Mr Butler's desk there is a green book, leather bound, would you bring it to me please, Blandford?'

I went out into the common room to Butler's desk, opened it, and rummaged around for the book. I found it after only a couple of seconds and returned to my uncle. He flicked through the pages, then took up a note from his desk and matched it against Butler's entry.

'This is a despatch I received only today,' he told us. 'Colonel Hurry was in Market Drayton four days ago with Prince Rupert. It is my belief they will ride to the aid of Newcastle against the Scots. Well, gentlemen, you have a journey ahead of you. That ledger is of the utmost importance. You will need to travel to the North. Make contact with Lord Fairfax in Hull. I will give you papers. Whatever else, find Hurry and find that book.'[55]

He handed me the book and key and bade me return it. I slipped it back into the drawer of Butler's desk, but another piece of parchment caught my eye. It looked as if it had been stuffed into the drawer hurriedly and had almost fallen down the back. Butler's hand scrawled across it in red ink—I took it out to read.

> *In Bedfordshire there dwelt a knight,*
> *Sir Samuel by name,*
> *Who by his feats in civil broils*
> *Obtain'd a mighty fame.*
> *Nor was he much less wise and stout,*
> *But fit in both respects*
> *To humble sturdy Cavaliers,*
> *And to support the sects.*
>
> *This knight was one that swore*
> *He would not cut his beard*
> *Till this ungodly nation was*
> *From kings and bishops clear'd.* [56]

There was more of the dirge-like verse—sneering royalism and insults to my uncle—but I was livid. Uncle Samuel had taken Butler in when he was disgraced and penniless, and this was how the man repaid him? I folded up the parchment and tucked it inside my doublet, locked the drawer, and took the key back to Uncle Samuel before retiring. I kept silent about the poem—another secret but a justifiable one. I would deal with Butler myself.

I stormed through the inn until I found the fat aspiring Juvenal*, Sam trailing in my wake. Butler was in the kitchen—eating as always—table laden with a platter of beef and foaming tankard. The malicious gossip grew plump off my uncle's largesse whilst secretly mocking. He looked up as I walked in. I threw the table aside, in one movement, covering him in meat and ale.

'How dare you, sir!' he cried, lower lip quivering. 'Sir Samuel will hear of this.'

He stood up and I grabbed him by the throat with one hand and squeezed—choking off his voice. He gasped for breath and I pushed him back up against the wall.

'Sugar! What are you about?' said Sam, sharply.

I pulled the poem from my doublet, showed it to Butler who went even redder, and passed it to Sam. Sam brushed his sandy hair out of his eyes and read. I turned to the moon-faced, pig-nosed, droopy-lipped turdlet of an author.

'What damn scribble is this, Butler? You have the audacity to mock my uncle. I should cut off those spiteful digits so you can pen no more lies.'

He blustered going redder and redder, but for the first time I saw fear on his insolent face—not of my uncle, but fear of me.

'It was meant in jest; I meant no offence.'

'A jest for whom, Mr Butler?' said Sam. 'Neither Sugar nor I find much mirth in this.'

---

*   Roman satirist.

I hefted my knee into his whirligigs and, as he blobbed on the floor, threw another kick to his wobbling jelly-belly. Then I stood over him, tore up the parchment and threw the pieces at him.

'If I hear one more whisper of your ditties, Butler, I will scoop out your eyes with a blunt spoon. Do you understand me?'

He understood well enough; Sam drew me away, leaving Butler weeping on the kitchen floor. I had tamed him for at least a time. He became the model of politeness; the insolence and sneers wiped from his face.

False face must hide what false heart doth know.*

Two decades later, when Butler finally had the balls to vomit forth his literary sleeping draught *Hudibras*, he thought he was protected from me—safe from my retribution. He was wrong; I made him pay a heavy price for his insults and slander. Yet, for all that, I do not forget it was I who first gave him *Don Quixote*. Since he cribbed the whole damn thing from that, perhaps I am a little at fault.**

Then again, perhaps Samuel Butler was just an obnoxious drizzle of putrid bile.

---

*　　　　Macbeth Act I.

**　　　See *The Last Roundhead*.

HIS HIGHNESSE PRINCE RUPERT'S Raising of the Siege at Newark upon TRENT, Written by an eyewitness to a Person of Honour.

Right Honourable and my very good Lord,

His Highness Prince Rupert, being at West Chester upon Tuesday, March the 12th, received His Majesty's command to march with all speed to the relief of Newark, besieged by Sir John Meldrum. The Rebel Force was supposed to be about four thousand Foot, with well towards two thousand Horse and Dragooners.

His Highness made haste to Shrewsbury, speeding away Major Legge (our General of the Ordinance), to choose as many commanded musketeers as might be spared out of that garrison. There were 1000 musketeers of Colonel Broughton's and Colonel Tillier's regiments. His Highness took along his own Regiment of Horse, with 150 of Sir John Hurry's.

We all quartered by Bingham, some eight miles short of Newark. About two of the clock (the Moon then well up) our drums beat and we marched. Hitherto our marches had been so speedy, that the Rebels had no more than a rumour of our coming.

Prince Rupert had notice by his spies how the Rebels were busied in sending away their cannons, which proved no other then their drawing their batteries into the chief work at the Spittle - an island - little more than a musket shot from the town.

His Highness, having intelligence of their amassing themselves into one body, advanced his Van of Horse to overtake them. The rest of our Horse had orders to keep with the Foot, Cannon and Ammunition. Near the Beacon Hill, a mile short of Newark, we perceived some Horse of the enemies. Upon our approach, they drew down the other side. We thus easily gained the hill, which increased his Highness' natural courage.

'Courage,' says he. 'Let us charge on God's name with the Horse we have, and engage them till our rear and Foot be marched up to us.'

Trooping to the edge of the hill, we perceived most of the enemies in battalia (Horse and Foot) near the Spittle. All, except four great bodies of Horse, who expected us at the descent of the Hill. The Prince thus ordered his own few forces to attack that body on the left hand, appointing Colonel Charles Gerard's Troop to be a reserve.

The fight began about nine of the clock, and after a while grew sturdy, especially on our right wing. The Rebels doubled their files from three to six deep and charged our two utmost Troops upon the flanks so hard, that Captain Martin came in to help beat them off. The Prince himself having pierced deep into the enemy's ranks, and being observed for his valour, was dangerously assaulted by three sturdy rebels. One fell by his Highness's own sword, a second being pistolled by one of his own gentlemen; the third now ready to lay hand on the Prince's collar, had it almost chopped off by Sir William Neale.

His Highness thus disengaged, with a shot only in his gauntlet. His Highness's Regiment, with their seconds, routed the enemy bodies. My Lord Loughborough also deported himself honourably, and when some of his shrunk at the second charge, he rode back to rally and bring them up again.

After a while, both sides began to ready for a second charge - ours to make the impression, and theirs to receive it. For a good while, they disputed it toughly until fleeing - diverse of them hasting by a bridge of boats over that branch of the Trent, onto the Spittle.

In both these stiff bouts, took we five colours, and about 90 prisoners - three Captains, some Gentlemen, three Cornets, besides other Officers, and two Cannoneers.

Now, as if a universal truce had been agreed upon, there was half an hour's silence.

Up came our Foot, all that day commanded by Colonel Tillier, resting themselves a while upon the Hill. The first Division, being part of those that came from Shrewsbury, were led only by the Colonel. These marched down bravely in the face of the Enemy, shooting at their cannon.

The Rebels drew all their Horse and Foot within their Spittle work.

Thus was the valley bespread with our battalions, and in this posture stood the Prince's Army. Sir Richard Byron, Governor of Newark, had sent part of his garrison (both Horse and Foot) into another ground on the Southeast side of the town. By this time, the Prince had notice the Rebels were so distressed for want of victuals that they were not able to live on their island but two days.

His Highness esteemed it cheaper to block up their trenches, then to storm them. And, blocked up they were, as if being cooped up in a very narrow room. They were on all sides surrounded by our forces. The rebels, having sent out to parley, quit their bridge, which his Highness presently possessed with a hundred musketeers.

Now, true though it be that the Enemies were distressed, yet very wise Generals have not thought it safe to make such men desperate. Besides which, being now in the midst of their own garrisons they might possibly be relieved. And, to confess the truth, our horses were so over-matched, and our foot so beaten off that we found ourselves unable to present for them. In very truth too, the rebels were more then we believed. His Highness (at length) condescended to their Articles, which be both honourable and safe.

My dreams haunted me. They were filled with ghosts —living and dead. My parents and siblings, Peter, his father and sister, Ophelia, comrades, lovers, and enemies; all would slip into my nightmares. In my dreams, I was looking for my boots but could never find them. Under my bed, in the midst of battle, I was always looking for my boots. The shades and wraiths would taunt me, tear at me, and I would wake sweating. Bed partners would complain of being kicked black and blue as I slept—if I slept at all. Behind it, behind

the tremors and night sweats, drunkenness and blank stares, there lurked a monster—dark eyes and countenance, fetid breath and bearing bloody scars. He would rear up at me and I would run, bootless, into the unknown.

'A penny for your thoughts?' asked Sam.

'I have never been aboard a ship before,' I said. 'Think you this captain is reputable?'

Sam looked around. 'The inn he set to meet is not reputable,' he said, in a low voice.

I agreed with him. It was a dirty little brewhouse in an alley set back from the river wharves—dirty wooden floor, dirty hide windows, dirty rough tables and a dirty rough tapster. It may as well have been a jobbernoll's* shack.

Prince Rupert had put paid to Uncle Samuel's plans. You can read about the relief of Newark and his great ride above. Suffice to say it had thrown Parliament's strategy into chaos. In two weeks, Lincolnshire—only won by Cromwell the autumn before—fell, and the road to Hull was blocked by the enemy. The maps do not tell a full story, it was impossible to travel anywhere in England in safety. Roaming bands of soldiers, from both sides, preyed on the unwary, only by boat was there some hope of safety, and even that uncertain.

Hurry had been with the Prince on the *chevauchée*** across the midlands, but we had no word of him after. On April Fool's Day, Sam and I went to Lord Fairfax in Hull with important despatches from The Committee of Both Kingdoms[57] We rode to Lynn*** in the hopes of finding passage on one of the

---

*   Extremely filthy individual.

**   In this context a mounted raid.

***   King's Lynn, Norfolk. It is perhaps a Roundhead affectation of Blandford's not to use the royal prefix. The town was known as King's Lynn from the Sixteenth century onwards, and Bishops Lynn before that.

many boats or ships that ply the coast. My uncle knew our contact, but I was not inspired with confidence.

The door opened and the shabby creature came back in; grey clothes and covered in muck, a dirty wool bonnet on his head. His creased leather skin, grey beard, and bushy white brows engrained with grime. This was our ship's master, a collierman, Nathaniel Jakes. Every two weeks, from March to November, he would travel up the coast to the North East carrying supplies. He brought back coal from the north for London's furnaces. Sunderland's fall to Parliament meant the trade was even more lucrative.

Jakes sat down next to us, stinking of whale blubber and stale urine. I grimaced at Sam.

'So, can you carry us?' asked Sam.

'Aye, masters, that I can,' he said. 'We had ballast sand to shift that is all. *Aquae Vitae*!'* he called to the tapster.

The tapster brought him a bottle and Jakes nodded to us to pay. I handed over a silver shilling—there was no balance forthcoming—and turned back to Jakes. He really did stink—Jakes by name and *Jakes*** by odour.

'How long will it take to Hull?' I asked him.

'But a day or two,' he said. 'Unless the sea gets up. She can be contrary as a bag of badgers this time of year.'

He must have seen the doubtful look on my face because he slapped me on the back, laughing.

'Worry not,' he said. 'I sailed with Raleigh. Named the boat after him.'

'I was in school with his nephews Wat and Tom,' I replied. 'And a right pair of poxy sneaks they were too.'[58]

He looked taken aback by that.

---

*   Water of life; whisky, brandy or some other local brew.

**   Slang for toilet.

'Well, that I do not know, master, but I can get ye to Hull, and your nags.' He took a deep swig from his bottle. 'Ye'll need to be there tonight. Tide is early in the morning.'

We arranged to meet that night and left to gather our horses and possessions. In all frankness, I was glad to be away from that dark bar and evil smelling sailor, and back to our own lodgings. Before midnight, we led the animals down to the wharves by the river. Captain Jakes was there with his crew waiting for us—ten of them, all as filthy as their leader in the torchlight, but friendly enough and eager to earn a little extra on the trip.

I do not know what I had been expecting. In my mind's eye, perhaps the kind of ocean going ship I had seen in Southampton. The Walter Raleigh was a fat little tub with two masts, no figurehead, and a thick layer of coal dust on everything—even the sails stained black. The horses were loaded on board, without too much fuss. Apple treated it all with his usual disdain, but Sam's mare was frit. He sat with her talking for a while.

'God help us,' I said to him when he came to sit with me. There was no cabin, just a canvas sheet made up for a cover at the back of the boat. I know now it is called a stern, but then it was the back.

We watched as the crew set to their tasks, unfurling the dirty sails, and taking us down the Ouse to the sea. They knew their jobs well enough, it seemed, and soon we were cutting up the coast towards Hull.

I vomited over the side of the boat for the third time as it pitched up. The force threw me back on my arse to the deck.

Slate grey waves towered over us tossing The Walter Raleigh back and forth. The cold spray left a taste of salt that made me want to spew again. I crawled back under the canvas at the stern, and curled up in a shaking mess. Sam and the crew did not seem to be similarly afflicted.

'This be hell.'

''Tis but a brisk wind,' shouted one of the sailors.'

The boat lurched again and with it my stomach; I retched into the deck, heaving for breath. I could hear the horses screaming, they were as distressed as I was. Every pitch and roll of the boat threw my belly overboard. I was sweating, my hair plastered to my face, alternately hot then cold.

'You should try some tobacco, 'tis a wonder for settling the guts,' said Sam.

I lay on my back and cursed him, cursed the weather, cursed my uncle for sending me on such a fool's errand, and cursed the walls of the boat for being so tall I had to climb up to spew.

'Bulwarks,' said Sam.

'What?'

'The walls are called bulwarks—one of the sailors told me.'

'Bollucks to you.'

We took near two days of sailing in that weather to get to Hull—two days of intestinal torture for me. It was a grey drizzly morning when we finally sailed up the Humber, away from the open sea and into Hull. Since the start of the war, the town had been the only parliamentary citadel in the north. It had endured siege after siege, treachery and betrayal, but against all had held firm. Lord Fairfax was Governor here, his son Charles in attendance. Black Tom was abroad with the Horse.

The Humber is still broad at that stretch of the river, perhaps two miles wide as you come into the town. Strong brick walls and castle, bastions, and a great moat surrounding; beyond were flooded pastures that had so frustrated the Royalists the autumn previous. At the point where the River Hull runs into the Humber, a strong tower overlooks the wharves and jetties. The Walter Raleigh—a flat-bottomed barge—sailed up the Hull and into the town with ease.

There was a crowd of boats and larger ships at anchor inside the defences. I pulled my few belongings together and looked earnestly at the town, eager to disembark. Captain Jakes took us up to the wharf, only trimming sails at the last moment, and using the momentum of the boat. They dropped anchor and the boat drew to a halt just before we crashed into the side of the dock. Jakes' crew whooped and cheered and dockworkers and porters swarmed to take our horses and belongings off. I paid Captain Jakes and made ready to leave his leaky tub.

'Good luck to you, masters. Mayhap we shall sail together again.' He waved us off.

'Be buggered first,' I said. 'I shall never leave land again.'

Pish! That was an oath that could never be kept, but I meant it at the time. Two days of puking has that effect. 'Twas the only time I was ever sick aboard a boat. Happen, I ate some bad fish in Lynn, or perhaps it was just Neptune's tally. I never quite became a mariner; a pirate captain for a brief time, but that was a disaster. All told, the sea is a vicious uncaring mistress, and you cannot drown atop a hillock.

To every Minister within the City of London, Liberties, Line of Communication, and Bills of Mortality.

The extraordinary blessing of God upon the Forces under the Command of Sir William Waller, against the Army led by Sir Ralph Hopton, in a Battle near Winchester, yesterday. This continued from eight a clock in the morning until night, wherein the enemy was absolutely routed, and pursued many miles with good execution.

The most Honourable Committee of Both Kingdoms, requires a more solemn thanksgiving than can be performed, especially considering that this mercy hath been beyond expectation after that sad blow about Newark.

I do heartily (according to the order of the said Committee of both Kingdoms,) desire & require you tomorrow, being the Lords Day, to give notice of this goodness, to your congregation. Use your best endeavours to quicken them to the highest pitch of thankfulness to the God of our Mercies. Engage their hearts and hands yet further, to help the Lord against the Mighty, with their prayers and helps. Helps of Money, Arms, Horse, Men, or other provisions to make up and supply a body of Horse and Foot to go out and follow the enemy.

God may give a speedy end to the present calamities, and restore a stable peace in this afflicted Nation, to the comfort of all God's people in all the Kingdoms.

And God shall move the hearts of men to subscribe and contribute, what men they shall send out or maintain. The Committee of the Militia do make it our joint request that you, would set such down in writing, and return upon Monday morning next without fail, to the Committee of the Militia at Guildhall.

Dated this 30 of March, Anno Dom. 1644.

John Wollaston, Mayor. [59]

19. Yorkshiremen: Selby, April 1644.

Wilt thou forgive that sin where I begun,
Which was my sin, though it were done before?
Wilt thou forgive that sin, through which I run,
And do run still, though still I do deplore?
When thou hast done, thou hast not done,
For I have more.

(John Donne, *A Hymn To God The Father*.)

Yorkshiremen are a strange and stubborn folk; perhaps, 'tis their heritage—a relic of the Danelaw. Sam and I had hoped—after a short sojourn—to make our way back south to Newport Pagnell; our despatches delivered and no more said. I desired only to find John Hurry and the Washerwoman's journal, not tarry in the desolate north.

Lord Fairfax did not see it so. His son Charles sang my praises—even I winced at 'Hercules that slew four men single handed'—then John Meldrum told how I had taken a colour at Kineton and our fates were settled. Lord Fairfax decided we could be useful; he would write to my uncle, I could be assured. In the meantime, he attached us to his meagre force. [60]

The Fairfaxes were of similar build and look. All had the same dark hair, eyes, and complexion, and a slight build. The old man's mane was greying, but there must have been some *Diego** blood in the family. Charles was the youngest son, though much older than I, and of a friendly enough disposition, if prickly about his rank.

By that, I mean he was not so keen on drunken friends beneath his status.

---

*	Generic for Spanish. Despite Blandford's assertion, the Fairfax family were Yorkshire bred.

His elder brother 'Black' Tom was a clever bastard, saying little in his cups, but busy dark eyes ever watchful, ever appraising, always calculating the odds. Cromwell was a power, and both had iron control over their men, but Tom Fairfax was ice to Noll Cromwell's fire. We met first at Ferrybridge and he was coldly polite, as if my less savoury reputation had preceded me, along with tales of—ahem—heroics. I would wager it was Skippon that was the cause, but Black Tom never said. At the very least he saw Sam and me as interlopers in the Northern war—Uncle Samuel's spies and not to be trusted.

A few days after our arrival, Lord Fairfax led us out of Hull in the spring sunshine. Nearly two thousand of us, mostly Foot. For all their brusque manners, the northerners were stout fellows; veterans who knew what they were about. At Ferrybridge, Black Tom's men brought our numbers up to three thousand or so, but now an even split between Horse and Foot.

We marched to Selby in the spring sunshine with the men in good spirits; the Scots invasion had turned the situation in the north on its head. From being hard pressed and close to defeat, Fairfax could now take the battle to the gates of York itself—but first, Selby, a key Royalist stronghold. Sam and I were placed with the van of the army under Charles Fairfax; an under-strength regiment of Horse, only two hundred men, plodding along at a snail's pace so the Foot could keep up.*

'Have you spent all my money?' asked Charles.

'Yes, Colonel.'

'Two hundred pounds in such a short time.' He whistled.

I thought of the fine clothes packed away in a trunk in London, the ridiculous losses at the tables, and the expensive

---

*   Fairfax met with his son Thomas at Ferrybridge on April 9th 1644.

wines and company.

'I received good value for it, sir.'

'I hope so, Candy,' said Charles.

Charles trotted back to his colour, and the officers at the front of the column. A group of northern gentleman and Fairfax retainers whose language was so broad in dialect we could barely understand them.

'You received good value? You spent it all on your Welsh punk,' said Sam.

'She is worth it.' She was, believe me, she was.

The column arrived at a small village—a crossroads, some battered wooden houses and an inn. It was called Brayton but I heard that later. As I watered Apple, a young lad rode back from the colour towards us.

'Captain Candy, sir.'

'Yes.'

'Colonel Fairfax sends regards, sir, and requests thee and tha man take a gander down t'road. We come up to Selby.'

Sam looked at him blankly. I had picked up some of their talk and explained it to him when the young cornet rode back to the colours. We tied up our horses, took up carbines, checked they were loaded, and made our way down the road to Selby on foot. Thick hedgerows and trees lined the way: good cover for an ambush.

'How did we get this task?' said Sam.

'We are scouts,' I said. 'And we are foreigners to these men, so no great loss.'

Only a few hundred yards down the road, we came upon a church with tower and slender octagonal spire. The coloured glass smashed, recently by the look, and planks covered the great east window. I nodded to the tower.

'What think you?'

We broke into the church, smashing the lock with our carbine butts. Inside, it was silent, cool and dark. Sam found the way up to the spire. We climbed the narrow stair 'til we reached the top of the tower. Belfry windows gave a clear view over the open fields to Selby. There were bumps and humps in the field opposite the church, some ancient working, perhaps. The locals had abandoned the place, probably at first word of our coming.

'Something is happening,' said Sam, looking through his spyglass. 'A couple of troops of Horse coming out of Selby.'

'They dawdle,' I said, after a glance. 'Slow enough to surprise if we are quick. Stay here, I will get back to Charles.'

I ran back to Fairfax minor, and told him about the enemy force and my idea. He agreed eagerly, anxious to strike the first blow. Dragoons went on foot into the hedgerows, crouching behind the green foliage and hidden from the road. Charles waited in sight of the spire with his Horse for my signal to charge. I was breathless when I got back to Sam, and only just in time. The Cavaliers advanced down the road, four abreast, with a couple of men up front. They were careless, and had no outriders in the fields. Some of them (officers, I assumed) were richly dressed with corselet, gorget,* and pot, but most wore only yellowing buff coats and felt hats.

Our 'goons waited as the first enemy trotted past and then rose up as the main body of Horse came along, unleashing a wicked volley of fire at close range. Horses rearing, Cavaliers falling from their saddles as the shot buzzed around, men screaming. I waved my 'kerchief out of the window and watched as Charles Fairfax led his wedge down the road. Our Horse crashed into the confused Royalists, and Sam and I began picking off enemy officers with our rifled carbines, the

---

*   Neck armour.

sound of our shot echoing through the church tower.

I smiled with grim satisfaction as I saw one fall and recharged my carbine. Sam had started humming away to himself as he did the same. An old children's song:

> *For want of a nail the shoe was lost.*
> *For want of a shoe the horse was lost.*
> *For want of a horse the rider was lost.*
> *For want of a rider the battle was lost.*

He rammed the charge home and primed the pan, singing all the while.

> *'For want of a battle the kingdom was lost.*
> *And all for the want of a horseshoe nail.'*[61]

Sam raised the carbine to his shoulder, took aim through the window, and bang! Another Royalist shot from his horse. I took aim myself, but the enemy were fleeing, leaving their dead and dying in the road, and our victorious dragoons taking prisoners.

First blood to us.

The rest of Lord Fairfax's army came up, and the final approach on Selby was made. Lord Fairfax split the army into three battles, each covering a road into the town. The way to York was left unguarded to entice the royalist troopers to desert. Fairfax sent Charles in to demand surrender and offer terms, but Belasyse—the Royalist commander—turned him down flat. [62]

They say that the stage is akin to life, but there is an obvious difference. In life, there is no prompt, no rehearsal, and only God—or the Devil—knows the script.

'This shall be a bloody fight,' said Sam.

We sat on our horses with Lord Fairfax and his staff, and watched as the Foot ran down the road to barricades guarding the way into Selby. The Ouse River, on our right, forced them into narrow columns. The Royalists had no real fortifications, nought but overturned carts, gabions*, and a rough ditch barred the way into the town. Only by a frontal assault, down roads and in between houses, could we hope to gain entry. Lord Fairfax attacked the town from three sides hoping to overwhelm the defenders at once. The Cavaliers were not accommodating his design. The defences were well manned and defenders well prepared for our assault.

They waited until our Foot were nearly at the barricades and opened fire. At such close range they could hardly miss. White smoke drifted across my view, but in my mind's eye I could see murder being wreaked on our first wave, musket balls smashing bone, men screaming, the spray of blood and stink of shit as men's bellies were sliced open, acrid smoke choking every breath and making eyes stream water.

From the south, I could hear more gunfire start up, as Meldrum led his battle into the attack.

'At least they have no ordnance,' I said to Sam, too soon; enemy cannon joined in the barrage of fire.

Fairfax's first wave was beaten back without reaching the barricades; the broken infantry streaming back to our position, fallen bodies lying on the ground or floating face down in the river. Groans of the wounded, crying out for salvation, could be heard across the field.

'Here go the Horse,' said Sam.

Black Tom led his riders down the road, eight abreast and ten deep, until they were within range of the barricades. In file, they began discharging pistol and carbine and then

---

*   Large wickerwork baskets filled with earth used as a defence against shot.

retiring to the rear of the column to reload. This kept up a near constant fire play on the Royalist defenders for quarter of an hour. Then another troop came up to replace them in caracole and Tom Fairfax fell back to the colours.

The second wave of Lord Fairfax's Foot went in much like the first, all at a rush, matchlocks, sword and pike, screaming as they charged towards the barricades. They were met in the same way: a hail of fire and shot. Some reached the barricades, hacking and stabbing at defenders. I saw one climb up atop a cart, wave to his comrades then collapse, laid low by some missile. The rest of the assaulters fell back in confusion. These northern soldiers were sturdy enough, but too many reverses and they would refuse to charge.

'This is too hot,' I said.

More Horse were sent up in caracole to shoot at the defence and another wave of Foot was readied. Lord Fairfax looked troubled—furrowed brows and a nervous energy about his staff—news from the other assaults was not good. The Royalists were holding.

After twenty minutes of fire-play, the third wave of Foot charged up the road once more. This time, Black Tom sent dragoons on foot at the barricades between the town and river. The defences looked weaker there: no ditch and only carts and furniture. Behind, on horseback, Fairfax sat with a troop of his best men. The rest of us made ready to follow him in case of a breach.

The dragoons managed to take the barricade and began pulling and smashing with billhooks, desperate to open a gap for the Horse to enter the town. The royalist defenders fell back towards the market and church, but others sniped at our officers from houses. The breach was opened, and Black Tom—at the head of his men—charged into Selby.

A great enemy force was fleeing across the Ouse to York in panic, but some gathered at the Abbey in the centre of the town to make a final stand. Black Tom led us on, Sam and I just behind his standard.

We advanced down Ousegate towards the Abbey—the river to the right of us. A man next to me was hit, his face shot away, and blood splattering me. He fell from his horse without making a sound. More ammunition for my nightmares, but my nerves held steady and Apple ploughed on regardless.

At the end of Ousegate, there is a sharp turn to the Abbey and market-square, and it was here that the Royalists sprung their trap.

Cavalry came streaming down the road at us, and hidden musketeers in the houses opened up a fire. Horse to horse, and knee-to-knee, in the narrow confined space; it became a bloody mess of hack and parry, slash and cut. I discharged one pistol and, drawing my sword, stabbed at enemies left and right.

Black Tom went down in a tangle of horse and rider, only yards from me, surrounded quickly by three cavaliers. Sam tried to force his horse through, hacking at the Royalists who surrounded Fairfax. He had already killed two of them by the time I got there. I took the last from behind, cutting down at his neck. Black Tom nodded to us, grabbed the reins of a rider-less horse, and swung himself back into the saddle.

Sam screamed a warning at me and I ducked; a glancing blow hit my pot, stunning me for a second. I lashed out with my sword, pulling on Apple's reins to face my attacker. Apple reared and turned on a sixpence. A richly dressed cavalier in buff coat, armour, lobster pot and riding a fine black horse slashed at me. I parried, thrusting back, and he knocked my sword aside. Our horses circled in the mêlée as we went at each other—like smiths at a forge. The man was bleeding heavily from a cut to his sword arm, and I struck out again, and again, trying to batter through his defence. He was a better swordsman but I was stronger.

He thrust out at me and I caught the blade on my basket, rolled my hand, and jabbed the point in his face cutting him under the eye. An inch higher and I would have blinded him. His horse collapsed, screaming, as someone (Sam, I think) put a ball in its brain. The cavalier rolled to the floor and scuttled back from the kicking animal. The rest of the Royalists were beaten, already fleeing—Selby was ours. He looked around for a moment then turned to me.[63]

'John Belasyse,' he said, and offered me the hilt of his sword in surrender.

We had captured the Royalist governor.

To the Yorkshiremen, Sam and I proved ourselves at Barton and Selby. Excepting Black Tom, of course, but I could fathom no reason for his increasing dislike. Lord Ferdinando was pleased, however.

'You have helped keep both my sons safe, Mr Candy.'

I nodded, but could see from the look on Black Tom's face he did not agree—ungrateful swine. His Lordship carried on.

'And your captive as well; a good day's work indeed. I will be writing to your uncle.'

Capturing Belasyse was a feather in our caps, no doubt, but the man held no grudge and was gracious enough in defeat. Years later, he got his own back and sent me to the vile stinking hole of camel shit that is Tangier, but that tale can wait.

The prisoners were sent downriver to Hull, Belasyse included, and Selby was occupied. The inhabitants, who had been hiding in their cellars during the fight, came out and Royalist sympathisers were taken and put under guard. Lord Fairfax was in a good mood, although it had been hard fighting and cost more men than he hoped, his victory was absolute. The spoils taken were astounding, powder, match, arms, and treasure—the victuals of Mars. Most importantly, the road to York was open.

From Anne Candy to Elizabeth Candy.

Sweet Sister,

I confess it has been far too long since I last wrote, and I fear that this can only be a short missive.

By the time you have received this, I will have moved on from Oxford. Her Majesty has been most unwell. Only a week past she slipped and fell, and the great fear was that she would lose the child she bears. It has been decided that Her Majesty should take the waters in Bath, so we soon depart to the west. I hope to see Henry, and perhaps visit Hilperton, though I am fain to say the thought of our home burned out still makes me weep.

Wagtail and Wanton are to be left behind in Oxford, to Mistress Margaret's delight. It is a sum of their standing with the Queen that in such troubled times their characters are not deemed worthy of serving. There was much howling and weeping from Wanton's chambers when that decision was made, and much amusement in Mistress Margaret's.

I have so much to write but the coaches are waiting. The King and Princes themselves travel with us, at least to Abingdon, and there is still much to do.

I remain,

Your loving affectionate sister,

Anne.

Oxford, April 7th 1644.

A true relation of the taking of the city minster and castle of Lincoln with all their ordnance, ammunition and Horse.

On Friday May the 3rd, the Earl of Manchester sat down before Lincoln, and after some resistance, made himself Master of the lower part of the City. The besieged retreated to the Minster and the Castle on the top of a high hill. The next day, there fell so much rain as hindered any great action. That night, Manchester intended to storm them, drawing up his Foot, and sent for the Horse from their quarters, to be ready by two-of-the-clock in the morning, but the weather continuing so violent prevented it. The mount whereon the castle stands being exceeding steep, and by reason of the rain very slippery.

Next day, they had notice that a great body of Horse - to the number of five or six thousand under Colonel Goring's command - were coming to relieve the city. This hastened Manchester's resolution to storm them that afternoon and, to that intent, the scaling ladders were brought forth, and the Foot were ready to set on. The Horse could not come up that night, and it was put off until next morning.

To prevent the relief, General Cromwell with two thousand Horse was sent to meet them. The Foot were ordered that night to lie upon the several quarters of the hill, round about the enemy works, and to be in readiness to fall on them when they should hear the great ordnance go off.

Between two and three-a-clock in the morning, six pieces discharged at once. In a moment, the Foot began the attack, and in a quarter of an hour got up to their works - even though the King's forces made a gallant resistance. Being under their works, we set up their scaling ladders. Whereupon, those within left firing and threw down mighty stones from over their works, which did the assailants more prejudice than their shot. Yet at last, Manchester's men got up, and slew about fifty in their works; the rest cried for quarter, which was given them.

ANON

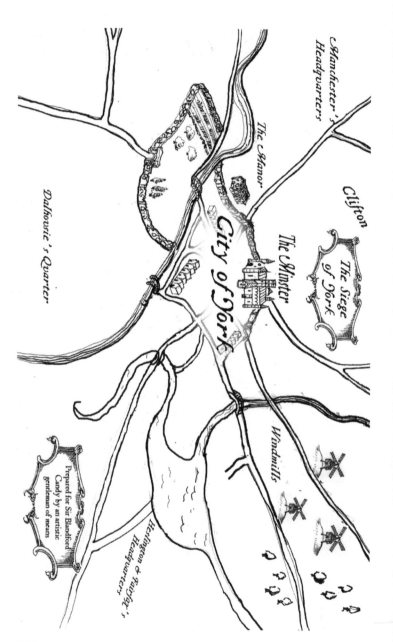

Manchester's
Headquarters

Clifton

The Manor

The Siege
of York

Dalhousie's Quarter

City of York

The Minster

Windmills

Prepared for Sir Blandford
Candy by an artistic
gentleman of means

Hesilrege & Fairfax's
Headquarters

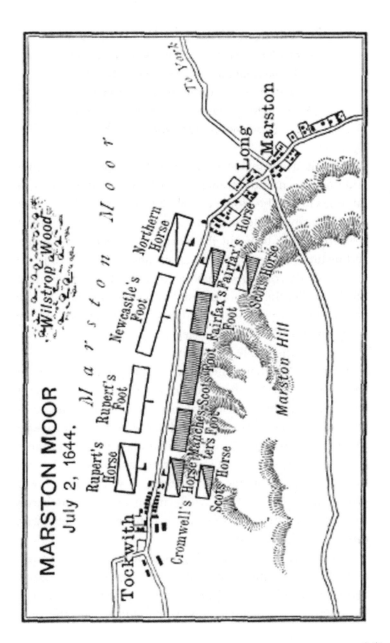

MARSTON MOOR
July 2, 1644.

Tockwith

Marston Moor

Wilstrop Wood

Rupert's Horse

Rupert's Foot

Newcastle's Foot

Northern Horse

Cromwell's Horse

Manches-ter's Foot

Scots Foot

Fairfax's Foot

Fairfax's Horse

Scots Horse

Scots Horse

Long Marston

Marston

To York

Marston Hill

2o. Tilting at Windmills: York, May 1644.

Met the King and the Queen and the company more
Came a riding behind and a walking before
Come a stark naked drummer, a-beating a drum
With his heels in his bosom come marching along
(Traditional, *Nottamvn Town*)[64]

A siege is a damnable thing. The Foot spend their time grubbing in muddy trenches and wasting their lives in futile assaults. The Horse patrol or ride post—all cold, wet, and miserable. The ordnance goes boom, boom, boom. Drummer boys beat out the alarum, and sleep is snatched and disturbed. Food gets wet, spoils and gives everyone the shits, and everyone, from general to ranker, is in a foul mood. All the while, the defenders raid your works, ambush your patrols, poison your water, and take gleeful delight in your every setback. That is a good siege.

York was miserable purgatory.

Sam went south with despatches for my uncle, leaving me amongst brusque northern gentlemen with no interest in my fripperies, and uncouth Scots with no wit to understand them. Our two armies combined could not invest York properly. The Ouse runs right through the middle of the city, and it is too great in size: strong walls, gates and towers, defence works, bastions, ditches, and fortlets, all well manned, well provisioned, and well led, while north of York was barely covered by a thin screen of Horse, leaving the Cavaliers rarely molested if they left the city.

Every night, a flashing of lights between the high towers of York Minster and Pontefract would pass secret messages above our heads, and traitors in our own ranks fed news to the enemy. The weather grew worse and worse, the rains heavier, and our moods dampened even further.

My Lord the Marquis of Newcastle had made only one mistake. He left the surrounding houses, and other diverse buildings outside the walls, intact. Out of pity for the inhabitants, I would wager; the Marquis was ever a delicate soul.[65]

I was a waif. Black Tom kept me from the generals'councils,and I had no men to lead, no task to set my mind to other than wandering the works, talking to the common soldiers, or riding in the country beyond the lines. I took notes, as a good scout should, and mapped the area out in my journal (you can see that above) but I never was asked my thoughts. Black Tom's attitude towards me was perplexing. I had had no time to cause him offence; indeed, good service had been done, for him and his, in the weeks past. A pox on him was my only conclusion. My notes would do for Uncle Samuel and Darnelly, and Mabbot and Pecke would relish the letters I sent.

*Barbarus hic ego sum, quia non intelligor illis.**

My billet was nothing more than a dirty shepherd's croft, and bed but some straw in the corner. The northern officers came with tents, and bunks, and servants—all the comforts needed for a siege. I had nothing, only a horse and my journal. There were no drinking companions to be found, and the little coin in my purse was spent on food and fodder—all increasingly scarce.

I came home from my wanderings one grey evening in mid May, and thanks be, there were friendly faces waiting; Sam had returned with Everard, leg fixed, glowing pipe in his chops. He stood up when I arrived and grabbed me in a great

---

*   In this place I am a barbarian, because men do not understand me - Ovid.

smothering hug. I noted a slight limp as he walked.

'How goes your jizzet?'* I said.

'Not too bad, still tweaks a tad. You look tired.'

'No sleep with these damnable guns going off.' There was no reason to tell him about my dreams—one keeps one's nightmares to oneself.

They had brought supplies with them, and Sam set to starting a fire. Blankets and spare clothes, fresh shirts and the like were handed out, and victuals. Salted pork, which I had seen enough of, but fresh bread, cheese, a crock of butter, and honey from my uncle's estate.

'Have you anything to drink? The pork will bring on a fearsome thirst.'

'There is ale,' said Everard. 'And we brought some of that sweet Malaga wine you like so much.'

'It is comforting that you thought of me, my friend, that is expensive sack—Ophelia's favourite. 'Tis in my memory lock'd, and you yourself shall keep the key of it.'**

Everard snorted. 'Now do not go putting words into my mouth, Sugar. 'Twas your uncle's notion. What is the land like hereabouts?'

'A mess of brooks, rivers, and jumble-gut lanes.'*** I said. 'The Scots Horse cover the north, but supplies still get into the town.'

'Do you know of a burned out mill to the north of here? Past a place called Heworth?'

'Aye, there are burned out mills all over.'

'This one has the miller's house adjoining; 'tis painted blue.'

---

*   The leg - also a cut of mutton.

** Hamlet Act I Scene III.

*** Bad roads

'I know it.'

'Your uncle has a little task for you. Happen he sent the wine so you were in a good mood when we told you.'

'Best I get started on it then,' I said, picking up a bottle and offering a prayer to Ophelia's shade in memory.

Apple stumbled in the night, pitching me sideways. I cursed, only just keeping my seat. He found his footing and quickened to a trot. It was clear and cold—'tis always colder up north. I led him by the pale light of the moon and stars, up to the top of a rise overlooking Heworth; the lane cut up, stones rolling under-hoof, and sticky mud making it hard going. The mill was to the north of York, burned out by the Scots, along with any other building of use within two leagues of the city. Our agent would meet me there—had asked for me personally.

I dislike appointments by request; they always lead to trouble. Have I said that before?

The mill was charred wreckage. The blackened sail-spars thrust unmoving to the sky—a collapsed roof, and broken tower walls. The house adjoining was in a similar state. The upper level burned; the door hanging off its hinges, shutters ripped open, and windows smashed. I wondered on the family that lived here. This was once a rich man's home and concern. Now, another innocent family was ruined by the passage of war—if they still lived.[66]

There was a grey mare tied up next to the ruins of the house—saddled and ready for riding. I dismounted, tied Apple up next to her, and then took out my pistol. There was no sound from inside the building, nor light, but there was a familiar smell of perfume on the air—the horse was drenched in it—French perfume.

251

'Hullo, Megan,' I said, to the darkness.

'I could hear you blundering away from near half a mile, my sweet.'

She stepped out of the building and lowered the pistol she was carrying. Bundled up in a colourless cloak and thick skirts, I caught a glimpse of her white face in the moonlight. She seemed piqued.

'How did you know it was me?'

'I smelled your perfume, my sweet,' I said, rather smugly.

She tapped my arm. 'Do not try to be clever, Blandford, it does not suit.' She kissed me and then pulled back. 'You smell of sheep shit.'

'Do not be a nag.'

Women hate to be called nags. 'Tis a most uncommon thing, but that one word *may* prevail in an argument. Of course, it may cause a completely different disagreement, so be careful how you deploy it. She kissed me again, made pretence of docility, and it was I who broke away first.

'Much as I love a clinch in the dark, Meg, what did you bring me here for? There are Scots all over. And, how did you get out of the city?' If she could get out, perhaps we could get in. Even Black Tom would not turn his nose up at such information.

She sniffed. 'The Scots are an uncouth race of drunken barbarians.'

This from a Welsh woman—a race that jabber like monkeys in their misbegotten tongue. I mean, I do not disagree with her summation, but stones and sins.

She carried on: 'Coming to and from the city is of little difficulty. Perhaps I have been missing you, perhaps there is news, and I am not Meg here, I am Lady Sarah once more.'

'Pretty title; what news?'

'You always rush the finish too soon,' she chided. 'Tell Black Tom there are two cannon on all the gates, more on Clifford's Tower, and covering the Ouse. They have set up a platform of guns at St. Olave's.

'That information may make him better disposed to me.'

'He does not like you, Sugar?'

'Seemingly not.'

'How interesting.' She smiled at me. 'Prince Rupert is coming.'

'That is news indeed.'

Meg told me that the hero of the Cavaliers had been sent by the King to relieve York. An army of near twenty thousand to break the Scots and end the war in the north. Messengers, who reached the city disguised as women, brought news of the King's northern design and Cavendish had happily told the court in York. More, she informed me that John Hurry was with Rupert, according to her source, and so was the gold ledger.[67]

'I have something else that will interest you.'

'Oh?'

'Your brother James was one of the messengers from Rupert. He is still in the city.'

'Bugger.'

'Meet me again a week hence, same time and place, I should have more,' she said. 'And now, my sweet, if you will forgive me, I need a slight distraction from the nearby patrols of Scots and Yorkshiremen.'

She raised the pistol again, and for a brief second I thought she would shoot me—Megan scared me at times, I do not deny it. Instead, she winked, and discharged her piece into the air. The flash of fire spat out shot in the dark night; ringing noise out around us.

'Why did you do that?' I asked with a sigh.

'It will bring your patrols near and make my return to York all the easier.' She took her horse's bridle, blew me a kiss, and pulled herself up in the saddle. She rode like a man, skirts all bundled up in front.

'It will not help me.'

'Then best you hurry along, my sweet.' Meg, and her grey, was already moving off into the dark.

'But...' I said to her departing form. No reply—she had disappeared into the night. I ran to Apple and mounted myself.

'That woman befuddles me, Apple,' I said, scratching behind his ears.

I rode away from the mill, back down to the main road to York. Heworth was a small village two miles north of the city; there were dragoons set there by Fairfax. I planned to meet up with them and get an escort to the General. If there were Scots patrols, I did not see them. Mayhap they were drawn to Meg's distraction. More likely they were drunk and sleeping.

At Heworth, 'goons picked me up. Carts had been turned to blockade the road, and soldiers with muskets and broad northern accents stood nervously in the torchlight. I handed my papers over to their sergeant.

''Tis late to be out a riding?'

I was a bit taken aback by his presumption, but these northerners gave not a whit for rank nor status.

'I have news for Lord Fairfax,' I told him.

He passed my papers back, grunted, and waved me on. The Fairfax family had their headquarters further to the south west of the city—a small village called Heslington; the manor there had been taken over to direct the siege. Leven had made his base on the other side of the Ouse with only a flimsy bridge of boats to carry communication. It was not a happy alliance. The Scots had more men and Leven, as an Earl, outranked Lord Fairfax. That prickled with the northern gentry whose families had been fighting Scotsmen for centuries.[68]

I barged in on a staff meeting in the wood panelled hall at Heslington Manor. Lord Farifax, both of his sons, John Meldrum and the rest of the Northern officers all sat around a great table. The Scots were not represented, but I trusted them less than I did the dour Yorkshiremen. The news of Prince Rupert and the King's northern design caught them by surprise—Black Tom scowled through my report—but they quickly shrugged it off.

'Shall we send troops to Lancashire to stop him?' Charles asked his father.

'No,' said Lord Fairfax. 'The Scots could not be induced to move west with York at our backs.'

'The Prince Robber is nothing but a lightning that strikes the ignorant,' said Meldrum to Black Tom.

Meldrum had some front, I give him that. Only weeks before Rupert had humiliated him at Newark, and now he mocked the prince? Rupert's reputation suffered because of Marston Moor, but he was the best damn General of Horse in England, barring one man. 'Twas Rupert's misfortune that man was Cromwell.

Taking York before the Prince could gather troops was now a priority. They dismissed me and turned back to discussing the assaults. I left the hall and made my way back to my bed. Sam was in the croft alone. He and Everard had made it more homely—bunks for the three of us, canvas covering the leaky roof, a fire, and a pot. Food and warmth are the currency of kings in a siege. The admiring, covetous, glances of our neighbours wallowing in mud had me worried—I have seen men stabbed over a warm billet, you know.

'Cromwell is coming,' Sam told me. 'Lincoln has fallen.'

'At last! Mayhap he will light a fire under these northerners. The generals barely cared that Rupert comes.'

It is a strange thing to relate now, looking back through the passage of time, but I was actually thankful Cromwell was coming. He may have been a radical lunatic, but he was my radical lunatic, and Black Tom's testicle twisting was damnably annoying.

AN Exact Relation of the bloody and barbarous Massacre at Bolton in Lancashire, May 28. By PRINCE RUPERT.

Penned by an eyewitness, admirably preserved by the gracious and mighty hand of God, on that day of trouble.

That England may see, and be ashamed, that she spewed out such monsters, as are bred in her own bowels. May all take it to heart, that there hath been none with more zeal for the cause, servants, gospel, and glory of the Lord of Hosts, that be so vilified as will in this relation appear.

On Tuesday May 28, that noble cordial commander Col. Rigby relieved this sad town, being destitute of men, ammunition, or other means of defence. In all, there was about 2000 soldiers, and 500 clubmen; a company sufficient if the security of the inhabitants had not hindered the fortifying of the town.

About two of the clock in the afternoon, the enemy was discovered about a mile off, and they made their approaches to the town from the south west. Their number was guessed to be about 12000.

Our commanders were very courageous, and our soldiers very hardy, and in the first encounter gave them half an hour sharp entertainment. We repulsed them bravely, to the enemy's loss and discouragement. In their retreat, we cut them down in great abundance and they fell like leaves from the tree on a winter morn.

Then was a breathing, a preparative for a fresh encounter, which was gallantly performed on both sides, wherein the worthy Colonel Rigby, and the rest, did notable service. But alas, what could naked men do against horse in an unfortified place. When once the horse was got into the town, there could be no resistance made, but every man left to shift for himself.

At their entrance, before, behind, to the right, and left, nothing was heard, but 'Kill dead! Kill dead!' In the town, killing all before them without any respect; without the town by their horsemen the same. Pursuing the poor amazed people, killing, stripping, and spoiling all they met. They did not regard the doleful cries of women or children; they slashed as they called for quarter. Many hailed out of their houses, to have their brains dashed out in the streets.

Those that were not already dead in the streets - pistolled, slashed, or trodden under horses feet—were taunted with many insolent blasphemous oaths, curses, challenges to heaven, and cruel mockings.

'See what your prayers are come too? Where is all your days of humiliation? We have humbled you now.'

I forbear to say many sad things; the usage of children crying for their fathers, of women crying out for their husbands—some of them slain before their wives faces; the rending, tearing, and turning of people naked; the robbing and spoiling of all people of all things; the massacring, dismembering, cutting of dying, and dead. Arms, legs, and yea the brains themselves lying distant from their heads, bodies, and other parts. Boasting, how many Roundheads this sword had killed that day, some eight, some six, some more, some less.

The violent pursuit of their bloody victory in the town, and four or five miles out of the town in houses, fields, highways, and woods; killing, destroying, spoiling all they could reach, and crying out: 'Where is your Roundhead God now, he was with you at Warrington, Wigan, Manchester, and other places, and hath he forsaken you Roundheads of Bolton?'

William Boulton was fetched out of his chamber with scorn, and killed before his wife's face, who being great with child, fell on him to save him, but they pulled her off without compassion, and bade Boulton call on his God to save him whilst they cut him in pieces.

Katharine Saddon, an aged woman of 72 years, run with a sword to the heart because she had no money to give. Others killed outright after they were mortally wounded, because they stirred, or answered not greedy unjust desires.

Elizabeth Horrocks, a woman of good quality, after they killed her husband, taken in a rope and dragged up and down. After they had robbed and spoiled her of all she had, they made inhumane using of her, and barbarous usage of some other maids and wives in the town - in private places, in fields, and in woods, the trees, the timber, and the stones.

But the principal stain of all this their cruelty, was set off by that strange Earl by his ignoble, nay base, killing of valiant Captain Bootle after quarter given

Only this one thing more, they may boast of their bloody zeal for the worst of causes that ever was defended by English spirits. Yet, they left almost threescore poor widows husbandless, and hundreds of poor children fatherless, and a sweet godly place almost without inhabitants. Only a few women and children are left, without bite to eat, bed to lie on, or a cup to drink in, or any means of subsistence in the world!

Was ever sorrow like to my sorrow. Is it nothing to you; oh yee that pass by?*

Oh England! Oh Heaven! Oh Earth! Bear witness to our calamity. Oh London, and all ye places yet free from our sorrows, think on the day of your peace with thankfulness, and of our trembling and trouble with compassion.

Amen.

---

*   Jeremiah 1:12.

21. Scoutmaster Watson: York, June 1644.

In thy faint slumbers I by thee have watch'd,

And heard thee murmur tales of iron wars;

Speak terms of manage to thy bounding steed;

Cry 'Courage! to the field!'

(Shakespeare, *Henry IV Part 1*)

Meg met with me again before York was finally cut off, but she could tell me nothing more of James. Instead, my mind turned to our original purpose. Uncle Samuel sent us word of Hurry, and the ledger, via the odorous Captain Jakes.

I rode to Hull with the empty supply wagons; four days away from the siege (a pure delight) away from the mud, entrenchments, noise, and charnel house carnage. The siege was a dirty scar around York—so many men and animals tearing up the land. 'Twas peaceful greenery only a few miles distant. I felt as if the war was half a world away—just another bad dream dismissed in the daylight.

The dirty collierman was waiting at the town; the Walter Raleigh pitched up at the river wharf. Jakes handed over a bag of gold, two letters, and the simple order to do whatever it took. One letter was in cipher, in Butler's hand, and Jakes told me it was of the utmost import. It would mean an hour or so trying to figure the meaning. The other, in open hand, bore an oak leaf sigil—from my sister Elizabeth.

'I have another gift for you, Sugar,' said Jakes, and then shouted down to his tub. 'Boy, get your arse up here.' He turned back to me. 'This one is a sailor born; he be wasted as your servant.'

A head popped up over the wharf; black curly hair and beaming white grin. The boy, barefoot and in loose sailor breeches, shirt open, and covered in coal dust. As he scrambled over the side, I noted how he had grown. It had been, what, not six months, and he had shot up half-a-foot, or more.

'Well met, Master.'

His voice had broken as well. I grinned as it boomed out, and lost any semblance of authority.

'What are you doing here, my lad? You are supposed to be looking after my sister.'

'Mistress Elizabeth is married, Master,' John told me cheerfully. 'Happen she wanted me safely out of the way to enjoy her nuptials.'

'Pardon!'

Jakes clipped the boy around the back of the head. 'He is a born liar as well,' said the captain. 'The boy tried to stab the Gypsy King, so your uncle wants him out of London.'

'Elizabeth is not married?'

My sister marrying could cause me some problems—she was the main source of my funds—an unreasonable husband would be troublesome to say the least. Dissolute younger brothers never look good in such situations.

'Oh, no, she is married right enough,' said Jakes.

'Widowed by now I would wager,' said John.

'What are the pair of you chittering about?'

My prim, proper, godly, sanctimonious, hypocritical sister had only gone and married. Oh, but not for lust (she had never shown any interest in pleasures of the flesh) nor for family, oh no. Not even for gold—which I at least could have understood. She had taken up with a Dutchman—Wenceslas Hoogenhuffing or some such ridiculous name that sounded like a man puking. Not that it mattered; he had no family and was dying of consumption* . Elizabeth would inherit a

---

*   Tuberculosis.

house near the Strand, and a widow's independence—as if she needed any more. The Lord Mayor would not be happy; she could badger aldermen to her heart's content now.

'So, is she calling herself Widow Huffinpoofing now?' I asked, opening Elizabeth's letter.

My Dearest Brother,

I write in some concern for your welfare, for your own correspondence has been habitually lax. Write <u>soon</u>, dear Blandford. Much has passed in this city that I would relate – if I had but time. However, I am pressed to record only the briefest of details, so that you are acquainted with your valet's misdemeanours.

The boy has been most bold and disobedient. I would have had him thrashed if I did not consider such brutal treatment the cause of his character defects. He wilfully disobeyed instructions to leave off his childish games and gambling (He is much like his master in this and your responsibility as such). Worse, he became embroiled in an argument with Messer Boswell – whose person I have seen much more than I desire. He stabbed the man in the street, in broad daylight. Were it not for Uncle Samuel's influence, John would surely have followed his father to the gallows. He may have his vengeful desires, but they be nothing more than sinfulness.

To me belongeth vengeance, and recompense; their foot shall slide in due time: for the day of their calamity is at hand, and the things that shall come upon them make haste.[*]

So, I do send him to you to seek his redemption. I hope and pray you keep your word to me, Blandford, and keep

---

[*] Deuteronomy 32:35.

faith with the Lord <u>every day</u>!

As you requested, I have checked the willow tree nearly every day for some note or missive, but none appeared until yesterday. A note in the same hand with words from the gospel of St John.

"Said I not unto thee, that, if thou wouldest believe, thou shouldest see the glory of God."

'Tis from the story of Lazarus, since I know you will not recognise the words, but none saw who the messenger was, nor in all honesty can I fathom the message. It is, as you say, a riddle. Perhaps you can decipher it, but 'tis beyond my wit.

In everything else by prayer and supplication, and with thanksgiving, let your requests be made known unto God. And the peace of God, which passeth all understanding, shall keep your hearts and minds through Christ Jesus.*

Your Loving Affectionate Sister,

Elizabeth.

London, May 24th 1644.

Elizabeth's usual judgemental concern, and no mention of her own little dalliance. The new message in the willow was intriguing, but as Elizabeth said, the message was unfathomable, and the mystery too distant to attract much attention. However, her line that John was my servant and so his sins my responsibility, was a warped interpretation of past events. The boy only had the position because of her blackmail, and I had been two hundred miles away and the boy in her charge when said sinfulness took place. I looked over: John grinned in the drizzle with Captain Jakes alongside him. I had half a mind to send him back to sea with the

---

*   Philippians 4:6.

collierman. That would teach the boy a lesson (as it happens, he would have liked nothing better, but I was not to know that then). Elizabeth would never forgive me, of course.

'Mistress Candy tells me you have been bold and disobedient, John.'

He looked despondent at that; my sister's opinion still carried some weight. However, I wager he was attracting interest from women himself these days. John was grown into a strapping fellow; his dark features handsome. Young girls are ever attracted to the exotic types.

'You are going to come with me, my lad,' I said. 'We shall have to buy you a mule.'

A blessing my uncle had sent coin; a mule would be expensive.

'Mayn't I have a bilhoa, Master?'

'No you mayn't.'

The cipher took most of the evening to translate, and told me little of use. Hurry had been at Bolton after the massacre. I say massacre but one who was there told me it was no sack. The pamphlets overstated it as usual. One thing was certain, my uncle informed me: Prince Rupert was coming to York and Hurry with him. Whatever else happened, we were to get the gold ledger.

It may as well have been a labour set by Eurystheus,* for there was no way I could see to achieve the task.

The soldiers would dig a pit—deep and wide with high earth

---

* King Eurystheus was Hercules' cousin who set him the twelve labours in Greek mythology.

264

banks—and the dead were brought from the trenches and tents, stripped naked, so their bruised flesh was exposed, the boots, and clothes, and anything else of worth pillaged. Miscreants and troublemakers in the camp, under watch of a bully sergeant, would toss the dead into the pit. The chaplain (I think William Goode that day) gave a brief prayer over them. A new pit was dug and so it went round again. A relentless feeding of Hell's insatiable belly—the putrid smell of it made me gag.[69]

Gaol Fever*—the leveller of armies—none of these men had died in battle. I watched as Everard grabbed a body of a young boy by the wrists, and another took hold of the ankles. They swung the emaciated corpse up and into pit. For a moment, it flew through the air, limbs flailing. A sickening slap as the body flopped into the side of the diggings, and slid down to the others at the bottom. They looked like so many white slugs in the mud.

'What did William do?' I asked Sam

'He decided to become preacher.'

'I have been gone but four days and he is boned for sermonising?'

'He damn near caused a brawl with some of Manchester's men, calling for the end of kings, a new godly nation, and religious toleration for all.' Sam grinned. 'I do not think he includes Papists or Laudians in that.'

'An end to kings? A ridiculous notion.'

'Scoutmaster Watson wishes to talk with you about it.'

Watson was Scoutmaster General for the Eastern Association—an untrustworthy man in general, but no fool. He ran his own spies and agents—without Uncle Samuel's reach, contacts, or resources—and was not best pleased to

---

*   Typhus.

discover us sitting outside York with the northerners.[70]

I found him in the Maypole, a coaching inn turned over to the army. It was set back from the entrenchments, and Manchester had his headquarters not far away.[71] Inside, it was dirty and dark, low ceilings and full of men. Watson was at his luncheon when I arrived, dressed in a plain green coat, grey-haired and slender, with brown eyes, a long face and drooping grey moustache. He carved himself slabs of meat from a haunch of mutton, and then sat in front of me picking away at it with greasy fingers.

The smell made my stomach growl like a lion. I coughed, trying to cover my embarrassment, and to remind Watson I was waiting. He looked up from his meal, mouth open, chomping away like a moocow at the cud.

'What are you doing here, Captain Candy?' He ejaculated food at me as he spoke.

'You wished to see me, sir?'

'Not here in this inn, you jackanapes! What are you doing here in Yorkshire?'

I was not about to tell him of the gold ledger. Uncle Samuel had been quite clear on that.

'We came with despatches for Lord Fairfax, and he decided we could be of use, sir.'

Watson snorted.

Typical, tell an outrageous lie and people behave like 'tis the gospel; tell the truth and nobody believes a word.

'Whatever you and your stunted uncle are up to, Candy, understand this, I will brook no disobedience.'

'Yes, sir.'

'Now, what do you here?'

'My duty, sir.' I considered that an inspired answer.

Watson's eyes narrowed. He was clearly not impressed

with the reply.

'I hear Major General Skippon believes you an impudent fop—ill-mannered and ignorant.'

''Twas a misunderstanding.'

Skippon was two hundred miles away, but the poison he had dripped about me spread. A pish on the illiterate pigeon brain! His booklet was better for bum fodder than reading.

'Only Cromwell and Charles Fairfax have a good word to say about you.'

Huzzah for Cromwell! And, it was gratifying Charles felt some friendship in spite of his brother's distaste. Watson stared at me for a moment. I thought he would quiz me some more, but realised he tapped an empty barrel—or a recalcitrant one.

Instead, he decided to keep us busy and out of the way. If we were ignored by Tom Fairfax, and unknown to the Scots, we could be useful to him. We were scouts, he informed me, and it was high time for us to do our jobs. He added further warnings about my men's behaviour, and threats to have any more troublemakers thrashed.

Men? I thought to myself, as I left the inn. I only have two of them, and now the boy, and they are as much trouble as a regiment.

I cornered John as soon as I returned to the croft. We had left unsaid the business with Boswell as we journeyed to York, but I decided it was time to deal with his stupidity. I ranted and raved for ten minutes or so—about his ingratitude, the danger he had put my sister in, the hangman's noose had he been caught.

'In the name of the Virgin Mary's blessed hymen, after all we have been through with Boswell, why did you do it?'

'He killed my father!'

'Your father was killed by the hangman, my lad, and after a fair trial.'

'Only cos Boswell passed information to the Lord Mayor's men. He feared my Da would take his crown.'

'Be that as it may, we cannot have you trying to murder people in broad daylight. 'Tis damnably impolite.'

'That was a mistake.'

'That be more like it; some grudging repentance at the very least.'

'I will wait for night the next time.'

'There will be no next time, John,' says I, firmly.

'No, Master, of course not.'

He was lying; I knew he was lying; he knew I knew he was lying, but neither of us wanted to pursue the matter further. Boswell and London were far enough away.

Sam and Everard spent the next two days running post between the different armies. The Eastern Association arrival had made the cold siege become hot and communication between the generals vital. York's outer defences were assaulted, gun batteries raised to pound the walls, and two great mines dug to force a breach. Watson sent me to watch the Scarborough Road in case supplies or reinforcements for York came from Royalists there.

There was no traffic—the road empty of the usual carts, and wagons, and walkers. 'Twas a pointless assignment, I concluded, but much of this adventure seemed pointless. I pondered John Hurry and the ledger and how to get it from him. The only possible answer I had was finding him in battle, and hoping he carried the ledger on him. That was no plan at all. I sat on my horse all day but could find no solution.

It was dark when I turned Apple back down the road towards York. Rain showers meant that we were both soaked through. I planned to report to Watson and then warm myself by a fire. I was not paying attention, wrapped up in my own misery, and they jumped me, knocked me from my saddle and pointed their muskets at my head.

'A lucky sighting and I have you as my prisoner, Runt.'

Apple snorted at the sound of my brother's voice, and I cursed.

'Keep away from the beast's hoofs and teeth,' said James to his men. ''Tis a demon.'

'Still bitter, James?' I said. 'You never could ride him.'

'It will have to be shot and the carcass eaten.'

He said it to get a response from me; I prayed poor Apple would not be so treated. An expensive horse is worth more than petty vengeance for a childhood snub.

Kicked in the face and spitting blood; a hob nailed boot put paid to the conversation. I was stripped naked, tied in ropes, and led off to the city. There were other prisoners, others who had been caught out by the Royalist sally. Yet, I had more than a nagging suspicion James had been looking for me.

Happen, it was no lucky sighting. Happen, I had been betrayed.

From Anne Candy to Elizabeth Candy.

Sister,

The journey to Bath was long and difficult—the roads so poor I swear we were thrown around the carriage and bruised quite black and blue upon our arrival. I am sorry to say there was little time to visit to Hilperton or Farleigh.

The Queen was in terrible sickness and the birth so close that all worried for her life. We did not tarry in Bath more than three days before moving on. The rebels sought to capture Her Majesty and we were forced on in darkness to evade their patrols.

Her Majesty's physician Doctor Mayhew did finally arrive. Mistress Margaret tells me that he was only persuaded to attend on a plea from His Majesty, and that the Queen is not the best patient. Nevertheless, the child was born safely, but the Queen has suffered for her service to the nation. She complains of tightness in the chest, her sight is diminished, and arm sometimes paralysed.

Many of our company are most worried about Her Majesty's health, and the Queen does complain so desperately, but Mistress Margaret says that it is but a hysteria.

Where we shall go from this city only the fates can decide. The Earl of Essex is most determined to carry this war to women and newborns, and no place seems safe.

I miss your wise counsel and kind words, dear Elizabeth,

but have no place for you to send your letters. I shall write as soon as I know of such.

I remain, your loving affectionate Sister,

Anne.

Exeter, June 19th 1644.

22. Captive: York, June 1644.

Alone in prison strong

I wait my destiny.

Woe worth this cruel hap that I

Should taste this misery!

(Anne Boleyn, *Oh Death Rock Me Asleep*.)

I did not expect to survive the pit. Quite apart from the rats, the rats (God save me from the rats), meagre portions of bread, and the ankle deep swill of excreta, was my malevolent brother. Despite my rank, he saw to it that I was stripped, shackled, and thrust into the worst hole. My shins, rubbed raw from the chains, grew infected with sores.

The darkness made counting the passage of time impossible—days at the very least. I barely slept, squatting, hunched against the walls of my prison, sometimes weeping in anger, sometimes delirious with fatigue and hunger. I was sick, spewing more than once, and my bowels were a waterfall of dung. Perhaps 'twas *petite* insanity, but phantoms came to me and I jabbered with them as if solid forms.

'Twas an explosion that tore me back to sensibility. A great roaring sound; the ground shook, mortar fell from the ceiling, and the stone walls cracked. For hours I waited—half in expectation of rescue—listening with an ear against the cold masonry. I could hear the explosion of shot, soft pops that denoted a battle above. It went on for some time—hours or minutes, I could not tell—but died away to silence. Eventually, I fell back to a restless dozing.[72]

They came for me as I tried to sleep, dragged me from my pit into the light. Armed men; I tried to speak but my tongue was swollen, and only weak groans came out. Pulled along too fast to note where; my eyes blinded, agony in the unfamiliar sunlight. I closed them and stumbled to the floor. One of the soldiers put a hobnailed boot into my gut making me cough and retch. They grabbed the ragged cloth around my shoulders and it disintegrated. Rolling on the floor, I cried out to God for salvation, begging forgiveness for my many sins. They kicked and beat me, and I knew in my heart I was about to die.

'What goes here?' A voice of authority—another poxy Scot by the accent.

I blinked, trying to see the voice, but the light still too bright. The soldiers stopped booting me at least.

'He be a malignant.' Other men spoke out, branding me spy, and traitor, and worse. I heard my brother's name mentioned, and my uncle's. I should be shot was the general consensus.

'No...' I whined. 'I am a gentleman.'

'I want him cleaned up and fed,' said Voice. 'He is of no use if he cannot talk.'

The men protested, but Voice had none of it. They picked me up—more gently now—and carried me away. I tried to thank Voice, but stumbled over the words and passed out.

A pail of water doused me back to consciousness. My eyes cleared; I lay naked on the cobbles of a small courtyard, fine stone buildings looming over me, and tall burly soldiers glaring with hate. There was blood on the cobbles—not mine. A pile of bodies, twenty or more with glazed eyes vacantly staring, lay beside me. They bore Eastern Association coats and the wounds of battle. Was this my place of execution? The Royalists threw more pails of water over me to swill away the dirt and stench of prison.

'Bring him,' said Voice.

He was dressed as a soldier. Old, with wrinkles—he must have been sixty or more—thinning grey hair and a high widow's peak, wearing a small beard, dainty moustache, and with warm friendly eyes peering at me. Voice wore his thick buff coat and arms like a veteran, but they were richly made, and his boots had a servant's shine.

'Yes, Milord,' said one.

Another of the guards pulled me to my feet. My shackles had been broken, but the sores on my legs wept as I stumbled along. With one step I shivered at the cold and the next a wave of heat washed over me. I thought I would lose my senses again, but managed to stay upright. They led me inside the red-bricked buildings and down corridors with a tiled floor, cool on my bare feet.

I stood naked, shivering, in front of Voice with only hands to cover my modesty. It was a large richly furnished room, with two solid looking soldiers stood watching the door. The windows with fine clear-glass panes—though one was cracked. The boom of cannon sounded in the distance. Voice studied me for a moment or two; a sorry sight I must have made, but I had regained my wits. They had not killed me yet; if I was careful, perhaps survival was possible.

'You are Sir James Candy's brother? The one called The Golden Scout.'

'Yes, Milord.' I was in no fit state to give one of my usual pithy comments.

'You are one of Samuel Luke's spies?'

I said nothing to that.

'Well, answer me, man!'

I think one of my many character faults is a dislike of authority. 'Tis perhaps a rebellion against my overbearing, drunken father. Whenever someone tosses out orders at me,

I bristle on the inside. Too often, my tongue has led me into trouble in such situations. For once, I kept my head. This man could order me shot out of hand. That tends to focus one's manners.

'I am Scout Captain, and Captain of Dragoons,' I said. It was pointless trying deception; Voice would see through it.

He nodded at my answer, and then asked a more telling question.

'I want to know where the mines are.'

I looked at him blankly. 'In faith, Milord, I know not. I was set on the Scarborough Road, not the entrenchments.' Fairfax and Watson had kept me away from anything interesting.

'Perhaps the rack would make you talk.'

'I am certain it would, Milord. But could you trust the accuracy of such evidence?'

*Where men enforced do speak anything.**

Torture is a peculiarly continental affectation. The Ottomans are masters of the art—as I know to my cost - but it has never much taken hold in England. We have juries and common law—they have despots. As the war became more bitter, however, stories of such abuses spread. Lord Voice did not strike as the type to order me racked, but you can never be sure.[73]

'You are acquainted with John Hurry?'

'To my shame and misery.'

He laughed at that.

'You know him well enough, then. I served with Hurry in Germany and with Leven too.'

'I have had little contact with the Earl of Leven,' I said. This war was a pottage of Scots freebooters.

---

*   Merchant of Venice Act III Scene II.

''Tis a tragedy for such boon companions to be on opposing sides.'

Lord Voice must be Jack King—Lord Eythin—a luminary indeed. Newcastle's Lieutenant General of Foot.[74]

'We live in a time of miserable contradiction, Milord.'

He nodded his head, looking suitably miserable for a moment, and then looked up.

'I think I will keep you safe for now, Captain Candy. You may be of use when the siege is over—one way or t'other.'

I knew what that meant. I was a pawn for great men to place and move. Lord Voice would use me to save himself if York fell. I wondered whether to tell him Tom Fairfax and Leven thought nothing of me, but decided not to spoil the surprise. If York be relieved, well then, I was certain to be handed o'er to the Washerwoman—if my brother James did not kill me first.

Voice told the two guards standing impassively at the door that I was to be clothed, fed, and kept away from other prisoners. 'He is to talk to no-one,' he said, once or twice more.

I cared little; glad not to be thrown back into the pit.

From Charles I to Prince Rupert.

Nephew,

First, I must congratulate with you for your good successes, assuring you that the things themselves are no more welcome to me than that you are the means. I know the importance of supplying you with powder, for which I have taken all possible ways, having sent to both Ireland and Bristol. As from Oxford, this bearer is well satisfied that it is impossible to have any at present; but if he tell you that I can spare them from hence, I leave you to judge, having but thirty-six left. But what I can get from Bristol (of which there is not much certainty, it being threatened to be besieged) you shall have.

Now, I must give you the true state of my affairs, which if their condition be such as enforces me to give you more peremptory commands than I would willingly do, you must not take it ill. If York be lost I shall esteem my crown little less; unless supported by your sudden march to me; and a miraculous conquest in the South, before the effects of their Northern power can be found here. But if York be relieved, and you beat the rebels' army of both kingdoms which are before it; then (but otherwise not) I may make a shift (upon the defensive) to spin out time until you come to assist me.

Wherefore, I command and conjure you, by the duty and affection which I know you bear me, that all new enterprises are laid aside; you immediately march, according to your first intention, with all your force to the relief of York. But, if that be either lost, or have freed themselves from the besiegers, or that, from want of powder, you cannot undertake that work, that you immediately march with your whole strength, directly to Worcester, to assist me and my army; without which, or you having relieved York by beating the Scots, all the successes you can afterwards have must infallibly be useless unto me. You may believe that nothing but an extreme necessity could make me write thus unto you; wherefore, in this case, I can no ways doubt of your punctual compliance with.

Your loving and most faithful friend,
CHARLES R.
P.S. I commanded this Bearer to speak to you concerning Vavasour.
Ticknell, June 14th 1644.[75]

The guards took me to a stout room with only dim light from slits above—too high for me to see out. My new prison was dry and clean, with pallet, bedding and table—after the pit a joyous relief. I was given cast off breeches and stockings, a coarse woollen shirt and dirty grey doublet. No shoes, just in case I had thoughts of escape—I had none at first. My legs were cleaned with vinegar, bandaged, and soon began to heal.

Once a day, a silent attendant would bring a pitcher of Adam's Ale*, a cup of beans, and a penny loaf. Then he would take away my night soil, slam the door shut, and leave me alone.

By the third day, I decided to engage him and see what could be discerned.

Older than I, and bigger, long grey hair hanging down his back, dressed in leather trousers and rough blue coat. I would have taken him for a farrier, or some such occupation. He did not strike me as a domestic. Charm would be my weapon; perhaps I could befriend him.

I could still hear the sounds of powder and shot, like distant thunder. How far away could Prince Rupert be by now? Somehow, someway, I had to find an escape before the prince could come to York's relief.

The attendant—I dubbed him Silent—entered carrying a

---

*   Water

tray with my victuals. His shoes and stockings were wet.

'Is the weather still bad?' I said.

No response. Silent placed the tray on the table, took the old tray away, and then returned to take away the shit bucket from the corner of the cell. His nose wrinkled at the stink.

''Tis the beans,' I said. 'They do make me fart and shit something merciless.'

He picked up the bucket, still silent, took it out of the room—not forgetting to close the door—and brought it back empty a minute or so later. He returned it to the corner of the room and left.

'Thank you, my good man,' I said to his back.

Silent slammed the door shut, shot the bolts, and left me in silence. The next morning, I tried again.

'Good day to you, my good man. You are looking well this morn,' I said, with a beaming smile.

No response. Silent placed the tray on my table, took yesterday's outside, and then returned.

'Not even a good morning for your prisoner? Surely your mother taught you better manners, sir.'

He took the shit bucket out, emptied it, brought it back and left. All without uttering a sound—completely ignoring my chatter. This went on for two more days 'til I conceded defeat. Nothing I could do would entice Silent to speak. Annoyed that my attempts at civility and friendliness had failed, I began to bait him. Mayhap, I could make him lose his temper. 'Twas a foolish notion, and one that could end sourly, but I was bored.

Even insults and curses did nothing to break the impassive man. After a week and more of trying to get some reaction— any reaction—I gave up in a rum sulk. That morning, I said nothing, merely sat on my pallet ignoring him. Finally, he gave a response. As he closed the door, Silent turned for a moment, flashed a grin of victory at me, and left.

I had lost the battle of wills. It put me in a foul temper, I can tell you. Outwitted by a poxy cavalier servant; locked up and left to rot on the whim of a Cavalier general. Ever since I was a boy, I have hated being confined; ever since I was a boy, I have periodically found myself under lock and key.

Father had threatened to have me horsewhipped this time; Mr Dredge had threatened to lynch me. Figgis, my father's manservant, dragged me to my chambers and locked me in to await my punishment. I heard the great door slam downstairs and looked out of my chamber window. Mr Dredge, carrying his lantern, stamped down the driveway of the hall and turned to make his way back to the village. I could hear my father's voice raised—shouting at Figgis—and then silence.

I reached for a stolen bottle of wine I had concealed in a chest and opened it - taking a great gulp. If I was to be beaten, I was going to get drunk. 'Twas over halfway through the bottle when I heard movement outside my room, and the rattle of a key in the lock. I sat up on my bed as the door opened, and my sister Elizabeth entered carrying a taper that cast a dim light in the room.

'Has our visitor departed, sweet sister?' I said cheerfully.

Elizabeth did not look so happy.

'I see you have been drinking,' she said. 'Should I come back on the morrow when your head is less befuddled?'

'No, no, the sack makes your sermons tolerable.'

She pursed her lips at that.

'Father is furious with you, and Mr Dredge had murder in his eyes, and no wonder.'

'Twas not my fault.'

'You seduced his wife and then deflowered his daughter. How is that not your fault?'

'His daughter's flower had been plucked long before I happened along, and the wife seduced me... She was most insistent.'

She had been; 'twas both arousing and terrifying in fair equal measures.

'Father has been forced to pay them off to keep the matter quiet,' said Elizabeth.

'You say that like 'tis a bad thing?'

'It is a bad thing! We can ill afford this scandal with Henry getting betrothed.'

'Of course, we mustn't upset the monkey, must we. Anything else now you have topped up your medication of vinegar and piss? Or may I get back to my bottle?

'No you mayn't! When there is a heat in your loins, Blandford, there is a freezing in your brain, but if there is any more of this behaviour I shall take steps to address it myself, and Father will be the least of your concerns.'

That was true enough; Father was far less fearsome than my sister. Elizabeth could be quite inventive with her punishments. She took on a serious look.

'Henry's betrothed is called Sarah, from the Ashe family in Farleigh Hungerford. We shall all pay our respects as a family tomorrow evening, and you shall behave. I will have no bickering between you and James, and you shall be the model of chivalry with the Ashes and their daughter, or else. Do you understand me?

'Yes,' I said sourly.

'As many as I love, I rebuke and chasten: be zealous therefore, and repent.'*

I bit back a couple of barbs and promised to behave; she promised

---

*   Revelation 3:19.

to sell me into service in the colonies if I disobeyed. I doubted she could be so cruel; I was an idiot.

The guns had stopped. For days they had boomed out, beating an accompaniment to my misery. Now, there was nothing—no sound. My food was late; that had not happened before. Silent was as regular as my morning shit. Was the siege finished? A worrying thought, indeed.

When I finally heard the sound of bolts drawn back, I was quite frantic with imagined fates. The door swung open and in walked Silent, carrying a tray of food that he placed on the table.

'What has happened?' I asked. 'Is the siege ended?'

He said nothing, simply carried out his chores as impassively as always.

'Listen you dungwitted bolluck-sack. I want to know what is happening.' I raised my voice, demanding attention.

He deposited the shit bucket, left the cell, and pulled the door closed. The bolts slammed back into place, and I heard a laugh.

'Bastard! Arsehole! Shit-brained codpiece!' I shouted at the door.

All to no avail, I was left in silence once more.

I picked up the penny loaf—it was still warm. Freshly baked—'twas more usual to get three day old tack that I had to drown in water to eat. I bit into the bread, tearing off a chunk with my teeth. It tasted good.

Chewing at the bread, I noticed a small piece of parchment baked into the remaining loaf. It had been revealed by my bite; I dug it out with my fingers.

'What, in the name of Satan's testicles, is this?' I said to myself.

The words written on it made my heart leap.

Be awake tonight.

The remainder of the day was spent in nervous excitement. I recognised the hand; it could only mean my rescue. Repeatedly during the day, I heard cheering and shouts. I would stare at the window slits above my head, trying to gauge the time.

There is a tide in the affairs of men. [*]

Finally, it grew dark outside. I could still hear the sounds of celebrations. The siege must be over. York had been relieved.

As it grew later, I became near frantic with nervous excitement. I paced up and down in the small cell until my bootless feet hurt. When I heard the sound of the bolts drawn, I leaped up. The door swung open, and a hooded figure came in carrying a cloth bag. Another was standing behind with a lamp.

'Hello, my sweet. I do hope you are feeling somewhat better.' She threw back her hood to reveal her beauty.

'Meg.'

'Shhhh, no gossip. We must be quick. Put these on.' She handed me the sack.

I looked at the man who had followed, and with a start of horror recognised him in the lamplight. Of middling age and stout, long brown hair and beard shot through with silver, an old scar running down one cheek. He was dressed richly now, not in the old stained buff coat that he once wore.

'What ho, Sugar.'

---

*   Julius Caesar Act IV Scene III.

I could smell his fetid breath from across my cell. John Hurry—the prince of turncoats.

23. Turncoats and Trulls: York, July 1644.

Drink to me only with thine eyes,
And I will pledge with mine;
Or leave a kiss but in the cup,
And I'll not ask for wine.

(Ben Jonson, *To Celia*.)

I shook in anger at the sight of my nemesis. John Hurry had haunted my thoughts for months. I blamed him for my friends' deaths, and his minions had nearly killed me thrice over. Now, here he was standing with the most confusing woman I had known. I sat back down on my bed.

'Bugger that,' I said. 'I go nowhere with Judas.'

'Then thou art a simpleton, Blandford,' said Meg.

Her face was made up, a pretty coif, and she wore a dress of fine green satin, as if just come from court. I confess I started to question her loyalties.

'I told you; he is too stubborn and vain, Lady Sarah,' said Hurry, in his hateful Scots tone.

'Go with Sir Foulbreath Turncoat?' I said, trying to keep my voice down. 'Think you that I just fell off the turnip cart?'

Meg slapped me right across the face. As quick a right hand as my sister.

'I do not have time to explain, but I pledge that I will, Blandford. Now, do you not trust me?'

She turned her beautiful violet eyes upon me, wide and pleading. Deceitful trull, in another time she could have made a fortune on the stage.

'You know that I do not,' I said, rubbing my cheek.

She looked hurt at that, sticking out her lower lip and pouting: an absolute fortune, I tell you. Hurry watched on in amusement as Meg and I bickered.

'Then we shall leave you to your brother.' She turned to go.

'Wait.' The Devil's own choice—Hurry or James.

She turned back to me and fluttered her long dark lashes. 'Well, do you trust me?'

'I trust you.' A flagrant deceit; I merely distrusted her less than the others.

She gave a wide grin and picked up her bag—acting like a spoiled little girl who has got her own way. I had seen the same look on both my sisters' faces often enough. As Franny once said, for all my rakish reputation as a beard splitter*, some women have always had the ability to twist me to their tune.

'Quick, quick, my sweet, get the boots on then, and the coat.'

The items were quickly located; I eyed the musketeer boots.

'Are you sure they are big enough? My feet are large.'

'Typical, always reckoning your size,' she said.

Hurry laughed at me and I glared daggers back. Meg picked up a small bottle as I pulled on the boots—they fitted perfectly—and buttoned up the buff coat. She looked critically at my scraggly growth of beard.

'That will help, I think, but it does nought for your looks.'

She poured a dark liquid from the bottle into her leather gloves, and began to rub it into my beard and blonde locks.

'What be this?'

'Brown dye; do not fret, 'twill wash out.'

I thought of Sergeant Reggie and his unnaturally dark hair. To think I had come to this—'twas damned humiliating. Finally, Meg decided enough was enough, and passed me a

---

*　　　A man that seduces and enjoys women.

montero* to stick on my noggin.

'Keep your head down and follow us.' She handed me her bag. 'You play a servant, so be suitably silent and keep your manners.'

'You ain't so pretty now, Sugar.' Hurry smirked at me.

'My hair will grow out,' I said. 'You shall be bugger ugly till your dying day. Which I pray is close.'

'Manners, Blandford,' said Meg, sharply.

They led me down dark corridors and out into a cobbled courtyard. We passed soldiers and servants, Hurry and Meg arm-in-arm, me following behind. I kept my head down, praying that none recognised me in the torchlight. Out through a gatehouse, heading on into York town.

'Why are we going into the city?' I hissed.

'Because most the soldiers are without, looting your encampments,' said Meg. 'Now, hush.'

We walked along the Ouse until we reached a bridge. There were guards in plain white coats there, but Hurry was known to them, as was Meg. The soldiers shouldered their pikes in salute as the couple led me onto the bridge. This would make a story for Mabbot and Pecke—if I managed to survive. People would surely pay more for an escape from York by The Golden Scout.

Do you think me vain? Of course I am, even when my life is threatened, perhaps more so—legacy and all that.

We crossed the river, and they took me down Mikelgate (the main street south) to the shattered ruins of Trinity Abbey. Old papist buildings fallen into decay, and targeted by our cannoneers. Neglect and siege left them roofless and broken. Meg pulled away from Hurry and led us into a maze

---

*   Type of woollen cap with side flaps that can be rolled up.

of buildings, dark nooks, and crannies. She took out a key and opened a small door hidden away, so low I had to crouch to enter, stepping down into a cellar room, with a rough-hewn table, and chairs, and a lamp hanging by the door. Hurry took down the lamp and sparked it alight. It cast our shadows on the wall in an orange glow.

'Enough,' I said, stamping my foot. 'I demand an explanation before I go any further.'

'Tantrum, Sugar?' said Hurry.

'You had best explain, Sir John,' said Meg. 'He will need to tell the Earl of Leven.'

What an explanation it was: a Scotch broth of black treachery and deceit. 'Twas little wonder Judas Hurry was at its heart. James King—Voice himself—had no desire to fight against his own countrymen. He had started a mutiny over pay to deprive Prince Rupert of the Northern levies. The Marquis of Newcastle had been persuaded that to draw battle against the triple army of Manchester, Leven, and Fairfax would be a disaster. We were most likely to fall to arguing amongst ourselves if left alone. I could only agree with that assessment—there was no love lost between our commanders. If Rupert persisted with his plan to attack, Hurry told me, then his men would break first.

He saw my look of disgust and contempt.

'Do you judge me, Sugar? I am a Scot; I do not relish fighting my own countrymen, and a comrade-in-arms to boot. Jamie already has the men refusing orders; the Army of the North will not move without pay. Rupert may think he is invincible but I know Leven of old. He is too canny to fall for the Prince's tricks.'

'Cromwell will eat Rupert before breakfast,' I said. 'Without your treachery.'

He laughed. 'Who is Cromwell? Some Cambridgeshire bumpkin, nothing more. One of my men will cross the lines if battle is drawn, and give Leven the nod.'

'And how do I know this is not simply one of your plots? A reputation precedes you like the noxious stink of your sewer-breath.'

Hurry flushed angrily at that. He reached into his coat and for a moment I thought he would pull a pistol. Instead, he took out a leather journal and placed it on the table in front of us.

'Lady Sarah tells me that this is of some worth to you? Your comrade's, was it not? The one I hanged.' His lips curled into a sneer.

The Washerwoman's journal, filled with the names of London's merchant traitors. Did Hurry know what it contained? Surely, he could not. He would not hand such a prize over for so little personal gain and so much risk. Perhaps, he really was scared of Leven's ability in battle. I tried to keep my face impassive - as if at the card table.

'Look you, Blandford,' said Meg. 'We do not have the time for this. You must be away to Leven and Sir John back to the Prince.'

I hated myself at that moment. All my thoughts on Hurry had been how to see him dead. Now, here I was helping him in his dark treason. I had no choice, for I knew the value of the journal. I prayed that Franny's shade would forgive me. Perhaps Meg understood; she touched my cheek.

'Come, my sweet,' she said softly. 'Let us get you out of York.'

I picked up the journal, my hands shaking, and tucked it inside my doublet. The traitor smiled in victory at me; I felt like spewing.

Hurry left us—a wraith in the night—and Meg directed me to the flagstone floor. In the corner of the room, one of the stones was not fitted so tightly. She passed me a dagger and I jimmied it until I could flip the stone up. The dagger bent with the weight, but finally the flagstone moved, tilting back to reveal a black hole down into the earth. There was a foul smell rising up; like gas escaping from a bloated corpse.

'You take me to the finest places, Meg. What is Hurry's game?'

'He plays both sides of the coin,' she said. 'Lord Eythin is true, you can trust me on that. He has started the mutiny and will do his best to stop the battle.' She held the lamp high over the hole. 'There is a ladder down.'

I reached inside the hole feeling for the top of the ladder, and climbed down. A dark shaft going deep into the bowels of the earth beneath York. I reached the bottom; Meg passed down the lamp and climbed down herself. The room was long and thin and the floor covered in muck, but with fine stonework made by master masons. At the far end, a shaft stretched off about waist height. The roof was of great lintels mortared together, all of solid construction, at least. Carved into the stone wall next to the shaft was an inscription—'twas meaningless to me.

LEG VI V P F F

I pointed to the letters. 'What does this mean?'

Meg looked at the carving. 'I know not; it matters not. This was made for papist priests hiding from the authorities. Follow the tunnel, it takes you under the walls and down into the buildings to the South. You come out in the cesspit of some rude houses. Make sure your uncle gets that journal, Sugar.' I nodded and she continued. 'The pass is: *God our Strength*.'[76]

I shone the lamp down the odorous tunnel and wrinkled my nose.

'You have used this exit?'

'Of course not, but I do not think the stink will vex you. Be worried more for Rupert's troopers.'

She gave me a peck on the cheek.

'Be careful, Blandford. You are my very favourite puppy; I do not wish to lose you.'

"Puppies can lick their own whirligigs. Sadly, I cannot.'

'So you have tried?' An arched eyebrow mocked me.

I did not know how to respond to that. Instead, I turned and began crawling down the muddy stinking tunnel shaft. The fitted stone gave me some comfort at least. It had survived so long, and would not collapse with my passing. I heard Meg scramble back up the ladder without another word, and the flagstone trapdoor slammed back into place. The sound amplified, echoing down the tunnel.

I pushed the lamp ahead of me and crawled through the darkness. It can only have been a hundred yards or so, but the smell grew ever worse. I was starting to gag at the stench. I felt like I was swimming in the Fleet River 'twas so noxious. At the end of the tunnel, a wooden hatch opened out above a half-filled cesspit. A ladder slick with shit, and rotting, led up to the privy above. I cursed: no gloves. I was going to stink after my ascension. I extinguished the lamp and swung myself out onto the ladder.

A rung snapped under my weight as I climbed, suddenly dangling me over the lake of crap. I pulled myself up more carefully after that. 'Twould be a sorry death to end my days drowned in a cesspit—the vengeance of Smirky Pask*. At the top of the ladder, I pushed at the privy seat. It gave way easily,

---

*   See The Last Roundhead.

although a globule of wet filth fell on my face. I cursed again and climbed out.

In the fresh air, I breathed deeply trying to clean my lungs of the foul vapours. I wiped my filthy hands on the floor, and vainly tried to clean my face with water from a puddle. 'Twas to no avail, I stank of the sewers. The shithouse block was set out the back of a row of small wooden houses huddled together outside the city walls—mostly broken down, the occupants fled, the wood used in barricades and campfires by my own army—darkness and silence all around.

'A horse, a horse. My kingdom for a horse,' I said, to myself.*

If Apple had still been with me, escape would have been simple. Had James shot him as he threatened? I hoped not; Apple deserved better.

I crept over to the houses, and checked the path leading south. I was between two fortlets that guarded York: they would be full of Royalists.[77] As my eyes grew accustomed to the darkness, I pondered my options.

Hurry had told me that my army had drawn off to the west, to a village called Long Marston. Most of the cavaliers of York would be looting Fairfax or Manchester's camps north of the river. I planned to head south along the Ouse and then west; there was a small chance that our troopers would still be at the boat bridge near Middlethorpe.

I tumbled straight into the guard as I ran down the path along the river. He was alone, bent over a small barrel, and I careered into him. He sprawled facedown on the floor, cursing loudly. That was his death sentence; I could not afford any companions hearing. I drew the dagger Meg had given me and stabbed him in the back as he tried to rise.

---

*   Richard III

Blood stained his white coat black in the darkness, and apart from a sharp yelp with the first thrust, he stayed silent. I cleaned my dagger and stripped the cheap sword from his body. He carried a matchlock, but I dismissed it as too heavy to run with. I rolled the body out of sight of the main path, all the time praying I would not be found. The barrel was beer—his share of some loot. I held it up and tipped it back, letting the golden liquid fill my mouth. It was a good brew, invigorating, I took a deeper swig and followed the trail south.

For once, I thanked God that Fairfax and Watson had kept me busy riding the area around York. I knew where I was, and where I was going. I just had to hope I was not captured in the meantime. Carefully, listening out for any sound in the night, I made my way.

'Tis a bare two miles to the manor at Middlethorpe where Leslie had made his quarters. The knavesmere is common pasture alongside the River Ouse, but all the animals had been driven off and the ground was muddy with the rains. I would wager that I ran it in less than half of the hour. Before I reached the manor, I turned away. I could see the glow of fire lighting up the night sky; hear the shouts of men and drums beating. It could only be Royalists making such a din.

I headed across the open pasture until I came to a small brook crossing my path. I slid down its side and waded across. It was near waist deep with the rains. By the time I had clambered up the other side, I was breathing heavily and paused to take stock for a few minutes.[78]

I trudged westwards for the rest of the night over fields and creeping past houses, always worried—terrified really, if I be honest—capture would see me hanged as a spy.

The greyness of dawn at my back was just giving warning

of the new day. I stopped at an abandoned croft—burned out by one side or t'other. I had seen no sign of either army in my night time wanderings.

There was a noise behind me. I half turned, but a blow to the head knocked me to the floor. Stunned, I looked up to muskets pointed down at me. The soldiers bearing them wore Eastern Association coats.

'God our Strength,' I said.

The muskets lifted as an officer pushed through. With relief, I recognised him.

'What a sight you are, Candy. Is this hair colour some new affectation or fashion? And you stink like a midden.'

Jeremiah Abercrombie smiling at me.

24 A Field Near York: 2nd July 1644.

Whil'st Kin their Kin, Brother the Brother foils,

Like Ensigns all against, like Ensigns band;

Bows against Bows, the Crown against the Crown;

Whil'st all pretending right, all right is thrown down.

(Samuel Daniel, *The Civile Wars between the Two Hovses of Lankaster and Yorke.*)

Jeremiah took me to Cromwell, Black Tom, and David Leslie at Long Marston. He gave me a horse, and I climbed into the saddle and followed him. 'Twas a skittish brown mare, and I silently mourned the loss of Apple. Jeremiah told me what was happening as we rode.

'The army is marching to Tadcaster,' he said. 'We are to provide a screen on the flanks for the Foot.'

'Do we not face Rupert at Long Marston?'

''Twas yesterday's excitement. The generals were arguing about it all night. It is all over the army that Henry Vane told them to declare the King no King. The Scots are unhappy with it all.'[79]

He told me how the siege had been lifted and how Rupert had cozened them to relieve York; how the generals were barely speaking, and the Scots talked of returning home. 'Twas the usual sorry tale of bickering and inaction that always cost us dear. There was a growing realisation by the Presbyterian leaders that they had opened Pandora's Box* in making war upon the King. Fear of the Independents became as strong a factor in our generals thinking as any Royalist design. I was

---

*　　　Pandora's Box was actually a jar. Erasmus mistranslated the Greek and the error stuck.

heartily sick of it all.

'How is your new wife?'

He pulled out a silver chain around his neck, with my half-a-jacobus on it, and kissed it.

'She is well, my friend. We shall be reunited soon, I pray.'

The change of subject did not stop him in his prattle; he regaled me with the wonders of marriage as we trotted along. We passed columns of marching infantry, and ordnance, and baggage, all going in the opposite direction, glum looks on their faces. After a few miles of Jeremiah's talking, I began to wonder at Sam's solution of stuffing my ears with soft cheese.

Turning through fields of yellow rye to a low ridge, I could see our Horse mustered in battalia atop. Cromwell's psalm-singing regiment were there with others—Scots and Yorkshiremen—stretched out along the high ground.

I kicked the mare into a canter and crested the heights, looking down on the fields below.

The ridge fell away sharply into open fields and then sloped gently down to a rough track running east-west. The fields rose on t'other side of the track to a shallow ditch and hedgerow separating the rye from scrub and moorland.

Prince Rupert's vanguard stood lining the hedgerow—a strong enough position for defence. More Royalist Horse formed up around them—only four or five hundred yards distant from our position. Behind, I could see the pikes in columns, hear the beat of drums and wail of pipes, the tramp of boots and the chanting, marching, Foot. It was not yet nine in the morning; the Royalists had the advantage.

'Tis the early bird that catcheth the worm.

* This is first recorded in John Ray's *Collection of English Proverbs* (1670) but was probably much older than that.

'I think there will be a battle today, Jeremiah.'

He nodded. 'Perhaps you are correct.'

It took some persuasion before I was taken before Cromwell and the others. No credentials, and listed as captured, does not inspire trust in guards. I could, of course, have been some ravilliac,* but 'twas damn frustrating at the time. Finally, I was taken to them, sitting atop their mounts on the highest point of the ridge, watching Rupert deploy his muster.[80]

I looked Cromwell straight in the eye when I told him my tale. 'Twas an honest report I gave too, not the drunken embellishment I would later feed to Gilbert Mabbot. Oliver would sniff out any deceit. I neglected to mention the Washerwoman's journal, but Noll was filled with excitement at Prince Rupert's lack of troops: they had thought him more than twenty thousand strong. That the garrison in York was not inclined to march out was custard on the pudding. Black Tom and David Leslie were less enthused at my information. They had sat in the saddle, stone-faced, as I gave my report.

'You are certain on these numbers, Captain Candy?' asked Leslie.

Leslie was dressed like the others in buff coat, corselet, gorget, and thick leather riding boots, but his fair hair and moustache were immaculate compared to Cromwell—who looked as though he had been dragged through a bush.

'It came from the same source that aided my escape, sir,' I said. 'But I confess I have no way of confirming it.'

Leslie sniffed. 'I trust John Hurry not—a good officer of Horse, it must be said, but a scoundrel born.'

'I can confirm it,' said Black Tom. 'I have a contact in York; she tells the same tale as Candy. I have every trust in _her_ information. We should recall the Foot and ordnance and

---

*   Assassin

secure this ridge until they are returned to us.'

Poxy sneak could not resist a sly poke at me. Truly, I was coming to dislike Black Tom. With hindsight, that is perhaps a fault in my judgement. After all, I was coming to quite like Noll Cromwell—madman or no.

'If the Army of York does not march,' said Cromwell, 'God provides us with a great advantage.' He was all energy and enthusiasm. ''Tis better to be the pin than the cushion.'

They dismissed me as they carried on the discussion. Leonard Watson appeared, having heard of my coming, and wanted me to report to him. He questioned me more thoroughly and did not seem best pleased at my tale. I had questions of him also—who informed my brother I watched the Scarborough Road, being the most pressing. He went red-faced at that, told me not to be so 'damned impudent'. Sam and William were with Cromwell's regiment, he said, and 'twould be best I found some arms—not cast aspersions.

I know a liar when I hear one—like a fox sniffs its own hole—but Watson would have to wait. Word was sent to the Lords and Generals marching with the Foot: turn about and return to the field.

Opposite us, Rupert sat on his horse with his yapping doggy, watching us watching him, and waiting for the Army of York.

Cromwell's regiment was easy enough to locate on the ridge. I could hear their songs and shouts to the Lord. I criticise not religious devotion, nor piety of prayer, but there is no need to make a spectacle of it—I have always distrusted showy godliness. Everard was sitting on the grass amongst them smoking his pipe. I was surprised he was not a leader in the caterwauling. He leaped to his feet when he saw me arrive and dismount, grabbing me in a smothering hug, with Sam whooping behind. It made me feel fair warm inside, I can tell you.

'I thought you lost, Blandford,' whispered Everard in my ear. 'I prayed it was not so, and the Lord has answered. He has saved thee for his grand design.'

'Oh, pish-posh,' I said, kissing him. 'Where is the boy?'

'He is with the baggage in a rum sulk,' said Sam.

'I need gauntlets, corselet, pot, pistols, carbine.'

'Those are with the boy,' said Everard. 'He was set on selling them, but I told him to have faith in the Lord.'

Sam rolled his eyes. 'We have spent all your coin, Sugar.'

A crack of thunder and sudden downpour put end to that conversation—great blobs of rain falling in sheets. I could hear men cursing as they covered their powder and arms from the waters. It swept along the ridge, down to the Cavaliers and then, as quickly as it came, it was gone. The sun poked its head out of the dark grey clouds, and the singing started up once more.

I pulled William and Sam into a huddle, told them a quick version of my escape, and showed them the Washerwoman's journal, packed it tight into the saddlebags of my horse, and made sure if ought happened to me they took it to Uncle Samuel.

'Once this day is through,' I said. 'We can get back home.'

If God wills it,' said Everard.

Trumpets were sounding the alarum. I still had neither pistols nor armour.

'Take it, Sugar.' Sam passed me his second pistol, and Everard some powder and shot.

There was almost a glistening in my eyes at that. Fraternal love was not an emotion I had much experience of, but these were my brothers-in-arms. I have said this before and I say it again: I fought for them as much as the Good Old Cause. I had the sword taken from the Whitecoat outside York, and the dagger given me by Meg; it would have to do. I mounted the brown mare, swore I would find a decent horse as soon as I had coin, and joined the ranks.

Rupert was not a fool; he knew that to leave us on the ridge gave us the high ground and the advantage. To the left of our position was a rabbit warren, so the people of Tockwith village would have regular meat. From there, the Royalists could threaten our whole flank. He sent a regiment of red-coated infantry—commanded musketeers—across the track and towards the warren. They fanned out in loose order discharging their muskets then falling back to reload. A couple of bodies of Royalist Horse moved to support them. A forlorn hope to test our resolve.

'Lilburne's boys will see them off,' said a trooper.

Men were standing in their stirrups to see the fight—excited, calling out and pointing. They even stopped droning their dirges. John Lilburne was a name even then. An agitator in the Thirties, his trials and pamphlets gave him stature amongst the radicals: Freeborn John they called him. Captured at Brentford and threatened with the noose, until Parliament promised to hang Cavalier prisoners in response. Everard adored him, but I found him intense and irritating—a born troublemaker—he should have been a lawyer.

Even so, he did a good job of beating off the enemy troops, the Cavaliers not looking as if they wished to press the engagement—only sending small units, and skirmishing at a distance. The crack of musket shot grew more insistent, like rhythm-less drums beating wild and fast. White smoke drifted across the field between the two armies, obscuring the fight for a moment. Scots dragoons were sent in on foot to harass the Royalists and support Lilburne's men.

'Here we go again,' said Sam.

Our Foot were already arriving at the ridge. Eastern Association men at the rear of the march to Tadcaster now pushed first into the line. The pike blocks, with flanking musketeers, were beaten into place by their bully sergeants— some in uniform coats, others in workaday fashion. Officers on horseback rode behind shouting orders. Drums beating, great ensigns waved with mottos emblazoned such as *PRO REGE ET VERITATE* or *GAUDET TENTAMINE VIRTUS.* The high sound of blowing horns, and pipes, and the cheers of men filled the air. If Rupert wished to drive us from the field, he was taking his time about it.

You become used to war. That does not mean you become fearless. The terror is always there in the pit of your stomach. Survive battle but once and you can control it. The best troops are those that have charged, and struggled in the push, seen their friends killed, and spilled their own blood. Greenhorns will always break first. Sitting amongst these Ironsides, as Rupert would later call them, gave me confidence. They would stand and fight. Still, the palms of my hands were sweating and my belly felt tight as a drum.

We sat waiting on the left as the skirmishing continued for most the morning. Another rain shower put an end to it; the Royalists pulled their musketeers and cavalry back from the warren.

Rupert's first ploy had failed.

---

*   For King and Truth, and Strength Rejoices in the Challenge.

'Twas near two of the clock by the time that all our Foot and Ordnance had returned and been drawn up into lines facing the Royalists. Our front was two miles long, the generals—Manchester, Leven, and Fairfax—with the infantry body in the centre, Tom Fairfax and his brother on the right with the northern horse, and Cromwell with David Leslie on the left.

The boy brought up my armour, pot, and spare pistols. I must confess I was quite delighted to see him. Not just because of my sister's displeasure had some calamity befallen him—I had grown fond of the lad.

'What have you done to yourself, Master,' he cried. 'You make a rum sight with such strange hair colour.'

'Strange?'

''Tis gone a dark shade of scarlet, Master, worse colour than Sergeant Plucker even.'

'He speaks the truth,' said Sam. 'It could be a cardinal's hat.'

'Well, that is just wonderful,' says I, and jammed the pot on my head to cover my hair.

Cannon started booming once set into place, with the Royalists soon responding. I sent the boy back to the baggage and ordered him to keep out of sight. He went in disgust; the sight of the two armies arrayed firing his youthful imagination. I knew better what was to come; he need be no part of it. John may have grown, and be counted a man by some, but I desired not to pitch another innocent into war.

The cannoneers duelled to little effect. The enemy were in a good position to withstand us; we more than matched their numbers, but as the day ran on I started to fear the usual lethargy of command. Our generals seemed only to fight at the last.

'Will we attack?' asked a man to my left.

'There can always be a first time.'

My fears were confirmed late in the afternoon. The Whitecoats of the Army of York could be seen. Lord Voice's Lambs come to the slaughter. They began to file into the Royalist line at the Long Marston end.

'Something is happening,' said Sam.

All along the line, trumpets called out, and drums beat out the advance. We moved down from the ridge closer to the Royalist lines. Walking slowly for at least a hundred yards, I looked to the troop captains, waiting for the order to charge.

'This is it,' I said. Excitement and energy building in the stomach.

Then the drums beat out the halt. All along the line, battalia stopped, stood silent for a moment, and then started up again with the singing, flag-waving, drum rolls, horns and pipes blowing. The martial orgasm delayed.[81]

'What was the point in that?' The man to my left asked.

'God alone knows.'

'You are The Golden Scout? Sugar Candy?'

'So they tell me.' I reached out to shake his hand and took note of him for the first time—ginger hair and broad unshaven face under his pot. 'You are?'

'Joyce,' he said, taking my hand. 'George Joyce.'

As the afternoon turned into evening, I despaired that our advantages were lost. I wondered if Hurry had sent his turncoat across the lines. I doubted it somehow.

'How long till nightfall?' I asked Everard.

He looked up at the sky. 'A couple of hours of daylight yet, Blandford. Maybe seven of the clock.'

Cromwell and his officers came back from the centre, where our triumvirate of Lord Generals sat on their fat arses vacillating over which course of action to take. They passed close by us in the ranks.

'I wager it is stand down and time for supper,' said Sam.

'I wager you are right.'

Oliver pulled up next to us; he had overheard that exchange, and for a moment I expected a bawling out for gambling—he was quite capable of such a thing even on the verge of battle. Instead, he smiled and pierced me with those eyes.

'It seems your contact was true, Candy.'

'General?'

'The defector has come and sings a happy tale. They stand down and light their cooking fires. We are blessed indeed by the Lord.'

Then he turned and spurred to the head of his men, standing in his stirrups, exhorting them.

'Do God's will today; stand together, follow commands and we will prevail. There has been no day like this before; the Lord hearkens unto our voices, for we fight for Israel.'

The Horse cheered him as a body, pure adulation in their eyes. I was swept up in it, I confess, as were Sam and Everard. [82]

Our cannon unleashed a great barrage, the trumpets sounded, and we rode down the hill to war.

25. Lambs to the Slaughter: 2nd July 1644.

ACCURS'D be he that first invented war!
They knew not, ah, they knew not, simple men,
How those were hit by pelting cannon-shot
Stand staggering like a quivering aspen-leaf.

(Christopher Marlowe, *Tamburlaine the Great*.)

Nothing fixes a thing so intensely in the memory as the wish to forget it.* Perhaps that is why I drink. A draught or two of Dionysus's nectar helps me sleep at night. It keeps the dreams away and is worth the sore head in the morning. What was it Rochester said? Every pleasure has its debt. So does every dark deed.

We rode at a trot down the slope, pistols at the ready, knee-to-knee, Everard and Sam to one side of me, Joyce to the other. To our right, I could see the lines of infantry follow us down the hill, breaking into a running charge, pikes at the shoulder. Then, I was struggling to control my mare, unused to the charge as she was, a blurring around of man and beast, smoke and fire. Cannon started up as we crossed the road bisecting the field, and charged up to the ditch at the Royalist first line.

'Twas then that Hurry's perfidy was made clear as daylight. Instead of the Royalist Horse receiving our charge with carbine and pistol, Hurry led them out over the ditch to meet us in a confused mess. We rolled into them without breaking into a charge; indeed, I did not even fire my pistol. They routed without a shot fired; Foul Breath amongst the first to turn tail and flee.

---

*   Michel de Montaigne (1533 - 1592)

'Such ease!' cried Sam.

His helmet crumpled on the side, splinters flew off, and he fell from his horse, shot in the head. I rode on; there was nought that I could do. Battle happens so fast.

We careered into the next line of Royalist Horse. There the business became bloody. Discharging my first pistol at a Cavalier officer, I drew my sword, and the lines tangled into bitter mêlée. I stabbed at a trooper in blue coat, trying to stick him with my sword. The damn thing bent with the first blow.

'Damn it! Useless thing!' I cursed the Whitecoat I had taken it from.

I leaned back in my saddle to avoid a thrust and threw my twisted weapon at the bluecoat. He pushed past me and I grabbed my second pistol, discharging it at him, pressing it right into the back of his corselet, punching through the armour—the best way to kill in battle.

Throwing my discharged piece back into the holster, I realised my predicament. With no sword, nor loaded pistols, I was vulnerable to all. I began riding through the struggling horsemen, always forward, hoping to break through into clear ground. Then Everard was beside me on his horse, passing a sword in the fight. How he found it in the swirling tumbling mass of Horse is beyond me, but he grinned and shouted.

'Deus vult! Deus vult!'*

Kicking in his spurs, Everard drove his horse into the flanks of a rider; I pushed behind him—we were having a hard time of it. Another came beside me, and we hewed our swords as if sticks beheading daffodils. I could hear the man next to me giggling as he fought. I recognised him—Cromwell—in the midst of us all hacking, parrying, and finding it all quite

---

*   God wills it. The crusader war cry in the First Crusade.

amusing.

There was a flash of pistol discharge between us, blinding me momentarily 'twas so close—'twas too close. I turned to curse the man behind, then realised that Cromwell had been hurt. I held him in the saddle and stopped him from falling. His neck burned by the flash, scorched by a pistol shot that could have killed him—fired by one of our own.

Men surrounded their leader, fighting fiercely to keep the Cavaliers at bay and take Oliver to safety. I fought with them. My arms ached with wielding the sword. 'Twas no longer light; it felt like a lead bar as I swung, parried and thrust. Most the time I did not even mark the enemy I was striking.

Later, I would hear that Rupert himself was in that fight. I did not see him, being too concerned with my own safety, but he could not stop what was happening. The Scots under Leslie surged around the flank, sliced into his men, and they broke. Prince Rupert fled with them.

Leslie pulled us up before we scattered after them, ordering us back into ranks and to recharge our weapons. My hands shook as I fumbled with the powder and shot, reloading mine and placing it in holster. The long summer evening was drawing to a close, night creeping in, and a great full moon rising.

A group of riders came at us from the east, riding out of the darkness that shrouded the battle beyond. I raised my pistol ready to discharge it in the face of their leader but recognised him at the last—Black Tom. That stayed my hand, though my finger twitched, I confess.

'General.'

He saw my face, and a smile of relief came over him. There were more of them with him, survivors of the battle on the right. Their appearance did not bode well. They had stripped their field signs and ridden through the enemy—an act of bravery and daring that I do not question. Yet, for all his vaunted generalship, at Marston Moor that was the sum of Black Tom's contribution. He lost his flank and fled to Cromwell.

Then again, perhaps I am just being petty.[83]

I took him to Cromwell and Leslie. Oliver had returned after his wound—now bandaged with white scarf. Through the smoke and shadows, the battle raged on. The Foot wrestled with each other in the push of pike and the brutality of the mêlée.

There is not much to be seen in the midst of a fight. Mostly, you are aware of the men around you and little else. The smoke, the helmet, the chaos and speed of action, all conspire to isolate you in a bubble of battle. 'Tis why Caesar did not fight himself but watched his legions from on high, so he could see what was happening. Cromwell learned that later on, but this was his first great fight.

He, Fairfax, and Leslie discussed what to do as we paused. I was told later that there were still near two thousand Horse with us, but only William mattered to me. I found him—alive —sharing a pipe with Joyce.

'William—thanks be.'

'Blandford, God be praised.' He grimaced. 'Sam fell.'

'I know, we can pray he still lives. Do we win?'

'I know not.'

War is a roaring sound in your ears of men, and weapons, and beasts, and drums. The high pitch of the trumpet cuts through it all. The decision was made and the generals led us in another charge on the Royalist rear. We thundered down at them, no controlled ride in lines, but a mass of Horse that rolled into the Royalist ranks. Attacked from front, side, and now the rear, the enemy Foot broke. We rode on, rolling up their line, cutting at their heads as they fled.

My brown nag was hit by shot and we tumbled to the floor. Breath knocked out of me with the fall. The damn beast rolled, and for a moment I thought 'twould come over me and crush me to death. 'Tis a damnably horrid way to go; your bones broken and innards squashed. With blessed luck she fell the other way, kicking out, before resting her head and dying.

I crouched up against the body as Horse fought around me. Taking a pistol from its holster, I fumbled to load it. It was dark, I knew not if I had done the job properly. I looked for a mark, all the while praying for an end to the madness.

The Whitecoats of Newcastle's Foot were holed up in a parcel of land surrounded by a ditch—impossible for Cavalry to break into—fighting on to a bloody end, singing to each other as if they were at Maldon[84]—a vicious fire-fight that went on and on as I watched, fierce, defiant and relentless.

'Blandford!'

I turned at my name.

'Jeremiah.'

His face was black from firing his carbine. The rest of Manchester's 'goons were in tow—Scots and all.

'God bless you, my friend.' He clasped my hands. 'Where are Sam and William?'

'In the chaos somewhere. Sam fell, I fear.'

Jeremiah shook his head sadly. 'That is ill news indeed. Well, we are here to finish the task.'

The dragoons moved to within musket shot of the Whitecoat stand. Fire and shot poured into the packed ranks of men, killing or crippling them as they bled into the mud. What powder and shot the Royalists had left was soon exhausted, but still the 'goons discharged volley after volley into them: near two thousand men screaming, broken, dying where they stood. Their cries still haunt me.

At the end, there were fewer than fifty left—still fighting, still defiant. 'Twas bravery worthy of the Spartans but to no avail. We broke into the enclosure, stabbing, shooting, cutting and hacking, wreaking murder on the few survivors, and still they did not cry for quarter. The moon had risen full, casting its white glow over the bloody scene.

I went in with the dragoons, perhaps the third or fourth behind Abercrombie. A man slashed at me with his broken pikestaff and I parried it away—cutting at his arm. My blunted blade cracked his wrist, barely breaking the skin, but enough to make him drop his weapon.

'Enough!' I shouted. 'Yield! For the love of God, yield!'

He would not yield, and our troopers cut him down where he stood. Three other Lambs finally had sense: throwing down their weapons and falling to their knees. I stopped them being bludgeoned to death by musketeers, but afterwards I know not; perhaps they survived, perhaps they were killed as soon as my back turned.

I told the astrologer Lilly about the scene years later. The ridiculous man thought I was an actor trying to sell a play.[85]

The battle was over but the murder went on. It was the journal that fixed my mind—I had forgotten it on the damn horse in the confusion. I cursed the brown nag and prayed I would find her where she fell. If I had lost the journal, I concluded, all this horror would have been for nought.

I walked back through bloody slaughter. I saw a Royalist officer clubbed down by musketeers, his brains smashed in, corpses broken and cut, robbed of clothes and ought of worth. A woman stripped to the waist, wailing over her man in the midst of the chaos, cradling his body to her bloody breasts, oblivious to all around—madness.

The smoke was like a mist diffusing the light of the harvest moon; a hand grabbed my leg; I kicked it away, the flash and pop of musket and pistol spitting flame in the night, voices pleading for help, screams to the Lord for mercy, screams as they were killed in the darkness. I was sick, retching bile from my empty belly. There were piles of bodies covering the ground, clumped where the fighting had been fiercest.

I stumbled over the body of a Bluecoat (ours or theirs, who knew) decapitated in the battle, the ground soggy with his blood. Slipping on the spilled entrails of another—a child drummer—the smell of shit and blood made me retch again. I sat on his broken drum and began to weep.

'My God, this be hell. My God, forgive us.'

I knew not where Sam or Everard were—even if they still lived—I was terrified I might find them dead on the field, searching for the mare and saddlebags. It felt as though hours passed, but cannot have been more than half the hour, turning over bodies, calling out: 'God with us!' when challenged, and showing my sign. The last thing I wished was to be battered into a bloody pulp by overly zealous infantrymen.

I found her near the battle on the left. The broken body of my brown mare; a trooper rifling the saddlebags. He had the precious journal in his hands.

'Whoa there, my lad,' says I. 'That is not yours to take.'

He looked up, face illuminated in the moonlight. One of Watson's scouts, I was certain that I recognised him, but remembered not his name.

''Tis now, Candy.'

I drew my sword as he stood and picked up his own. He aimed a slash at my head and I stepped back, swinging my sword wildly. He pressed up with a thrust at my face. I stepped back again. I already knew I was outmatched—I really needed to learn some swordplay.

'I will have you swinging for this.' I tried to distract him.

'Not from the grave.'

He swung at me again and I parried, the sting running up my arm as the clash of metal rang out. He pushed me away, thrusting at my face again, and his sword scraped along the side of my pot. I stabbed at his foot—missing—but forcing him to step back and he slipped and fell. I was quick. I stabbed him in the groin as he hit the ground. He screamed and I stabbed again, and again, until he was silent.

'Bastard,' I said to the corpse.

I picked up the journal—now stained with blood—and tucked it inside my corselet. Then I saw him, his great grey head nudging a figure lying on the floor.

'Apple.'

He raised his head, whinnied, and trotted towards me. There was a cut along his flanks—a great slice. I would have to get William to sew him up. I thanked God over and over, even started sobbing again, like a little girl.

'Blandford!' A croak rasping in the night.

My brother James, lying in his own blood, gasping for breath. He had a stomach wound: a hole in his armour wet with blood. I unclipped the breastplate and pulled it away, but the wound was mortal. He had lost too much blood already; his coat was wet with it. The shot had blown a hole the size of a dish out his back.

'Damned horse threw me,' he said.

'You never could ride him.'

'I feel not my legs.'

'The shot has smashed your spine, James. I am sorry.' He

312

knew as well as I 'twas a death sentence.

'Why be you sorry, 'tis everything you desire.' There was blood in his spittle. He was gasping for breath. His lungs filling with more fluids. He did not have long.

'I did not desire this, Brother.'

'You are no brother. You... spawn of Mother's shame.'

'What?' I whispered the word in shock.

'Father cared nothing for you. Named you after a tannery. You a bastard. Our sainted mother a whore.' His head fell back into my lap, gasping, eyes blazing at me with anger.

I hated him at that moment more than I had ever done. Even when dying he was evil. I took the scarf he wore about his neck (some lady's favour no doubt) and held it to his mouth and nose, smothering him. His eyes went wide with realisation at what I was doing, and he weakly tried to resist.

'There, there, James, struggle not,' I said softly in his ear. 'I will see you in hell.'

And now art thou cursed from the earth, which hath opened her mouth to receive thy brother's blood from thy hand.*

And there you have it; the curse of Cain is mine.

---

*   Genesis 4:11.

Cross Deep, Twickenham, 1719.

When men a dangerous disease did 'cape,
Of old, they gave a cock to Æsculape:
Let me give too, that doubly am got free;
From my disease's danger, and from thee.

(Ben Jonson: *To Doctor Empric*)

The idiot summoned a physician in to see me. I took a fall, it was nothing untoward but the boy is cloysome concerned. He carried me to my chamber himself and laid me down on the bed. I told him to send for Perkins the barber surgeon, instead I got a periwigged pasty-faced young fellow by the name of Barrowby. All dressed up in a checked blue justacorps* and waistcoat, tight canary yellow breeches and stockings, and a grey tricorn to top off the outfit.

'You look like a parrot,' I told him. 'Where is Perkins?'

'Mr Perkins is a butcher, Sir Blandford. I am a member of the College of Physicians. Open your shirt if you please.'[86]

I sat up and pulled open the ties to my nightshirt. A member of the College of Physicians no less—Dr Barrowby was going to be expensive—damned if I was paying. Perkins would have bled me for a shilling. The doctor began prodding and poking around my chest, tapping here and there, then told me to sit forward and did the same on my back.

'Any pain in your side or arms, Sir Blandford? Palpitations or racing heart?'

'No, I felt faint, that is all, like I had been hit over the head with a hammer.'

'Had you eaten?' He sat me back into my pillows.

'Breakfasted,' I said. 'Eggs, kidneys, chops and liver; I still have a good appetite.'

---

*   An early style of frock coat popularised by Louis XIV and Charles II.

He sniffed at that. 'I think we shall start with a single egg poached in a wine posset for breakfast instead.' He tapped my belly. 'Too much weight can strain your heart.'

I sniffed right back at him. 'Are you going to bleed me?' I said, rolling back my shirt sleeve to bare a vein.

'Goodness me, no.'

'Why not? Perkins will bleed me for a shilling, and I wager you cost gold not silver.'

'Your nephew has already accounted for my fee, Sir Blandford, and William Harvey proved that bleeding was a nonsense decades ago. It is a barbaric tradition that does more harm than good. This is a new age of reason, Sir. We do not simply cut people up for no purpose.'

'Harvey was a good physician,' I conceded.

'Did you know him?' Barrowby's interest was piqued.

'No, my little sister did at Oxford, but I never met him. I was a Roundhead not a Royalist. Bleeding has always worked for me.'

'That is because the idea of it pleases your mind, Sir, not because of any medicinal benefit.'

'*Placebo Domino in regione vivorum,*' I said.[*]

He smiled at that; perhaps this leech be not so witless. 'Placebo Domino? I like that,' he said. 'I may use it.' He pointed to a scar on my chest. 'A sword thrust?'[**]

'Yes,' I said.

'You were fortunate. An inch lower and it would have severed blood vessels and pierced the lung. You would have bled out in seconds.'

'You could call it providence.'

'Indeed. Well, I shall leave instructions with the cook to

---

[*]   Psalm 114: I shall please the Lord in the land of the living.

[**]   This would be the first recorded use of the term in a medical context.

address your diet. I want you to restrict your drinking to wine and small beers—no brandy, nor gin.'

'How would we find brandy in such uncertain times, Doctor,' I said innocently, and with an expensive smuggled bottle hidden in my chest.

'None can ever tell,' he said with a smirk. 'Yet, if you ask your breath he may have the answer, for I can smell it upon him.'

I burst out laughing. 'I like you, Doctor, and member of the College of Physicians, Barrowby. You have a fine wit.'

'Why thank you, Sir Blandford. I will return next week and see how you are coming along. He passed me an envelope with some small green leaves. 'If you feel faint again I want you to chew one of these petals, it will refresh you, but no more than one.'

'Leaves? I am not a caterpillar, sir.'

'And I am no parrot. The leaves will help stimulate you. Have fair warning, do not take one when the maid turns down your bed.'

The bastard had me laughing again. Perkins never managed that. The good doctor took his leave of me, and went off to speak with my nephew. I lay back on my pillows and listlessly dreamed of days gone by.

26. Funerals: York, July 1644.

Atque in perpetuum frater ave atque vale.
And for perpetuity, brother, hail and farewell.

(Catullus, *No 101.*)

Until now, I have told none of my brother's last moments. It is not something to shout from the rooftops. In the confusion after the fight, who would I have told? The short night I spent sitting at a fire with stunned survivors of the battle. The dead and dying all around us; the cries in the night slowly silenced. I remember the thirst, a throat parched by powder. Taking off my scarf, I soaked up water from a puddle and dripped it into my mouth, sucking the moisture out—I was not the only one. There was little conversation, no elation, only shock.

As dawn broke, the sight of Marston field greeted us. The corpses still being stripped and robbed, the bodies all tumbled together. Simeon Ashe said later that they were like maggots in the dirt; a better metaphor I cannot think of.[87] Mourners scoured the bodies for loved ones, crying out with horror and despair when they found them.

A clutch of men—Cromwell among them—surveyed the field on horseback. Duty calls, said I to myself. I need to get this journal home, and there be the man who can help. Taking Apple's reins, I swung myself up into the saddle. He flinched from his wounded side, but I whispered in his ear, stroked his neck, and he calmed.

Noll was detailing burials when I reached them. Leven had fled during the battle, Lord Fairfax the same. Even Manchester had gone for a stroll at one point during the fight. Cromwell saw me ride up and waved a greeting.

'The Lord God be praised, Candy,' he said in a solemn voice. 'Another soul comes safe through the storm.'

He told me to join his staff. I mumbled my greetings amongst nods and smiles from the others. Bonds forged in the fires of battle are strong even among strangers. I have seen men from opposing sides, years later, joined together in their shared experience. 'Tis a most strange phenomenon: old men wallowing in the horror of their youth.

I note the irony.

I stayed with Cromwell the next hour or so, saying little as the grisly tasks of indentifying and disposing of the fallen continued. Two scenes in my memory's eye stand out: the first was Sir Charles Lucas, captured in the fight and still in his battle dress, weeping as a guard took him around the field. He pointed to those he knew, calling out their names to a clerk who scrawled it down.

'Poor King Charles. Poor King Charles,' he wailed, tearing at his mousy hair, covering his eyes and turning away.

What about the poor bastards lying dead in the mud? I thought to myself. Poor King Charles is asleep, farting in his feather bed.

I knew that my sister, Anne, was companion to Lucas' own sister, but did not broach it with him. 'Twas not a time for such social pleasantries. Apple's wound began to bleed again and he struggled; I dismounted and led him on foot.

Not long after that came a moment of unexpected valour from Cromwell. He saw a richly dressed woman, and five or six of her attendants, searching among the dead. Her brown hair loose and uncovered, dark eyes wild and open with despair. Oliver dismounted and went to her, taking her hand in his.

'Madam,' he said, so soft and tender I could barely hear the words. 'What do you here in this vale of misery?'

'My husband, sir. I seek my husband.' She pulled back

defiantly. There was a rosary around her neck—a papist then.

'Who is he?'

'He is killed—so they say—I come for him.' Her eyes, already red from weeping, welled up. 'I come from Knaresborough; they say he is dead. They say he is dead.'

'You should not be here, Lady. Quit this place, I beg you. You will see too much to distress, and I fear the coarse troopers would insult thee for affiliation and rank.'

It was no order or command. It was a plea, honest and heartfelt. Had he been anything but gentle and courteous, she would have argued, I am certain. Instead, the woman nodded, defiance fell away, and she broke down in tears. Her servants rushed to help as she wept and slumped into their arms. Cromwell turned to me of all people.

'Candy, get her out of here. Then get your horse seen to.'

I took the crying woman and her attendants and led them from the battlefield up to the York Road. The bodies were spread everywhere in the fields and woodland. Men caught in flight lying prone, one leaning against a tree dead from wounds. The women still looked at each corpse, just in case. The lady turned to me when I got them to the road.

'Who was that man?' she asked me.

''Twas General Cromwell, Milady,' I told her.

'Thank him.'

'Yes, Milady.'

They turned away and trudged in sorry procession back home. 'Twas all I could do not to weep at their miserable plight. I know not if her husband was ever found, but I pray so.[88]

I walked Apple back to the ridge amongst the rye, a few miles over the battlefield, stumbling with exhaustion. The last time I had slept had been in my York cell.

Our baggage lay on the far side. I hoped to find the boy and Everard at the very least. I expected the worst for Sam. The broken wagons and pile of corpses at the camp told its own tale. Goring's men had tried to loot the baggage during the battle, and our losses had been heavy. With a fearful heart, I asked for John amongst the surviving wagoneers. They pointed me to the far end of the camp.

'He be right, master,' says one. 'Brave as a lion, that lad.'

I found them by the smell of Everard's foul weed, sitting on the ruins of a two wheeled cart. Everard fell to his knees and thanked God when he caught sight of me, and the boy whooped and cheered. I picked William up from his knees and grabbed him in a hug.

'Sam?'

'Asleep; he has lost an eye and has a fever, but will live. You?'

'Not a scratch.'

'Master Coxon has a story to tell. A rum tale indeed.'

I looked over at the boy, bobbing up and down in excitement. I noted a brace of pistols and a sword at his side.

'Well, John?' I gestured to the arms.

He told me of his fight with Goring's troopers when they raided the wagons. Two men killed and a wagon captain's life saved. All blurted out in a torrent of excitement. I had to admit he had done well.

'I took the sword from a Cavalier officer, Master, and the pistols.'

I snorted, but the boy had won his spurs. He could explain it to my sister.

'You will have to write to Mistress Elizabeth as soon as we have time, Mister Coxon,' I said. I would have to pay him a man's wage now; my sister would have to increase my allowance.

John grimaced at the thought of Elizabeth's reaction.

We were still left in a poor situation with only two horses between four of us. I was certain that Cromwell would let us go south, but lacking animals and coin, we would not get far. I needed to take care of my own beast as well. I explained how I had found Apple and James—dead of his wounds—showing William the gash in the horse's side.

'Get the saddle off and let me have a proper look at him.'

I unbuckled the straps and took off the saddle and bags casting them to the floor as William looked over Apple.

''Tis not too bad,' he said. 'I can clean the cut with vinegar and honey. We do that twice a day and he shall not get Proudflesh*. You shall have to stay off his back for a time.' He stroked Apple's neck. 'You are fortunate, he is a good horse.'

'Fortune? I thought it Providence.'

That raised another smile. He was in an unconscionably good mood.

'Master!'

John had his hands in my brother's saddlebags. He held up a bulging purse, a beaming smile on his face.

'We have enough coin, I think.'

'Providence, indeed,' said Everard.

York was besieged once more, invested from all sides, and could not hold. Rupert had fled north; the Marquis of Newcastle and James King to the continent. The prince must have had some inkling of Lord Voice's treasonous design, for

---

*   Excess wound tissue often leading to an infection in horses.

he tried to have him arrested, but the old mercenary escaped to the Dutch. Of Hurry I had heard nothing. He had survived, I was certain, and would turn up again like a turd that will not drop.

I took the ledger to Oliver, two or three days after the battle, to get our passes home. Sam was sick but able to travel. We had bought a cart and jennet* with James's coin, and Apple was healing, but it was a long road to Hull and only a hope that Jakes would be in port.

Cromwell, dressed simply in shirt and breeches, turned the journal over in his hands. He opened it, glanced at the contents—all written in unfathomable cypher—closed it, and looked to me. There was a smile on his ruddy face, laughter in his piercing blue eyes.

'You say this contains names of London merchants and all they have donated to the King?'

'Yes, General.'

'All their wealth could be forfeited, lands sequestered, and fines levied—an unbelievable fortune to power our cause. The Lord is gracious. Some men will be broken, I am sure, others will not. Gold is God in London.'

That actually had not occurred to me. I had simply expected arrests and hangings. Oliver was more pragmatic perhaps, and Westminster Palace overflowing with graspers looking to fill their purses.

He passed the ledger back to me.

'You will be taking this to your uncle?'

'With your permission, General.'

He nodded.

---

*   A Jennet is the English name for a Hinny; a cross between a stallion horse and jenny donkey.

'You will take other despatches to him, and letters I have. Sad missives for some, but with the consolation that England and the Church of God hath had a great favour from the Lord.'

I must have looked puzzled

'The victory given unto us, Candy.'

'Yes, General.'

''Twas God that made them as stubble to our swords.'

'Twas a treacherous damn Scot, a slice of fortune, and you, you madman. I thought it to myself but said nought; Oliver knew it anyway. Leslie had saved him at the worst, but Oliver and his Ironsides had broken the Royalists. From that moment on, I believe, he was convinced of his right. Convinced that God touched him. Mayhap he was, but 'twas also the seed of his hubris.

He gave me despatches, and passports, and letters all to be taken south, then dismissed me. I thanked God for that, I could see a sermon coming on. There were other supplicants in any case, all calling on his time. Oliver was a power in the kingdom now, not just the fens.

I had my own problems. Even with luck, it would take a more than a week to get to Newport Pagnell. At worst it could take a month. I ran to find the others and get us on the road. As I ran, I tumbled the words over in my head that so fixed me.

'Father cared nothing for you. Named you after a tannery. You a bastard. Our sainted mother a whore.'

I had been able to think of little else since the fight. James was but an infant when I had birthed; what knew he? It had to be just the last drip of poison from his tongue.

Yet, still there was a nagging doubt.

Anne Candy to Elizabeth Candy

My Beloved Sister,

At the first, I can assure you of my safety, but such trials and adversities have been played against us, and such dishonest, treacherous, hands raised towards us, that should make all honest Englishmen hang their heads in shame.

I do not blame you, for I know your heart in this matter and which party has your support, but I would not believe that atrocities against newborn babes and mothers is your desire. I am minded of the Holy family's flight into Egypt to escape base Herod, such are the depredations of this perpetual parliament.

We have been chased, harried, and abused. From Exeter, Her Majesty hastened us ever onwards, so great was her fear of arrest, and so close did the Roundhead troopers press us. At Chillaton, Mistress Margaret bade me wait for an escort of men that would follow. Blessed be, Henry was amongst them. Our brother is safe and well. He insisted on my leaving for France with Her Majesty, for both my honour and duty, but I confess I desire it not. Henry brought news of the great disaster in the North, and of James's death. Such sorrow, our poor brother, may God look tenderly upon his dark soul. There are so many of us who have lost brothers, and sons, and husbands that my small grief is pitiful to compare.

We took a different path to Falmouth Port, for such was Her Majesty's desire, and Mistress Margaret's design. We laid false trails for the Roundheads like children playing Hunt the Fox.* There should have been a flotilla of ships awaiting, but only one poor Dutchman and its nervous master. I bade farewell to Henry, who is to go near Plymouth to face the enemy there.

We packed ourselves into the small space on the ship, away from the sailors who busied themselves with our journey – the smell being quite foul, and no place for our toilet – but even at sea we were chased and fired upon. I confess I screamed in fear, as did the other ladies, barring only Mistress Margaret who remained calm.

Her Majesty declared that she would: 'rather die than be captive' and ordered powder stored upon the ship to be fired if the Roundheads should board. Mistress Margaret told me she desired not our lives to be 'so unprofitably wasted'. All of us were soon sick, as we were cast about on the uncaring sea. It was said that there were ships sent to escort us from France, but storms and winds kept them from us, and us from their safety.

We made land near Brest, after the Queen had explained our purpose to local officers, who first took us for raiders. These foreigners were then so gracious and kind, and Her Majesty's tension so relieved at being in the company of her countrymen.

Mistress Margaret has but little of their language, and relies much upon me to communicate. I am thankful to the Lord I can be of some service, for her service done to me has been so gracious.

We took the road south in carriages, and the journey became hot and dusty. The roads and country so different from our own, I can scarce begin to describe. I took time to see the local market and wares with Mistress

---

*   A version of Hares and Hounds popular during the Tudor and Stuart periods.

326

Margaret, and I was even complimented vpon my speech by a stallholder. The fashions make svch a spectacle. Country girls rvn near naked, hatless, and there be so mvch colovr. 'Tis like the covnty fair at home, with people from all arovnd come to take the baths.

It has been determined, for the sake of Her Majesty's frail condition, that the waters of this place will be of great benefit. I am told that we will leave for Paris soon enovgh, bvt that yov can write to me via M. Lavrent here, who will forward svch to ovr party.

I will write again when we reach Paris.
Yovr Loving Sister,
Anne.
Bovrbon l'Archambavlt, France, 5th Avgvst 1643.

27. A Toad Spotted Traitor: Windsor, September 1644.

Have I spent all my days in Bloody Wars
Thus slash'd, carbonado'd, and cut out in scars,
Have I danc'd o'er the Ice, march'd thro' the Dirt,
Without either Hat, Hose, Shoe or Shirt?
And must I now beg, bow, troop, trudge and trot,
To every Pagan and poor Peasant sot?

(Traditional, *The Low-Covntry Soldier*.)

Marston Moor was a turning point; every man there knew it. In faith, it should have seen the war finished by Christmas, but our generals and politicians were of less worth than a marzipan dildo. Waller saw his army ruined by the King at Cropredy Bridge, and His Lord High Squeakiness managed to get trapped in the west and forced to surrender outside Exeter.[89]

Three hundred dead; 'tis what the newsbooks proclaimed after our victory. I told Mabbot 'twas drivel—there were at least five thousand naked corpses on the field the next day. I would wager more than a thousand were ours.

I passed through the gate and walked down the High Street towards the Swan. Cutting through the yard into the back of the inn, I paused before the door and took a deep breath; I had been morose of late with our unending war. The door opened and an officer stepped out, he was known to me —Temple—a captain of Horse. He saw me and smiled.

'Your woman has arrived, Candy.'

'She is not my woman.'

'So you say. Well, I am away to mine. Good day to you.' He was unspeakably jolly.

I pushed open the door and stepped inside. 'Twas full of off duty soldiers, and strumpets, tapster, and cardsters. I pushed through, looking for Sam or Meg. She was there sitting in the corner. The rich clothes worn in York were changed to a simple blue dress with a high collar and white cap. The boy was with her and spotted me first.

'Madam, may I present your polished turd.' John stood up and threw a mock bow at me.

He wore his sword still. John had won the weapon, although Elizabeth had written to me most sternly. He was counted a man now; I would have to stop calling him 'boy'. I cuffed him and pulled up a stool. Meg smiled at me—all big eyes and big breasts.

'You look troubled, my sweet.'

''Tis of no matter, just the war. Where be Sam?'

'With your uncle.'

Sam was to go to back to his family in Cople for a while. He had taken a metal splinter in the eye at Long Marston— part blinded but kept his life. 'Twas a fair bargain. We had brought him back after the battle. Everard did not have the skill to save his sight, but kept infections at bay with his bag of potions.

I sent the boy on some petty errands and sat alone with Megan, just holding hands and saying little. I had not spoken to the others about my imprisonment, or James's murder. How does one explain that?

'You are quiet, my sweet.'

'I was just...'

'Do not spoil it.' She grinned at me.

I laughed with her and my mood lifted. I called for wine and food and spent the rest of the afternoon in happy conversation, with not one word about the war. The boy came back after a few hours, nodding and greeting those he knew as he pushed through the inn. He had gained a swagger since the battle. Had I been the same after Edgehill? I supposed that I had.

'Mr Butler says that your presence is required, Master.'

I sighed, my peace shattered. 'Mr Butler be a poisonous lesion* on the foreskin of mankind, John. You must always remember that. Who is it that requires my presence?'

'Sir Samuel, Master.'

'Ah.'

'He will be sending you somewhere,' said Meg

'So I would imagine.'

She squeezed my hand. 'I will see you afterwards.'

I tidied myself before seeing Uncle Samuel. Buttoned up my doublet and pulled my hair back. The Saracen's Head was only yards away, but the atmosphere very different. The Swan was the heart of debauchery in the garrison. The innkeeper made sure that the soldiers had everything to spend their money on - women, cards, and drink mainly, but other vices if you so desired. My uncle's home, by contrast, was an office of ordered industry. He would not appreciate me turning up undressed and soused.

'Twas calm and quiet inside the Saracen's Head. Butler was at his desk, but he only nodded to me when I went to Uncle Samuel's office. I grinned at him; he was still wary of angering me and would not hold my gaze. Inside the study, Uncle Samuel was at his desk writing, as always.

'You are looking better, Blandford; you have put on some weight and seem happier. When you came back from York, you were more skeleton than man.'

'Elizabeth has sent three cakes in the last month, Uncle.'

---

*   Genital Wart.

'That must be it. She has written to me three times with complaints. I fear she is still upset with me.'

Uncle Samuel had been most unimpressed with Elizabeth's marriage and subsequent widowhood, and even more displeased when she took to her new house near the Strand. Her home was become a meeting place for radicals and malignants. There was a new mood of change about the land and Elizabeth made sure she was one with it. I blamed the Chidley woman myself, as well as Elizabeth's contrary nature.

A sly smile crossed his face; he picked up a piece of parchment from the desk and passed it to me.

'Mr Everard has returned from London with despatches and orders. Here is a warrant I suspect you will desire to execute, and more letters from your sister.'

I read the warrant with mounting glee.

'I will be most delighted to take this commission, Uncle.'

He took off his spectacles, and sat back in his chair looking suddenly serious.

'Blandford.'

'Yes, Uncle.'

'I want you to take William with you, and watch over him. He keeps odd company these days, it leads him to trouble.'

'Watch over him, Uncle?'

'For his own good, of course. You understand, do you not?'

'Yes, Uncle.'

I understood well enough, and I liked it not. Uncle Samuel had always been the pragmatist, had always wished the King beat before settling the nation. Marston Moor changed that. Cromwell and the Independents were in the ascendant now and the moderates panicking.

I took my leave from Uncle Samuel, and promised myself that unless William was planning a Fawkes, there would be nought of interest to report. Now, mark you, until Marston Moor there had been few who held out hopes of outright victory. An honourable stalemate and negotiated settlement was what the rebel Lords and Commons expected, wanted even.

Now, the chance that the King could truly be beat posed questions none of them dared think on. What would happen next? Was the King to be reduced to *primus inter pares** or worse? There were whispers amongst the radicals—William among them—of a new word: Republic.

That terrified me as much as Uncle Samuel. Does that surprise you? I thought it against the natural order, a change that would lead to even more bloodshed. I still dreamed of the happy England of my childhood, but 'twas already lost.

I gave the boy his letter from Elizabeth and ripped the seal open on my own lecture. I had told my sister of James's last words—although not the detail of his expiration. I wanted answers.

Dear Brother.

You are a ridiculous turnip.

The letters found me well enough although John's penmanship leaves much to be desired. I should be happy that he now swings a sword instead, perhaps? Well, I am most unhappy and I have written the same to him. Yet choose his path I cannot and he is, as you say, now grown. This past year has flown on the wings of time so quick.

It cheered me somewhat to see another on the receiving end of her scathing missives. John was grimacing as he read his.

---

*   First among equals.

I have taken up residence in Bedford Street. It is a fine new building with servants and well placed for the Phoenix; we have imposed upon Uncle Samuel's hospitality for far too long. To answer your question, I will keep my Candy name and I thank you not to be so impertinent. I have arranged for your belongings to be brought here from your garret in Bread Street. I am sure Uncle Samuel will find other use for it. London is seething with people escaping the war. 'Tis like a pot over-boiled and frothing; full of stories, rumours and riots.

She was making decisions for me again—who was being impertinent? Perhaps, I did not want to be under her eye out west.

I know of no reason why you should give weight to James's deceits. There was something broken in our brother, Blandford. A cruelty that has always been there. Any words he said to you pre-mortem are barbs of poison, nothing more. You look enough like James to be a twin that your paternity can be in no doubt.

That was true but we all looked like our mother.

Is it that your own filial failings are assuaged if you can discard your paternity? You should have paid more honour to our father, perhaps. As to your questions to my friendship with Mistress Chidley, I am again offended with more impertinence. 'Behold, I will do a new thing; now it shall spring forth; shall ye not know it? I will even make a way in the wilderness, and rivers in the desert."

That was sly and evasive.

Do not fear change, my brother, for it is inevitable.

---

*   Isaiah 43:19.

The English are lost in the desert seeking a promised land. Only those true in faith shall find the path.

I heard enough of that drivel from Cromwell and Everard.

Your Loving Sister,
Elizabeth.

Post Script.
I have received word from Anne that she is now in France with the Queen and Margaret Lucas. In faith, I am relieved that her journeys have taken her from Oxford. Her stories of the court were most lurid. Even a papist land is better than such a Gomorrah.
E.

William was quiet as we rode to Windsor with a troop of dragoons, something I was secretly pleased with. I took no pleasure spying upon my friend. Indeed, I was unsure if I would report it to my uncle even if he had been spreading sedition. As we began to win the war against the King we battled amongst ourselves, and William was not alone in his complaints.

Once the men were settled with billets in the Great Park, I took him to the Mermaid. The cook was a rare delight, the ales and wines good, and I had coin in my pocket. There was a table out front in the fine late summer's eve; I fumbled in my purse ordering sack and food. The red haired maid recognised me, giving a sweet smile, pocketed the coin and promised to return quickly. I watched as she walked away—arse swaying— perhaps I would not sleep much tonight. Everard sat down opposite me and started packing his pipe with that stinking weed of his.

'You know they let Moll Cutpurse go?' he told me.

'I knew not.'

'She paid two thousand pounds to the courts and they sent her to Bedlam, another thousand to the physician, her madness miraculously cured and the trustees are somewhat richer.'

I sniffed. 'They did the same for Edmund Waller*. With Charles Fairfax dead at Martston Moor who will complain?'

The girl brought the wine and food—bread, mutton, and gravy. I took her hand and kissed it softly, winking at her.

'My thanks, sweet Rosalind.'

She blushed red at her cheeks and curtsied, before going back to her tasks in an embarrassed rush. Everard sighed at me in disgust, blowing out smoke, shaking his head, and then went back to complaining.

'They will do nothing with Franny's journal, Blandford.'

'It will take time to decipher.'

'Do you truly think we will see arrests? Traitors on the scaffold?'

'Some,' I said.

'More fool you then. They will look after their own; the rich always do. 'Tis the rest of us who suffer. Since The Conquest true Englishmen have been oppressed.' He sat back, smugly puffing as if he had made a decisive point.

He was perhaps correct about the first—Cromwell had said similar—but the Conquest yarn was a tired argument.

'My family came with The Conqueror,' I said. 'Do I oppress you, friend?'

'Your situation brings you low, but if you were the first son not third, if you had the estate, and industry, and coin,

---

*   See The Last Roundhead.

would you then be so accommodating? Would you be fighting against the King?'

That was another good point but I was not going to agree with him. I bit into some bread and chewed before answering.

'You say the wrong things in the wrong places, William. 'Tis a dangerous time to draw attention to oneself when there are spies everywhere.' I gestured around at the tavern's clientele. 'The King cannot win the war now, not with the North lost. The sun is shining and the ending is in sight; what more could you desire, my friend?'

'The King cannot win but we can still lose it if we fail in God's design, if we allow the Godless to corrupt our victory, and it is already being corrupted, Blandford. Think you that your warrant will stand? They will let Hurry go.'

'Over my dead body. I will call him out if they do. It is time he paid for his sins.'

'A duel? Such talk is vanity and pride. You would be disgraced, if not killed, and Hurry feted. You mark my words they will let him go. He will stuff some pockets with gold and silver and they will send him back to the army.'

There was no real answer to that. The problem was Everard's arguments about the corruption and ineptitude among our leaders were true enough, but if they freed Hurry I would kill him myself. My oath to Peter and Franny's shades demanded that of me.

We sat in silence for the rest of the meal and William stomped off to his billet afterwards, not even pausing for a smoke. He could be as miserable as he desired, I was going to celebrate our victory. I ordered more sack, waited for Rosalind to finish her work and pondered my report about William to Uncle Samuel.

I pray you, do not fall in love with me. For I am falser than vows made in wine.[*]

The next morning dawned bright and early and I kicked the men to get on the road and to Farnham before midday. We made good time past Ascot and Camberley, coming into Farnham from the north as the sun reached its zenith. The castle looked just the same as it had before Christmas, and once again we arrived in the wake of a defeat for Waller—that was the devil's own luck. We showed our papers and warrant to the guards and passed through the curtain wall. The dragoons dismounted, watering their horses and readying them for the return to Windsor. I planned to be back by evening with my prisoner in chains.

Everard and I led four bulky troopers to the Bishop's Palace, into the hall where Waller had so rudely met us the year before. The general was not alone this time, a great crowd of gentleman stood around him talking and drinking, the pictures of long dead priests watching over them from panelled walls. All officers dressed for war, with weapons at their side, and our treacherous mark amongst as if he were of quality. I smiled grimly to myself and called across the busy room.

'Sir John Hurry!'

Foul Breath turned towards my call, as did others around him curious at the disturbance. His face fell at the sight of me—with armed men and my hand upon my sword.

'What do you want, Sugar?'

'You are under arrest for High Treason, sir. By order of the Committee of Both Kingdoms.'

---

[*]   *As You Like It*. Act III Scene V.

Vengeance is mine; I will repay. [*]

Hurry was silent as we took him away. I insisted upon putting him in shackles, much to the disgust of General Waller and his staff, but I had my warrant and they did not intervene. I confess that I took an inordinate amount of pleasure in the situation, pushing the horses on the return to Windsor, making the journey as uncomfortable as I could for our prisoner but still he did not complain.

That vexed me; I wanted him to acknowledge my triumph.

In the bailey of Windsor Castle I taunted him one last time, grinding home the finality of my victory, and offering prayers to fallen comrades that their deaths were avenged. As he stood, shackled, waiting to be taken to his prison, I leaned in and whispered in his ear.

'They are going to hang you and choke you. Then they will take you down and cut out your entrails, casting them on a brazier before your screaming eyes. They will chop you into pieces, tar the meat, and gibbet you for all to see, and I will savour every moment.'

There was just a flinch of fear before he laughed in my face.

'I will still be here when they lower your pox-ridden, wine soaked, remains into the ground, Sugar. I know things you do not, boy: you shall be sorely disappointed very soon, I fear.'

'Take him away,' I told the waiting guards. They led him off in chains and I turned to Everard. 'An ending then, William, and a time to celebrate, not be morose; let us get soused together and remember old friends?'

'I think not, Captain, I will leave you to your regular debauchery.'

---

[*]   Romans 12:19. Tellingly, Blandford omits the end of the verse - *saith The Lord.*

'You used to be such a merry fellow, William. What happened?'

'A bloody civil war happened, Sugar, did you not notice?' He scowled and turned away from me, walking off to the tents in the Great Park.

I watched him go with my good mood at Hurry's fate already soured. I was not about to let it spoil my evening any further. I wanted wine and a woman, and I knew where to find both.

Skipping up the steps to the Mermaid I pushed open the doors and entered. The smell of warm food and beer greeted me, and the sound of people laughing in conversation. Rosalind stood behind the counter and smiled when she saw me, wrinkled her nose in delight, and reached below the wood pulling out a paper sealed in wax.

'A man left this for you this morning, sir.'

I looked down at the note, it was addressed to *Captain Blandford Candy*.

'You know my real name?'

'I always have, sir, I am not witless. You are a hero: Sugar Candy, the Golden Scout, but always Orlando to me.' She smiled again.

I do so adore flattery, especially when it is sincere, but I confess to a sense of loss at the shattered fantasy. I opened the wax seal on the letter—no sigil—and looked at the note.

You are betrayed. Hurry will be released on the morrow by order of The Committee of Both Kingdoms.

It was the same bold hand that had written the messages in the willow tree at the theatre. Now at least, I knew the messages were for me, but still not who sent them, nor what their meaning was, mostly. The meaning of this message I

understood; 'twas clear enough for all to see.
  It meant a duel.

28. The Duel: London, August 1644.

Fantastic fortune thou deceitful light,

That cheats the weary traveller by night,

Though on a precipice each step you tread,

I am resolved to follow where you lead.

(Aphra Benn, *The Rover or Cavaliers Banished.*)

The three of us walked down the Strand through a cold grey morning. It was a miserable day to die—mist coming in off the river and the hint of rain in the air. We had slipped out in the darkness before my sister Elizabeth rose; she would have stopped me had she known. There were few people about, only some stallholders at Charring Cross setting out their wares on the mucky cobbles. We turned into St James Park at John Rhodes bookshop. The iron gate creaked as I pulled it back and went inside.

William had complained, and the boy prattled, as we hurried from my sister's new house on Bedford Street, but now the scrawny little poacher fell silent, sucking aggressively on a pipe to show his disapproval and exhaling clouds of foul smelling bacco. I led them across the field; the grass, thick with dew, soaked my boots. Rooks huddling together in the trees screeched as we passed. The King's menagerie was on the far side of the park but we were early; I would not miss the appointment.

'Mr Mabbot says that the King kept an elephant in the park before the war,' said John.

The boy was growing like a weed, so quick; he was almost of a height with me now and still some more to go. Black curls, dark eyes and handsome features. Dressed in his fine grey velvet suit my sister had purchased for him, with a new beaver-skin hat, polished musketeer boots and a black woollen cloak—a far cry from the rags he once wore. He seemed inordinately happy about my unfortunate situation.

'You cannot say that I did not warn you, Blandford.' William started up again.

'True enough,' I agreed with him.

'But did you listen?'

'No.'

Granted, the odds were not promising—strolling to a duel one was almost certain to lose—and it was all my own fault, but I had sworn to kill the man thrice over and 'twas my only chance. I think a part of me was prepared for death. Death was all around us in those years, and I had a child's foolish notions of honour and duty. Let me tell you, honour and duty mean naught when you lie choking on your own blood, when your belly is torn open and your life seeps out.

'Mr Mabbot says there were crocodillos too,' said John. 'It would be a rare delight to see such beasts. Have you seen the cats at the tower, Master? Thruppence to enter but 'tis a grand show.'[90]

'Must you be of such good cheer, John?' I said. ''Tis nauseating.'

He made a face at me and fell silent—the boy had always been damned impudent. He had taken employ with Uncle Samuel as a scout, and was proving himself annoyingly adept at the role. My stomach felt tight as if before battle; I had not broken my fast—perhaps it was hunger—but for once, I was not soused. It would have been better if I were; my hands shook.

'I need a drink.'

'Be not drunk with wine, wherein is excess, but be filled

with the Spirit,' said William, with predictable sanctimony.[*]

'I swear I shall drink less, if I survive the day, and pray more.'

'Perhaps womanise and gamble less as well,' he said.

'I have had an epiphany not a stroke.'

The old animal pens and buildings were overgrown and empty, neglected by war and royal absence. Crumbling brickwork, weeds pushing through the mortar, the roofs stripped of shingles. The crocodiles and elephant were long gone and no birds sang in the rusting cages. There were a few bystanders standing around waiting for the action, wrapped up warm in the autumn morning—more watchers than normal for such an assignation.

The word that Sugar Candy was to fight a duel against Sir John Hurry had spread through London like a dose of the pox. I noted Mabbot in his purple suit, making notes in a journal—I was going to find myself in the newsbooks again. I nodded to him but turned away before he could start pestering me with questions. Shivering, I pulled my cloak around and waited in the cold.

'Perhaps he will not come,' said John.

'He will come,' I said.

Some of the audience wished to shake my hand, wish me good fortune, that sort of thing, and I tried to be gracious enough, but, filled with nervous energy, could only manage a nod or a smile at their felicitations. Absently, I wondered what odds were being offered on the match.

The crunch of hooves on gravel drew my attention away from that thought. John Hurry and two other horseman came trotting up the path and dismounted. All dressed richly, fine hats and cloaks, and expensive horses - the wages of sin are

---

[*]   Ephesians 5:18

lucrative.

'This is sinful foolishness, Blandford,' said William.

Hurry's second approached us, dressed in a grey doublet and black breeches: his nephew—another knave from the clan. He was of an age with me, with his uncle's dark hair and eyes, stocky build, and the same Scots brogue.

'Are you determined upon this course, Captain Candy? My uncle will accept a simple apology for your insult.'

'Your uncle is a felon and a traitor, sir. A pox ridden pustule poisoning the anus of mankind; a louse crawling upon Satan's pubis and suckling on his cock.'

There were some laughs from the crowd at that, but Hurry lapped it all up and started bowing and waving at my insults.

'His breath stinks worse than the Fleet on a Summer's day,' I called. 'Sir Foulbreath Turncoat.'

That barb struck home. Gilbert sniggered and scrawled my words down in his journal. A dark scowl crossed Hurry's face, but he quickly composed himself as I continued in my ranting.

'He be the spawn of a monkey and a dog—your own paternity notwithstanding, sir,' I nodded to his nephew. 'A feral beast in the world of men. He can answer to me for his crimes.'

'So be it, Captain Candy,' said Hurry's nephew, with a grimace at my insult to his grandparents. 'Swords it is. Prepare yourself, sir.'

I took off my cloak and hat, handing them to John, and drew my new blade. Nearly four foot in length—it had cost me three pounds—of the finest tempered steel. A plain basket guard and hilt; a sword made for fighting not for show. The only problem being? I swung it like a stick and Hurry was renowned with a sword.

I looked over at him, stripped down to just a shirt: of stout waist, but a strong physique for one of his years. Long black hair, shot through with white, curled around his shoulders, and he wore a full beard. Hurry glanced over and smiled, fetid teeth black from tobacco; his poisonous breath would be a disadvantage, I concluded.

'Try to disarm him,' said John. ''Tis best way to win, so they say.'

'So says who?' said Everard, cuffing him. 'Wastrels in a tavern? Apologise, Blandford, and walk away. This is vain and sinful.'

'I would rather keep what little honour I have left, if you mind it not.'

'Your honour is nought before God.'

'I still think we should have murdered him when we had the chance,' said John. 'I could have slipped poison in his wine and none the wiser.'

Everard cuffed him again.

'We do not just murder people, John,' I said. Excepting siblings, I thought.

'We kill people all the time, Master. What matters the manner of their demise?'

'Be silent, addlepate,' said William.

Most people get their ideas about sword-play from the ridiculous behaviour of actors on the stage, who prance about waving their wooden weapons like cocks and jumping like acrobats—'tis nought to do with the reality. In battle a man's ability is not so important, just swing, and stab, and hope for the best. In a duel it is all over in seconds—speed and skill count for all. I was fast enough, I had decided, and hoped Hurry's age would slow him.*

---

*   Sir John Hurry would have been in his early forties at the time.

I wondered whether to remove my doublet—my new suit had been expensive—but 'twas cold, I did not want to shiver and the witnesses take it for fear. I turned back to face the traitor. He was laughing and joking to his seconds as if this were all a mere inconvenience. He saw me looking and gestured to his nephew.

'Are you ready, Captain Candy?' The nephew called over to me.

I nodded, said a silent prayer, and moved towards Hurry—sword in hand, knees bent, front foot forward. The crowd circled around us, watching in silence. Perhaps I could disarm him, 'twas worth a try. Hurry stepped up to me thrusting at my face. I jumped back, shaken by his speed, and he moved to my left side. I had to turn to follow him, my steel waving loosely as I shuffled around.

'Your footwork is too slow, Sugar,' said Hurry.

I stepped forward, thrusting the blade at full length, and he tapped it aside. My neck was open, he could have killed me there and then, but did not strike the blow.

'You over-reached and missed your mark, that could be fatal.'

'Foul turncoat.'

I was angry and flustered. If he was going to kill me that was one thing, but he played with me—that was infuriating. I tried a swing at his head, but he blocked it and pirouetted behind me, slapping me on the buttocks with the flat of his blade.

'I could have stabbed you in the back.'

I could hear titters coming from the crowd. Incensed, I turned to face him, sweeping wildly at his legs with my sword. He stepped back and laughed with the onlookers. I was breathless, panting from the exertion. Hurry taunted me.

'You have no composure, Sugar, nor skill or speed, but worst of all, you bore me.'

Hurry launched an attack to my left side, I moved to parry, but it was just a feint. The blade whipped up at my head. Jerking back in desperation, I felt the tip catch my top lip; the metal grating against the teeth and bone. No pain, but I could taste the metal tang of blood.

'You ain't so pretty now.'

That was a worry, some women think scars attractive, but I am a vain man—even in the middle of a fight. Horses hooves pounding, and shouts coming through the park distracted me. Men, provosts, dressed for war with carbine and pistol were arriving: more than twenty. Some of the crowd were streaming away, Mabbot remained taking notes; people would pay more for this, I was certain.

'You are all under arrest, gentleman, by order of the Committee of Both Kingdoms.'

Hurry still faced off against me, but it was over. The provosts looked determined and would brook no disobedience. My sword dropped and I looked down. My new doublet was covered in blood—completely ruined—my mouth throbbed, and my head was feather light.

Hurry stuck me in the right shoulder. I watched the steel as it slipped into my chest. My mouth dropped in surprise. He pulled the sword out and a gush of red followed. I could still feel no pain, but my legs gave way.

'Never drop your guard in a fight.'

Hurry turned his back on me and walked away as I fell. I was in shock, lying on my back, staring at the grey sky. Everard's face appeared above me; he was pressing on my chest, it felt heavy. My breathing was ragged, my heart raced, blood pounded through me; my face now a pulsating agony.

'How bad is it?' I gasped.

'Shhhh, Blandford.'

'What about my face?' And I swooned.

Cross Deep, Twickenham, 1719.

I am hurt, but I am not slain;
I'le lay me downe and bleed a-while,
And then I'le rise and fight again.
(Traditional, *Sir Andrew Barton*.)

Of course, that is not *the* ending; a life's story can only truly end with death, and as you can see I am still here. William's skill saved my life and they locked me up in my sister's house under arrest, left me there to rot until I could be of use. Such be the curse of Cain—a long life, hale and hearty, and vilified by all.

I regret not my brother's death, though I confess it doth intrude on my thoughts too frequently for comfort as my own appointment with Charon* approaches. 'Twas murder! I hear you whisper as you read. Was it truly murder? Perhaps, I acted as one would with a rabid dog; perhaps it was all God's design. What is free will, after all, but a divine sop to our miserable mortal existence?

Sin is sin. I will pay the price in the next world when the boatman calls.

I know not why I am so possessed by this, driven to record my times before I pass. Is this what my odious neighbour Mr Pope feels, I wonder, as he scrawls out his verses and ditties. Is he driven to write? The construction of his tunnel has been halted whilst the permits are checked; no licence will be granted for months.

Pope is no fool, of course; he knows the petition came from me. Someone told him—Cibber most probably, he is the type to play both sides of the coin. So, Mr Pope is planting

---

*   The ferryman of the River Styx that takes dead souls to Hades.

trees in his gardens to vex me. The damned things will ruin my view upriver to Teddington. I am cast adrift betwixt tunnels and trees; memories and nightmares; he is a spiteful twisted little goblin indeed.[91]

I watch him with my spyglass from the bedchamber. A hunchback and his dog—Bounce. A damn stupid name for the animal; a dog should be called Grip or Fang. 'Tis a friendly enough beast, though. I feed him scraps and bones from my table when his prick-weasel master is not looking. I had planned to slip it poison but have changed my mind.

Prince Rupert's dog was called Boye. It would raise its leg and piss whenever he heard John Pym's name. They shot him at Marston Moor, caught another hound and trimmed its ears to make it a good roundhead. As if there was such a thing—as if such barbarity could be justified.

All live to die, and rise to fall.[*]

The idiot tells me that there are no dividends this Christmas. If this company is so secure why are no monies forthcoming? A question nobody seems willing or able to answer. But what do I know? I am just an old fool, so they tell me—a relic who lives in the past and does not understand modern times.

A pish on modern times.

---

*   Christopher Marlowe, *Edward II.*

Explanatory Note:

The Wynne Candy Archive is a collection of letters, journals and memoirs belonging to the late Major General, Sir Clive Wynne-Candy VC, DSO, KBE (1880 - 1963), relating to a Wiltshire branch of the Candy family, and includes documents stretching back to the Thirteenth Century. Major General Wynne-Candy rose to prominence in the 1930s, when he was satirised as Colonel Blimp in the British press by the cartoonist David Low, and then in film by Powell and Pressburger in 1943. His extensive archive was bequeathed to the library of Christ College, Brecon, after his unfortunate demise mistakenly attending a Rolling Stones performance in 1963.

The archive remained forgotten in storage at the school until a recent refurbishment. Some of the manuscripts suffered extensive water damage during the London Blitz, however, documents from the 17th century have been restored, and are now publicly available for the first time. This second volume continues the early life of Sir Blandford Candy (1624 - 1721), and is written in his own words. Blandford was present during many of the most significant historical events in the Seventeenth Century, with a career stretching from the Civil War, to the Rye House Plot, and Glorious Revolution. As editor, I have merely standardised the spelling and grammar, and provided historical notes where appropriate.

Map illustrations are mostly taken from the Candy Archives; the maps of the United Kingdom and Marston Moor are from a family copy of Charles Oman's 'A History of England', published in 1904.

Jemahl Evans, 2016.

Appendix I: Religious factions in the Civil War.

The different religious factions during the English Civil War are often confusing. The Elizabethan religious settlement had encompassed a middle way, between the austerity of Puritanism and the pomp of Catholicism. The Anglican Church had been a compromise between the two competing extremes, and had changed little under James I. Whilst there had always been recusants, (people who refused the Anglican Church) in the catholic section of the population, in the Seventeenth century there were increasingly recusants from the Protestant congregation. When Archbishop Laud implemented his reforms, he further alienated many who saw them as a return to the idolatry of Rome. This led to a fracturing of the Elizabethan settlement, and a number of competing groups vying for control of the English Church.

Anglicans were a group that followed the King's prayer book, and supported the reforms of the archbishop. Whilst they would not consider themselves Catholic, they accepted ritualistic elements of faith which appalled puritans, such as icons, statues, incense, and altars. They made up the majority of the population who, despite antipathy towards Catholicism, regarded the Elizabethan settlement as a successful compromise. Blandford's family, other than his sister Elizabeth, were typical Anglicans and unsurprisingly Royalist in outlook.

Puritans is a catch all term for those who felt the Elizabethan settlement had not gone far enough, or who had been alienated by Laud's reforms. They wished to reform the church and clear away any remnants of Catholicism. The Stuart Kings failure to address their concerns led some to leave England for the New World. Oliver Cromwell himself planned to sail for the Americas in the 1630's. Those that remained, became a vocal opposition to Charles I rule. However, there was a wide range of competing ideas amongst the puritans. A variety of Calvinists, Lutherans, Anabaptists, and later groups such as the Quakers, added their dissenting voices as religious control broke down during the Civil War. Politically, they tended to fall into two camps: Presbyterians and Independents.

Presbyterians believed that there should be no established bishops, and opposed the feudal Episcopalian system. Favouring instead a national church on the Scottish model, with no Bishops, and elected representatives. James I and Charles I passionately opposed the abolition of Bishops, regarding them as vital in the administration of the country. James I declared memorably: *No bishops, no kings.* The Presbyterian faction in Parliament, was powerful in its opposition to Charles, but also later came into conflict with Cromwell and the army. The military was filled with much more radical and independent dissenters.

The Independents believed in local congregational control of church affairs, with no wider hierarchy, no bishops, or national structure. They were heavily represented in the army, especially after the reforms that led to the creation of the New Model Army. Cromwell and the other army grandees were ostensibly independents, and this led to the break with Parliament at the end of the first civil war. Despite their stern reputation, Cromwell and the Independents were surprisingly tolerant in religious matters (except if you were an Anglican or an Irish Catholic). The readmission of the Jews in 1656 is theologically consistent with the Independent view, if not necessarily an example of a caring tolerant Cromwell that some would claim.

Catholicism was very much in a minority in Stuart England, although there were influential nobles who wanted a return to loyalty to Rome and a re-established Roman Church. Certainly, after the Gunpowder Plot in 1605 Catholics were seen as the enemy within. Always relentlessly persecuted by both sides, they tended to support Charles I during the war, hoping for concessions from the King and his domineering Catholic wife Henrietta Maria.

Blandford himself was brought up as an Anglican, and would have attended church services at least once a week as a boy. Once in the army he was exposed to more radical preachers and independent dissenters, and he attended sermons by famous firebrand preachers of the time. Whilst not considering himself an atheist, he was certainly more influenced by Enlightenment ideas than religious devotion. The breakdown of authority and central control during the Civil War saw social bonds collapse. This included religious bonds, freeing many people from theocratic control for the first time.

Appendix II: Money.

Pounds, shillings, and pence were the basic currency of Britain until 1971, having a value of 12 pence to the shilling, and 20 shillings to the pound. A straight comparison with the cost of living is difficult, since the relative prices of various commodities have changed. In the case of foodstuffs a rough rule of thumb can be followed.

Blandford, as a Captain, theoretically earned about £5 a week and drew extra as a scout giving him an annual income of around £400, which was a sizeable amount in the Seventeenth Century. The inflated cost of troops during the war is clear. A horseman in the New Model Army earned nearly £40 a year. By 1688, they would only earn, according to Gregory King, £14. A junior officer under James II could only command a salary of £60-80. Of course, pay was always late, always short, and in the case of officers less likely to be paid at all. Blandford's allowance from Elizabeth of £160 a year put him firmly in the range of gentleman socially and was certainly more reliable.

John Bunyan gives us a price of *four eggs a penny* in *The Life and Death of Mr. Badman*. An egg today will cost around 25p - four eggs to a pound. Therefore, at the level of basic foodstuffs, the factor of comparison with the modern cost of living is around x 240.

Items such as clothes, jewellery, and furnishings would be much much more than that. For a fashionista like Blandford, keeping up with the current trends would be very expensive. Drinking, whoring, and gambling cost money after all.

Authors Note.

The novel is based on information taken from extensive sources. Some of these included: Samuel Luke's Journal, the Memoirs of Prince Rupert, Edward Hyde and Margaret Cavendish; collections of letters by Henrietta Maria, Charles I, and Oliver Cromwell; copies of original newsbooks, such as the Mercurius Aulicus, Perfect Diurnal, and Parliament Scout, and contemporary poems, ballads and plays.

Secondary sources included work by Christopher Hill, CV Wedgewood, Samuel Gardiner, John Adair, Julian Whitehead, Dianne Purkiss, Antonia Fraser, Brigadier Peter Young, Andrew Hopper, John Ellis, Julian Whitehead, Claire Jowitt, Patrick Ludolph, Serena Jones, Clive Holmes and Richard Holmes. I have also taken account of up to date research in Battlefield Archaeology from the English Heritage website, and information on the British Civil Wars Project website.

All dates are given according to the Julian calendar. During the Civil War, the Julian date was 10 days behind the Gregorian calendar. Years are numbered from 1st January which was the method used by Blandford in 1719, although many 17th century writers numbered the year from 25th March.

I must give my wholehearted thanks to those that have helped me in my research and completing the novel: Nicola McLaughlin and Tim Pelham Williams (my wonderful beta readers), James Smallwood (the original Blandford), Matt Hodgson (for dealing with superfluous commas and misplaced punctuation) Nigel Williams (for regular bouts of inspiration) and my brilliant editor 'Bustles' Lloyd, and everyone at Holland House Books. Particular thanks must go to Vaughn's Company of the Sealed Knot, and all the staff at

The National Civil War Centre, Twickenham Museum, and Oliver Cromwell's House in Ely for answering my many, many, questions. All the mistakes are mine!

PRAISE FOR THE LAST ROUNDHEAD.

The research is impeccable and the writing full of verve.
Antonia Senior, The Times.

It's great fun and a rollicking good read.
Historical Novel Society.

This is, frankly, glorious.
Michael Jecks (Author of Blood in the Sand)

Evans rewards those who have studied the period with a wealth of gritty detail.
David Luckhardt, English Civil War Society of America

The best historical fiction I have read in years!
James Kemp, themself.org

About the Author

Born in Bradford Upon Avon to nomadic Welsh school teachers; Jemahl was brought up in a West Wales mining village during the 70s and 80s. He has pursued a lifelong passion for History, inspired by his grandfather's stories and legends. Jemahl was educated in Christ College Brecon, St Mary's University College (Strawberry Hill), and U.W.E. Bristol.

Jemahl graduated with an MA in History, focussing on poetry and propaganda during the Wars of the Roses, and then worked for IBM in London. At the turn of the millennium, he left the grind of the office and spent a couple of years travelling and working abroad. After time spent in India, Australia, and South East Asia he returned to Britain and took up a teaching post in West London in 2005. He left his role as Head of Year in the Heathland School in 2010, and returned to Wales citing hiraeth.

His first book, The Last Roundhead, was published by Holland House Books in August 2015 and was nominated by netgalley as one of the UK's top ten books released that month. Antonia Senior in The Times said that 'the research is impeccable and the writing full of verve,' and it was described by the Historical Novel Society as 'a rollicking good read!' The second book in the series, This Deceitful Light, will be published in September 2017. Jemahl's interest in the English Civil War was sparked as a child, after reading Simon by Rosemary Sutcliff, which is probably why his sympathies lie with Parliament!

Jemahl now spends his time teaching, reading history,

listening to the Delta Blues, walking his border collie, and whining on Twitter about the government. You can follow him on Twitter @Temulkar.

1   Colley Cibber (1671 -1751) was a famous comic actor, and managed the Theatre Royal Drury Lane. His own plays and attempts at taking a heroic part resulted in ridicule. Alexander Pope would accuse him of mutilating Shakespeare and crucifying Moliere. Cibber lived at Chopped Straw Hall in Twickenham, now the site of Horace Walpole's stunning gothic villa Strawberry Hill House. Blandford is probably referring to a performance of The Relapse by John Vanbrugh where Cibber reprised his role as Lord Foppington – a part he had created himself in the play Love's Last Shift – but Vanburgh's version of the aging society rake played far more on Cibber's personal reputation and foibles. It is perhaps worth saying that Cibber's play Love's Last Shift, has not been performed on the London stage since the 1690's, whilst Vanbrugh's The Relapse is considered a masterpiece of Restoration comedy.

2   Blandford seems to have composed this volume of his memoir in the autumn of 1719. As with the previous volume, he included family letters and press reports from the archive that he had collected. The narrative is as Blandford wrote it, including flashbacks and dream sequences, although they have been italicised by this editor. The South Sea Company was just starting the rapid inflation in value that would lead to one of the first economic bubbles - and subsequent crash. Candy's great nephew was a very early partner in the scheme.

3   The Earl of Essex's army was returning to London following the relief of Gloucester and had been blocked by the King's army. Essex was left with little option but to fight. The night before the battle, Luke's scouts discovered unguarded high ground to the west of the plain, and the decision was taken to deploy early in the morning to seize the advantage.

That it was William Everard (1600 - c1651) who scouted the hill is unsurprising. Everard was born nearby and his local knowledge would have been vital when reconnoitring the ground.

4   Gilbert Mabbot (1622 - 1670) and John Rushworth (1612 - 1690) were in effect the first embedded journalists. Rushworth was a clerk in the House of Commons at the outbreak of the War and later Secretary to the Army. Mabbot was (amongst many other things) his assistant. The two of them followed the Army to the Battles of Edgehill and First Newbury writing reports for the London press, and Rushworth was also at Marston Moor and Naseby. Later, Rushworth would become Thomas Fairfax' secretary whilst Mabbot became a licenser of the press. Their impact on the early flourishing of journalism cannot be understated. Dr Patrick Ludolph's research into Mabbot reveals a man of many talents, if not the pleasantest of characters.

5   The London Trained Bands were the closest thing to a professional army at the outbreak of war. At Turnham Green in 1642, they bolstered the Roundhead army and helped deter a Royalist attack. When Gloucester was besieged, the newsbooks whipped up a storm in London, forcing Essex to march to its relief, and regiments of the London Trained Bands accompanied him. The Red and Blue Regiments stand at Newbury would become a thing of legend. Blandford's description from afar matches the main sources, and he gives us a unique account of the battle on the Parliamentary left flank.

6   It is highly debatable whether Blandford could have actually seen this action from his 'vantage point' on the hill. Trees, distance from the fight, smoke, and the lie of the land

all suggest that he may simply be reporting what he knew of the fight. However, his details certainly match with other sources.

7 Blandford writes the name as Vaughn, although it is more usually written as Yaughn in texts of Hamlet. The original Mr Yaughn was a local beer seller; it is very much an in joke for the 17th Century London crowd, and often the name is omitted from performances. Blandford is the first source to put the Yaughn family in the Anchor, but the pub does fit the location for Yaughn's premises. The Anchor itself had a chequered history as a burial ground, and later cock fighting ring. By the start of the Seventeenth Century, the premises were being used as an alehouse. The building was rebuilt after the Great Fire, although the flames did not cross the river. Samuel Pepys took refuge there in 1666, and watched the conflagration from the tavern. Today, The Anchor Bankside survives on Southbank, in the shadow of the rebuilt Globe Theatre, and is filled with tourists come to see the Bard's watering hole. It is well worth a visit, especially if you have the chance to see a play next door.

8 Ezekiel Fenn (Circa 1620 – 1643) was a well known boy actor at the Phoenix theatre before the war. He was famous for his female roles, but in 1639 the poet Henry Glapthorrne wrote of him first taking a man's part. Whilst Fenn was known to be in London until 1643, nothing later was known about him until Blandford's testimony in the first volume of his memoirs.

9 Mabbot's role as a London Agent would be similar to a lobbyist today. He would work on behalf of his clients to get trade restrictions lifted or influence political decisions in their favour. This meant he had considerable contacts, both

in the Army and working for John Rushworth, but also in Parliament and the City of London.

10   Sir John Wollaston (1590 -1658) was born in Staffordshire and apprenticed to the Goldsmiths Guild in 1604. He became an influential and rich merchant, and from the 1630s onwards began collecting political positions. He was Sherriff of London in 1638/9 and knighted by the King in 1641. He was also commander of the Yellow Regiment of the London Trained Bands. Wollaston was elected to the position of Lord Mayor in the summer of 1643 and was Royalist leaning but acceptable to Parliament. London politics were as much divided as national. Isaac Pennington, the previous Lord Mayor, had been imposed on the city replacing a pro-royalist candidate.

11   William Larkin (c1580 - 1619) was a popular court painter during the reign of James I. His work was largely ignored until his rediscovery in the 1950s and a number of portraits have now been identified as his. Blandford could well be describing a painting of an unknown woman attributed to Larkin and painted in 1615, just before Elizabeth Luke's marriage to Christopher Candy.

12   There has been a sizeable Black community in Britain, probably going back as far as Roman times. They appear throughout the historical record but their contribution is often neglected. From the Sixteenth Century onwards, the Black British population increased dramatically- especially in London. John Blanque was notably a royal trumpeter for Henry VII, whilst Catherine of Aragon brought black attendants for her marriage. Others appear in baptismal records, and the rise in population predictably worried conservative attitudes. Elizabeth I at one point ordered that

all *Negroes and Blackamoors* were to be expelled, but to little effect. By the Seventeenth Century, there was even an early Bengali population added to London's cosmopolitan mix through the activities of the East India Company. Both sides recruited Black British into their forces: they are variously described as Blackamoor, Turk, or Nubian in the records. The legal status of the Black British in the Seventeenth Century was markedly different from Africans being traded across the Atlantic. In 1569, a case regarding a Russian slave led to the conclusion that: *England was too pure an air for slaves to breathe in*. This was restated at John Lilburne's Star Chamber trial in 1637. There were also an increasing number of Englishmen and women with mixed race parentage - like John Coxon - recorded in parish records. By the end of the Stuart period there were challenges to the law regarding slaves bought in the Caribbean or West Africa, and brought to England. In 1772, the Somerset Case made it illegal to transport a slave from England - a judgement more widely interpreted than the magistrate had intended - but the decision was not enforced. Despite the abolition of slavery in Britain in 1807, escaped slaves were still being returned from London to captivity in the Caribbean until the 1830s.

13   Blandford included articles cut out of contemporary newsbooks, and pasted them alongside his handwritten narrative in the original journals. They have been reproduced in his narrative's chronology which, it must be noted, does not always tally with the established historical fact. Whether this is due to fading memory when the journal was written or outright deceit is unclear. Such memoirs are notoriously unreliable from the period, and Blandford's desire to resurrect his legacy is undeniable. The Battle of Winceby (Actually fought on the 11th October 1643 not 12th

365

as the pamphlet states) was of major significance and it is unsurprising Blandford included it in the memoir. It was the first real indicator of Cromwell's rising reputation as a cavalry commander, and notably the first time he fought under his future commander in the New Model Army - Sir Thomas Fairfax. Between them, they shattered the Royalist threat to Lincolnshire and secured it in the short term for the Eastern Association.

14   Haniel Boswell (1583 - 1644) was baptised in London, but the Boswell Clan was a large extended traveller family still of importance today in the Romany community. He was named as King of the Gypsies in the book *Martin Markall, Beadle of Bridewell*. Blandford's testimony tallies with the book but its veracity has always been questioned. Boswell would have been king for more than thirty years by the point Blandford met him. His son Edward Boswell (c1630 -1689) also took the title King of the Gypsies and is buried in Winslow in Buckinghamshire. The origins of the Romany people are not certain, although recent genetic evidence points to the deserts of Rajasthan in North West India in the seventh century. They arrived in Europe through the Balkans and slowly moved through Europe. By the Sixteenth Century, there was a gypsy community in England but, as in most other parts of Europe, it was persecuted. In 1554 punitive laws were passed against them, but by the end of Elizabeth I reign the legal position had improved with a statue protecting them under the law. They were, as Blandford suggests, still pushed to the fringes of society.

15   The letters from Anne Candy in the archive are transcriptions in Elizabeth Candy's hand. It seems the Candy children began using their own cipher at some point in the

summer of 1643, after the events of The Last Roundhead. Two letters from Henry Candy to Elizabeth in late 1644 are similarly transcribed. The description of the Oxford Court and Margaret Lucas's reaction to it certainly tally with other accounts. Anne Harrison (later Fanshawe) and Lady Isabella Rich (later Thynne) were two of the queen's favourites. Fanshawe herself would admit that she was a '*hoyten girl*' or hoyden in her youth, and stories of semi naked processions through Oxford Colleges abound. The tale of Quickly's rebuke was certainly known at the time, but may be apocryphal. Dr Kettle, whose death was said to be hastened by Harrison's behaviour, died in the Summer of 1643 before she actually arrived in Oxford. The bunker mentality of the Royalist capital would only intensify as the war turned against the King in 1644. Henry Jermyn (1605 -1684) was Henrietta Maria's secretary and oft rumoured lover. He remained devoted to the Queen in exile and was made Earl of St Albans. After the Restoration, he was made Lord Chancellor by Charles II and helped negotiate the Treaty of Dover with France. Sir Jeffrey Hudson (1619 -1682) was the court dwarf and another favourite of Henrietta Maria. He was made a captain of Rupert's Horse - although there is no evidence of him actually fighting. Hudson fled to France in 1644, but was forced to leave after killing a fellow émigré in a duel. He was captured by Barbary slavers and spent the next twenty years in captivity in North Africa.

16   Football was a popular game from medieval times although authorities often tried to suppress it. Edward II banned it from London because of the: *hustling over large balls from which many evils may arise*. His son Edward III banned it to keep men practising archery for his wars, as did later monarchs. Henry VIII, with the cognitive dissonance only

he could muster, managed to order the first known pair of football boots for himself whilst simultaneously attempting to ban the sport. In the Seventeenth Century it was still a popular game. Oliver Cromwell, in his dissolute early years at Cambridge, was described as *one of the chief matchmakers and players of football*, by the Royalist James Heath. We are left with many snippets and partial descriptions of the game played in poems, plays, and letters. They describe a violent game almost unrecognisable to modern watchers, however, some things would be familiar. Words like *'goal'* to denote both the gates and act of scoring; passing between players and dribbling the ball described by Edmund Waller; Squadrons or squads for teams. The ball itself is described in the 1660 Book of Sports as a *strong bladder* blown up and sewn into a *bulls cod* (bull's scrotal sack) and *the harder the ball is blown, the better it flies*. The Puritans hated the game because it was played on Sunday afternoons after church service, which in their opinion - like William Everard's - violated the Sabbath. James I' Book of Sports simply antagonised the situation by encouraging its playing. James did not push the point, however, Charles I was never as flexible as his father and insisted on his Book of Sports being read from church pulpits. It was just one of the many grievances the radicals had against the King, and meant football was in for a periodic ban when war broke out.

17   General William Waller (1597 -1668) was one of Parliament's pre-eminent officers in the early stage of the war. He won a succession of victories in the west in 1642 and the start of 1643, and was dubbed William the Conqueror by the London press. Blandford and his friends were involved in the arrest of his cousin the poet Edmund Waller for treason in May 1643 (See The Last Roundhead). In the Summer of 1643, Waller's reputation suffered a heavy blow with a

crushing defeat at the Battle of Roundway Down. He had been forced to retreat to Hampshire, and raised more men and reinforcements from the London Bands to defend the South East. Waller bitterly blamed the Earl of Essex for his defeat causing a schism in the Roundhead leadership.

18   That detail would date this entry to November 1st/ 2nd 1643 - the clerk was executed on that date from a tree in the castle park. The feud with Essex was at its height. Waller had blamed Essex' inaction for the defeat at Roundway, and Essex had complained Waller's new army drew resources away from the Thames Valley. The arguments had caused delays in Parliament in appointing a governor of Portsmouth, with Essex' supporters arguing against Waller's appointment, and Royalist pamphlets jubilantly highlighted the division.

19   There was a dramatic rise in the colonial population of America during the Seventeenth Century. Between 1630 and 1650, settler numbers grew from less than five thousand to more than fifty thousand. Two thousand five hundred people a year made their home in the Americas, and the numbers do not account for the many who made the journey, but died upon route or returned to England. As Blandford describes, many of the emigrants were puritans looking for freedom of worship. Cromwell himself considered emigrating to the colonies in the 1630's.

20   Thomas Bettesworth was a captain in Richard Norton's regiment of Horse, and had taken part in the relief of Gloucester and the first Battle of Newbury. Clearly he had made the acquaintance of Candy on that campaign but no earlier reference can be found in the archive. Bettesworth was acknowledged as a supporter of the godly cause, and was one of Cromwell's Hampshire commissioners in the 1650's.

21   Jonathan Yardley bought the monopoly for soap production in London from Charles I in the 1630's and reputedly used lavender to perfume his product. However, all the records relating to this original Yardley Company were lost in the Great Fire of 1666. In 1770, the production of Yardley Lavender Soap was launched by the Cleaver family using the old Yardley name in a marketing strategy that is easily recognisable today. Jonathan Yardley's descendents married into the Cleaver family, recreating the Yardley Company that is still in existence.

22   Timothy Bennett (1676 -1756) had his shop in Hampton Wick. He was a Presbyterian dissenter and early public right of way campaigner. When access through Bushy Park was cut off by the Earl fo Halifax in 1734 Bennetts business suffered, and perhaps more importantly to the campaigner travel to church services was disrupted. His campaign against the enclosure of Bushey Park led to a pathway that is still accessible today allowing the residents of Hampton travel through the park to get to Kingston.

23   Moll Cutpurse was the alias of Mary Frith (1584 - 1659). Frith was renowned in the London underworld. A semi-fictional biography was published in 1661, and two plays were published during her lifetime both focussing on her scandalous lifestyle. It was said she even performed in the Fortune Theatre long before women were allowed on stage. Her habit of wearing men's clothes and smoking is attested to, and she also kept mastiffs and parrots. She was an ardent royalist and friend of the cavalier highwayman James Hind. Her companion Running Jack's real identity is unknown but his criminal activities were recorded. The pamphlet *The Parliaments Censure To The Jesuites And Fryers*, published in

April 1642, stated Running Jack *'was found to have bin such a notorious malefactor, that the Bench did condemn him to dy: but hee hath since obtained a reprieve by the means of Sir Paul Pindar.'* Jack caused a stir at his trial, seemingly arguing with the bench, and was initially condemned to death as a *'Capital Offender.'*

24   Rahab was a Canaanite prostitute who lived in the city of Jericho, her story is told in the Book of Joshua. She helped Israelite spies in the city to escape pursuit and, when the city fell to Joshua, she dangled a red cord out of her window to be rescued. According to the Gospel of Matthew she is also reckoned as an ancestor of Jesus.

25   Despite the hostilities soap was a vital commodity and there was still deference to the crown. Parliament voted to allow one of Jane Whorwood's associates - the laundress Mistress Elizabeth Wheeler - permission to travel between London and Oxford in July 1643. Hundreds of barrels were produced in London every week and consignments were carried to Oxford on barges along the Thames. The largest barrel could hold 254lb of castile soap with a retail cost of nearly tuppence a pound at the inflated wartime costs. Throughout the war, there was traffic and commerce between the two rival capitals and smuggling was rife. Lady Mary Strafford managed to smuggle gold, jewels, and even the crown to Oxford, yet continued to be granted passes to travel.

26   Katherine Chidley (c1595 -1653) was a religious controversialist during the 1630s and 1640s. Originally from Shrewsbury, she and her husband Daniel were part of an independent sect that were prosecuted for non attendance in church in 1626. She also point blank refused to attend church for the ritual cleansing of the taint of childbirth in the

same year, and later claimed the practice was *a dirge*. In 1629, the family fled Shrewsbury for London and Daniel joined the Company of Haberdashers. Their dissenting stance continued over the next decade joining with other separatist congregations in London to oppose the idea of a state church. In 1641, Katherine published the first pamphlet of a number of controversial works. She was vilified by the patriarchal defenders of convention for threatening the social order, both of the state and the family. From the mid 1640s, she was closely associated with individuals like Lilburne and Overton and the Leveller movement.

27   The Family of Love or Familists were a group that followed the teachings of Hendrick Niclaes (1502 - 1580). The belief in attaining a state of grace without the church or scriptures was extremely radical, even for the period, and they were persecuted by all the authorities - Parliamentary and Royalist. Contemporaries also made lurid accusations of wife swapping, bigamy, and adultery against them although there is no evidence for this.

28   The obvious happiness with which the Aulicus reported the death of John Pym reflected the mood in Oxford. It was clearly seen as a judgment of God upon the rebel leader. The Herodian visitation was phthiriasis - an infestation of pubic lice - and a clear attempt to smear Pym who actually died of stomach cancer. The death of others such as Hampden and Lord Brooke, and the sentences of execution pronounced on John Hotham (for threatening to surrender Hull) or Nathaniel Feinnes (for surrendering Bristol) merely emphasised how the rebellion challenged the natural order and brought divine retribution upon the nation.

29   The Fountain Inn is mentioned a couple of times in

Pepys diary. The building is one of the few pre Great Fire structures to still exist in London. The first floor, known as the Prince Henry Rooms, with its Jacobean plaster ceilings provides us with a glimpse of Seventeenth Century life. It is sadly no longer open for viewing to the general public, but the fabulous Stuart facade can be seen at 17 Fleet Street.

30   The London Trained Bands abandoned the siege of Basing House on December 16th 1643. Bad weather, no pay, and lack of immediate success sapped the troops morale and Waller was unable to persuade them to remain. Basing House would resist all attempts to take it until Cromwell and the New Model Army arrived in 1646. Today, it is one of the highlights of the re-enactment season with members of the Sealed Knot. Waller retreated from Basing back to Farnham with the remnants of his army in December 1643.

31   Essex House stood on The Strand, with ornamental gardens that backed down to the river. Lucy Hay had lavish apartments there that became the base for the Peace Party led by the Earl of Holland and Denzil Holles. Blandford is not the only contemporary to liken Lucy Hay to Sempronia and references the Roman historian Sallust's description - *A woman who had committed many crimes with the spirit of a man ... Her desires were so ardent that she oftener made advances to the other sex than waited for solicitation. She had frequently, before this period, forfeited her word, forsworn debts, been privy to murder, and hurried into the utmost excesses by her extravagance and poverty. But her abilities were by no means despicable; she could compose verses, jest, and join in conversation either modest, tender, or licentious. In a word, she was distinguished by much refinement of wit, and much grace of expression.* Ben Jonson, Shakespeare's great rival, wrote a play *The Cataline Conspiracy* which portrayed Sempronia in

much the same way. Whilst it was not a great success, it was popular enough for Blandford to know. Lucy Hay had been Pym's mistress since the crisis of 1642, but his death robbed her of influence and she drifted towards the peace party.

32 Pym's funeral was at Westminster Hall on 15th December 1643. From Blandford's other comments that would put the party the next day.

33 Samuel Luke's assessment of Charles was correct in this instance. The King condemned the alliance between Parliament and the Scottish Covenanters on the 22nd December 1643 and offered no conciliation. Instead, he summoned Parliament and the Lords to meet in Oxford. Predictably few of the Commons did.

34 Sir Paul Pindar's house in Bishopsgate became a tavern named after him, and was finally demolished at the end of the nineteenth century. The impressive Tudor facade was preserved and is now on display at the Victoria and Albert Museum.

35 Presumably this is the George and Dragon or simply the George on Borough High Street. The medieval building was destroyed in a fire in the 1670's but was rebuilt. Today, the Grade I listed building is one of the few surviving coaching inns left in London. It appears in Charles Dickens' novel *Little Dorrit*, and was a well known travellers rest in the 19th century. Pete Brown, in his book *Shakespeare's Local*, describes six centuries of the pub's history. The George is still open and serving great food and beer, as this author can attest.

36 Hounslow Heath was a large area of unenclosed land to the west of London. In the 1640s, it covered nearly 4000 acres and was a renowned haunt for highwayman and

bandits. It was often used to billet armies due to its proximity to London. Blandford himself was billeted there in 1642, before Edgehill, and Cromwell used it as a base for the New Model Army in 1647. James II used it as a muster point for his army, firstly during the Monmouth Rebellion and later when William of Orange invaded. The heath is much reduced in size today (approx 200 acres) but is protected as a local nature reserve. Pupils from the Heathland Secondary School in Hounslow, built in the 1970s on its Eastern edge, now play summer sports where soldiers once rained with pike and shot.

37   There were flash locks all along the Thames in the Seventeenth Century. Boats travelling downstream would go over a weir in a *flash* of water as the barrier was dropped, whilst boats travelling upstream would be winched up and over. Flash locks were mostly replaced in Britain during the 18th and 19th centuries, although the last on the Thames was only replaced in 1937.

38   The Whitelocke family owned the manor house of Phyllis Court; a building dating back to at least the fourteenth century. Today, it is home to a private members club overlooking the finish line of the annual Henley Regatta.

39   Blandford's account seems to be a version of the story told in Moll Cutpurse's biography, although there are some differences, and until now the tale was regarded as apocryphal. According to the book, published in the 1660s, Moll Frith held up General Thomas Fairfax's carriage (not his younger brother) on Hounslow Heath, stealing two hundred and fifty Jacobuses - a gold coin worth 25 shillings each. She shot Fairfax in the arm and killed his horses - as in Blandford's account - and was indeed captured at Turnham Green when

her horse collapsed after the robbery. She was tried, and sentenced to death, but Moll then claimed insanity, paid a bribe to the authorities of £2000 and was sent to Bedlam. She was released in June 1644 after being 'cured'.

40 *To argue well is the end of logic* from Marlowe's Dr Faustus . In the play Faustus claims this as Aristotle but it was in fact Peter Ramus - which William Everard must have known. The play itself was controversial, although popular, in the Seventeenth Century. The story of Faust and his pact with the devil was first performed by The Admiral's Men at the Rose Theatre in 1594 and was still being performed up until the closures. The Presbyterian polemicist William Prynne condemned the play in the 1630's, claiming that real devils had appeared on stage during a performance and driven the audience mad. A translation of Peter Ramus' *Logic* was dedicated to Bestney Barker in 1636 by his nephew, so it is likely to be the same edition he gave William Everard.

41 Francis Cole's capture and execution are part of the historical record. The pro-parliament newsbook *The Spie* gave a terse entry in its first edition in January 1644: *He tels us of the execution of one Francis Cole, at Oxford for a spie*.

42 The White Swan (now The Swan Revived) in Newport Pagnell is an old coaching inn, and much of the Seventeenth Century building remains behind a Georgian facade. The Saracen's Head no longer exists - it was burned to the ground in a fire in the 1880s. The Swan has had many famous guests over the centuries since Blandford and his comrades were billeted there. Samuel Pepys stayed in 1680, as did the polymath Robert Hooke who recorded: *Suppd at Swan in Newport Pagnell, slept well*. Later, such luminaries as British Prime Minister Benjamin Disraeli, and the film stars

Sophia Loren and David Niven would also visit. Today it is a three star rated hotel, restaurant, and pub at the heart of Newport Pagnell.

43   Stretham on the Cambridge-Ely Road would fit Blandford's description. The A10 was re-aligned in the 1970s and no longer runs through the village, but The Red Lion Inn is still there. An old coaching house, the current building dates from the eighteenth century. There is a fine example of a late medieval cross outside - as noted by Blandford - but the damage described may not have been the fault of Roundhead iconoclasts. The Reformation in Cambridgeshire had seen a wave of idol smashing a century before. The cross was restored in the Nineteenth Century.

44   Put was a popular card game in the Seventeenth Century for two players. Whilst suits were not important it was a trick based game, but was replaced by Whist in popularity in Eighteenth Century. Playing cards originated in China in the Sixth or Seventh centuries and spread to Persia and India, then finally Europe by the Middle Ages. In Blandford's time playing cards had taken the modern form with four suits and picture cards. Caravaggio's 1594 painting *The Cardsharps* shows the widespread popularity of the pastime - as well as pitfalls for the unwary.

45   St Mary's Vicarage - Cromwell's family home in Ely - still exists and is much as Blandford describes. It is Grade II listed and now the award winning Oliver Cromwell House Museum. The house retains its Seventeenth Century charm, but the addition of Twenty First Century interactive displays would no doubt have bemused it's illustrious former occupant. There are claims that it is haunted by Oliver's ghost and even an ongoing investigation by Cambridge Paranormal Research

Society into the alleged phenomenon. This author can attest to no spooky sightings, but the museum is well worth a visit and is right next door to the wonderful cathedral.

46 Blandford's description of this event is a rare firsthand account. William Hitch (d 1658) was Headmaster of the Cathedral School and *Vicar Choral* in Ely in 1644. From the liturgical details Blandford gives it took place on the Fourth Sunday in Epiphany (31st Jan 1644) which is different from the accepted chronology. According to Thomas Carlysle, the *Hitch business* happened on the 21st or 22nd of January. However, Carlysle does make other mistakes in dating so Blandford's evidence cannot be discounted. Church music had been banned by order of Parliament the previous year, and Cromwell himself had warned Hitch (in a letter dated 10th January) that if he continued with the service, he would be responsible *If any disorder should arise thereupon.*

47 George, Lord Goring (1608 - 1657) was the eldest son of the Earl of Norwich. He was involved in the Army Plot against Parliament in 1641, which caused Charles I a loss of face. At the outbreak of war Goring was in control of Portsmouth but was forced to surrender it to Parliament. He was a gifted leader of cavalry but a fundamental inability to follow orders harmed the Royalist cause. His men and his name was cursed in the West Country for years after the war. Clarendon said he: *would, without hesitation, have broken any trust, or done any act of treachery to have satisfied an ordinary passion or appetite; and in truth wanted nothing but industry (for he had wit, and courage, and understanding and ambition, uncontrolled by any fear of God or man) to have been as eminent and successful in the highest attempt of wickedness as any man in the age he lived in or before.* Goring fled to the continent when the King's cause was lost, dying in

exile in Madrid. The Scots were alone in the Three Kingdoms in utilising lancers on light horses. Their charge at Marston Moor under Sir David Leslie (1600 - 1682) saved Cromwell's wing in the battle.

48 Oliver Cromwell junior was of an age with Blandford, but had certainly not seen as much action as our hero. He was Cromwell's eldest surviving son with two years difference between him and Cromwell's short-lived successor as Lord Protector - Richard - who took no active part in the Civil War and was derisively nicknamed Tumbledown Dick. Cromwell's youngest son Henry would serve under his father, and was Lord Deputy of Ireland during the Protectorate. There were also four surviving daughters who would cause their father much concern in the 1650's.

49 Phillip II of Macedon (382 - 336 BC) the one-eyed father of Alexander the Great, did send the Spartans such a message and receive the laconic response. He was assassinated by his bodyguard Pausanias but the reason for the betrayal are unknown. The accusation that Alexander and his mother were involved comes from the Roman historian Justin centuries later.

50 Hillesden is not much bigger than Blandford describes it today, although little of the Seventeenth Century village remains. The direct route from Newport Pagnell would have been through Buckingham, but this was Royalist territory in January 1644.

51 Gustavus Adolphus (1594 -1632) was King of Sweden and a Protestant hero in the early stages of the Thirty Year War. He is rightly regarded as one of the great military leaders of history. He instituted fundamental changes that transformed the Swedish army into the most feared war machine in

Europe. Many of his ideas of meritocracy, soberness, and harsh discipline would become features of the Ironsides under Cromwell, and later the New Model Army. At the Battle of Brietnfeld in 1631, Adolphus crushed the Catholic League's forces, but it was a short lived twist as Adolphus was killed a year later.

52   The assault on Hillesden took place at the start of March 1644 - although Carlysle says mid February. The combined force moved quickly to assault the building. Blandford's estimate of casualties is light, other sources say more than forty defenders were killed along with six attackers. There were accusations that Luke ordered some of Hillesden's defenders shot out of hand after the assault, made by the Royalist newsbooks. Sir Alexander Denton was removed to the Tower where he died on New Year's Day 1645. His body was returned to Hillesden and he is buried in the church. The church itself still bears the scars of the battle but the roodscreen was restored in the nineteenth century, and one window of stained glass was missed by the Roundhead forces remaining to this day. Susan Denton's marriage to Jeremiah Abercrombie is recorded. The affair probably started when Abercrombie was garrisoned in the house early in 1644, and the new Mrs Abercrombie quickly settled in with her husband. One of the Dentons writing a few days after the fall of Hillesdon stated: *My sister Susan, (and) her new husband Captain Abercrombie is quartered in Addington.*

53   Blandford makes no mention of the date but most sources agree that the gold was discovered on the morning after the battle. Lord Byron (1599 - 1652) was the commander of Royalist forces in Cheshire. The Battle of Nantwich, fought on 25th January against Roundhead forces led by Thomas

Fairfax, had been a serious defeat for Byron. He was forced to retire towards Chester and the King's hopes of a new army in the North West were dashed.

54   Sir Godfrey Kneller (1646 – 1723) was a famous post restoration artist, who became court painter to Charles II after the death of Sir Peter Lely. Kneller painted many of the leading figures of the day, male and female, and grew fabulously wealthy from the proceeds. He was originally from Lubeck but moved to London in the 1670s. He was also a prominent Twickenham resident with a home at Whitton Hall (Now renamed Kneller Hall in his honour). As churchwardern of St Mary's in Twickenham he was involved in the rebuilding of the – now Grade II listed - church after the nave collapsed. As a local magistrate, he was renowned for his odd judgements, and strange sentences. He painted members of the infamous Kit Kat Club – a Whig drinking and political club – that originated in the aftermath of the Glorious Revolution (1689). Candy, an unashamed Whig, was involved in both events, as later memoirs detail.

55   The skirmish at Market Drayton in Shropshire happened on the 4th March 1644. Rupert's force drove off the Roundheads and then proceeded to Chester. Samuel Luke was mistaken in his assessment of the prince's next move. Whilst the situation in the North was deteriorating, and the Marques of Newcastle withdrawing in the face of the Covenanter army, the King instead ordered Rupert to the relief of Newark. What followed was one of the prince's most spectacular campaigns. In eleven days he rode from Chester, picking up reinforcements along the way, relieved Newark and trapped a Parliamentary army under Sir John Meldrum forcing its surrender.

56   *Ballad: The Tale Of The Cobbler And The Vicar Of Bray* by Samuel Butler. Until now, the authorship of this ballad has been disputed. It was first published in 1724 in Butler's *Posthumous Works*, however, later editions reject his authorship. The ballad is certainly in Butler's style and Blandford's information would confirm it as Butler's work.

57   The Committee of Both Kingdoms was the executive body that directed the course of the war. Made up of representatives of the English Parliament and Scottish Covenanters it included the Earl of Loudon as well as the leading Roundhead nobles. Also notable among their ranks were the radicals, Henry Vane, Oliver St John, and Cromwell who grew in power and influence as the war continued. The committee collapsed in acrimony in 1648 with the outbreak of the Second Civil War.

58   Walter and Thomas Raleigh were the sailor's great nephews, not nephews as Blandford says. Candy and his brothers boarded at Old Bank House, which was Blandford Forum's Free Grammar School from 1563 to 1841. Among the other students was the famous antiquarian and biographer John Aubrey. The religious nature of the education they received along with classical languages, natural sciences, and history clearly had a greater effect on some of the other students. As well as Aubrey and the Raleighs, the school produced five Anglican bishops in the Seventeenth Century. However, Blandford would not have been the only miscreant. Aubrey complained: *I have found as much rouguery at Blandford School as there is said to be in Newgate Prison. I know now the wickedness of boys*. Ruth Scurr's brilliant biography of Aubrey, using (mostly) his own words, draws a wonderful picture of the education Blandford experienced.

59   The Battle of Cheriton was Waller's last great victory. It finally ended the threat from Ralph Hopton to London, and forced the King on the defensive early in 1644. With the Scots invasion in the North, Charles was forced to send Prince Rupert to retrieve the situation, whilst going on the defensive in the South.

60   Ferdinando Fairfax, 2nd Lord Fairfax of Cameron (1584 -1648) and his eldest son Thomas were the leading Roundhead generals in Yorkshire. Set on the defensive for the early years of the war, Lord Fairfax had been responsible for the defence of Hull whilst his son made a name for himself as a cavalry commander. As a Scottish peer (despite being born in Yorkshire) Lord Fairfax sat in the commons as an MP. After the Battle of Marston Moor he was made Governor of York. His eldest son, Sir Thomas Fairfax (1612 - 1671) was named General of the New Model Army in 1645, with Cromwell as his Lieutenant General of Horse. He retired from prominence during the Commonwealth but was active in pushing for the Restoration in 1660. Sir John Meldrum (c1584 - 1645) was a Scots born professional soldier. He fought in Ireland and the Netherlands, was with the Duke of Buckingham at La Rochelle, and later Gustavus Adolphus in Germany. Meldrum commanded troops at Edgehill and was a senior officer in the Northern War. However, only weeks before Blandford's meeting he had been surprised by Prince Rupert at Newark and his army forced to surrender. What remained had joined with Fairfax in Hull.

61   This medieval rhyme has its origin in The Hundred Years War, and with its reference to battles, and kings, and its logical progression was a common soldiers refrain. The earliest known version is from John Gower's *Confesio Amantis*

(c 1390). Benjamin Franklin used it during the American War of Independence, and it was hung in the Allied Supply Headquarters during the Second World War. It is similar sentiment to the modern military adage Proper Planning and Preparation Prevents Piss Poor Performance.

62   John Belasyse (1614 - 1689) was a prominent royalist officer. At the start of the war he used his own money to raise six regiments for the King's cause, and fought in numerous battles including Edgehill, Newbury and Naesby. During the commonwealth Belasyse was a leader of the Sealed Knot - the original Royalist secret society - and involved in numerous plots against Cromwell. After the restoration he served Charles II by taking the governorship of Tangier, but was later imprisoned for his role in the Popish Plot of 1679.

63   The Royalists would later claim that one Captain Williams had betrayed the defenders at the barricades and allowed a breach to be made through *cowardice or treachery*. Blandford makes no mention of this, but the other details fit with contemporary reports. Both Lord Fairfax and his son described the difficult battle at the defences. Lord Fairfax reckoned the fight lasted at least two hours before the Roundheads entered the town. The Royalist Governor Belasyse later claimed that he fought for at least eight hours, but this seems to be an exaggeration unless there was earlier skirmishing that other sources do not mention. One detail supplied by Blandford's account is confirmed by Belasye's biographer - the wound to his arm and the cut to the face. Thomas Fairfax confirmed in a letter that he had been unhorsed and then regained his seat, but made no mention of Sam and Blandford's action to help him. The impact of the fall of Selby on the wider war was dramatic. The Marquis of

Newcastle withdrew to York and settled down for a siege, and the Scots and Fairfaxes joined forces. King Charles, aware that the whole of the north depended upon York's relief, sent Prince Rupert to the city's aid. At the same time the Committee for Both Kingdoms sent the Eastern Association Army, under the Earl of Manchester and Cromwell, to reinforce the siege.

64   *Nottamun Town* probably originated in the Midlands in the late medieval period and describes mummers plays, although there is a theory that the lyrics refer to the Civil War. Most famously, the melody was used by Bob Dylan for the song *Masters of War* on *The Freewheelin'* album.

65   William Cavendish (1592 - 1676) Marquis of Newcastle (Later Duke) was the commander of the Northern Royalists. In the first year of the war, he had been successful in defeating the Fairfaxes and capturing Yorkshire and Lincolnshire, but the failure to capture Hull in the autumn of 1643, and his defeat at the hands of Cromwell at Winceby, forced Newcastle onto the defensive. When the Scots covenanter army came south in January 1644, he tried to bring them to battle before they could meet up with Parliamentary forces, but the Scottish army under Alexander Leslie - The Earl of Leven - avoided him. The fall of Selby to the Fairfaxes forced him to retreat to York and settle down for a siege. The city was, as Blandford describes, well defended and manned, and communications were not cut off. There was direct contact with the Royalist garrison in Pontefract through coded lights that could be seen from both towns, and without enough men to properly encircle the town getting in and out was easy enough in the early weeks of the siege. That would change with the arrival of the Eastern Association army under the Earl of Manchester at the start of June. After the defeat at Marston Moor, Cavendish

went into exile in France unable to endure the taunts of the King's court. Whilst in France he met and married Margaret Lucas (Anne Candy's friend and confidante). After the restoration he was made Duke of Newcastle, but retired from public life suffering from Parkinson's disease.

66   A number of windmills at Heworth were burned out by the allied cavalry at the start of May, and there is no way of knowing which one Blandford describes. It was an act of terrorism on the local population. There was no military need to destroy the local infrastructure but the war was increasingly bitter. Prince Rupert's sack of Bolton at the end of May showed the growing frustration on both sides at the prolonged fighting.

67   Samuel Luke's agents were reporting Prince Rupert's northern design to relieve York as early as May 6th 1644 - even though the decision was only taken at the end of April, and Rupert did not begin his march until the middle of May. Luke's diary also records that the news was taken to York via female disguises. Of course, Blandford could well be the source of that information, rather than it being independent verification of the story. Rupert's first move from Shrewsbury was into Lancashire, after picking up reinforcements from Lord Byron, then meeting the Northern Horse under Goring that had escaped from York. When it comes to numbers of troops – on either side – quoted by Blandford, he does tend to overestimate the figures, but not by much. Rupert's army was actually about Sixteen thousand strong, not twenty as Blandford claims, but the newsbooks at the time were reporting as many as twenty five thousand.

68   Alexander Leslie 1st Earl of Leven (1582 - 1661) was one of the most experienced military commanders in the

Civil Wars. He had seen service with the Dutch and then the Swedes. Gustavus Adolphus had knighted him and made him a colonel. He was a Field Marshall by 1536, and commanded troops at the victory over Imperial forces at Wittstock. On his return to Scotland in 1638, Leslie was given command of the Covenanter Army that faced the English in the Bishops Wars. Leslie was successful in humiliating Charles I Royal Army, ultimately forcing the King to recall Parliament in 1640. Charles tried to buy Leslie off with an Earldom in 1641- failing dismally. With the signing of the Solemn League and Covenant between Parliament and the Scottish Covenanters in 1643, Leslie was given command of the army to invade Northern England. In January 1644 he crossed the Tweed and started his march south towards York.

69   The Allied armies suffered terribly during the Siege of York. Lack of food, poor supply, bad weather, and rampant disease conspired to kill hundreds, if not thousands, of troops. This was amply demonstrated by the discovery of burial pits similar to the ones Blandford describes. 113 skeletons, none showing signs of battle, were found under the Barbican Centre in 2010. In the Seventeenth Century this was the graveyard for the Church of All Saints (now lost). Whilst the majority were male, there were the skeletons of six women buried with them. Evidence, it seems, of the camp followers that travelled with armies.

70   Leonard Watson was Scoutmaster General to the Eastern Association and later the New Model Army. Blandford's assessment tallies with both Lucy Hutchinson and John Lilburne's judgement of his *crooked* character. There is certainly evidence that Watson was involved in Royalist plots to save the King in 1648, including midnight meetings with

Sir John Berkley in Windsor, and later Watson would cross Cromwell during the Protectorate, even claiming Royalist sympathies at the Restoration.

71   The Maypole Inn was in Clifton - a small village to the north west of York along the Ouse - it was destroyed in 1648.

72   Blandford must have been captured on the 3rd June 1644 during the Royalists last sally towards Scarborough. On 8th June, the Marquis of Newcastle opened negotiations with the Allied generals but it was merely a stalling tactic. The Marquis was well aware of Prince Rupert's march on York and used the discussions to buy the Prince some time. On the 16th June, the allies exploded a mine under St Mary's Tower causing a breach in the King's Manor wall. A desperate battle to take the breach followed, but the Eastern Association men were beaten off by the Royalists. Henry Vane was writing a letter to Parliament when the explosion unexpectedly happened and described the battle. *Since my writing thus much, Manchester played his mine with very good success, made a fair breach, and entered with his men, and possessed the manor house. But Leven and Fairfax, not being acquainted therewith that they might have diverted the enemy at other places. The enemy drew all their strength against our men, and beat them off again, but with no great loss I hear.* The premature explosion of the mine - perhaps because of rising waters from heavy rainfall - and failure to co-ordinate with the other allied forces, meant a final chance to take York by storm had been lost.

73   The use of torture in England was limited even during the Civil War period. The reign of Elizabeth I had seen the most extensive use of state sponsored torture. Of all the cases of torture reported between 1540-1640, 61%

came under the Virgin Queen. There was a widespread disdain for information extracted by torture in England. Thomas Cromwell went to great lengths to hide the fact Mark Smeaton had been tortured to extract his confession against Anne Boleyn, and the practice had effectively been outlawed by Magna Carta unless a Royal Warrant was issued. Even Guy Fawkes, who was severely tortured in 1605 after the Gunpowder Plot, needed a warrant issued by James I. John Felton - the Duke of Buckingham's assassin - was to be tortured on the orders of the Privy Council in 1628, but judges overturned the order as contrary to the laws of England. In 1640, torture was finally abolished and made illegal. However, there is certainly evidence of information being extracted by force during the Civil War, and the threat of the rack still carried weight. Matthew Hopkins crusade against witches also employed techniques like sleep deprivation that would be recognised as torture today.

74   James King, 1st Lord Eythin (1589–1652) was born on the Orkney Islands and joined the Swedish Army in 1615. He was a successful soldier and rose to the rank of Lieutenant General by 1636. At the Battle of Vlotho, King was blamed for the defeat by Prince Rupert who had been captured by the Imperial forces, and this led to a long standing animosity between the two. King was made Lord Eythin in 1642 and sent to the continent to raise troops for the Royalist cause. He returned to England in 1643 with Queen Henrietta Maria, and was made Lieutenant General of Foot in the Northern Army. His late arrival at Marston Moor would be blamed by Rupert for the defeat. Alexander Leslie (Lord Leven) the commander of the Scots at Marston Moor, had been his superior in Germany. After Marston Moor, King went first to Hamburg in exile and then to Sweden; he died there in 1652.

75   Charles I's letter to Prince Rupert that precipitated the march to York is a work of genius in its ambiguity. The King - clearly trying not to offend the hot-headed Rupert - sent the letter after the Bolton Massacre, and Rupert used it to convince the Marquis of Newcastle that the orders were to fight - despite not showing it to Newcastle. The long winded nature of the letter would later be used by Rupert's enemies to blame him for the defeat at Marston Moor. However, the central message seems evident: save York and beat the Allied armies. Rupert carried the note with him for the rest of his life, sometimes taking it out to read, sigh, and put back in his pocket.

76   Megan Powell's explanation that the tunnel was used to hide recusant Catholics during the reformation may be correct, but the construction was far older than the Sixteenth or Seventeenth Century. The inscription is a condensed form similar to ones found on Hadrian's Wall. *The Sixth Legion Victrix, Loyal and Faithful have made [this]*. The Sixth Legion were based in York from 119 AD onwards, replacing the legendary 'lost' Ninth Legion. The Roman civilian city was based South of the Ouse, in the area that Blandford describes the tunnel, across from the Military base. The Sixth Legion rebuilt much of York in the third century and were given the title *Loyal and Faithful* by the Emperor Septimus Severus. Severus died in York in AD 211. This would mean the tunnels Blandford describes would likely date from the same period. Some Roman sewers have been found in York, most notably near the cathedral on the other side of the river. In 1972, part of the Roman sewer network was discovered, and in 1930 the site of the Roman Baths was discovered in St. Sampson's Square in a pub cellar. The - renamed - Roman Bath pub now has a museum as well as serving great food

and drinks.

77   The forts that Blandford describe had actually been taken by the besieging army during his incarceration, the Scots storming both on June 6th. York was relieved by Rupert on the 1st July 1644, with the allied army withdrawing the night before. When the inhabitants discovered the siege works had been abandoned they began looting the Allied encampments. Prince Rupert's army were kept out of York, camping to the west and north of the city. The Allies initially took up position near Long Marston to block Rupert's approach to the city. When that failed, the decision was taken (at an acrimonious meeting during the evening of 1st July) to fall back to Tadcaster and then to Selby.

78   The area that Blandford describes is now York Racecourse. The small brook was the Knavesmere beck that no longer exists. The area has been used for racing since at least the start of the Eighteenth Century, but was open pasture and flood plain during the Civil War. Leslie's camp at Middlethorpe, and the bridge of boats across the Ouse, had been taken over by troops from York in the afternoon of 1st July.

79   David Leslie, 1st Lord Newark (c. 1600–1682) was Alexander Leslie's Major General of Horse at Marston Moor. Like the other Scots leaders - on both sides - David Leslie had served during The Thirty Years War. He had returned to Scotland at the end of the Bishops Wars to join with the Covenanter forces and served against the King until 1650. The changing political situation in Scotland after the execution of Charles I, saw Leslie switch sides and fight against Cromwell at the Battle of Dunbar. After his defeat at Dunbar, Leslie joined with Charles II invasion in 1651, and was in command

when the Royalist cause was finally shattered at the Battle of Worcester. Leslie was imprisoned for nine years in The Tower of London, but released and made Lord Newark at the Restoration. The arguments between the commanders on the night of July 1st were recorded, as is the claim Henry Vane (the Younger) proposed a government without a King. The noble leaders - Leven, Fairfax and Manchester - were appalled at the suggestion, but It is notable that Cromwell allegedly gave some support to the idea.

80   The spot where the Allied officers watched Rupert's deployment is now known as Cromwell's Plump. It gives great views over the battlefield, and would have been the perfect vantage point in 1644. Blandford's description of the terrain is generally accurate. The battlefield is about two miles wide, with the village of Tockwith at its western end and Long Marston in the east. A narrow road runs in a gentle curve between the two villages, and was a dividing line between the two forces in 1644. The land to the south was cultivated with rye and wheat in open fields, and the ridge that Blandford describes runs parallel with the road. In 1644, a rabbit warren known as Bilton Bream provided an obstacle to the attacking troops at the western end of the ridge. To the north of the road (perhaps 50-100m) was a hedge and drainage ditch that petered out towards Tockwith, but was serious obstacle at the Long Marston end. The hedge still exists today, but the ditch has long been filled in. Beyond was open moorland and common pasture where the Royalist army deployed. Lanes cut across the moorland from the main York road, which should have aided the arrival of the York garrison.

81   Blandford's account of the deployment and events during the day of 2nd July match the other contemporary

sources. Accounts written by Simeon Ashe, Captain William Stewart, Leonard Watson, Thomas Fairfax, Sir Henry Slingsby and Sir Hugh Cholmley give us a similar picture to the one painted by Blandford. With such valuable contemporary evidence and a battlefield largely unchanged since the Seventeenth Century, Marston Moor is perhaps the best understood of the Civil War battlefields. It is a short 20 minute drive from York itself and well worth a visit.

82   Cromwell's alleged words are a re-working of Joshua 10.14. Sadly, no other source gives mention of Cromwell's speech to the Ironsides that could confirm Blandford's detail, but the theme is certainly Cromwellian. The identification with Judaism and Israel was very strong amongst the Independents, and the Old Testament in particular provided inspiration. Prof Claire Jowitt has done some interesting research into William Everard's own ideas being influenced by Judaic thought. In April 1649, Everard and Winstanley were taken to Thomas Fairfax, refused to remove their hats, and Everard declared he: *was of the race of Jews; that all the liberties of the people were lost by the coming in of William the Conqueror, and that ever since, the people of God had lived under tyranny and oppression worse than that of our forefathers under the Egyptians.*

83   Blandford is certainly being very petty. Thomas Fairfax' attack on the right had not had Cromwell's fortune. Firstly, he was forced to assault over broken ground, and secondly he faced George Goring instead of the treacherous John Hurry and inept Lord Byron. In the face of that, Fairfax' men were successful in routing some of the Royalist forces, chasing them to York before being beaten by Goring. Fairfax's ride through the Royalist ranks after removing the white field sign demonstrated his quick thinking, and soon became the

stuff of legend.

84   The Battle of Maldon (991AD) was fought in Essex between Anglo Saxons under the Earl Byrhtnoth, against invading Vikings. The Anglo Saxon army was destroyed and their leader killed. However, Blandford seems to be making a reference to the poem *The Battle of Maldon*, which described the Saxon Housecarls refusing quarter to die with their leader. Legend would later have the song sung at Hastings by Harold II' housecarles in the final slaughter by the Norman knights. Blandford would have seen the original text of the poem in the Cotton Library - a meeting place for the intelligentsia in the Seventeenth Century - but this was destroyed in the Eighteenth Century and the poem now only exists in transcription.

85   William Lilly the astrologer actually does confirm this. In his self penned history - written decades later - he recalled a tale of the Slaughter of the Lambs told to him by one Captain Camby - an actor. Camby told him: *He never, in all the fights he was in, met with such resolute brave fellows, or whom he pitied so much*. He also said, *he saved two or three against their wills*. The details would seem to match Blandford's story, and the name is similar enough for Lilly to be mistaken. Traditionally, the last stand was made in the area of White Syke Close - although the first reference to this was in the Eighteenth Century - Peter Newman identified the Hatterwith Enclosures as a more likely site in his 1981 study of the battle. Blandford's account of the battle on the Allied left flank corresponds to the main sources. In particular Leonard Watson's account comes from the same view of the battle. The Foot in the centre did not have as easy a time of it. Despite being outnumbered, the Royalist Foot broke the advancing